REFINING
FIRE

REFINING FIRE

PRODIGAL JOURNEY

LINDA PAULSON ADAMS

LDStorymakers, Inc.

This is a work of fiction, and the views expressed herein are the sole responsibility of the author. Likewise, characters, places, and incidents are either the product of the author's imagination or are represented fictitiously, and any resemblance to actual persons, living or dead, or actual events or locales, is entirely coincidental.

Refining Fire

Published by

LDStorymakers, Inc.
P.O. Box 468, Orem, Utah 84059-0468

Cover images copyright © 2004 by PhotoDisk

Cover and book design copyright © 2004 by Linda Paulson Adams

LDStorymakers is a registered trademark of LDStorymakers, Inc.

ISBN 0-9749241-1-3

Printed in the United States of America
Year of first printing: 2004

10 9 8 7 6 5 4 3 2 1

to Liisa

SUMMARY FROM

PRODIGAL JOURNEY

The year 2023 changed the course of American History forever.

A nuclear attack destroyed Los Angeles—led by the Reverend Alluvius Blankenship, a fundamentalist Christian leader—rendering the entire West Coast unsafe for human habitation. Convinced that the current U.S. President was the long-foreseen Anti-Christ who would bring about the Tribulation prophesied in the Bible, he and his followers believed that destroying him would prevent that event.

No visible Tribulation arrived, but Blankenship was convicted for crimes against humanity and executed. His followers quietly disappeared.

The impact of his actions did not disappear with his conviction—exactly the opposite. Evangelical Christianity was crushed, memberships in every religion dwindled from that point forward, and the expression of any type of faith became ridiculed, suppressed, and feared.

The ash cleared, and as the sun brightened, Alyssa was born to Joan and Chuck Stark, second daughter in their family. The oldest, Lauren, was the favored child, and Alyssa was raised feeling she was unwanted and unloved.

When Alyssa was five, President James Antonine Garrison drafted a New Constitution, eliminating presidential term limits—and the amendment on freedom of religion. Silence was preferable to public objection. J.A. Garrison, known as "Jag" by his cronies, legalized many things once outlawed, in the name of this new freedom—gambling, narcotic trade, prostitution, and most forms of federal regulation.

In this new world, nearly anything could be purchased legally . . . for a price.

When Alyssa was nine, the formation of the Atlantic Subduction Trench destroyed the East coast with tidal waves, earthquakes, and fire. As a result, construction boomed in the Midwest, and the former Kansas City became an enormous capital—an architectural menagerie. Within it, the President built himself a Presidential Palace, which became the Ninth Wonder of the World.

The immense capital became known simply as Central City. Larger than the entire state of Maryland, bordering Des Moines on the north, Omaha on the west, and Springfield on the south, it contained the largest urban population on earth by many millions.

This was the era in which Alyssa came of age.

Joan, her mother, had maintained a long friendship with Beverly Richardson. Beverly held Joan together in rough moments, providing a voice of reason. But as time passed the friendship grew rocky. Beverly and her husband, Phil, had four children—Isaac, Peter, Julia, and Andrew—a few too many, in Joan's opinion.

Peter and Alyssa were best of friends throughout childhood, as Alyssa's family made the trip from Des Moines to the Richardsons' farm in eastern Iowa quite often. In their early teens, a secret romance blossomed between them, and Peter and Alyssa shared their first kiss on the Fourth of July in the middle of a cornfield.

It was their secret—no one would ever know.

Unknown to Alyssa at the time, Beverly was also pregnant with twins, adding further points of strife between the two women. Without warning, Joan cut off all contact with the Richardson family when the Richardsons chose to align themselves with an organized religion—The Church of Jesus Christ of Latter-day Saints (the Mormons).

An atheist, Joan could not understand this bold choice in a time when religion of any type—especially Christian faith— was frowned upon. She forbade Alyssa to contact Peter ever again, forcefully removing her daughter from her only true friend.

Her mother was prone to rage and violent outbursts, and Alyssa held real fear of a severe beating should she disobey. Her relationship with Peter was severed. Joan's abuse of her daughter also worsened once Joan deprived herself of her longtime friend and confidant.

After high school, Alyssa escaped from her home in Des Moines and took refuge in Central City, attending college with her new friend, Debra Gray. Once safely away from home, Alyssa tried to contact Peter, only to discover that he was in China doing humanitarian service—with a fiancée waiting at home. Beverly had heard false rumors about Alyssa's reputation, and wasn't thrilled with the thought of Alyssa coming back to haunt Peter's life, potentially ruining his virtue. She never passed the news on to her son that Alyssa had called.

Alyssa's father passed away during her sophomore year in college, and she turned away from Debra's support, discovering instead a dangerous and addictive experimental drug known as Elation. Alyssa experienced terrible hallucinations under its influence, and soon these strange creatures were visible even while she was sober.

After recovering from a near-fatal overdose, and with Debra's help, Alyssa overcame her addiction. She then began an ill-fated romance with her former drug dealer, Robert Giles. Rob led a double life, working for Victor Caldwell, head of the Federal Department of Research and the inventor of the drug. Elation had been placed on the market for research purposes, and Caldwell sought a test subject who could communicate with the beings that he had discovered on special equipment—beings which sometimes became visible to Elation users.

Rob's assignment was to find a subject—Alyssa—and bring her in to be used as a permanent emissary with these strange beings against her will, and kept on small doses of the drug indefinitely.

Rob thought he could play both sides of the game, but was forced to choose between his work and his growing love for Alyssa. He came clean, explaining the grave danger she was in— danger he had placed her in, and which he now shared.

As a result, they were both forced to go into hiding. Rob begged her to go away with him to Montana, but Alyssa refused, aware that Rob was intertwined with her worst mistakes, and strangely unable to forget Peter.

Shortly thereafter, Rob vanished—without Alyssa.

Around this same time, President Garrison passed into law the infamous Article 28. The Article stated that religious belief was a proven, dangerous psychosis, as evidenced by the Rev. Blankenship and his followers, Osama bin Laden, and other noted religious figures throughout recent history. Therefore, all persons professing such beliefs were to endure mandatory psychological "correction" of this disorder, or face worse consequences.

Debra—recently engaged to her boyfriend, Jon Pike, and privately a faithful Mormon—now revealed that she was at risk. She asked Alyssa to come with them to Northern Iowa, where she, her family, and members of her church would build an experimental community near Sioux City named New Hope. They hoped that local authorities would look the other way if they kept to themselves, and allow them to live in peace.

Religion of any kind had always made Alyssa uneasy. She was uncomfortable with things that could not be explained, seen, or touched, and the political climate was too unfavorable. She chose a different path, and the two soon lost contact.

Meanwhile, Peter experienced his own trials. In his mind, no one could ever compare to Alyssa, and the previous girlfriend married someone else before Peter returned from China—to his ultimate relief.

But soon after his return, Peter was swept off his feet by a beautiful woman named Jackie—a woman who professed to share his values, hopes, and dreams. Two weeks before their planned wedding day the truth came out—Jackie was cheating, her values false, her entire character a lie. Peter felt lost. Throughout that relationship, he had disturbing dreams about Alyssa, who called through the mists of time, "Wait for me . . ."

As Article 28 came into full force, the Richardson family experienced the trial of their lives, and Peter set romance aside indefinitely. Phil, his father, was kidnapped and never found. Local police were not sympathetic, and the family was left to worry and wonder.

Seventeen months after his disappearance, however, a strange note in Phil's handwriting appeared on their back door. It assured them that he was all right, although he could not be with them as yet. Beverly drifted, depressed and lonesome, all the more confused about what may have happened to the husband she loved, unable to give him up for dead and move on. Peter took charge of the farm, his older brother long since married and moved away. His youngest brother and sister, Jordan and Kellie, fraternal twins, were young and needed a father figure. The weight of responsibility shifted to him.

After leaving Debra, Alyssa lived in a hidden slum of Central City for two years—The Gardens. The President controlled the media, and made it sound as though he had erased the problem of poverty entirely within Central City. But it was not true. It was merely hidden from public knowledge. The government allowed the Gardens to exist, but placed strict regulations on its inhabitants, including mandatory birth-control shots for zero population growth.

In The Gardens, Alyssa made new friends, who became like close family, and she discovered personal peace and happiness for the first time in her life.

One fateful phone call changed that. Her best friend, Margret, with her children Marcus and Natty, ran to escape death threats from her psychotic ex-husband, Ralph DeVray, and once again Alyssa was left alone. She later learned from a nurse that the mandatory shots were permanent—she would never have children. Having recently lost her job, and feeling hopeless, she began to wander the streets of the slums.

Meanwhile, Victor Caldwell was secretly developing a genetically-engineered virus, a biological weapon designed to erase the President's problem of the remaining poverty in the City—through death. Aided by a strange being, known only to him as the Caretaker, and seeking fame and glory for himself, Caldwell designed this secret weapon to eliminate the poor population of Central City . . . and the President himself. With the Caretaker's persuasion, Caldwell hoped to place himself in charge of the nation, once the disease had done its work.

The President's conflicting actions and international policies aggravated the Middle East, and oil barons enacted a long-term embargo against the United States. Oil became scarce, gasoline a rare commodity. Prices soared as the cost of shipping multiplied. All petroleum-based products became precious and difficult to obtain, and travel became impossible for all but the very wealthy; plane tickets were more costly than large gemstones.

Technology soared in all other areas except transportation. President Garrison carefully manipulated and controlled what technologies were allowed, preventing solar or electrical replacements. He hoped that American citizens, deprived of their automobiles and the familiar ease of travel, and suffering inflation rates never before seen, would approve and even demand the war of complete conquest that he wished to wage against the Middle East.

Military officers cleared out the slums where Alyssa lived, forcing recruits at gunpoint from among the impoverished non-citizens to use on the front lines in the impending war with the Middle East. Alyssa was caught in the middle of an anti-drafting riot, shot in the leg, and left for dead.

A stranger approached Alyssa and healed her injury instantly. He warned her to leave the City at once, then vanished.

Alyssa traveled on foot until she discovered a familiar place— the Richardsons' farm. Peter still lived there, helping his mother run the farm and raise his younger siblings. Alyssa learned of Phil's mysterious disappearance and the strange note he had left. She accepted an offer to stay with their family, feeling in a strange way that she had finally come home.

Caldwell had seeded his new biological weapon into a reservoir east of Central City. The disease was carried by water and fluids, which produced enormous amounts of oxygen as a byproduct of its metabolism. Guided at every step by the Caretaker, Caldwell sealed off or rerouted pipelines to ensure the deadly virus would reach its intended targets.

But one can not always account for human error . . .

In Central City, the pipelines leaked, and the disease escaped the boundaries Caldwell thought he could control. His own laboratory, saturated with excess oxygen from the organism, erupted in flames, and he died in the fire, meeting the Caretaker after his death.

Explosions resulted throughout Central City—not only in the slums—and word came that a terrible plague was taking over the Capital. The President himself was ill.

Alyssa realized on hearing the news that most—if not all—of her friends could be dead.

Even this was not the most startling news to Alyssa's heart. At the Richardsons' home, she saw a portrait of her disappearing stranger and learned that this man was none other than Jesus Christ himself . . .

❧◆❧

PROLOGUE

April 19, 2045

Phil Richardson swayed with dizziness. His hands were tied behind his back, his arms crushed between his body and the back of a metal folding chair. His ankles ached, swollen where rope cut into them. He had a blindfold on so tight that his head pounded. He couldn't see light.

His sense of smell told him he was in an old wooden barn used for storing alfalfa hay and not animals. Time blurred; he didn't know how long he had been here, if it was day or night, or how often his captors had questioned him.

What they wanted had floored him: temple recommends. For a price.

Once Article 28 passed, it was hard enough to keep a few U.S. temples open and maintain entrance restrictions. Precautions unneeded in previous decades had been set in place.

Phil was under sacred covenant that he would never allow the unworthy to enter their holy sanctuaries, and as second counselor in the Liahona Stake Presidency, he possessed final authority to certify a recommend. His captors needed not only his signature but his thumbprint—and his cooperation later on to keep the unholy sale a secret.

The sum they offered initially was large, but not tempting. He'd rather give up his life.

He only hoped he wouldn't have to.

"I say we shoot him and get us an easier one."

"You know what Al went through to pull off this job, C.J." There were two voices; one was scratchy and hoarse, the other had an odd squeak on certain vowels, or when he seemed excited or tense.

"Yeah, but he ain't so easy as the others." That was the scratchy voice; the other had called him *C.J.*

Phil tried to make a distinction, listening for the squeaky one's actual name, but it seemed that C.J.'s only appellations for his friend were unpleasant and foul. Phil decided to think of him as "Squeaky," instead.

"Al said—"

Phil turned toward their voices. "Even if you had valid recommends, you could never impersonate good enough Mormons to get in."

A fist hit his jaw, hard. He fell, knocking over the chair. Dirt. Dirt in his mouth, and stickiness. Blood.

A kick struck his back near the kidneys. Phil moaned. It had to be a steel-toed boot. The chair clattered, kicked across the barn floor. Another kick landed in his belly. This version of torture was no refined art, but pain was pain, and he hurt.

"Sign the paper or die, freak. Forget the money. I'm tired of being nice."

Phil said, "You call this nice?" Patience, and all hope for a diplomatic resolution, faded as pain increased. "Tell me why you want to get in the temple!"

"Listen," said the scratchy voice—C.J. "Make it easy on yourself and cooperate. We'll get in with or without your help, and you won't corner the market no more, either way. You might as well be on the side what's gonna win." Another blow struck his ribs. It felt like a metal pipe.

Phil spat out, "I'm on the Lord's side, and He *will* win!"

He was kicked again. "Them secret powers ain't doing you no good now, are they?" The squeaky voice laughed, an ugly sound.

More blows to his ribs, knees, head, and torso followed. Fervent prayer was all that helped Phil not to cry out in pain, terrified for Beverly and his children, unwilling to show them either how much it hurt or the depth of his terror. Silently he gave thanks these men hadn't gotten his family too. Yet.

C.J. said, "I told you, stupid, they bleed just like anybody else."

"Of course I bleed!" Phil said. "I'm human, and I don't have 'secret powers.'" He busied his mind trying to figure out if he'd heard the squeaky one's name.

"I seen it," Squeaky said. "They got mind control. Jeff's been telling stories for months down at the store."

"Now look who's crazy," Phil mumbled. Pain swirled through him, a red haze. "It's just the Priesthood," he added. As though holding the Priesthood was "just" anything. *I take it for granted more than I should. Could I control minds? If I had to?* His memory searched for a scripture reference to it, but drew a blank.

"He said something." Another kick, not so hard: a warning. "Something priest stuff. Cough it up, you—" The squeaky one launched a string of descriptive words regarding his low opinion of Phil.

"The powers of the holy priesthood cannot be handled or controlled except on conditions of righteousness," Phil quoted through his fog of pain, surprised the words came clearly. "It isn't secret. It's the power of God to act in His name, and the Lord won't allow its abuse. If I did confer it on you, it might damn your souls to an eternal hell. Is that what you want?"

"Ain't no hell but the one you're living in," the squeaky one said. "Give it to me now." He called to his partner, triumphant. "I told you. That's way better than them dumb storehouses that Al—"

"Shut up!" the scratchy voice hissed, with a curse.

Storehouses? A vague thought connected.

"Come on, give it to us—now." Squeaky.

"It won't work unless you—"

"Now!" the squeaky voice yelled, too high-pitched.

"I have to lay my hands on your head, so you'll have to untie me. Besides, how do you expect me to sign all those papers with a blindfold on?"

"The idiot thinks we'll untie him!" C.J. hooted.

Squeaky joined in, with some expletives. "Like we gonna let him see our faces before he takes the oath."

Phil didn't like how that sounded. But he kept going. "Listen, it's not a repeat-after-me chant. I'm serious, I have to lay my hands on your head. That's how it's done."

He had zero intent of conferring the Holy Priesthood of God on these two creeps, but it was true he'd need his hands untied, and then he might have a fighting chance.

Recommends . . . storehouses . . . it came together. They might not want to enter the temples at all—they wanted access to the Bishop's Storehouses: food and goods without price. The Church membership had recently switched over to a trial system of economics, cooperative, united in purpose, sharing commodities equally for only the price of serving one another. Falsifying valid membership would potentially give these creeps a free ride. The security breach could even shut down the system . . . and maybe all the remaining U.S. temples.

Phil's mouth went dry. He had to escape, tell someone of this new danger. Maybe cooperation was best; if only he got out alive, said anything to please them, maybe he could warn the higher authorities. "If I sign, will you let me go?" He fought off the nausea of pain and terror building in his gut.

"Sure." It wasn't at all soothing.

"I don't believe you," Phil said.

Squeaky spoke. "You can't go home looking like that. You'll have to wait a while. And my feet hurt from kicking you, so forget the money."

"I understand," Phil said. He wouldn't have taken money in any case.

"I don't trust you," C.J. said. "There's a vow of secrecy first. Then the initiation rites."

Squeaky gave his ugly laugh.

"Vows?"

"Yeah. You blab and we slit your throat. You and your whole family."

Bile rose in his throat. It stung and burned.

Secret oaths and combinations. He swallowed. "I don't like those terms."

"I suppose you could sign without the vow."

Phil was silent. *Yeah, and shoot me before the ink dries.*

An accidental laugh from C.J. confirmed that thought.

"Wait, do we still get that Priesthood?" Phil heard C.J. give the squeaky one a shove. Then more cussing.

Phil wondered about that; if coerced, he could always make something up that sounded official but was in fact mumbo jumbo. That was a definite possibility. He might still have a shot at escape.

He tried a different tactic. He couldn't take their "vows"—no matter what they were. Best to get them off the subject. "Mind control, is that what you want—to control Al? That's easy. We do it all the time for kicks."

"I told you," Squeaky gloated. "Show me how."

C.J. said, "Al won't be happy about this . . ."

"We control Al's head, we *make* him happy. See?"

"Stick to the plan!" More cursing ensued as both voices launched vulgar insults about the other's prowess.

As if on cue, Phil put in, "See? I just made you two fight. Easy."

"He gives me the creeps," Scratchy said, and poked Phil in the belly with the metal pipe-thing. It stayed there long enough this time for Phil to recognize the shape: a double-barreled shotgun.

Despair set in.

Of course they would be armed. He was getting beaten with a *shotgun*? Most likely loaded? They weren't just mean, they were stupid. He fought down a new surge of horror. They could have blown his face off already, by accident!

"Just kidding, all right? If I had mind control, wouldn't I make you let me go?"

"He has a point," Squeaky said.

"Don't mess with me, man!" C.J. gave Phil's belly another poke.

Suddenly, Phil's entire being was filled with light. The Spirit took over his words and spoke through him, as it often did when he administered blessings. The stories of Alma and Amulek in prison came to his mind. The walls split in two and crumbled, and they walked out free men.

"I have authority from the Most High God, that if it was His will, I could break these bonds and strike you dead where you stand. That is no secret power; it is the very Priesthood you have mocked." He felt the truth of it surge through his bones. His mind became clear and lucid, and his fear dissipated, replaced by renewed faith. God was with him.

He paused. There was something else. Before Alma and Amulek were imprisoned . . . worse things had happened, and the Lord hadn't stopped it. It was true that sometimes the Lord allowed the righteous to perish, for a witness against the wicked at the last day. Phil felt dread and the strength of the Spirit simultaneously. "The choice to set me free is yours. Release me, escape with me, and rid your lives of evil. You can still be saved in the kingdom of heaven. But if not, know this: if you kill me, you shed innocent blood of the Lord's Anointed, and shall be held accountable before God at the last day."

"He's freakin' glowing," Squeaky said.

"I prophesy that if you kill me, your lives shall end the same way you end mine, even as Abinadi cursed the priests of King Noah, who took his life. I recommend you don't choose anything too painful. Would you like to know what happened to the priests of Noah?" His Irish streak couldn't help tossing in the last two sentences.

"Why should I care?" C.J. said.

"Because every last one of them was burned alive after they burned Abinadi . . . hunted down like animals and burned the same way. It wasn't at the stake, either, it was more like they beat him with burning sticks until he was dead."

"I'm outta here!" Squeaky squeaked.

C.J. yelled, "Don't leave me alone with this freak!"

Running footsteps sounded, and a heavy door opened and slammed shut.

Then, only the sound of angry breathing.

"So do you want to know why?"

"Why *what?*" the voice was terse.

"Why the priests were hunted down. What they did."

"*No.*"

There was no questioning that response. Phil went silent.

In a moment a thought wafted into Phil's mind: *Call him Clovis.*

Phil hesitated; his voice came out hushed. It formed into a fuller thought. "Why are you so afraid of me, Clovis?"

He heard something heavy hit the ground—the shotgun, perhaps?—and a scrambling to pick it back up.

"Everyone calls me C.J. Only my mama called me Clovis."

Phil veiled his surprise. "The Lord told your name to me." He felt a glow of pleasure. That was a far more specific revelation than the general feelings and impressions he was used to.

"I don't believe in no God," C.J. said, and spat.

"The J is for . . ." Phil waited, hoping he wasn't asking too much. No; it came like a whisper. *Jefferson.*

"Jefferson," Phil said aloud.

The man's breath came heavy, loud, angry.

Phil continued, feeling his way through the impressions coming to his mind. "I remind you of your father, and you hate him . . ."

That feeling struck his gut, a lightning bolt of unchecked pain, sensation more than words. It was terror, revulsion, disgust; so powerful and miserable a revelation of the abuse this man had suffered that he was filled with unmistakable compassion for his captor. It surprised and awed him that forgiveness could come so fast and be so complete.

Yet it was.

He said, "I can't help reminding you of him, but C.J., I'm *not* him. Please. Let me help you. Untie me and come back with me. We can help you. Don't worry about the vows you took—we can work that all out. I'm sure of it. Listen. I would *never* . . . C.J., what he did was cruel and wrong." Phil paused. "He—"

"Shut up! *Shut up!* I don't believe in no freakin' psychics neither!" C.J. yelled.

A shot went off.

Phil's body jumped as a shower of pellets struck his abdomen. His legs curled up to his belly. It couldn't be a direct hit, but it stung, badly. "Did you mean to do that, or did you just miss?"

The man retreated at a run and the door opened.

Phil cried out, "Wait! Help me! Free yourself of—"

"Any more funny stuff, freak, and I'll shoot to kill!"

The barn door slammed.

Silence.

Phil lay on the hard cold dirt. Had he pushed too hard?

No, he only said the words he felt strongly prompted to say. C.J.'s reaction . . . something had gone wrong. But what? Phil had to conclude it wasn't his fault. What to try next, he didn't know.

Pain commanded all his attention.

His shirt clung to his skin, sticky with blood. His ribs hurt far worse than the sting in his belly; they must be broken. He fought the pain, praying any bleeding would stanch on its own. It should; the shot couldn't have penetrated too deep. He had no way of knowing.

Soon drowsiness overtook him and he slept.

* * * * *

Phil woke to a soft glow, confused.

Was his blindfold off?

Diffused light seemed directly in front of him. His immortal soul longed to reach the source with a nameless, deep-rooted hunger.

Slowly he understood. Death.

His first thought wasn't wonder, or concern for his family, or any of the things he expected he would think of at this moment. It was: *If I have to be a martyr, couldn't it be more . . . spectacular?* Bleeding to death on a barn floor was hardly a heroic way to go.

He hadn't gone far when he felt himself yanked backwards, hearing words that resonated with deep familiarity.

Phil panicked: he was going the *wrong way*—why?

He saw his body below as it lay on a barn floor in a pool of blood. Next to it stood a shining being in pure white robes. Light filled the barn.

The next moment, he felt *zipped* back into his body.

He sensed every living cell, from the skin on his toes to every bone in his feet, to his ankles, and upward. In perhaps an instant, a wealth of information about his body's systems flooded his intelligence. His mind processed information faster than he knew was possible.

It was wholeness, communion, oneness; a sense that after eons of existence, he had completed the final stage in an eternal design. He filled his lungs. His brain sorted each separate scent, labeling. Another moment told him breathing was a pleasant habit, but unnecessary.

His captors had taken his glasses. Yet now he could see in more perfect detail than when he was younger and had no need of them. Colors were clear and sharp, and it seemed there were *more* of them. The straw seemed to sparkle.

The being of light leaned over him, smiling. It was a man with a young-looking face.

Phil exclaimed, "You're an angel!"

The being laughed softly. "Yes."

The one thing Phil did not feel was pain. He sat up easily, no longer broken and bruised. Even the arthritis pain in his left hand was gone. Not dead, then; healed? A near-death experience?

He felt *young*.

"This is incredible," Phil said. His wrists had no bruises, although rope had rubbed and chafed the skin raw. A large bloody hole rent his shirt where the buckshot had gone through.

He lifted his shirt and found smooth, new skin. On impulse, he pushed up his right sleeve to find the large scar from when he slipped off the baling machine, twenty years ago.

It was gone.

He looked at the angel. "What just happened to me?"

"Welcome to immortality, Phillip," the angel said, smiling.

Resurrected? Phil was dumbfounded.

He stretched his left hand. It flexed easily. Knowledge of every tendon, ligament, and muscle in his hand flowed into his brain.

"I am Stephen." The being raised him to his feet.

"But why was I resurrected?"

"You are greatly blessed to have this gift given you. I was separated from my body for over two hundred years, and it was most unpleasant," Stephen said.

"Were you the Stephen who was stoned in the Bible?"

"Of course not. But I was named for him."

"Of course not?"

"*That* Stephen is very busy and is assigned to Europe. Were you expecting someone famous? Moroni? Father Adam? Perhaps Joseph Smith? I have the authority, and I am perfectly qualified."

"No, I wasn't 'expecting' anyone at all. Forgive me, I'm just very confused." This was not going anything like angelic visitations recorded in scripture.

Phil blinked, sorting it out. He had half-expected that death might be a result of the kidnapping. The other half hoped he would get free. But he never expected *this*.

"You couldn't have helped me escape, instead?"

"We cannot underestimate the power of agency. Clovis exercised his free will. I gave you his name; he chose not to believe or to help you. I fear for his soul."

"*You* gave me the name?" Phil asked. "It got me shot!"

"No, Phillip. The name was sufficient; the Spirit confirmed this to his soul. He was not as past feeling as he seemed. He rejected that witness. I'm terribly sorry. But it is done; and these men shall not retain your body for sport."

"I just want to go home." Phil was plaintive. Homesickness struck with greater yearning than any feeling he had ever known. "I miss my wife and my children."

The angel regarded him with compassion. "I'm afraid that won't be possible, Phillip."

"But why?" Tears welled up. He was acutely aware of the formation of each tear, and each pathway they took down his cheeks. It was distracting enough that he stopped.

"Living with them as an immortal is neither allowed nor recommended at this time."

"If I was dead, I could visit them in spirit. I won't get to see them at all?"

"There are commandments which you must learn and keep before any such visits may be allowed. Your family must not know of this; yet you are far more able to protect and help them now than you know."

"Won't my kidnappers go after my family, when they don't find my body?"

"Your family is safe. Clovis and Jack shall know exactly what happened to you." Stephen grinned.

So Squeaky's name was Jack.

"Why can those miscreants know, but not my own family?"

"Your family—" Stephen began, when the barn door opened behind Phil. It was night. "Welcome them," Stephen instructed.

"Can they see you?" Phil whispered.

"They shall see both of us. In the meantime, try not to glow."

"What?"

Stephen put a finger to his lips and motioned Phil to turn around.

He turned and said, "Hello, C.J., Jack," nodding to each in turn, instinctively knowing which was who before either spoke. The door creaked to a close.

Jack said, "What the hell! How'd you get free?" He aimed a semi-automatic at Phil's chest.

Brilliant light flooded the barn, and Stephen spoke in a voice of rumbling thunder: *Thou shalt not murder the Lord's Anointed! A curse is upon you for rejecting the Holy Spirit, and the word of God taught you in your youth!*

The angel floated several feet above them in the air. *"Cease to torment the Saints of God, or suffer the fulness of His wrath to be poured out upon your heads!"*

The guns dropped, and both men fell to their knees, covering their faces. The semi-automatic weapon discharged, and a shower of bullets ricocheted through the barn.

Jack recovered first and reached for his gun. "It's a trick!"

"What do I do?" Phil called.

Stephen's voice spoke to his mind: *There is no danger. Let the bullets pass through.*

Jack fired a steady stream. C.J. fired wild, aiming first at the angel, then at Phil.

Let the—what? When the volley hit his chest, he understood. The bullets passed through without harm; the sensation reminded him of being stitched up while numb. He grabbed the shotgun barrel, yanked it out of C.J.'s hands, and tossed it away.

C.J. curled up and cried, "Don't hurt me! I believe!"

Jack's gun clicked, empty. "Why can't I kill you?" His voice squeaked as he reloaded.

"Because C.J. already did." Phil was enjoying this.

"What?" C.J. uncurled and sat up.

"You some kind of ghost?" Jack fumbled with the clip.

"No. Thanks to C.J., I am now an immortal being, with more 'special powers' than you ever dreamed of."

"What'd you do to him?" Jack kicked the man on the floor, insulting his intelligence with a plethora of curses.

"Nothin'!" C.J. kicked back with one foot. "He scared me with some hocus-pocus mind trick and took a stray shot in the belly. It weren't no direct hit."

"There's a mess of blood over there." Jack eyed Phil's belly.

Phil took the semi-automatic. "But nothing underneath." He raised his shirt just enough to prove it, then gestured toward Jack with the gun. "Bet this has a nasty kick."

"Don't mess with that!"

Phil aimed for the rafters, pulled the trigger, and emptied the clip into a beam. Chunks and slivers of broken wood rained down on them. He tossed the gun aside.

C.J. faced the angel. "I didn't mean to kill him! Lord have mercy!"

Stephen glared down. "Murder, not mercy, was in your heart. You left him to die. You failed to check on his condition or tend to his injury. You have shed innocent blood, and I fear it shall go hard for you in the Final Judgment."

Time to go, Stephen's voice came to Phil. *Come up here.*

How?

Directions came to his mind, and air currents moved under his feet as he ascended to Stephen.

"Thou shalt no longer destroy the Saints of God," Stephen bellowed. *"If thou wilt of thyself be destroyed, so be it!"*

The next Phil knew, they were outside, on top of the barn roof. Phil's heart pounded. He sat down, gasping for air.

"Why are you panting?"

"Adrenaline?"

"Inform your body to slow its systems."

"Oh." His heart rate slowed as he commanded. "I get it."

Stephen stared down at the roof. "They mean to say they killed you and destroyed your body, to appease their boss' anger."

"How are you getting this?" Phil said.

"Can't you see inside?"

"It's a solid roof."

"Try."

Phil made a frustrated noise and stared. Barn shingles.

"I've forgotten; you have much to learn. Regard the obstacle. Look through the spaces between the molecules, not the particles themselves."

Right, Phil thought. *Look at individual molecules.*

"When you are first learning, it is helpful to imagine the interior."

Phil kept staring. Shingles. "I can't do it. I'm sorry."

"You shall have to practice."

"So what are they saying?" Phil said.

"You can't hear them, either?" Stephen asked.

"No." Phil felt he was turning out less-than-expected.

But Stephen only nodded. "Clovis is arguing with Jack. He says, 'what's the point of killing them if they come back to life?'" Stephen laughed. "That was the concept we wished to teach."

"What happens now?" Phil asked.

"That is uncertain." Stephen's brow furrowed. "The rumors that follow should frighten them enough to cease the storehouse raids. I hope the kidnappings will stop."

"There are others?"

"I'm afraid so."

"I hadn't heard of any."

"This group of rebels arrived recently from Nauvoo, having failed in their efforts there."

"These men sounded local."

"Yes, they are. But the heads of their organization are not. The more evil of them may yet torture their victims without the mercy of death. Still—your disappearance and the rumors surrounding it will divide their ranks. They will not be as strong hereafter."

"We should have been warned!"

The angel hushed him. "Clovis swears to spread the truth. Jack's beginning to agree. I shall help them."

A thud sounded, and the men ran out yelling.

Jack said as they ran, "It's like vampires or aliens or the undead!"

"Whatever it was, I don't ever want to see one again!"

Their voices faded into the distance.

"What did you do?" Phil asked.

Stephen grinned. "I helped that broken beam fall to the ground and shorted the electrical circuits."

"What happens to my family?" His heart ached. Alive, yet separated . . . *Beverly* . . .

"They are protected. If you appeared to them, they would be too calm afterwards and seem to know something. Spies may be watching. Surely you can see the danger."

Phil nodded, anguished.

"As difficult as it seems now, the easiest path never promotes the most growth."

"I'll appreciate anything I'm allowed to do for them." Phil shivered in the night breeze.

"You're also cold?" Stephen asked.

"Aren't you? It's freezing out here."

The angel sighed. "You require physical orientation," Stephen said. "Come. I shall take you to One who is a far greater teacher than I." His eyes sparkled.

Phil prickled with excitement and worry at once.

"You realize you must ascend to the Father before much longer, Phillip."

Ascend to the Father.

The words penetrated Phil's soul with electric fire. Each day since his baptism he strove to live well, to be prepared for that eventual day. His heart raced in spite of himself.

"I fear you ought to check yourself over for stray shot. I'm not certain whether it all dislodged . . . generally one is buried properly and . . ."

Phil barely heard him.

Stephen stopped and touched Phil's shoulder. "Fear not. You have laid down your life for His sake. The Father is well-pleased."

"I hope so." Phil tingled with anticipation.

"It shall not seem long before you are reunited in peace," Stephen said. He stretched his hand out to Phil and smiled. "Time is far less meaningful where we shall be. Come."

Phil took his hand, and they were away.

September 25, 2046

Phil sat on the roof of his own stable watching Beverly and the children exercise the horses. It was a brilliant fall day with terrific weather.

Peter turned Teancum, Phil's dappled gray stallion, in tight figure-eights. Phil was amazed by his son's expertise. Jordan and Kellie rode together on their pony, squealing with delight as Andrew chased after them on his mare. Beverly spurred Abish, her sorrel mare, into the chase, but Peter held the anxious stallion steady.

Phil tapped a folded piece of paper against his palm. After seventeen months, he had received permission to give his family word of his safety. The note encouraged Beverly to be faithful, and assured her of his continued love, although he was not yet able to be with her.

He longed to hold her, brush the hair from her face, kiss her passionately . . .

Yet anger gnawed at Beverly's faith day by day.

Phil ever prayed that she would turn her grief over to her Savior. Still she clung to it. This work was for Jesus alone; laying her terrible burden at His feet would speed them back together, but until then, she wouldn't be ready to hear the whole truth. He hoped the note would help.

Andrew opened the far gate, leaning sideways from the saddle. The twins whooped with joy as they all broke into a gallop. Two dogs ran after, barking. Phil focused long-range as they galloped away. Beverly shone in the golden light.

He could cross that distance in less than a beat of her heart. But not today. Though he knew they were sealed for eternity, and this time apart would one day seem brief, he ached with longing.

With effort, he turned to the house.

Phil stood and walked across the roof, floated his body easily to the ground, and started for the house. An old black Labrador appeared, sniffing the air, staring, confused. He growled and gave a short, low bark.

Phil slowly made himself visible to the dog. "Bobbsey, it's me. Hush." Bobbsey wagged his tail and was quiet. Phil scratched the dog's ears. "Good boy." A thought came to him. "Is that hip still bothering you?" The dog limped with arthritis, which modern medication hadn't cured. Phil laid his hands on the dog's head. Moments later, he said, "It shouldn't trouble you any more, old boy."

Thank you, he heard in his mind. The dog licked Phil's hand and trotted off, tail wagging. The limp was gone.

Phil went invisible again. *I'm going inside to get the tape now*, he prayed.

Be careful, came the instant answer.

He pulled his body through the glass pane of the back door.

It was alluring to touch the familiar things of his own home; he felt a powerful urge to sniff Beverly's pillow, wrap his arms around it, and bask in her warm, sweet scent. But it might leave traces of his presence. He was strong, and held back.

He found the tape in the desk drawer. He snapped off a piece and returned it, careful not to move the smallest molecule of dust out of place as he went.

Then he stopped short. A fresh loaf of homemade bread rested on the kitchen counter. Tears stung his eyes as the scent beckoned him to take at least this small memento; eating was a pleasant occasional experience. He thought about how he and Beverly used to share the heels, fresh out of the oven.

Closer inspection showed both ends of the loaf were missing. Phil smiled. That made it easier. Which of his children picked up that trait after him? Or had she taken both ends for herself?

He slid his body easily through the glass, but the tape stuck to the inside of the door. He hadn't worked with sticky molecules before. He grunted with consternation and focused harder; the tape came through. He taped the note to the center of the door.

"Don't forget to erase fingerprints," a familiar voice called. Phil jumped.

Stephen stood in the yard, holding one of the barn cats.

"What are you doing here?"

"I was sent to keep you company at a difficult moment. Fingerprints?"

"Right, fingerprints," Phil said, mildly disturbed Stephen was sent as backup. But if he was less strong, he'd have eaten that bread, or held Beverly's pillow in his arms and wept until they came home. This was his first test.

He looked at the paper fibers on a microscopic level. There was a thumbprint. *Tsk.* He rearranged the molecular surface of the paper to wipe it out.

The cat lay nestled in Stephen's arms, purring loudly, kneading his forearm with her paws.

"That's Micah," Phil said, puzzled. "She never lets anybody hold her."

"I know." Stephen scratched the cat between its ears and down its spine. "Congratulations, little mama. Five kittens coming soon," he cooed.

"That one's always hiding," Phil muttered. "Beverly must not have caught her yet for spaying."

Stephen let the cat down gently. "Thank you, Micah. Take good care of your babies, and you shall let Beverly catch you next time, understand?"

The cat meowed and sauntered back to the barn, calico tail high in the air.

Phil breathed in the familiar, crisp spring air of the barnyard, anxious to leave while he could still manage to tear himself away.

The two ascended together.

He and Beverly had fought the morning of his kidnapping over how to discipline Andrew. She had refused to kiss him goodbye. She agonized over it now, he knew. Neither knew it was their last chance for—who knew how much longer.

He ached from the emptiness of leaving.

September 15, 2047

Phil stood by a bubbling stream and watched Alyssa Stark whittle a stick into a sharp point. Her wheat-blonde hair was ragged and matted; one leg of her jeans was torn to shreds and bloodstained.

Phil reached the fish before she did and spoke to them. "The Lord Jesus your Creator asks you to feed this girl who approaches." He peered into the water. He *felt* a volunteer in there; a faint twinge of fish-fear registered in his mind, with a vague sense of obedience.

He hoped it was enough.

Moments later Alyssa reached the spot, took aim, and thrust the spear into the water. She dragged the point along the muddy bottom and drew it out. A catfish wriggled on the end of it.

Phil thanked it.

It tried his patience to watch her try to light a fire. He itched to grab the knife and stone away from her and do it himself—which would scare her right out of her skin, never mind the added danger that she might recognize him. He had little practice in disguising his looks.

Finally, a tiny spark lit.

A breeze whipped up and blew it out.

Try using pine needles, Phil thought, careful not to make it too overpowering.

"Should just eat this thing raw," she mumbled. She rubbed her arms for warmth in the chill breeze. Phil realized she was cold. He'd forgotten about cold.

Alyssa hunted for tinder and returned with a handful of pine needles. She would never realize it wasn't her idea. The next spark ignited the needles, and with a little help from Phil, it kept burning. Soon she had eaten roasted fish.

Night fell.

Alyssa sat by the fire, quiet, warming herself, staring into the flames, her hazel eyes reflecting different colors in the firelight; green, blue, gray.

You could try going home, Phil suggested.

Alyssa tended the fire.

Phil sensed tangible anticipation in the air. A great deal of future happiness hung on this choice, including that of his second son.

She wasn't thrilled. *Home* was hardly the same word to her that it was to him. Yet it could be, in time.

The penetrating voice of the Spirit said, "*Go now.*"

Alyssa jumped.

Again the Spirit spoke. "*Go now. Go ye out from Babylon, for the hour of her destruction is at hand!*"

The urgency in the voice thrilled him.

Alyssa stood as if to bolt. She bounced on her legs. "Who's there?" she asked, drawing her knife, looking in all directions. "I need rest before I go. Sleep. And I need daylight. I won't know where I'm going. I need water, and food. Let's be practical here." Alyssa sat on the ground with a thump.

After a long pause, she said, "Okay. I'm going."

Phil's heart swelled with joy.

And [an angel] cried mightily with a strong voice, saying, Babylon the great is fallen, is fallen, and is become the habitation of devils, and the hold of every foul spirit, and a cage of every unclean and hateful bird.

And I heard another voice from heaven saying, Come out of her, my people, that ye be not partakers of her sins, and that ye receive not of her plagues.

For her sins have reached unto heaven, and God hath remembered her iniquities.

Therefore shall her plagues come in one day, death, and mourning, and famine; and she shall be utterly burned with fire: for strong is the Lord God who judgeth her.

The merchants which were made rich by her shall stand afar off for the fear of her torment, weeping and wailing,

And saying, Alas, alas, that great city, that was clothed in fine linen, and purple, and scarlet, and decked with gold, and precious stones, and pearls!

For in one hour so great riches is come to naught . . . And as many as trade by sea stood afar off,

And cried when they saw the smoke of her burning, saying, What city is like unto this great city!

. . . And in her was found the blood of prophets, and of saints, and of all that were slain upon the earth.

—Revelation 18:2, 4, 5, 8, 15-18, 24
Holy Bible, KJV

CHAPTER I

EASY MONEY

Heavenly Father, are you really there?
And do you hear and answer every child's prayer?

—"A Child's Prayer," verse 1
Janice Kapp Perry

Margret DeVray was out of money. A crumpled scrap of paper in Alyssa's handwriting lay in her pocket, with the name of some town still too far away, where friends might be, and shelter. *New Hope.* Alyssa's gift of all her savings had gotten Margret and her two kids, Marcus and Natty, from South Central City to West Des Moines.

Margret's ex-husband Ralph was far behind, and her moves were untraceable. She breathed easier. One phone call, three seconds of his distinctive voice, and she ran like a scared fox.

Did you think I'd forget, Margret? he said, gloating.

She shuddered, remembering, and crossed herself; what if he hadn't called at all, and appeared at the door before she could escape?

She had trusted too much in the Gardens, staying too long, forgetting the day of her discovery might come. The Gardens felt so safe and hidden.

She wouldn't make that mistake again. If Ralph was still trying to carry out death threats after four years, he wasn't likely to stop.

She wished for the millionth pointless time that she'd never gotten involved with that psychopath. You can't pick 'em by their looks, that's for sure. And she got pregnant with Natty on the first time with Ralph. Rotten luck. Marcus' father had refused to marry her, and Papa was already angry with Margret's behavior and her single, irresponsible motherhood, embarrassing the family and casting off her devout Catholic upbringing.

Ralph was willing . . . so she did what she thought was the right thing this time, even though Papa hated "that nasty white boy," and she wasn't that much in love with him.

She didn't catch on how twisted the man's mind was until after the wedding. He changed instantly, scarring her leg on their wedding night with a vicious knife wound, his first threat against her ever leaving him.

She had escaped when Marcus was four and Natty was just learning to crawl, and they lived in fear of his finding them ever since.

Stay focused. She couldn't wallow in the past; survival was key. Rotten as it was, the present wasn't the nightmare that living with him had been.

She couldn't settle in and get a job just yet. She had to keep running. And most places wanted work history, citizenship, and ID, which she either didn't have or couldn't afford to give out. It left tracks. After a single, failed attempt, she discarded prostitution as a viable source of income; she just couldn't go that far. Outright theft wasn't that easy, either, with electronic surveillance everywhere. Strange that sex could legally be sold for any product or price, but picking a pocket or snitching a few apples for her babies would send her straight to prison.

Article 28 had killed off charities, soup kitchens, homeless shelters. She had little choice but to keep moving, to avoid getting arrested for transience as well.

She could almost give up . . . but they would take her children away, and she couldn't bear to lose them. They slept behind buildings, industrial parks, anywhere they could find to hide for a day, and move on, hopefully one day closer to their destination.

She stooped to foraging out of dumpsters behind restaurants at night while the children slept. Neither Marcus or Natty complained. Much of it was barely touched; bread, salads, even fresh fruit. Not perfect enough for pampered taste buds, but it fed them well. She discovered that cold salmon in beurre blanc at seven a.m. wasn't so bad after all.

Marcus woke up slightly when she returned. "Are you back, Mama? Did the restaurant give you something yummy?"

"They sure did. We'll eat in the morning." She wrapped her arm around him, running her fingers through his wavy black hair.

"Sing me a song, Mama," Marcus mumbled, drowsy.

She hummed an old song that reminded her of Bert's constant gospel singing, "Amazing Grace." She never learned all the words, yet the tune calmed her, and her harried breathing slowed.

One night the trash pickup came before she did; the dumpsters were all empty. They hiked at least three miles through back alleys the next day and still she found nothing. By lunch their bellies were long empty, and Natty complained the loudest.

She took a risk. She walked the kids to a large grocery store. "Here's the plan. We go in, and put stuff in the cart like we're shopping, eh? You follow?"

Marcus nodded.

"We'll snack as we go. I'll say we're paying for it on the way out. Then we'll duck into the bathroom, ditch the cart, and leave."

"But Mama, that's stealing," Marcus said.

Like she thought he wouldn't figure that out. She sighed. "I know."

"You taught us never to steal."

"I know that too. Marcus, *niño*, this is an emergency. I don't have any money left or any job and it's the best I can do today. Just this once, it will be okay."

Marcus thought long about it. She could see the turmoil that brewed in his amber eyes. Eight years old and so pure. *I was mean by his age,* she thought. *My sweet baby—he'd rather starve than do anything wrong.*

Natty, only four, whined in her ear.

"What happened to the restaurant people?" Marcus asked.

"They didn't have any leftovers today." That was true, in a way. "It won't *look* like stealing," she added.

"There's no money at all?"

"None. Baby sister can't go hungry, Marcus. Neither can you."

He looked at Natty. "I can't think of another way, either." He squeezed his eyes shut.

"Good boy." She hated tarnishing his natural goodness.

On the way in, a security guard asked for ID as she put Natty in the cart.

"Yeah, I got ID, what's it to you?" Margret asked.

"Sorry, ma'am, you look—May I see it, please?"

"Excuse me? I don't look like I can shop here? I've had a hard day, all right, Godzilla? I work graveyard, then come home and clean house before I go to my other job. My man don't do squat, and I don't get much sleep. I don't need this routine every time I come in here. This is your last warning, hear?"

"But I've never seen you before." He furrowed his brow, a single, furry line wandering across his forehead.

"And you work every shift?" She had to look way up. He was big; she surprised herself to be taking this on. Must be desperation.

"I'm sorry, ma'am. I was gonna say you look sick is all."

Her Hispanic accent came on thick. "Listen, you racist pig, I am way too tired to put up with this crap. Sorry if I look so *bad* to you."

His eyes narrowed. "I don't like how you called me Godzilla. Your ID, please?"

"It's buried in my hand, idiot. This one." She held up her right hand, middle finger extended, and moved past before he forced the issue.

"He wasn't nice," Marcus said.

"He's prejudiced because we're Mexican. Remember that."

"I thought we were black."

"We're both. He's still racist."

"I want an orange." Natty leaned out. "Over there, Mama."

Margret mumbled to Marcus, "Follow my lead. Don't stuff yourselves. Watch me." Her mouth watered as she piled oranges into a produce bag. The citrus scent clung to her fingertips.

Margret compared canned goods as if checking for sales. They accepted the tidbit samples employees handed out, and Margret put packages of the samples she liked in her cart, making every effort to be polite and gracious, painfully aware of how bedraggled and smelly they were.

Marcus held up gourmet cookies. "Can I have these?"

"Not this time. We'll get these instead." She grabbed the store brand and tossed it in the cart.

"Can I have one now?" he asked, hopeful.

"Go ahead."

Soon the cart was full of discreetly opened packages of prepared food mingled with produce and meats; it looked normal enough. She didn't fuss when Natty whined. Nobody messed with them—whether in spite of or because of their ratty appearance, she didn't know.

Natty announced, "I have to go potty, Mama!"

"Is your tummy full, honey?" Margret whispered.

"I hafta go," Natty said, bouncing in the cart.

"Come on, Marcus. Time's up."

The restroom was in the back. She left the cart and they went in. "Come with me, Marcus."

"I'm too big for the girls' room, Mama."

It was unlike him to complain, and she hadn't expected that to be an issue. Her whisper was harsh. "I'm sorry, but you gotta go with us. I can't risk losing you!"

"Okay." He stared at his feet.

She washed their hair, faces, and hands in the sink. She had grabbed a brush; she should have added a pair of scissors. Their hair was more matted than she realized, and she could have cut it all off.

Natty had fun standing under the automatic dryer, giggling.

Margret crossed herself, grateful they were alone and undisturbed. They went out. With Natty balanced on her hip, holding Marcus' hand, she turned down a different aisle toward the exit.

"Miss?"

Sunshine beckoned through the plate glass doors. She squinted.

"Miss?" the voice repeated.

Surely he couldn't mean *her*. But it was more natural to look back than to plow on ahead. So she turned.

There was a man pushing her cart. *Caramba!* Her cart. Her eyes went wide in horror. That was it, opened packages and all.

Margret stopped short and held her breath. "Yeah?"

"Did you forget this?" He had a warm, friendly smile.

She trembled. Marcus squeezed her hand, their knuckles going white.

"No." It wasn't exactly a lie; they hadn't forgotten. "I needed a certain brand and they don't have it here. Do you mind not getting into my business?"

He persisted. "I'm almost positive I saw you with this cart. I noticed you back in produce."

"You noticed me back in produce?" It occurred to her that maybe he was single. But she was an unlikely pickup—ratty and stinking and dragging two kids. "Tell me what you really want, and I'll see what I can do, buddy. You work here?" Maybe he was plainclothes—even worse.

"No, no, I don't work for . . . Listen. I don't know how to say this, but I can help," he whispered.

"Help with what?" She kept a guarded eye.

His voice stayed at a whisper. "You can take all this home. I mean it."

"What makes you think I want it?" She tossed back her curls.

"I saw you eating, back there . . . the children . . ." His smile faded. "I'm sorry, I thought maybe . . ."

"Wait," Margret said. Maybe he was for real. "Don't go. We could work something out."

She looked him over. Back to Plan A. Or C. Whatever that once-failed idea was. He wasn't *muy* good-looking, but not bad. Even on ordinary non-financial terms he might do. She shifted Natty on her hip.

"We can discuss arrangements," she smiled.

"Great! Let me take this through the line for you."

"No, we'll never eat it all."

"Your kids are much too thin. Take it."

They rolled the loaded cart out into the parking lot. "Where's your car?" he asked.

She laughed. "My car? Look at me! What planet are you from?"

He smiled. "Bus, then?"

They headed for the stop at the far end of the parking lot.

"But this is the long-distance line to Sioux City . . ."

"I know," Margret said. "So what's your name?"

"David. And yours?"

"Margarita Juarez." Marcus tugged on her shirt. She waved him off with a *shh*.

"That's a pretty name," David said.

They reached the stop.

Margret seated Marcus with his sister and fished out the cookies. "Eat. Watch your sister. Natty, be good." She kissed her daughter on the chin. "I'm going to talk to David some more, all right?"

She caught him by the hand and pulled him out of earshot. "Now, about those arrangements." She forced a smile. "You'll get more than you paid for. I'm very good, eh. And that food's worth a lot to me. Anything you like, you got it. I can do it all."

"Excuse me?"

"What you see is what you get." She tilted her head, showed off her body. "Does your car have tinted windows? Or I'll go with you wherever—your place, a hotel, just so my kids don't know, eh? And the deal's *off* if you want the kids." She had to be clear; that was how her first attempt went sour.

"Wait—you think I want to sleep with you for this?"

"Buddy, nobody hands out that much money." She folded her arms. "What else do I have to pay with? *Nada*."

"You're not paying me back, and definitely not that way."

She was half insulted. "Why, are you gay?"

He was flustered. "Margarita, that's not my way any more than it is yours."

"You think I don't want to, is that it?"

"That's beside the point."

"Then what *is* your point?" she asked.

He paused. "You don't have a home, do you?"

"What do you care?"

"Tell me the truth. Please," David said.

Margret sighed. "We're traveling."

"Where? And with what means?"

"I don't owe you answers about my personal life, mister."

"That bus is coming in a few minutes, and you're not getting on, are you? You don't have anywhere to go or any money to get there."

"I do too," she retorted. "Listen. David. I'm extremely grateful, but we were fine. If you don't want to trade, fine. But don't bug me about my life, eh? I *don't* owe you that. Take my offer or leave me alone."

To her surprise and shame, he pulled out his wallet and took out several bills, shoving the money into her hand.

"I'm not taking any more of your money unless I work. I'm a seamstress. I can do lots of stuff, mending, laundry, gardening. Anything." She tried handing the money back, but torn by need, her hand wouldn't budge.

"Just get your kids to safety, Margarita," he said, closing his hands around hers. "Promise me."

"Sure, I promise."

"Hurry. You do that, call it working for me, and we're even." His broad smile returned, with straight, white teeth. He walked away, back through the parking lot.

She looked closer; the bills weren't twenties, they were hundreds. She gasped. "David—wait!"

But he didn't turn back, and she didn't run after him to see if he'd made a mistake. She shoved the money in her jeans pocket and hurried back to her kids. No sense arguing with fate.

"What were you fighting about?" Marcus asked.

"We weren't fighting. He gave us bus money. Want to ride the bus?"

"Yeah!" Natty brightened up.

"See, sweetie, we didn't have to steal after all!"

"I knew it would be okay," Marcus said, relieved.

"What do we do with all this food?" She looked through her bags, nervous laughter escaping her lips.

"Eat it!" Natty squealed and clapped her hands.

"Yes, sweetie, we'll eat it!" Margret hugged her daughter.

In her efforts to seem like a normal shopper, she had thrown a lot of food in the cart that she couldn't use. Plus, ten heavy sacks of groceries were too much to carry far. If she had only understood, she'd have gone back and picked different stuff. Instead she had raw roast beef. Rice, potatoes, onions. Tin cans—and no can opener. *Estúpida.*

She separated the things she couldn't cook, carry, or eat raw from the practical stuff, and kept six bags. If only she hadn't rushed. She was grateful, but kicked herself for not doing better.

Well. It got them out of town with money left over, even though bus fare wasn't cheap. Their legs could use the break. And they could eat a real dinner that evening.

The bus west to Sioux City came up with a whoosh and squeal of brakes, and they climbed aboard.

* * * * *

As they traveled, a passenger had a coughing fit. The bus stopped. The man was forcibly hauled off by other passengers and left at the side of the road. Margret hushed Marcus' questions, frightened. "Whatever you do, *niños*, don't cough, eh?"

The other passengers wore fearful, nervous expressions, and no one argued the man's treatment was unjust. She was silent. There were times questions did more harm than good.

* * * * *

They disembarked at Shelby, Iowa. The passengers acted so strange; snatches of whispers made out Central City like it was the source of ultimate evil. She got too nervous to stay on the bus any longer.

Best no one knew where they came from.

* * * * *

"Kids ain't allowed in this pub," the bartender said, an older man with bushy, white eyebrows.

"Give me a minute, I'm watching this." Margret indicated the TV screen. Something big was up.

The broadcast was unreal. Some disease taking over Central City. And half the City was burning.

"You're not drinking. Give me a reason to let you stay." He held out his hand.

She ignored the gesture—she wasn't about to pay to breathe the air. "I ain't heard any of this, all right?"

"Ain't you got a TV?" he frowned.

"No. Gimme a few minutes, eh."

Marcus sat on a barstool, looking down at his feet. Margret held Natty on her lap next to him.

"What's Mandy Tyler doing as anchor?" she asked. Mandy was just a regular reporter.

"Where you been, lady? They're all dead."

Dead?

Mandy Tyler's face showed terror. That woman usually had a face of stone, except for that polite TV-smile, no matter what story she covered. Except this time. "A special election is announced—"

"What?" Margret asked.

The bartender said, "It's that toxic flu thing going on. Man, lady, you *are* out of it. It's killing everybody in Central. President Garrison, reporters, politicians—didn't you see the Palace blow up? General Horne's ordered a quarantine. Nobody goes in or out."

That explained the odd behavior of the people on the bus. Margret caught her breath in a sudden, sharp gasp.

Alyssa— Bert—

Papa! All her estranged siblings, cousins, aunts and uncles. Multitudes of others she knew.

Dead?

Ralph? A shiver ran up her spine.

"Tyler's on the air because she was out of town when the disease started and didn't catch it. The usual guy, old Everton, he died right away."

"I miss Alyssa, Mama," Natty said out of the blue, burying her head in Margret's chest. Sometimes the girl had uncanny timing. "Can we go see Alyssa?"

Margret ran her fingers through her child's wavy, matted hair. She blinked away tears. "Not now," she said, finally, when she could speak without choking up.

She could barely comprehend the scope of the destruction.

Mandy Tyler went on, "General Leopold Horne has requested surviving citizens of Central City to check in at designated sites. At these checkpoints, we can begin restoring your lost information. Your citizenship and rights may be lost otherwise. Main Central City servers have exploded, causing permanent data loss."

The picture zoomed in on a completely destroyed location in Central City. Margret recognized famous landmarks smoldering in ruins.

The bartender said, "You're too young, but I remember when Blankenship nuked L.A. Couldn't get clear pictures through the ash, but that was worse than this, except for casualties."

The news anchor listed off checkpoints from a long list. A map showed up in a corner of the screen.

"I hope we're not a checkpoint," the bartender said. "I don't want all them people coming here."

"From satellite photos, we estimate a minimum of two million lives have been lost to this disease. There is worldwide panic that this toxic flu virus will spread into an Extinction Level Event. General Horne reassures us our fears are unfounded and that it *will* be contained within the quarantine boundaries. If this disease proves to be genetically engineered, as we all suspect . . ."

"You ain't from Central, are you?" The bartender glared at her.

The question startled her. There was only one right answer. "Never been there."

She gave Marcus a fierce look as his mouth dropped open. He shut it.

He said, "They say it only spreads by water and body fluids— but they don't know squat. Germs go everywhere."

The bartender news anchor continued, "As viewers well recall, rather than facing a second Civil War after passing of Article 28, President James A. Garrison allowed Utah to secede from the

Union. Today we have confirmed that four other states—Florida, Montana, Nevada, and Arizona—have submitted petitions this week to follow Utah in secession. This request comes now, not over religious issues, but through the desire of these States to govern themselves until the leadership crisis is resolved. Again we remind you to vote in the upcoming election—"

The bartender scoffed. "Ain't nobody running against Horne, what's the point?"

Video came on the screen of marching soldiers in fatigues, tanks rolling in near the southern outskirts of the City.

"U.S. troops have been mobilized to patrol the quarantine perimeters under the direction of General Horne. His expected attack on the Middle East has been postponed due to this major repositioning of troops. The downside to this is that the oil embargo will continue to drag on. Gasoline prices have suffered yet another sharp hike."

An image of a lake came up on the monitor.

"UN officials are searching for motives among remaining terrorist factions. We do know that the organism was seeded inside a government-owned reservoir east of city limits, pointing suspicion to someone or some organization on our own U.S. soil."

After repeating the list of checkpoint stations once more, the broadcast switched over to local news. Sports. People were playing organized sports in the middle of all this?

"You got your news report, lady. That's all the patience I have," the bartender said.

"I'm leaving, all right? Thanks."

"Mama, you told a lie in there," Marcus said as they left the pub.

She groaned. "Weren't you listening? He would have hurt us if he knew we were from Central! Couldn't you tell he was scared?"

"It was still a lie," he said, sullen.

"I wish me and your old pal Bert hadn't taught you so good, niño." A wan smile flickered across her face. "I protected us. We're not sick, but he wouldn't have cared."

She hated how every day made it harder to justify herself to him.

* * * * *

Margret decided to head to the countryside and come up with a makeshift camp. She dared not waste precious money on soft motel beds. Tempting, but stupid. They'd been fine on cement, and dirt would be an improvement.

At a convenience store north of town she bought a lighter, for starting fires, and a few other things that looked useful. She asked casually, "I'm looking for a place called New Hope?"

The clerk wrinkled her nose. "That's Mormon country. You one of them?"

"Do I look like it?" Margret laughed. Her multiple earrings jangled.

The woman sized her up. "Come to think of it, no. What do you want to go up there for?"

"I'm just curious. Aren't they weird?"

Margret only remembered Alyssa saying her friends were Christian, not tacking on *Mormon*. She narrowed one eye. Maybe she should stop for good in Shelby.

"It's hardly a tourist attraction," the woman said. "They're not so interesting as the Amish. You want to see different, go see them. They ain't too far neither. Mormons use electricity and computers and all that, and their clothes ain't even too funny. If you ask me, they just got a bad deal from that Article 28. Those I've seen look almost normal. Nice folk."

"You've been there?"

"Nah. We get a few come through here on their way to or from Utah Nation. You go back out north on 59 about eighty miles. It's northwest of Holstein a ways. They say you can't miss it."

"Thanks. Come on, Marcus. Natty."

She'd forgotten to watch them. Marcus clutched a comic book in his hands, and Natty had her grubby fingers firmly attached to a package of bubble gum, which she was working on opening.

"Marcus, weren't you watching your sister? I'm sorry, ma'am, they know better. Come *on*."

"Okay, Mama." Marcus put the book on the rack, with some effort, and went to the door.

"It's all right." The woman leaned over the counter. "I had kids. I know how it is."

Margret reached to separate the package of gum from Natty's determined fingers, but as she did, something in her heart softened. They had so little for fun, and nothing lately. They were only kids.

She pulled out a little more of the precious money. "I'll take the gum. And the comic book."

Marcus let out a startled noise. "No, Mama! I was only looking, honest."

"I know. Let me do this, okay?"

He shook his head no, his eyes like saucers.

"Go give it to the lady so she can ring it up."

Hesitating and open-mouthed, he did so.

On the way out, she mussed up his hair. "Smile, *niño*. Live a little." A sudden sob choked her throat, but she held it back so he wouldn't hear.

"All right, Mama." He looked up with a wide grin, clutching the book with both hands like it was solid gold.

They were close to their destination, with easy directions. Margret felt better than she had in weeks. It would still be a long march, saving the rest of the money for food, but she made up her mind to go—it was a real place, even if it *was* filled with Mormons. They ought to be friendly, if she remembered right.

On the bright side, Ralph would never dream of looking for them *there*.

CHAPTER 2

THE RIGHT HAND

> *American Toxic Flu, or ATF, was released into the world on September 17, 2047.*
>
> *The name is inaccurate; it never was a flu virus. Three small letters do not convey the horror of its toxicity, the vicious symptoms ravaging its victims before death, or the death toll counted in tens of millions. Our reactions seem to mirror those who lived through World War II, once the horrors of Auschwitz were fully realized and understood.*
>
> *We soon came to think of every event as either "before" or "after" Outbreak . . .*
>
> *Crushed by greater loss of life than we'd ever known, Alyssa asked so many questions about life and death and our beliefs in those first weeks with us that she about drove us crazy. At first she doubted, especially in our lifestyle; it seemed too rigid and imposing overall, although she had mostly followed it, without knowing. It wasn't as much of a lifestyle shift as she imagined.*
>
> *. . . Alyssa's startling spiritual gifts became apparent almost immediately. She did not always think of them as blessings . . .*
>
> —Beverly Richardson,
> Richardson Family History

General Leo F. Horne heard of an outbreak of a strange and fatal disease through the emergency hotline. He'd been in the field surveying practice maneuvers for the upcoming war with Saudi Arabia when he was called in. It was a chill night, and his blood froze once he understood the implications.

Horne watched on the screen as President James A. Garrison, his confidant and friend—"Jag" for short—died a gruesome death over the course of a four-day illness.

Horne took Garrison's last video calls privately. "Get me out of here!" Jag screamed, blinded by the disease. The sight of the empty sockets wrenched his stomach. He'd seen battle. Gore was no stranger, but this was his Commander-in-Chief, his mentor and father figure. He couldn't show emotion—not here—not when terror was foremost, above grief. He could do nothing to save his friend.

"Come on, Leo! Do something! We're all dying in here!"

"I can't," Horne replied. "You're not getting out. This is bigger even than you."

No tears fell from his cold, chiseled face. The quarantine was absolute.

He cut the connection, and did not answer again.

Twenty hours later, word came that the President was dead.

* * * * *

At thirty-eight, Horne was young to be the top General in the U.S., but he was well-qualified. Jag recognized his potential when he was a young soldier and Jag was first coming into his Presidency. Horne took risks, and Jag liked it. The risks had paid off: Horne was promoted fast through the ranks, to the disgruntlement of many older generals. Soon, even they had to concede his strategic brilliance.

The President became a trusted ally, and Horne trusted few men. Jag affectionately called Horne the Right Hand. So did the rest of the military, all divisions, as they grew to appreciate his skill and strategy.

In turn, Horne mentored his troops the same way, his goal to be the father most of them never had—that he'd been deprived of, himself. He commanded their respect, absolute loyalty, and obedience, and worked hard to earn it. Often he did maneuvers in the trenches side by side with his boys, refusing to get soft in HQ offices, requiring the same physical conditioning of himself as his boys, and more.

Now the man who made him what he was, was dead—along with the Vice President, the rest of the Senate, and nearly all the

House. It would be a while before a meaningful vote could be organized, restructuring the governing bodies.

It fell to him to lead.

His troops were currently marshaled east of Central City for imminent transport to war in the Middle East. Central HQ offices were teeming with the virus. Horne had no family. He stayed out with the troops. Uncomfortable quarters, but safe from disease.

ATF had to be addressed. He postponed the war he had so carefully plotted for years, discouraged that the country would have to wait even longer to restore its oil supply. He'd been looking forward to blowing those rats out of their holes once and for all.

Horne didn't send the troops home—they were needed right here. He ordered a quarantine around the perimeter of Central City and marched his soldiers out to enforce it, laying siege to his own capital. He would do whatever it took to contain this thing.

He rang up Dr. Joel Kensington in Des Moines. "You're heading up the project to find a cure. Fast."

"You forget I'm a civilian, General. I don't take orders."

"You'll be paid well. Listen. Victor Caldwell is dead. That leaves you as the top geneticist in the United States. Get to the bottom of this. ASAP."

On the screen, Kensington looked startled, as if Horne had woken him from a sound sleep and the man believed he was still dreaming.

"Caldwell's dead? You know for sure?"

"The entire building blew up with him inside it. Security records show he checked in that morning, and didn't check out. Satellite photos show nothing left in that rubble. It's safe to presume as much."

Kensington accepted this with a nod.

Horne continued, "I don't need to explain the rewards, financial and otherwise, that you stand to receive for being the one to solve this puzzle—do I? I'm offering you a great honor. You'd do well not to refuse it."

"I understand." There was a pause.

"What is it?" Horne asked. "Be quick, I'm a busy man."

"I may need special clearances . . . access to records . . . permission to use whatever procedures that might be required." Kensington licked his lips. He was not known for his ethics. Caldwell, at least, was better at covering his tail, better at diplomacy with his superiors.

Horne didn't have to think. "Granted. I don't care how you do it. Whatever it takes—any equipment or lab you need, say the word and I'll acquire it for you. Money is no object—not with the entire human race at stake. The only thing you can't do is violate quarantine."

"But—!"

"No exceptions! This thing is fatal, Kensington. If you work inside the quarantine zone, you and your staff will likely all die. Then I'm back to square one with no answers. I don't have the time, for one, and I can't afford to lose your expertise. This thing had to be engineered. You have to reverse its effects."

"It would speed the process considerably to have active test subjects!"

"It would only speed the process of your death. Haven't you seen the reports I sent you?"

"Begging your pardon, sir, but you're not the scientist here."

"I know that. Are you refusing the job and the terms?"

"No—no, I'm not. I'll do it, General."

"You can call me Sir."

"Yes . . . Sir."

"Good."

America would have to deal with military law—his law—until the crisis was over. And he liked being called *Sir*.

* * * * *

For no rational reason, one evening Horne found himself suddenly craving a good Havana cigar.

Horne banned smoking in all forms from his troops. It made them weak, unhealthy, unable to fight the good fight.

He hadn't smoked, himself, in years.

The craving intensified to the point he could not rest. He battled a great deal of frustration with the circumstances fate had dealt him, but he lost the fight against this tobacco craving.

At 19:32 hours he stalked to the nearest temporary barracks. They were little more than hard reinforced plastic tents, not designed for long-term housing. If this went on through the winter, he'd have to do something. They weren't designed to hold out a twenty-below Midwestern wind-chill.

The soldiers snapped to attention.

"At ease. Listen. You're good soldiers—the very best. I know you follow all my orders to the letter. But listen, if any of you have a cigar smuggled in your gear, I need one now."

"Sir?" the nearest said, startled.

"I need a cigar!" he bellowed. "Somebody in here has to have one!"

"Sir, possession of cigars is against regulation, sir!"

"I know that, Corporal. This isn't inspection! I need a good smoke!"

"Sir, does this change regulation, sir?"

"No! Just find me a cigar. Fall out and search the barracks! There will be no punishment unless you fail."

They scattered.

"The generous donor remains anonymous!"

*　*　*　*　*

Thirty minutes later, a trembling young private approached him in his office with the contraband. Thunder rumbled outside as the door opened; another storm was coming through. Odd for this late in the season. He hated this dratted unpredictable Missouri weather—hot one September day, freezing wind the next.

"Sir, your cigar, sir!"

"At ease. Private, is there more where this came from?"

"I did not inquire, sir!"

"Find out, in case I need another one."

"Yes, sir!"

"Good work. What unit are you from, soldier?"

"Special Unit 5-3-9 dash 8-2-1, sir." The young man relaxed slightly.

Horne smiled. "Your unit provides my best soldiers. I'm sending my best girls to your barracks tonight—my treat. All night. And tomorrow, your unit is excused from maneuvers. You'll need the rest."

The soldier's face barely changed, but Horne saw in his eyes that the news pleased him a good deal. He looked at the name badge. "Private Right Hand Hawk. Tell me . . . what was your number before you became a soldier?"

"Sir?"

He lowered his voice and looked him in the eye. "You know *exactly* what I mean, Private."

Right Hand Hawk was near undone, trembling. "8-8-5, sir!"

"Ah. I remember your file. Excellent performance in training sims. Remarkable aim and reflexes. Nearly as good as my own."

Recovering, the soldier fought back a smile, working to keep his expression stoic. "Thank you, sir!"

"You're quite young yet."

The private stammered. "Begging your pardon, sir, my age is unknown. I passed all tests for entry into the service. Sir."

"I'm aware of that, soldier. I'm offering to look it up in your file if you like." Horne noted the glimmer behind the eyes, the hungry curiosity.

"Please—that's not necessary, sir."

Horne was pleased. The proffered tidbit would smolder in the boy's mind a long while, cementing his loyalty. "Dismissed."

Right Hand Hawk saluted.

"By the way, soldier—"

"Yes, sir?"

"Good choice of name. I like it."

"Thank you, sir!"

"Sometime we'll sit down together and you can explain it to me."

"I'd like that, sir!"

Horne returned the salute and the soldier left. He sat and chewed the end of the cigar a long while before lighting up. How do you plan a strategy against an unknown enemy? Mother Nature gone berserk? Or human evil? A human culprit was the simplest explanation.

He had to find out who did this, how, and why.

And how to beat it before more people died.

CHAPTER 3

RECORD KEEPING

Peter gave me this journal for my birthday. He says keeping a journal is important, but my life is just not that interesting. Who'd want to read about me?

I'm still surprised that I got out of Central City just before Outbreak. Strange to think I should be dead. It hurts so much when I think about my friends there.

Still it's good to be at this old farm again. It always felt safe. Always. And the house smells good. It does bring back memories, but these are good ones. It feels so much like home . . . the kind of home I never had. I loved this place when I was little. I used to imagine Beverly could be my mother and Phil could be my dad . . .

Phil's been missing a long time. Beverly's not the person I remember. She seems so sad.

Beverly cut my hair. It was so ragged when I got here. Margret was last to cut it before this, a lifetime ago. It's a small thing, but I feel so much better.

While Beverly was cutting, we talked about Joan. So it's shorter than she meant to cut it. Ha ha. No really, it is. It's just below my chin.

Last week I dreamed about a terrified little boy living in a steel cage. There were rows of cages, like a laboratory, but big ones with humans inside, not mice. Creepy. It made no sense, but I couldn't get back to sleep.

Last night I dreamed about him again, the same boy. I can see his face so clearly, as if he were a real person. He was out of his cage, afraid and surrounded by flames. He didn't know where to go and he couldn't see me. I couldn't help him. I hated that feeling—like watching someone fall off a building.

I'm afraid to talk about it, in case it means I'm crazy.

I get weak-kneed around Peter. I wish I didn't. Eight years apart is a long time. I can't help remembering how he kissed me, when I was fourteen and he was sixteen, in the cornfield, the last time we saw each other. It was the Fourth of July. It's unlikely to happen again—he's afraid of me or something. Or he hates that I lived in Central City so long, like it was a pit of evil. Well— that's not far from the truth.

It is nice to be out of there . . . I do miss Margret, but she was gone anyway. I miss the rooftop gardens, even though there's plenty of dirt and gardening here to go around. I worry about Marcus and Natty too. If they all made it out of the City in time. If they had enough money.

If if if if if. I may never know.

After being homeless so long I look like a skeleton. Beverly stuffs me full, but I haven't gained much weight. I hope Peter doesn't come in and read this. This must be why people hide diaries and why I never kept one before! Mother was always poking in my stuff. Guess this gets shoved under the mattress, huh.

I need to write more about my healing, but I don't know if I can do it justice. Meeting Jesus himself? How many people alive can say they've done that. And who will believe me? Besides Peter and Beverly. It's obvious Andrew has issues with what happened to me. I'm so busy with farm chores, and morning comes so early, I don't know when I'll have time or not be too tired or feel up to writing it. It's amazing people live this way . . . that I'm living this way.

Well, I gotta go. Writing this has been very strange.

—Alyssa Stark,
first journal entry

Alyssa sat on her bed with her journal and a pen, re-reading her first few entries so far. Peter said to write down everything that had happened to her recently, before she forgot. But how *could* she forget? She ran her fingers through her short blonde hair.

She studied the words scribbled down the pages. Her writing was disjointed, skipping from one topic to another. She'd barely mentioned her birthday. That came shortly after the day Peter asked her to stay with them. They remembered it before she did—she'd lost track of the date. She asked them not to make a big deal out of it. She felt she was causing enough attention just by being there. Peter dug through his things and found this blank journal to give her. It was made of plain lined paper with a hardbound, dark green cover. It wasn't the fanciest present she ever received, but it was nice of him.

As she looked through her words, she realized she wrote a lot about dreams. She'd been having strange dreams ever since she arrived—weird, yet more vivid than reality.

She'd forgotten to write down the first dream, about Bert and Mary from the Gardens, and added that in. She wrote how Crazy Mary had found her lost baby; of Bert singing in a heavenly choir, telling her she was home now, safe in the arms of Jesus.

Shortly after that, Peter had asked her to stay as part of their family. Alyssa thought again how right it felt to call this place home. *Is that what the dream meant?*

Maybe it only meant Bert was dead. Or nothing at all.

There was no way to know. Once General Horne proclaimed martial law and enforced a strict quarantine, no one could get in or out. Most communication grids were down as well.

It was chaos everywhere but here.

The uncertainty nagged at her. She liked knowing things. Precision. Math. Things she could measure, examine, depend upon.

The spirituality she felt awakening in her soul also unsettled her, deeply. It couldn't be seen or proven. She couldn't explain it. It wasn't logical. But it *was* felt—and it would not be denied.

Every day it grew, if slowly: an awareness there was more to her life than a brief mortal existence, a hope, a great love enveloping her in its powerful arms. Like a long-dormant seed in dry earth, finally watered and beginning to sprout its first tendril, soon it would burst through the surface to the light, sending out deep taproots, bursting forth with green, new leaves. She felt its approach.

She couldn't quite explain that, much less explain why she was not afraid.

She wrote down how the Richardsons held church services in their home. Peter said they used to have a chapel, but arsonists burned it to the ground, and the restrictions of Article 28 didn't let the members rebuild. Sunday, she had watched with interest as Peter and Andrew blessed the sacrament of the Lord's Supper. After that, the family spent two hours teaching one another from scriptures and church texts, singing hymns to recorded music. Fraternal twins Kellie and Jordan sang their favorite children's songs with enthusiasm, which had made Alyssa smile.

She moved on, changing topics. There was something important she'd forgotten to write.

Victor Caldwell is missing and presumed dead.

Alyssa checked on that immediately after news of the outbreak. She found out the Federal Department of Research building, where Caldwell worked, had exploded. She hoped he was inside when it blew. The newscast didn't say.

Caldwell was the man she blamed for everything wrong in her adult life. He created the powerful drug Elation. It nearly killed her before she recovered from a frightening addiction. Without that, she wouldn't have been so involved with Rob—if at all. He was her dealer first, then dated her, even proposed to her; but he was also an undercover federal agent, working for Caldwell. She once had feelings for him, true, and still wondered if he had escaped Caldwell's grasp—or not—but remembering that relationship always filled her with poignant regret.

Rob vanished as he planned, and she escaped separately to the anonymity of the Gardens, refusing Rob's offer to go with him to rural Montana.

Caldwell wanted Alyssa to serve as a human ambassador to the strange beings he had detected, beings to which Elation gave her a terrifying access point. Beings which may or may not be real.

A disquieting thought rose in her mind. *Is Elation why I'm dreaming now? Flashbacks? What about the stranger . . . the portrait . . . the man the Richardsons say is Jesus Christ?*

What is *real?* she wondered. *And how do I know?*

She didn't write any of *that* down for future generations.

Her recent experiences, from her miraculous healing, to arriving at the Richardsons' farm, to the revelation that she had been healed by Jesus himself, were overwhelming. Peter had given her books to read, along with the journal—the Bible and a *Book of Mormon.* She'd skimmed through them—but the volume of information to absorb could give her a headache, if she let it. She put the journal away, took the other two books down with her into the living room, and settled on the couch next to Beverly, who was working on a cross-stitching project.

The news was on, as usual. Since the outbreak of the new plague, no one ever turned it off. It was getting late, but only the young twins, Jordan and Kellie, were in bed.

"Hey," Peter said, a greeting.

"Hey." Alyssa opened her books.

Peter seemed to be watching her more than the TV, but that had to be her imagination. She tried not to look over too much.

On top of everything else, she got a giddy feeling sometimes when she looked at him, which she was unsuccessfully trying to squash. She wound up thinking about the blue of his eyes or how his hair had changed since they were kids, still blond but staying in place; it didn't fall in his eyes anymore. He wasn't a scrawny kid anymore either, but tall and well-built.

But they had already started out fighting. She was sure her current attraction was a remnant, a leftover from their shared childhood. Nothing with substance.

Alyssa had the strange feeling someone was missing. Of course: Phil. As soon as she placed it, she sensed that absence keenly. The twins were asleep; Isaac, Peter's older brother, and Julia, his younger sister, weren't in the room either, but they were each married and living elsewhere, not *missing*. Alyssa glanced at Beverly, sure that Peter's mother felt the loss of her husband more keenly than it showed.

The TV report caught her attention. "The virus begins like a common flu, with coughing, nausea and fever, but quickly worsens. By the third day or sooner, connective tissue around vital organs begins to deteriorate, causing intense pain and discomfort for the affected patient before death ensues. Eyeballs disconnect from their sockets—"

"We can change the channel," Beverly offered, distracting Alyssa's attention.

"I have a strong stomach—I've seen worse firsthand. Hospitals down in the slums are ruthless. You don't want to get sick without insurance."

Andrew grunted and wrinkled his nose. At her, or the picture on the TV?

"What happens?" Peter asked.

"If your body can survive without it, they're allowed to take it out to pay your bill," she explained.

Bringing up the Gardens made Alyssa think about Margret and her children, wondering again if they had made it out of Central City before the quarantine was enforced. She missed the kids as much as she missed her friend. She was glad for the twins' cheerful company during the day. They were close to Marcus' age.

She felt a wistful longing, and on placing it remembered her own dead ovaries; she shook it away. Mandatory, government-regulated shots taken during her time in the Gardens had systematically killed off her ova and any chance for a child of her own. There was no point in spending emotional currency on that. It was done and could not be undone. She rubbed at the back of her neck, tension bothering her.

"Are you okay?" Peter said.

"I just miss my friends more than I ever thought. When I left, I . . ." Her voice trailed off. Her thoughts took her back to the dismal day she learned the truth about those shots, the day after Margret left. After that, she began to wander, homeless, to find her way out of the City, nothing left to lose . . . or live for.

She looked up to find Peter staring at her. "When you left, you—?"

"Hm?"

"You stopped in the middle of a sentence."

"I'm sorry. I don't know what I was going to say." Shyness welled up. He wasn't ready to hear about anything difficult she had been through, any more than she was ready to tell it—not after the arguments they had right after she got here. Her previous homelessness bothered him in some deep way that she didn't understand.

She drifted between poring through the books and watching the broadcast. Most of the regular anchors had died of ATF. The new reporters seemed more human, dark circles under their eyes that makeup couldn't cover, their words slurring with fatigue.

The station replayed satellite footage of the Presidential Palace, burning. It was the Ninth Wonder of the World, and it had burned to the ground.

"How long is that General Horne supposed to stay in charge?" Andrew asked.

Beverly said, "They called for an emergency vote next Tuesday, to officially make him President."

"Is anyone running against him?" Peter asked.

"It wouldn't do us any good if they did, since we can't vote anyway."

Article 28 denied persons of religious faith the right to vote—until they gave up their beliefs, or turned themselves in for psychiatric "therapy."

Alyssa shut her books, too much information swimming through her brain, refusing to be sorted out. The company was fine, but the discussion had been rehashed many times over, and her eyelids were heavy.

She told them all goodnight and went back upstairs.

The bed was warm and comfortable, the quilts solid and heavy on her body.

That was real enough for now.

She snuggled in, and in spite of her worries, jumbled thoughts, and fears, she fell asleep immediately.

That night she dreamed again.

In the dream her mother, Joan Stark, fought with Alyssa's older sister Lauren. It was silent, no soundtrack, no voiceover. Torn photographs and a ruined artist's portfolio lay strewn on the floor. Lauren was in the photos; Alyssa did not want to see, but did. They were explicit, disturbing, and pornographic. Lauren threw a drink in her mother's face. Joan knocked her down and kicked her with the toe of pointed shoes, shredding more photographs with bony, aging fingers. The dream shifted and Alyssa became Lauren. Joan's screams became audible: *Slut! Whore! Tramp! You ruined her. It was your bad influence. This is all your fault. Your fault. Your fault!*

Alyssa woke panting in a cold sweat. Her ribs ached. It was a remembered pain; her body never forgot that undeserved beating. Her father's voice echoed in her mind, *I'm sorry, I'm so sorry* . . . and for a moment she almost felt his arms around her, a flutter, an imagined touch.

She slipped uneasily back into sleep. As she drifted off, she heard murmured words, a splash of clean water, an underwater bubbling, a rising up out of deep water.

A remote part of her mind connected what it meant, this thing that would heal, help, make whole, and teach her the meaning of her dreams.

It was the sound of baptism.

CHAPTER 4

MICAH

Our tests reveal the Missouri River has contaminated the Mississippi at St. Louis, on southward to the Gulf. Please inform all citizens immediately of the risk.
However, the ATF virus/bacterium does not survive in cold salt water. We are greatly relieved.

—Dr. Joel Kensington,
memo to General Horne

Alyssa fed the chickens with Peter's mother, Beverly, as the sun peeked its shining arc over the Iowa hills. It was a crisp spring dawn. Alyssa yawned; her sleep had been all but restful.

Beverly scooped a hen under her arm before exiting the chicken yard and latching the gate. "Always ask me how much to feed them. Sometimes they get leftovers. Other times they need the vitamins in the feed itself."

"Always ask." Alyssa's mind swam through a thick fog of exhaustion.

"After a while you'll get a feel for it." Beverly moved across the farmyard. Alyssa followed.

"What leftovers do they eat?" she asked.

"Oh, chickens will eat anything," Beverly said. In one fluid motion, she laid the chicken flat on an upended log, brought a hatchet out of nowhere and lopped off its head.

Alyssa squealed and covered her mouth, shocked such an embarrassing noise came out of her throat.

"What?"

Blood spurted from the headless body, which to Alyssa's horror flopped off the log and ran about the yard exactly like the saying. An old black dog came up next to the chopping block and gave Beverly a low, plaintive whine.

"Oh, all right, Bobbsey, take it," Beverly said, impatient.

The dog snatched the head and trotted off.

"Remind me to get Andrew to take him to Dr. Creaver. He thought the arthritis was permanent, but he hasn't been limping. I keep forgetting to check up on that."

Alyssa thought she might throw up.

Beverly finally looked over and saw her face. "It's *dinner*, Alyssa. This is a *farm*."

"I know," she nodded, still holding her mouth.

The chicken body flopped lifeless in the dirt. Beverly picked it up by the feet and let the blood drain. Andrew's Keeshond, Mimi, left off a losing battle with Bobbsey for the head and licked the dirt where the blood pooled.

Alyssa shut her eyes.

"The chickens are not pets," Beverly said. "This is what we keep them for. This, and eggs."

"I know."

"Peter prays over them first, but I've been farming too long to care. To me, it's a dumb chicken that cooks up nice and juicy. I'm sorry—I didn't think to warn you."

"I don't think I can *do* that." Alyssa recalled Beverly's fluid, emotionless swing.

"We won't make you. Sometimes I pretend the chicken is one of the men who took Phil, and it feels really good." She blushed.

Alyssa raised her eyebrow. Her childhood image of Beverly as Peter's sweet, kind mother was evolving rapidly.

"Lucky for you we're not restocking the beef freezer until spring," Beverly said.

"Don't tell me! I don't want to know."

Beverly laughed out loud.

Alyssa took a few steps backward and bumped into Peter. "How long have you been standing there?"

"Long enough," Peter laughed. "She can muck the stables with me, Mom."

Beverly said, "She doesn't have to kill them, but she does have to learn to pluck them."

"I don't want to pluck a chicken."

"You'll get used to it," Beverly called.

It made her cross and nervous to bump into Peter like that. Her defenses were down. "Can I please be a vegetarian?" she asked on the way to the stable.

Peter laughed. "Mom won't let you. You need animal protein to build muscle, skinny. You're all bone."

"Thanks a lot."

"I didn't mean it in a bad way. But you *are* bony."

"I don't think I can eat dinner."

"The main thing is not to get attached. Dad never lets—Dad never let us name the chickens. He got after us real bad if we tried. Don't you remember?"

She noticed an odd catch in his voice. "No," she answered.

"With Dad gone, I keep after the twins. Don't pet the baby chicks. Don't give them names. Don't get excited when their feathers grow in. Dad always said, 'Eating roast chicken is easy, but it's impossible to eat a dish named Frances. You'll cry buckets, and your mother will be mad nobody ate.'" He made his voice deeper, to sound like Phil. She'd forgotten how he used to do impressions of people they knew. He was pretty good. At the moment, all it did was emphasize the hole Phil's absence left.

Peter held the stable door, and she went in first. "Does that explain why you pray over the chickens first?" she asked.

Peter made an exasperated noise. "She told you that? Why?"

"I gather she thinks it's funny."

"Do you?"

"It's nothing to be embarrassed about. I think it's sweet," she said, in a matter-of-fact tone.

"I can't believe she told you that."

"Why not pray first?"

"Can we talk about something else?" Peter handed her a mucking shovel.

"Sure," Alyssa laughed. "The horses?"

"This big guy is Teancum, our stallion. He's sixteen hands tall." The horse was a dappled gray Appaloosa with a jagged blaze down his nose. The name was three syllables, Tee-*AN*-cum. "That's a funny name," she said.

"Dad named him after a Book of Mormon hero. You'll read about him later, I'm sure. He was a war hero, stubborn and determined, so it fits this guy well."

Teancum nudged her with his nose.

Peter said, "He's sniffing you for apples."

"Sorry, boy, I didn't bring any," she said, making a note to have an apple in her pocket for him next time.

"He likes you." Peter's tone held wonder.

"Why shouldn't he?" Alyssa stroked the soft nose.

"He doesn't warm up to everybody, that's all," Peter said.

There were six stalls and four horses. The others were Abish, Beverly's mare; Lucy Mack belonged to Andrew; and the twins rode old Thistle to school.

Memory called up Joan's anxious face, a lit cigarette locked between her pointing fingers, screaming. Joan had caught Alyssa in the Richardsons' stable. She was just looking. She hadn't touched the animals. *I've told you a thousand times, child, don't go near the horses! The last thing I need is you trampled to death or maimed. You'll be in a wheelchair the rest of your life, do you hear me?* Alyssa was about eight years old. Joan's anti-horse lecture on the way home had lasted the entire two hour drive.

She pet Teancum's soft cheek. "Peter, do you remember Joan never let me near the horses?"

"I wondered why I didn't remember riding with you." He paused. "Should you call your mom by her first name like that?"

"Who cares?"

Peter let it drop. "You'll have to ride if you want to go anywhere. We'll start you on Abish . . . unless you want to ride with me, on Teancum."

"Won't that be too heavy for him?" She imagined clinging to Peter on the back of this majestic horse, and felt a thrill of excitement, weighed down by fear.

"Remember how big Dad was? Is? Was?" His discomfort with not knowing the correct tense was palpable. "Teancum can carry a much heavier load."

"Let's wait and see," she said.

"Sure. Meanwhile, it's time you learned about tack."

Peter went to Thistle's stall and showed Alyssa how to put on the bit and bridle.

Beverly came in as Peter was hefting the saddle over the pony's back.

"You're not riding now?"

"Just getting Thistle ready for the twins, Mom."

"Andrew's supposed to do that before he leaves for work." Beverly hunted around the loft, in the feed bins, in corners, kicking piles of straw, moving saddles.

"I'm just showing Alyssa how. Andy won't mind. What are you looking for?" Peter asked.

"Micah. She'll go in heat again if I don't find her soon," she groaned.

"I haven't seen her this morning," Peter said. He peered into Teancum's stall, then looked closer in Thistle's. He kicked a hump of straw in the far corner. A calico cat streaked out in a blur.

"Thanks!" Beverly rushed out.

"Is that cat Micah?" Alyssa said.

"Yeah. We have enough barn cats to keep rodents down, and don't need more, but she keeps having kittens. She's wild. We haven't caught her to have her spayed yet."

"There's a gray kitten hanging around my room," she said. It was fuzzy, with a loud purr.

"It's probably Micah's," Peter said. "The twins must be hiding it up there—Mom doesn't like the cats in the house. Don't tell on them, okay?"

Alyssa smiled. "Got it."

"It'll be our secret?" Peter said, then turned away fast, as if embarrassed he'd said it. Words from long ago.

Alyssa panicked inside. "Sure," she said, keeping her voice calm. Not the right answer. On purpose. She should have said, *our secret*. Why not? Her heart beat too fast.

At that moment out in the yard, something fell with a huge, metallic, thumping clatter. Alyssa heard what she thought was a fantastic curse. "Did she just say what I thought she said?" Alyssa asked.

"Probably," Peter grinned, "If she's after that cat."

Alyssa shook her head. *Her* mother used that language—and Margret, and she used to herself—not Beverly. She had to laugh. The tense moment was gone.

They went outside to meet her.

"Are you all right, Mom?" Peter asked.

Beverly came toward them. "I'm fine. Knocked over half the big milking jugs and the shelf of number-ten empty cans. I have a job for you, Peter—Dr. Creaver's waiting. I caught the cat. Hurry and take her in, before she finds a way out of that crate."

Alyssa became aware of an unhappy cat yowling somewhere. She got a better look at Beverly. "My gosh—are you okay?" she exclaimed. There were scratches all over her forearms.

"Oh, this is nothing." She dabbed at one of them.

Peter laughed. "You should have seen her last time. I'm surprised your cheek didn't scar!"

Beverly laughed too. "Yeah, she went for my eye. I'm lucky she missed. If I didn't know better, I'd swear she let me catch her. Do you think cats get tired of having babies?" she wondered aloud. "No—stupid. She can't possibly know why I want to catch her. She's just wild."

Beverly wiped a spot of blood off onto her jeans. "Peter, when you get back you need to call your brother Isaac and find out what's wrong with the second tractor. It's not running right." Peter nodded and turned to go.

Beverly said, "Alyssa, come with me and we'll get that chicken plucked."

Alyssa waved him a quick goodbye. There was no putting it off. No further chance to figure out what Peter meant, implied, or meant to imply, by his earlier comment. The last time he said that to her . . . was right after he had kissed her. She wished his eyes didn't sparkle such a bright blue in the sunlight. It made everything that much harder. He probably meant nothing—it was just a slip. Something to forget.

* * * * *

An unexpected, late-season storm came up that afternoon and everyone was stuck indoors. The twins played Monopoly on the floor; Peter sat in the brown recliner, opposite Alyssa, and she felt strained. She felt a magnetic pull towards him that about made her crazy. If the feeling persisted much longer, she feared she would fall at his feet, begging him to remember what they almost had. She hoped, in time, that being around him would get easier, that she would stop remembering the fun they had as kids, the feelings and secrets they once shared, everything leading up to that first, last, wonderful kiss . . .

Whoa. She had to stop that pattern of thought, fast. Alyssa struggled for something to keep herself distracted. The news was on, as it always was lately. Andrew soaked in every detail on every channel, flipping news stations during commercials. She learned to numb herself to it. Otherwise it hurt too much.

Outdoor work had been planned for the day, but it had to wait. Dishes were done; laundry was even done, except for what people were wearing. She and Beverly had caught up on everything the day before, down to tossing out the last mismatched socks. Beverly was even taking a rare nap. There was little to do. She could go to her room, but she didn't want to be holed up alone, listening to the rain.

Her mind wandered through a few more pointless thoughts, until it landed on something that ought to be neutral, stories she hadn't heard firsthand. The Richardson family had sent out two successful missionaries. Peter was the last. Isaac, the oldest, had served in Idaho—much less exotic than serving among the Chinese, new to democracy and Christianity, as Peter had. Shortly after Peter's mission, all American missionaries were called home, due to new laws making it illegal for U.S. citizens to serve proselytizing missions anywhere; this was a precursor to the fateful Article 28. Peter's next younger sister, Julia, was preparing to go when the change happened. Peter said she still vocalized her disappointment.

Isaac married his girlfriend Anna on his return from Idaho, and they now had a young daughter, Kira, and baby son, Ike Junior. Earlier, when Peter called to check on the tractor problem, Alyssa had said hello to Isaac and his family on the phone. It was strange to think Beverly was a grandmother. After the phone call, she asked to look through their photo albums, to straighten herself out on how these other two siblings had grown up. Julia lived in a nearby town, married less than a year to her husband, Derek. She knew the room she was in used to be Julia's. The clothes she now wore used to be Julia's. Even many of her chores used to be Julia's. It was a little weird.

Alyssa gathered that serving a church mission was, apparently, an expectation the older kids grew up with, something no one expected would ever change. Andrew was the right age to serve. He had mentioned wistfully at dinner once that he wished he could have gone.

She wondered about Peter's missionary service. He hadn't mentioned it much so far. She drew up her nerve and asked, "So, Peter . . . What was it like serving in China?"

"Oh, *no*," Jordan interrupted. "Why'd you bring that up?"

Peter's eyes got instantly far away. "It was so great. I could have stayed another two years. On P-days we helped the members plant rice paddies, and I got to teach *and* learn agriculture along with the gospel."

"P-days?"

"Preparation days. One day a week we did laundry, wrote letters, went grocery shopping, and did service, instead of teaching."

Alyssa relaxed and listened. Jordan and Kellie moaned they'd heard this or that story a thousand times, but she didn't mind— it kept Peter talking. She was learning too. By evening she could count to ten in Mandarin with the twins' help, and Peter informed his mother he was cooking Chinese for dinner.

"No, we're having stuffed chicken," Beverly said with a yawn. She'd just gotten up from her nap and her hair was tousled. Alyssa stifled a chuckle.

Peter looked over at Alyssa, then back at his mother. "It'll keep for a day or two, Mom. You're tired. Let me cook. Besides, she won't be able to eat that tonight. Let her adjust."

She yawned again. "Oh, twist my arm. All right."

* * * * *

Peter's love for China was even more evident as he stood over the wok. Alyssa laughed to herself. She hadn't seen him this animated since . . . childhood. It was charming. *No—he is not charming, not cute, not sweet. He's just Peter.*

"They don't carry authentic Chinese rice at the storehouse," he complained to everyone in general.

"It's impossible to get imported rice, Peter," Beverly said. She sat at the dining table, letting her son take over.

He poured the rice into the cooker. "They could try."

"I understand *you* were the one who asked about his mission, Alyssa," Beverly said dryly. "Did we forget to warn you?"

Alyssa suppressed a giggle. "I guess so. Does he always get this way?"

"Yes!" everyone said at once.

The wok sizzled as he threw the first vegetables in.

Andrew poked his head into the kitchen. "Peter's cooking Chinese? Not that fried chicken-feet thing, I hope?"

He laughed. "I fixed that *once,* specifically to gross you out, and it worked."

"You let me eat a whole plate before you told me what it was!" Andrew laughed. "I about puked!"

"People *eat* chicken feet?" Alyssa knew what chickens walked in—she cleaned the pens. Eating chicken *meat* would be hard enough, after today. Her mind replayed Beverly's effortless swing of the ax. She could still feel that rubbery skin against her fingers. She had scrubbed her hands for fifteen minutes after doing the plucking, and they still didn't quite feel clean.

Peter was making this dish with beef. She was relieved and grateful for that bit of mercy.

Peter answered her question. "Yes. They love chicken feet over in China. I can't get Mom to put them in soup, though."

"Dog food," Beverly muttered.

Alyssa looked from Peter to Beverly and back again. "Is this a joke?"

Peter shrugged. "Chicken feet flavor the broth."

"I don't want that flavor in my soup!" Beverly laughed.

"Please say he's not doing the chopstick thing," Andrew said.

"You know the rules!" Peter called.

Andrew groaned and shuffled back down the hall.

* * * * *

After blessing the food, Peter stood at the head of the table and explained "the rules."

"Again, I apologize for the inferior quality of the rice," he began.

Andrew said, "Yeah, yeah, yeah. We heard you the first hundred thousand times."

"You could have made Lo Mein," Beverly pointed out.

"It's not my best dish." Peter cleared his throat. "It is a mortal sin to eat authentic Chinese cuisine with *silverware*." He waved a fork in his hand, then tossed it over his shoulder into the sink.

"Nice shot," Andrew said.

"Thank you." Peter made a proper Chinese bow, hands pressed together at his chest.

Beverly said, "That was a clean fork."

Peter ignored his mother's heckling. "I refuse to watch my handiwork desecrated by American utensils. Does everyone remember their chopstick lessons?"

"We remember," came the chorus.

Alyssa understood why Andrew groaned.

Peter took the complaints in stride. His eyes sparkled.

"How often do you cook Chinese, Peter?" Alyssa asked.

"Often enough to make us tired of his speech," Jordan said.

Alyssa rarely used chopsticks. She remembered how her late gourmet-chef father Chuck had shared Peter's opinion, but always let her have the mercy of a fork.

She had the distinct impression such would not be the case tonight. If she was hungry, she had to learn, and fast.

Beverly indicated the proper position. "One holds steady, the other moves like a pencil, see?"

Alyssa said, "I know, I'm just not good at it."

Beverly corrected her grip. "Like this."

Jordan giggled.

She got a small bite to her mouth. The tiny taste she got was succulent and tender. "Peter, this is *good.*"

"Thank you." He bowed again.

"You're really good with chopsticks, Andrew," Alyssa commented. His plate was almost empty.

"Do or die. A guy's gotta eat."

"So why'd you fuss before dinner?"

"Because I'd rather use a *plain old fork,*" he said, stabbing a slice of beef fork-wise and putting it in his mouth.

"Unacceptable etiquette!" Peter laughed.

Everyone else's food disappeared faster than hers. She laughed with them, when bites dropped away just as she got them to her mouth, but she was so hungry that it was hard to stay in good spirits.

She made a mental note not to ask Peter about his mission ever again.

CHAPTER 5

MEDICAL TESTING

We hereby decree that any person exhibiting symptoms of the American Toxic Flu shall submit to a mandatory blood test. Persons testing positive shall be euthanized by lethal injection and cremated immediately.

Scientists have discovered the following:

1. *The ATF organism was released into the core water supply of Central City via an elaborate system of pipelines;*
2. *ATF spreads only through water-based sources, including any bodily fluid, and not by air or casual contact;*
3. *No person contracting ATF has survived;*
4. *The organism causes extreme pain and suffering before death due to the degeneration of connective organ tissue;*
5. *The ATF organism continues to survive in the deceased host for an undetermined period;*
6. *The organism can be destroyed by extreme heat or radiation, but only at levels toxic to human life.*

Therefore, without enforced euthanization and cremation, it will be impossible to contain the disease to the contaminated area. All human life is at risk. We urge all nations, governments, physicians, and individuals to comply.

—ATF Proclamation #2,
United Nations Council

Debra Pike was unexplainably throwing up. Her husband Jon worried it was ATF, but she insisted the nausea began before Outbreak. She suspected a normal virus, or some other type of infection. ATF didn't last this long; once you caught it you were dead in four days.

After Outbreak it was hard to be calm. Stress wouldn't help her get well either. She knew that. But Alyssa lived in Central City, and was not the type to ever leave it. Debra left much behind to carve out her post-Article 28 life in this remote corner of Iowa, where maybe the government would look the other way and let them live and worship in peace. Of all the sacrifices, the only thing she missed was Alyssa.

It was lucky they were thriving here at all. No, not lucky—the will of God made all things possible. Utah had seceded from the nation, with President Garrison's approval; that helped a good deal. The majority of other U.S. members fled to Canada or Mexico, where they could worship without risk of arrest and enforced therapy treatments to "cure" their beliefs. Many more had just dropped out—almost half. So far, New Hope and its mirror communities kept a low profile, co-existing in peace with their neighbors, basing their rights on a loophole in current law; the Church owned the land without a lien, which meant they could more or less do as they pleased on it.

Some days tried her faith, sure. Living with her parents hadn't been a thrill, before these apartments were built and they could move in. But overall, life here was wonderful.

Debra focused on her many blessings. She loved Jon to death, and her heart about burst with the intense love she felt for their newborn son, Zachary. He looked like Jon too; tight nappy hair, dark velvety skin, big brown eyes with long, curled lashes.

The only thing missing from the perfect picture was Alyssa. In her heart Debra had adopted her as a blood sister—so what if she was blonde and pale—and had cared for her with her life. It was Deb who got Alyssa through the Elation overdose and recovery period. Debra had begged her to come to New Hope with them. But Alyssa wasn't the religious type—she didn't want to be caught up with all this.

Debra understood that choice. But their years together, best friends in high school and on through college, meant so much. They'd fallen out of contact shortly after Debra moved. And hard as she prayed, she felt no comfort. Deb couldn't leave the apartment or turn on the satellite or talk to anyone without hearing more details. That meant she spent too many waking hours wandering in morbid daydreams, wondering how Alyssa may have died, or if she might escape the quarantine, or . . . or, or, or.

On top of that, the puking. Nausea worse than anything she ever had. For all she knew, it could be plain old worry, and not an illness at all. She just wanted it to stop.

Zach wasn't an easy baby, either. He was a fitful sleeper and fussed if she ever put him down. Motherhood was more of an adjustment than she expected—with four younger siblings, she thought she knew everything before Zach was born.

She was so wrong!

And being sick was awful. Days went by where she never got out of bed. She just lay with the baby on the bed and nursed him as long as he wanted, getting up only for food, water, or restroom breaks. She kept an old trashcan by the bed for puking into.

She hated it. She liked to-do lists. Getting her housework done. Scheduling things, planning menus, volunteering for others. It was hard to accept that she needed help, herself.

Her mother, Taletha Gray, offered that help as much as possible, but Deb's three brothers and baby sister needed her at home, too.

One evening her mom was over, making several pans of lasagna to freeze. Jon was working swing shift at the hospital, on ER duty this rotation.

"Have they run any tests?" her mother asked from the kitchen, stirring the sauce.

"I hate getting blood drawn. I hate needles."

Taletha smiled. "I remember."

Debra folded the last piece of clean laundry. They'd been digging through baskets for clean underwear for a week. The last clean pairs were gone for sure. She hated letting it go, but she wasn't up to hauling it out to the laundry facilities. She'd ask Jon to do it when he got home. She didn't want to ask her mom. She was helping plenty already.

"You've had blessings?" Taletha asked next.

"They weren't specific. Have faith, it's in the Lord's hands, that kind of thing. I take Echinacea and Vitamin C and raspberry leaf, but it all comes back up. Oh—" Deb clapped her hand over her mouth. "Mama, that sauce *reeks.*"

"You love my lasagna."

"I do, but did you have to use fresh sausage?" She felt a renewed urge to vomit. "I don't mean to complain—you're helping so much." Debra stopped before adding she could never eat the stuff. Well—it was okay—Jon would.

Her mother laid out the first layer of noodles. "Debra, have you had a pregnancy test?"

"That's impossible, Mama."

"Impossible? You haven't got your groove on since Zach was born? Baby, that's not healthy. I know you had all those stitches, but—"

"Mom!" Deb blushed. "The groove is going just fine, thank you."

"Then it is not *impossible.*"

"But I'm nursing. I haven't had a cycle yet. And we were careful." A twinge of worry came. *Were we?* Zach took over a year to conceive. Prevention had never been much of an issue.

"And your husband is a doctor and he hasn't asked you this question?"

"I'm not that fertile to start with."

"It explains the nausea and fatigue."

Debra said, "But with Zach I never even threw up. And I couldn't possibly be more than . . ." She reached the answer with dismay. "Nine weeks." Far enough along to be sick.

"Smells are bothering you."

"That's normal when you're queasy." She'd have to run to the toilet any minute now. Deb looked at Zachary, bouncing in his baby seat, alert and happy on his own for the moment.

Why didn't I think of that myself? She shook her head. "But nine months apart!"

"Maybe ten. Debra, people manage. Weren't you lecturing *me* on faith the other day?"

Deb sighed. "Yeah."

"God won't give you a trial you can't handle."

She sighed again. "I'll ask Jon to bring a test home."

* * * * *

Zach woke up from his nap while Debra was in the bathroom with the test.

Jon went to pick him up. "Hush, hush now, Daddy's got you."

Zach's little fists were clenched, stiff. Jon bounced him gently and wrapped a blanket over him.

"It's okay . . . it's called waking up. It's not so bad, once you get used to it."

Zach kept wailing.

"You're right," Jon said, snuggling him. "I never got used to it either." Then, sniffing, he noticed waking up wasn't the only problem. A warm sticky spot on his arm confirmed it.

He had to strip Zach down to nakedness to get him clean; the mess went halfway up the poor baby's back and down his thighs.

Jon made a noise of half disgust, half compassion, as he pulled the sticky diaper off.

Zach was not pleased with the whole process and kicked out his tiny brown feet, first one, then the other. Jon had a hard time getting clean pants on his legs once the diapering was finished.

"Is he okay?" Deb called from the bathroom.

"Just a blowout," Jon assured her. "He's fine now. Just mad."

"He's hungry," she told him. "But I had to throw up, I'm not done with this yet."

"We're okay out here. He'll be fine, baby," Jon said. Zach was fussing, but more calm now that he was clean.

Jon waited outside the bathroom door, pacing the floor with a fussy Zach, beating a horseshoe-shaped path around their bed. The room was small. There was nowhere else to go.

Moments passed like hours.

At the sound of her voice, he stopped pacing and looked up.

"Jon?" Debra's voice quavered. "It's positive."

She began to cry. She came out minutes later blowing her nose. He gave her a hug, the baby between them.

"I don't feel so good, I have to lie down," she said, and climbed into bed.

His feelings leapt all over the place, mostly with concern for his wife, but also with joy that another new life was coming to them. He was also relieved her illness wasn't dire or mysterious.

Obviously, Debra was not feeling joyful.

"In some ways it's good to know there's an explanation," he offered.

"I suppose," she said. "Bring him to me, please?"

He laid Zach by her side to nurse.

The baby latched on eagerly, expressing his frustration with the few minutes' wait.

"Ouch! Slow down, there," Debra said, stroking his wooly black hair with her fingers.

Zach made angry little grunting noises as he fed.

"He's sure telling me!" Deb laughed, and it relieved some of the tension Jon felt. "Don't you make me wait thirty seconds too long, Mama! Oooh!"

"Fierce little guy, isn't he?" Jon smiled.

He knelt by the bed to bring himself to her eye level and took her hand in his. "We'll get through this together, Debra, I promise." His heart swelled with love.

CHAPTER 6

SEEING ETHER

And it came to pass that when they had all fallen by the sword, save it were Coriantumr and Shiz, behold Shiz had fainted with the loss of blood.

And when Coriantumr had leaned upon his sword, that he rested a little, he smote off the head of Shiz.

And after he had smitten off the head of Shiz, Shiz raised up on his hands and fell; and after he had struggled for breath, he died.

—Book of Mormon, Ether 15:29-31
[paraphrased]

"**P**eter, I *saw* this!"

Alyssa sat cross-legged on the couch with her *Book of Mormon*. Vivid memory swept her like a windstorm as she reached the final battle of the Jaredites in the book of Ether. It was as though she had physically stood in the battlefield looking over the carnage and destruction. She knew the details of their armor, their faces, the carved patterns on the sword hilts.

But where? . . . When?

"Saw what?" he asked.

"Shiz and Coriantumr. I saw it happen, just like this."

"No kidding?" He sat down by her.

It snapped into place and she gasped; an Elation trip took her there. Years ago. *That shouldn't be possible.*

She couldn't tell Peter *that*. He didn't know about her ordeal with the potent drug; she doubted he would understand. She said, "I was so angry with them—this entire civilization, destroyed, down to the last person. Then a man came and told me, 'Their kingdom shall be given to another.'"

"Was this a dream?"

"On a drug trip" was a crummy answer.

The Richardsons avoided all recreational drugs, alcohol, coffee, and tobacco; things that could destroy physical freedom and health. She'd never eaten so many vegetables and whole grains in her life. "It was like a dream," she decided to say. "A long time ago."

Peter asked, "You mean, before your leg was healed?"

"It makes no sense, I know."

"Maybe you have the gift of visions."

A chill ran up her spine.

"Maybe it was given to you to be a witness of the truth, once you found it."

She felt the warm glow she was beginning to recognize as the Holy Ghost, or the Spirit.

But how could I see truth on Elation?

She half-worried her old hallucinations would return. Thankfully, her days were too full of new chores and tasks for her to dwell on it.

Her dreams were another matter. She was grateful when they were only ordinary or unremembered. Peter could be right, that it was the gift of visions; but for what purpose?

* * * * *

Late that night, another dream came.

A flock of sheep grazed on a grassy hill. Alyssa had soft fleece and little hooves for feet. She bounded off with joy, but soon she was far from the flock. She cried out, a lamb's bleat.

A gunshot echoed; pain hit.

The bullet crushed her hind leg. A thunderstorm arose, and with it the baying of wolves on the scent of blood.

Her blood. The wild, hungry sound filled her with icy fear. The wind swallowed her tiny bleat for help.

A massive wolf rose over the crest of a brown hill. Flecks of spittle flew from its jaws. More wolves followed at a dead run.

She twisted in powerless agony.

Three crosses stood at the top of the hill. *Crosses . . . Calvary . . . Jesus.* She cried out: *Save me!*

The pack leader slid back on his haunches with a yelp. The pack tucked tail and fled, whining. Strong arms gently scooped her up and cradled her. *Alyssa, Alyssa, my sweet child*, a voice said, tender, kind, and piercing.

Something about it gave her déjà vu.

Alyssa looked in his face. It was the man who healed her, who saved her from certain death; the same face in the portrait hanging in the Richardsons' living room. She spoke his name reverently, with awe and gratitude: *Jesus.*

He smiled. He stroked her lamb fur between her ears, on her forehead, her cheeks. She trembled under the gentleness of his touch. He spoke soft, tender words; words that filled her with light, with sure knowledge that she was loved completely. She gazed in his eyes and bleated softly how she longed to see him again, wishing she'd known when he healed her what she knew now.

I am with you always, Alyssa, he said.

Then she was awake and the room was dark and she realized that she had been dreaming.

"Don't go!" she whispered. *"Don't go!"*

She tucked into the fetal position and wept softly, but with an agony of longing. She shivered in spite of heavy quilts, and desperately tried to sleep, to rejoin the beautiful dream.

* * * * *

Sleep did not come.

But it was so real. Her own thought jarred her.

Real? Maybe reality needed a new definition. It had to include more than the five senses. Everything in her being told her so.

The sense of déjà vu persisted.

Not another flashback! She had seen this exact scene before, but she was not the lamb the first time. She had wished to be, and was not, and in despair and shame had melted into a raindrop. She took in a sharp breath, startled: *His face. It was the same face then, too.* From the moment she met him in the City, even half-dead from infection and blood loss, she felt a familiarity, an odd sense she had seen him somewhere before. But how was Jesus in the middle of a drug-induced hallucination?

And why had the scene returned, only changed?

The first time, she had yearned to be cradled in those gentle, rescuing, merciful arms. She also remembered her intense shame and the sadness and disappointment in his eyes.

She hugged her knees tight to her chest and listened to the quiet stillness of the night.

If both were me . . . past and future . . . how confusing.

In the dream, he spoke a perfect language, every nuance and meaning perfectly transferred. Alyssa struggled to remember the exact words, but they were gone. But the feeling of his words remained; she felt as full of light, as dearly loved, as she had within the dream.

She took out her journal, frustrated that English was not sufficient to translate everything she felt in her soul. Only his last sentence stuck, which she would never forget:

I am with you always.

CHAPTER 7

SISTERHOOD

> *Morning sickness is getting worse. My milk is holding up, good thing. I'm not ready to quit yet. Zach's fierce nursing helps. I'll have to quit soon enough, but he won't take a bottle anyway. I get him to sleep nursing and then whenever I try to put him in his bed, he wakes right back up and screams.*
>
> *Today his diaper blew out all down my shirt. It was so sticky and gross. Yeah—I threw up, all right. He pooped again all over, before I even finished changing his diaper. Taking care of him is so much harder than I ever expected. He's beautiful, and I love him more than any love I've ever known, but . . . it's impossible to care for his needs, and be so sick at the same time.*
>
> *I wish I wasn't pregnant. Which is awful. Some people can't have children at all. I ought to thank the Lord my God for this great blessing. But it doesn't feel like a blessing. I've lived close to the Spirit most of my life, doing everything right, but this is too much. And I'm not naive enough to think that laying this burden at Jesus' feet will make my morning sickness vanish.*
>
> *What Mom said is true. Where's my faith now? It feels like it's plumb gone.*
>
> *I have moments where I wish I had that fatal flu instead. I'm so ashamed to admit that.*
>
> —Debra Pike,
> personal journal entry

Roberta Pike, Jon's mother, dragged Debra to their weeknight Relief Society scripture study class. "I'm too sick," Debra complained, when her mother-in-law showed up at the door.

"You've missed too many weeks. It's not good. And the Spirit tells me you have to be there tonight, Debra," Roberta said.

So she went. You didn't argue with Roberta when she felt the Spirit. Whether it was indeed the Spirit, or Roberta's own ideas, Debra often questioned; but she never questioned *Roberta* on the subject. Nobody did.

Debra sat at the end of the semi-circle of about a dozen women. She sat leaning over in her chair, wrapped in a home-made quilt. She'd placed a small trashcan on her left, just in case.

The group read chapter thirty-two of Alma aloud, on the nature of faith, and began to discuss it.

"I still don't see why I have to be here," she mumbled to Roberta. She was more tuned in to the motions of her stomach than the Spirit, terrified she'd have to use the trashcan, not make it out to the bathroom in time. *Steady . . . breathe.* She was among friends, but she didn't exactly want to puke in front of them.

Roberta mumbled back, "Hush, child. It's your favorite topic." Her voice was deep and resonant, even in a whisper; she sang tenor in the ward choir.

Debra cursed her dumb luck, not for the first time, that they lived in the same ward as her in-laws. *My mother would let me stay home*, Debra thought. *She'd let me sleep, and take care of the baby for me.* Zach was being cared for—watched by teen girls in the nursery. Jon was on his last two nights of swing shift, so she'd had to bundle Zachary against the October cold just to get to the church, and he hated getting his coat on. Such a pain.

While her mind wandered, the room had gone quiet. What? Oh. Sister Lana Vernon, the president, had asked for personal stories about faith. No way was she speaking up—she had nothing to say tonight.

Sister Soong spoke up. "You all know my favorite story."

Yes, Debra knew it. Amniocentesis showed the Soong's sixth child should have Down's Syndrome, but he was born perfectly healthy. Crabby as Debra was, it failed to move her this time. She got thinking that maybe the lab just mixed up test results, putting this family through pointless heartache and worry.

Before, she had always assumed the baby was miraculously healed before birth. Right—of an extra chromosome in every cell? Come on. It strained even her imagination of miracles.

Jennie Soong finished with, "By the time Nash was born we had prepared for it, even though every blessing I had told us he was okay. And he was. But until then I didn't know what 'okay' was going to mean. We learned the trial of faith always comes before the witness."

Yeah, Deb thought to herself, *the lab must have blown it.*

As the women went through other stories, none of it made sense like it used to. She tended to think her faith was maybe . . . a little stronger than a lot of the other sisters'. She didn't have issues with doctrinal points like some of them did. And her testimony itself wasn't waning; she still felt deep in her bones that the gospel was real, as she once testified to an unbelieving Alyssa. That wasn't the problem.

She just couldn't figure out what God thought He was doing.

Only her journal knew her true feelings. It was whiny, and she didn't dare complain out loud. It was a pregnancy. Others couldn't conceive at all—and she knew that pain a little, from the long year it took them to conceive Zach. She remembered the hot anger she used to feel towards any sister complaining about an unexpected pregnancy. *They should be grateful. That's such a blessing!* Her own condemnation came back to haunt her now. She hadn't understood.

Still others had permanent disabilities or illnesses. This challenge was hardly as major. This was such a garden-variety normal event that her intense feelings surrounding it shamed her.

Then again, a baby was forever. And she couldn't imagine *two.*

These women wouldn't understand.

You were supposed to want babies. Spirits in Heaven were waiting for good homes. In such an evil world, who could deny them bodies, life? If she said *no,* what if that spirit then had to go to a terrible home instead? Debra couldn't live with that, whether it was true or not. She did want more children—just not this close together. Jennie Soong had seven babies in nine years, and not one of hers sounded as hard to care for as Zach. They were quiet and sweet and obedient. Debra loved Zach, no doubt—but he screamed so much. There wasn't anything medically wrong; he just came that way. High-strung, nervous, demanding.

It totally drained her.

The anti-emetic her doctor prescribed was wearing off. Great. With Roberta hustling them out the door, she forgot to take more, or bring it along. Her tummy wobbled and complained, threatening.

Octavia Hunsaker said, "I know my faith is weak when I'm scared. Fear drives out my faith till there's nothing left inside and I feel hopeless." Octavia was among her closer friends in New Hope.

Debra listened to that and it struck her like thunder: she was *terrified.*

She started to cry. Which set off the nausea. She grabbed the trashcan and set it between her legs—the bathroom felt suddenly much too far away. *Breathe . . .* maybe she could hold it off. Tears fell against the plastic liner with a funny crinkle-splash sound.

Roberta wrapped her arm around her shoulder. The embrace set off Debra's stomach, and up came dinner, right in front of everybody.

Humiliation piled on top of her careening emotions. Her body shook, and she leaned into Roberta as other sisters jumped up to bring her tissues and words of consolation. She wished she could melt away into the carpet. Anything but get this much attention.

But the tears wouldn't stop coming, and it was all she could do not to howl. She felt so awful.

Someone handed her wet paper towels from the bathroom. Sister Vernon took the trashcan away and changed out the liner, adding to Debra's mortification.

Roberta and Octavia helped clean her up. She shook from the physical shock of vomiting and crying so hard and having her feelings pile up on top of each other.

Finally she gained enough composure to say, "I don't know where my faith went. I'm terrified of having another baby. I can't do this. I can't! Then I feel worse even saying that. Or feeling it. I should be grateful! Right? Babies are blessings!"

Octavia said, "Deb, Thaddeus and Kisha are fifteen months apart. I wasn't ready. I wondered about you at first, but you seemed fine, spiritually at least. Me, I got so depressed. I cried all day for months. I cried when Kisha was born, too. It took me a while. Good thing she's so cute, I couldn't help falling in love with her!"

Debra tried to smile, then shook her head and started up crying again. "It's just too hard."

Jennie Soong said, "Boy, I know that feeling. Debra, I'm so sorry. Why didn't you tell us?"

Debra looked up, surprised. "You?"

"Hey, I love my kids, but I'd have done anything to keep them from coming that fast," Jennie said with a smile. "We did, too—tried everything known to man! Nothing worked. When my uterus came out with the last baby—remember?—it was such a relief to know I was done, I didn't care once that it was gone. Thank you, and goodnight!"

A laugh went around the room, even from Debra, amidst her tears.

If these sisters felt like strangers to her, Debra realized it was her fault. She hadn't made the effort. It had grieved her so much to lose Alyssa that she didn't make any close girlfriends ever since. Octavia tried, and they did a lot together, but emotionally, Debra kept her distance. Plus, she had Jon for closeness. Family on both sides kept them busy.

But busy didn't mean support. More women chimed in, with their own stories of feeling inadequate, unprepared, desperate, angry, eventually finding resolution in Christ. She felt their unity, love, and support. She had expected judgment.

Strength in sisterhood—essential to her Black heritage, as well as in church—gave women support not found elsewhere, and she had failed to draw from that deep well.

It was time; she needed more than Jon alone could give. Or even her mother.

She took a deep, sniffling breath and squeezed her eyes shut. "I'm so angry," she confessed. "I'm mad at myself. I'm mad at Jon. I'm mad at God. How can I love anything when I'm so angry with Him? It hurts to feel like this. I hate it. I hate that I'm pregnant. Why can't he just take it away like it never happened?"

There. The worst was out. She bawled again, terrified she'd said as much out loud.

"You don't want that," Bess Ryan piped in.

Debra opened her eyes.

Bess shook her head. "A pregnancy is a pregnancy is a pregnancy, and they don't all end with a healthy baby. Being so sick is a good sign your baby's all right."

Several others fervently agreed.

"No, I didn't mean I want the baby to die," Debra affirmed. "That would be worse. I mean, I want to go back in time and be more careful, or something!" She tried to laugh, and a few others laughed with her, relieving a little of the tension. What she wanted was the impossible: not to have this happening at all. "Zach is so difficult. How can I manage two of them?"

Sister Vernon said, "Each child is different, no matter how many there are. You never know. Somehow it works out. It really does."

Octavia said, "I think we should all pray for Debra. Sisters?"

Sister Vernon said, "I was about to suggest that."

There was a general murmur of agreement. The women all knelt by their chairs, and Octavia started her prayer first.

When she finished, Jennie Soong took a turn, and so on throughout the group. The prayers were sincere and earnest, some short, some longer.

The Spirit filled the room with its overflowing power, and for the first time since she took the pregnancy test, Debra was filled with a sweet peace that she had been missing. She wept more, but now with tears of gratitude. All these kind, loving words were offered to the Lord in her behalf.

She was overwhelmed by it.

She conceded that maybe it *was* the Spirit that moved Roberta to get her to come tonight. She had the brief, wry thought that there'd be no living with her after this, and let it go.

It was Debra's turn to pray last of all. It took her several minutes to get her voice to start, to know what to say. She spilled out the myriad of feelings in her heart, unafraid, unashamed, buoyed up by the pure love saturating the room.

As she prayed on, her anger and pride dissipated until there was none left.

"Dear Heavenly Father," she begged, "Please make me grateful for this baby . . . Please help me understand Thy plan for my life. Help me accept it, and come to know and understand Thy purposes. Help me stop fighting things I can't change, which are Thy will . . ."

CHAPTER 8

TARGETED

*Yes, superheating the river water should effectively
destroy the American Toxic Flu organisms.*

—Dr. Joel Kensington,
memo to Pres.-General Leo F. Horne

A soldier presented Horne with a large manila envelope. "Here's
the intelligence you requested, President-General, sir."

"Thank you. Dismissed."

Once alone, Horne opened it and spread its contents on his
desk. It was good work. Satellite photographs pinpointed the
locations of five small settlements, scattered throughout Iowa,
Illinois, and Nebraska. Various schematics and papers detailed
the available intelligence on each one.

He frowned. Ground troops wouldn't do. Maneuvers outside
his quarantine patrol would be noticed and questioned, and with
the nation in chaos, controlling the media was impossible. Jag
had worked long, hard years to position, cajole, and bribe the
appropriate personnel until his propaganda machine became a
fine-tuned art. Nearly all those so positioned, loyal to the
President and his views, were dead. The media was a total mess.
Disastrous. He wouldn't stay in power long if they found him
taking out civilian settlements.

He studied the diagrams and topographical maps. He studied
the roads. He saw one satellite zoom-shot and cursed a hearty
blue streak. Atop a large building, proud and defiant, a flag flew:
Old Glory, outdated and treasonous, not the President's new flag
design for the new age of reason.

Sedition. If he wasn't sure before, he was now.

Horne had never agreed with Jag on that.

When Article 28 passed, Utah petitioned to secede from the
Union rather than comply. Horne argued it shouldn't be allowed.

"The loonies have to have somewhere to go," Jag reasoned. *"A lot more than we expected are refusing treatment. They're rebelling."*

"This is nonsense!" Horne yelled. *"Haul them in for treason! Put them on public trial!"*

"I remind you, Leo," Jag said through clenched teeth, *"This is not a military state. When there is a flood, the water must find a place to drain. If they have their place, the public will not be alarmed, and we shall appear both benevolent and generous."*

Horne was obliged to admit that it wasn't worth open civil war. Keep it quiet.

So Utah was allowed self-government in exchange for a heavy flat-rate tax.

They're like weeds, Horne mused. The whole bleeding state of Utah wasn't enough. Outposts like these cropped up everywhere like zits. The land needed a good stiff cleansing to rid themselves of these demented vermin.

Among his papers were copies of land titles. There was some loophole in the law; if they owned the land free and clear, they believed they could declare independence from the Union and its laws on their property.

Jag was gone. It was Horne's country now. And it *was* a military state . . . for the time being. To him, that soil was still American soil. He didn't need a flock of these mini-Vatican type states in his country.

History proved that religious lunatics were dangerous. Too many good people died due to Reverend Blankenship's zealotry twenty-odd years ago. Before him, there was Osama bin Laden. That war took his father away . . . and in a way, his mother.

His mind found its way back to scant childhood memories. A different breed reigned at the turn of the millennium; select sects of Islam calling America the Great Satan. His father fought in the Great War on Terrorism and came home in a body bag in 2012. Leo was five and a half years old.

He shut off the memory flow before it took him through his mother's ensuing depression and suicide, before the string of revolving-door foster homes and the nameless rage that ruled him before he enlisted in the service. That was before he found

direction, before purpose. The military saved his soul. Serving as
a Green Beret hadn't killed his father . . . religious zealots had.
They robbed Leo Horne, stealing his childhood, his parents, his
security, his chance for a whole and complete life. Through
recent history they caused only war, death, suffering. He never
quite got over that rage.

These outposts had to be shut down. Worry nibbled at the
back of his mind. He didn't know what they were up to, and
couldn't risk open battle against a weird sect of Christians. It
galled him. Power at his command to correct Jag's error, and he
lacked both secrecy and public sympathy.

There had to be a way. He had no intention of letting them
stay put.

After hours perusing documents and schematics, Horne
smacked his hand on the desk in satisfaction.

"Good old Jag . . . you're more brilliant than I gave you
credit for," he muttered.

The diagrams were clear: a built-in safety valve, ready
and waiting to cut them off in an instant, wired into the
communications routing.

Two schematic plans lay side by side on the desk. At first
they looked identical. On closer inspection, Horne found the
first was the one given to the settlements; the other was the
true tech layout. Their whole connection to the outside world
was housed in one communications building, through which
was routed a single tie-in to cellular service, worldwide web,
television, and satellite. All the redundant loops circled around
their settlements, but did not tie in. The settlements, however,
believed they did.

Without communication, they could never pull off an
operation of mass destruction, if they were planning one.
Their commerce and available goods were carefully tracked by
satellite surveillance; they didn't have weapons. They maintained
a self-sufficient economy, water supply and power. Equipment
they couldn't manufacture on site had to be purchased from
outside; which meant anything from light bulbs to computer
hardware. Their goods—mainly organic produce, herbs, and

rustic handmade items—didn't fetch them enormous fiscal profits from outside.

Their medical services and labs were top-notch, though. That generated outside income. He could enforce sanctions. Without replacement parts, without income, rebuilding their servers would be physically and fiscally impossible for a long time.

Throwing that one switch would send them back to the Dark Ages.

* * * * *

President-General Horne watched the giant holoscreen as a missile arced upward. Ruby light flashed through the clear blue sky, trailed by white smoke.

Horne thought the colors were fitting, patriotic. Millions of television viewers were tuned in to watch him single-handedly save them from infection, disease, and certain death. The missile would irradiate the rivers and destroy the teeming ATF in their waters, making the world safe.

He would be a hero.

Would his father have been proud? He had little room for sentimentality. He pushed the thought aside, an annoying gnat, not sure how that got through his defenses.

The missile turned earthward toward its target.

"Is it safe?" someone murmured in his ear. A civilian physicist. He'd forgotten the man's name.

"The public better believe it is," he replied. "Nothing short of this will purify the water. You know that."

The man moved away.

The Missouri River loomed large on the screen. The missile opened and shot out its laser, boiling the river below. Steam enveloped the missile and it disappeared from view. Its guidance system would keep it tracking east along the center of the river for several hundred kilometers, superheating the water and killing ATF organisms. Similar missiles stood ready to launch along the Mississippi, firing in sequence north to south. The operation over the Mississippi would begin firing in a few minutes.

Satisfied, Horne stepped into a private office. "How are these doing, Corporal?" he asked.

In this office, five smaller missiles were tracked by satellite, each appearing on a separate screen.

These were not broadcast to the public.

He returned the salute of the Corporal on duty and put him back to work, asking for a status report.

"That one—on the left—its trajectory is off, Sir, but there's still time to fix it." He began keying into the computer.

"Corporal, stop. That's an order."

"Sir—it won't hit the tributary. It's headed too far north."

"That's a terrible shame. *Wait.*"

They watched the satellite relay.

The corporal cleared his throat. "Sir? Permission to speak freely?"

"Granted."

"I see buildings. People could be down there, sir."

"Are you sure you see people?"

The corporal faltered.

"There are no buildings on *my* map," Horne explained. "If there *are* buildings in that location, it could only be an illegal outpost of Article 28 violators, who are not, technically, *people.* Do we understand one another?"

Light dawned in the other's eyes. He grinned. "Sir, I see no people—my mistake. Begging your pardon, sir."

"Granted."

"These other four appear to be going off trajectory now as well, sir."

"All is well." The General smiled.

The first descended to its target, letting out its beam of light. A single building exploded into flame. Horne clicked his tongue. "That should do," he muttered.

"Sir?" the corporal asked.

Horne cleared his throat. "It appears that missile has misfired, Corporal. It must have been due to tragic computer error."

The other grinned. "Another round, sir?"

"No; that's a warning shot," he whispered. Louder, he said,

"We'll have to leave those little rivers alone for now. No ATF was reported found in them. It was simply a safety precaution gone awry."

The corporal muttered under his breath, "Sir, if the tributaries were infected, they're all so close to the settlements that—"

General Horne clapped the corporal on the shoulder. "Great minds think alike, soldier." He paused. "You do realize this conversation never happened."

"I fully understand, sir."

"And it would be wise to delete all records of this immediately."

"Consider it done, sir."

Horne returned to address the media and herald his success.

Chapter 9

TRIAGE

> *I've been wondering . . . I was healed by a miracle . . . were my ovaries healed too? I don't want to bug the Richardsons about finding out, making them all feel sorry for me or anything.*
>
> *No dreams last night. That's a relief.*
>
> *And for the first time in my life, I know what I have to do. I can't explain why I feel so sure. But I am. I haven't told them about my decision yet either.*
>
> —Alyssa Stark,
> personal journal entry

New Hope filled with screams, shrieks, and shouting for help. Debra grabbed Zach from his cradle and ran out of her apartment into the commotion.

"What happened?" she called out.

And what was that explosion?

Her stomach churned, morning sickness mixed with dread, and she threw up on the curb. She had to wipe her mouth with her shirt. Gross.

Jennie Soong ran over to her, with her three youngest kids in tow. "Debra, there you are. You all right?"

"I'll be fine as soon as I find Jon!"

"Come with me!"

It wasn't long before they saw the flames leaping into the sky. The communications building stood burning with raging fire. They stopped short, appalled by what they saw.

Debra went into action first. "I'm going to find Jon!" she called, and ran for the hospital. She saw him coming her way, and ran to meet him. "Jon!" He hugged her, and in his solid embrace she wept with relief. "You're alive!"

"Debra, you're all right! You're all right. You're all right." He couldn't stop repeating it.

They held each other in the middle of the panic, baby Zach sandwiched between them, wailing with fear and distress.

"The comm building exploded," she told him.

"I saw the fire," Jon said. "Come on, we have to help."

"What about the baby?" she asked. "What can I do?"

"People might be hurt. I'm a doctor, I have to get there."

Debra agreed and hurried with him.

The volunteer firefighting team was already there with the New Hope fire truck, hosing the flames with chemical foam. It was like throwing a handful of sand on a bonfire.

"Who's hurt?" Jon yelled through the noise and commotion.

"Dr. Pike! Dr. Pike! Over here!" someone called.

He ran off to give aid.

Debra slumped against a store front and tried to soothe Zach. But her pleas of, "Don't worry, baby, everything's gonna be okay," were flat-out lies, and he sensed it.

She watched the flames shoot impossibly high, tears streaming down her cheeks. Billows of black smoke roiled up and away on the breeze, miles high.

"It was a bomb or something," said a woman nearby, someone she didn't know by name. "A red light came down from the sky."

"They were irradiating the rivers today with lasers," another said. "I was watching it on the news when the TV went out and that explosion rattled everything like an earthquake."

"It shook the whole house!" someone said.

"My whole apartment building shook," Debra added.

Around her, small groups gathered and talked and waited. And prayed.

* * * * *

Jon couldn't come home until the next morning, exhausted, worn, and dejected. He looked ill.

He fell into Debra's arms and wept bitterly. She'd never seen him cry like that.

"We lost nineteen," he finally got out, and gave their names. "Twenty-six more are still in the hospital, two critical. Brother Teasdale looks like he'll die. I've never sewn up so much damage in one day in my life. It was awful, Deb. We did everything we could . . . ."

"Why?" she cried, as they held each other.

"It was that General Horne." Jon's shaky voice solidified into rage. "A nasty trick. The technology we worked so hard for, gone, in one shot. Along with so many *lives*—"

"He hates us," Debra affirmed.

"And we can't do anything about it!" He squeezed her tight.

"Oh Jon—don't squeeze, I'll puke," she warned.

"I'm sorry, baby, I forgot. I'm just so angry."

"Me too."

"We lost our satellite uplink, our phones, everything. No contact with the world. President Weber just left for Sioux Falls to get to a phone and inform Salt Lake. And I bet this won't even make the news. Nobody cares about us," he sniffed. "It's like they don't think we're even human."

Debra was flustered, trying to comfort him when there was no comfort. "Probably no one except us knows it happened, Jon. Horne won't let this out if he can help it. Besides, with ATF and everything else going on, we're just a blip," she said. "What could anybody out there do against him? Even if they did care, which you're right, they don't."

Jon pulled her tighter. "What's carrying me through is knowing our Father cares."

"Not enough to stop this," Debra said, grim. She knew it was mean and wrong as soon as the words left her mouth. "Sorry," she whispered. Whether she meant to apologize to the Lord, or Jon, she wasn't sure.

"He doesn't always stop everything, Deb." Jon wiped tears off her face.

"I know. I know," she said.

They clung to each other as if letting go would stop their hearts.

CHAPTER 10

SIENNA

> Dr. Kensington concurs that deceased, contaminated organisms pose a serious threat of infection.
>
> I have ordered my soldiers to begin a systemic air strike over Central City, beginning at the southwest and proceeding northeast, initiating a controlled chemical burn of all biological material remaining within the perimeters. The areas surrounding the southwest corner are the least populated, and we therefore risk less danger of detection until the chemical incineration is well under way.
>
> I have formally decreed the airspace of Central City a no-fly zone; any media or other aircraft attempting to fly over the maneuver will be shot down.
>
> I do not come to this decision lightly. After careful deliberation, I feel this is the only course of action capable of both containing this virulent, toxic disease within City limits and safely disposing of the massive amount of diseased bodies. We expect this ongoing maneuver may take weeks in order to ensure thorough destruction of any contaminated material.
>
> —President-General Leopold F. Horne,
> Confidential Report to the President of the U.N.

Ever since Outbreak, the news was never off at the Richardsons'. Andrew sat every night in front of the screen, absorbing the details of the broadcast. Jordan was the second most interested, fascinated by the medical details of the disease, much to his twin sister's disgust.

It was well into October. The weather had turned cold and windy. Leaves fell off fruit trees in the orchard, and the two dairy cows lowed every morning and evening to be milked.

The roosters crowed to herald the morning. Chickens were fed, eggs laid and collected. Horses whinnied in their stalls, waiting to be exercised. Songbirds flew south. Acorns littered the front lawn from the huge live oak tree. Nature on the farm seemed unaware of the tragedy playing itself out not so many miles south.

Alyssa studied every book the Richardsons had to give her. Joan had never allowed any sort of religious study, and everything she learned fascinated her. She felt answers to her prayers, a glowing, burning sensation within her ribs that just felt *right*. She didn't always understand, but she started to listen to, and trust, that new feeling.

She wished the chores could start later in the morning, but she was getting used to the early hours. She wouldn't dream of not helping—the Richardsons gave her everything she needed. She wanted to do what she could to repay their generosity. Still, by evening she was worn down. Her energy wasn't back up to speed. She remembered pulling all-nighters for projects in college, and didn't know how she ever managed it.

One evening, Peter sat in the brown recliner opposite the couch, while Jordan and Kellie played Parcheesi on the floor, directly in front of the TV. Beverly sat with her needlework, reading glasses perched on her nose.

Alyssa settled on the couch by Beverly with a book. "Hey there," she said to everyone. Beverly smiled and made space for her.

"Hey," Peter said back.

"Doubles!" Jordan yelled. "Ha!"

"Don't block me!" Kellie said. "Jordan!"

"Jordan," Beverly chided.

"I'm playing fair! Kellie just wants to win."

Alyssa smiled. Jordan looked so much like a younger Peter that it was like looking into the past. She felt another painful longing for her dead ovaries, and shook it away. What was done could not be undone.

Kellie stuck out her tongue. "I don't have to move my blockade."

"I didn't do that to *you!*" Jordan said.

"So?" Kellie smirked.

"Solve the problem or put it away," Beverly said.

Jordan moved a piece. "You're on *her* side," he mumbled.

"You know I don't take sides. Should we put it away *now?*" his mother asked.

"No," Jordan grumbled.

On the TV, anchorwoman Mandy Tyler said, "With us tonight is Dr. Joel Kensington, in charge of National ATF Studies. At the forefront of everyone's mind has been whether the river irradiation President-General Horne ordered has been effective. Environmentalists are up in arms over the incredible damage to wildlife and fresh water sources."

Alyssa looked up from her book. "Not him again," she said.

Kensington was a heavy, middle-aged black man, bald, with a bushy salt-and-pepper beard. Alyssa noticed him most for his droning, monotonous voice, worse than a tired college professor.

He said, "Ms. Tyler, we must understand, the water was not potable, since it was contaminated. And ATF is incredibly difficult to destroy. Heat irradiation was a sure way to destroy it."

"Right, that's why the UN requests infected bodies to be cremated immediately."

"Correct. Also misunderstood is that the fish were already infected with ATF, or would have been presently. I commend President-General Horne's swift actions. Without him, we might all be dead, with ATF spreading throughout the globe. It is an aggressive, fatal disease. Thanks to his quick thinking, the rivers, *and* the human race, are once again safe."

"The end justifies the means." Ms. Tyler paused. "Dr. Kensington, what can you share of your findings regarding American Toxic Flu?"

"First of all, Ms. Tyler, it isn't a flu virus. It's difficult to pin this bug down in that its DNA contains elements of both virus and bacterium. Antibiotics are ineffective due to its viral nature, yet its bacterial components confound efforts to develop a vaccination."

Peter interrupted, "What's he saying, in English?"

Andrew said, "Shh. Listen, why don't you?"

Dr. Kensington droned on, "Frankly, this DNA strand is not something any of us have seen before. We simply don't know what we're dealing with."

"So, the ATF virus *was* genetically engineered?" Mandy Tyler asked.

"I am only authorized to say it appears that way," Dr. Kensington replied. "Even with recent advancements in genetic engineering, basic scientific theory assumes that combining two unique life forms into a single, new, viable life form cannot be achieved. Therein lies our hesitation. We don't know what this thing is, or even how to classify it. We still have no clues on where it originated, except that the organism did not evolve in that reservoir by accident."

"Good news and bad in the same statement, then?"

The doctor nodded. "Yes. While it does not appear to be a product of natural evolution—"

"—Somewhere, someone created this thing and unleashed it on millions of innocent victims," Ms. Tyler finished for him.

"It unfortunately appears that way."

"Thank you for being with us tonight, Dr. Kensington." The anchor turned to the camera, filling the screen so the doctor vanished. "More questions with unsatisfactory answers . . ."

"I'm glad *he's* gone," Alyssa said. "Man! Boring!"

"Kensington knows what he's talking about," Andrew said. "Not like that babbling Tyler lady. She speculates too much."

Kellie said, "Would you *roll*, Jordan? I'm *waiting*."

"Okay, okay." Jordan took his turn.

The broadcast switched to local news.

"Our top local story tonight reminds us all of the need for gun safety. Clovis Jefferson Davis, known to friends as C.J., died today in a tragic accident. Mr. Davis was allegedly cleaning his gun when it unexpectedly discharged, shooting himself in the abdomen. The body was discovered around 3:00 this afternoon. Surviving him is his wife, Sally."

Video of the wife came on. She was mousy and rough-looking, exhibiting copious tears. "I was over to my sister's house for the weekend," she blubbered. "She been goin' through a divorce, see, and havin' a real hard time. I tole C.J. time and again, be careful cleanin' that thing. If they'd only of found him sooner . . . he might still be with us." Her sobs became incoherent, and the screen returned to the local news anchor, Kevan Frank. "An autopsy is scheduled for tomorrow morning to rule out foul play. We interviewed Davis' hunting partner, Jack Vi—"

Peter flipped off the TV. "Get ready for bed, kids."

"I wanted to hear about that guy," Jordan said.

"You're so gross," Kellie said.

"Didn't you get your funny feeling, Kellie?"

"I did not."

Jordan insisted, "I know you did. I *felt* you feel it."

Kellie said, "Hush!"

They locked eyes for a few moments. Jordan looked away first. "I just want to know what it meant," he said.

"You've got school in the morning," Peter said. "Get your jammies on and come down for prayer."

Alyssa stood, stretching her arms and neck muscles. "I think I'll turn in after family prayer myself."

"Already?"

Could he be disappointed? Alyssa wondered. She was too worn through to give it much thought. "4:30 comes early," she said.

The honest truth was, a single idea would not leave her alone, but she didn't know how to tell them. She wanted time alone in her room to mull that over. She had prayed over it for some time. Nothing ever felt more right. By now she was anxious.

It had to be soon.

* * * * *

"I want to be baptized," she announced the next morning, at breakfast.

After an initial clatter of silverware, there was silence.

"What?" She took a bite of her eggs. It was fun to watch the looks on their faces.

Beverly was first to recover. "Well, that's wonderful!"

"Lovely," Andrew said, his tone flat.

Kellie and Jordan said, "Hooray!" at the same time.

Peter was speechless.

Alyssa swallowed and managed a wry grin.

"When?" Beverly stammered.

She shrugged. "How about tonight? Is there deep enough water anywhere?"

Peter found his voice. "There are a few people you have to meet first, some interviews and things to do. Protocol stuff. And we'll have to ride out to the reservoir."

"Okay, is this weekend too soon? I didn't see anything special on the calendar."

"It could be, depending," Peter said.

"Have you read—" Beverly started.

"I finished the Book of Mormon a week ago. I've thought about this for weeks. Yes. I'm ready."

"Well—this is incredible. Let's celebrate," Beverly said. "We'll have a party, tonight. Peter, you can grill for us. This is terrific!"

Andrew gave Alyssa a hard look. "Nice move," he said.

"What?" she asked, confused.

"I'm late for work," was his only answer. He put on his baseball cap and went out.

"Don't ride Lucy too hard, she'll get sick," Beverly called.

"I know how to take care of my own horse, Mom." The French door slammed, vibrating the panes of glass.

Beverly rubbed her forehead, her breakfast half-eaten.

Kellie put her backpack on. "Come on, Jordan, it's time for school." Jordan gulped down his last bite of oatmeal, and the pair kissed their mother goodbye and went out the same door.

Alyssa asked, "Why does Andrew have such a big problem with me?"

"You're hardly the cause of his problems," Peter said.

"That doesn't answer my question," she said.

"He's getting flak at work," Beverly asked.

"What flak do you get at a vet's office?" Alyssa asked.

"Some people want to blame us for ATF, and they're bugging him about it at work," Peter explained. "He's not sure where he stands right now."

"He's not thinking of getting treated, is he?" Alyssa felt panic. That would be awful.

"No—not that he says, anyway. It's just not easy right now."

The first part of what Peter said sunk in. Alyssa said, "How can they blame you for ATF? You guys aren't geneticists."

"Not our family, the Church," said Peter. "Of course it's stupid."

"I'll say," she added.

Jordan poked his head in the door. "Andrew didn't saddle Thistle before he left. He's *supposed* to do it on the days he works. We're not big enough to get the saddle on."

Beverly looked up with a sigh. "Peter?"

"I'm on it."

He went out with his little brother.

It was just the two of them, but Alyssa lowered her voice anyway. "None of this explains to me what Andrew said—'nice move,' like that. What's he talking about?"

Beverly finished off her glass of juice before answering. "I can't be sure. He may have meant that if you want acceptance in the family, baptism is a good place to start." She looked Alyssa in the eye.

"That's not at all why I want to do this!" Alyssa said, shocked.

Beverly seemed to relax.

"Beverly, when did I ever care about fitting in? Look at me! When I was growing up, if I didn't do everything I was told, I paid dearly for it. But this is *not* the same thing. Nobody's forcing me to read these books, or pray, or do any of that. I'm doing it because I want to. Who is he to question my motives? He doesn't know what I feel inside!"

Peter's mother smiled. "Don't worry. He'll come around."

* * * * *

Peter grilled thick steaks with garlic, potatoes, and steamed vegetables on the side. Alyssa devoured hers off the plate, glad it wasn't chicken.

Beverly brought out a cake for dessert.

Alyssa was surprised. "When did you make that?"

"While you were mucking the stalls," Beverly said. "I wanted to surprise you. I didn't make you one on your birthday—you insisted on not making a big deal out of it—so I figured, why not now?"

"You didn't have to do that for me."

"I wanted to. Besides, this is like a new birth for you."

"That's true."

Andrew groaned.

She ignored him. "How big a piece can I have?" Alyssa teased the twins, who were vying over who got to use the knife.

Kellie said, "Big as you want. You're getting baptized!"

"Leave some for us though!" Jordan said.

Beverly handed Alyssa the knife. "Do I really eat that much?" Alyssa asked.

Beverly's only reply was a smile.

The twins' excitement was contagious. Even Andrew was affected. "Great cake, Mom," he said, his mouth full.

"So this party was a good idea?" Beverly asked.

"Hey, I never pass up cake."

Beverly asked, "I take it work went well?"

"Yeah. Sienna came in," Andrew said.

His mother's brow went up. "What for?"

"Just to see me."

"She didn't try bringing her cat in again?" Peter took a bite of cake.

Andrew blushed. "Okay, so she doesn't own a large animal! Dr. Hilbert talked to her about that, but he doesn't mind. He thinks she's hot."

Peter rolled his eyes.

Alyssa tried to fit in. "She doesn't own a horse?"

"Her family still runs their car," Andrew said.

Alyssa raised an eyebrow. *Spoiled and rich.*

"She asked me out tonight, and I'm going."

"You know how I feel about her," Beverly started.

"Dr. Hilbert likes her," Andrew said.

Beverly's mouth twisted. "He's not one of us. Neither is she."

"Mom. I can handle myself."

"I'd feel better if she came over and got to know us."

"That's stupid and pointless."

Peter said, "Andrew, Mom only wants—"

"Don't start!" Andrew pointed at Peter with his fork. "Sienna's pretty, she's nice, I really like her, and we're going out. That's all."

Peter muttered, "Sure it is."

"She's picking me up in an hour. She's letting me drive."

"*What?*" Beverly exclaimed.

Peter said, "That's not safe! You barely learned to drive when the embargo began."

"What traffic is there? Two cars an hour, if it's busy."

Beverly asked, "Where will you go?"

"Mom, I'm nineteen years old!"

Beverly stared at him until he answered.

"Maybe a double-feature. Then ice cream or something."

"Fine." She gave a heavy sigh.

"Cut it out, Mom. The sighing. The melodrama. You know it's not easy dating around here. Look at the luck *Peter's* had, huh? I — am — going."

Alyssa was curious what Andrew's comment referred to. But everyone picked up their dishes and cleared out. She wasn't finished with her cake; it was fluffy, tender, and delicious. She'd gone without proper food too long not to appreciate something so wonderful, made especially for her.

Finally she brought her plate to the sink, where Peter was washing dishes.

He'd started the dishwasher; only pots and pans were left. She rinsed out one of the round cake pans.

"So what's wrong with Sienna?"

Peter finished scrubbing a pot before he answered. He handed it to her to rinse. "Andy's faith is weak enough without distractions like her. Mom and I believe she's leading him on, but he can't see it. And she's *my* age—I went to high school with her. I know her better. But he won't listen.

"She's also divorced and has kids, but they aren't her husband's. Excuse me, that's two kids by *two* somebody else's, *while* she was married." He held up two soapy fingers.

Margret almost fit that description, Alyssa thought. The last time she saw Margret, she was hurrying to the train station with Marcus and Natty, hoping to escape her psycho ex in time. Alyssa worried for the millionth useless time what became of them. She thought of Margret's many scars, and said, "Sometimes people have good reasons for leaving."

"Yeah. Sienna's ex-husband had excellent reasons. Coming home to find her in bed with someone else had a lot to do with it. And it may just have *something* to do with why we don't want her anywhere near Andrew."

His face turned bright red.

"I get it." Her mental image shifted from Margret to her sister Lauren. Her nose wrinkled.

Peter looked vulnerable, more attractive when he blushed. She cleared her throat, forcing her eyes to focus on the dish in her hands. "Does Andrew know?"

"Yes, but he thinks he's invincible. Of course he isn't. You see why we worry."

"Yeah." Her throat was dry. She rinsed another dish. The Richardsons' church, soon to be her own, taught a code of sexual purity that made perfect sense to Alyssa, requiring no change of heart—or behavior, on her part. Lauren with all her promiscuity was never happy, incomplete, never satisfied, and, she observed, Margret found no happiness in a random-sex lifestyle, either. Long ago she vowed never to live like that, and she had never broken that vow.

Rob was tempting, though . . . she shook her head to clear that thought away. He hadn't persuaded her far along that path, and hadn't pushed for more.

She was more grateful for that restraint now than ever.

* * * * *

Peter tried not to watch Alyssa too closely as they worked side by side. It was unpleasant having to tell her what he thought of Sienna. Thankfully she didn't push the matter too hard.

They'd fallen into this evening routine, working together on the dinner dishes; neither had discussed it, but it was becoming a habit, talking quietly about the events of the day. The only hard part was pretending that he didn't ache with longing when she stood so close to him.

He'd nearly slipped the other day, talking with her on the couch about her dreams. It was all he could do not to kiss her then. It wasn't the right time. She was recovering from multiple emotional shocks, developing a faith she never experienced before, plus struggling with a blossoming spiritual gift that neither one of them understood. He didn't want to add a confession of love to her problems. Or at least, when he did eventually tell her, he didn't want her to take it as a problem.

"Peter?" she said quietly. She ran water over a pan, suds swirling down the drain.

"Yes?" His feelings bubbled up and overflowed. He suppressed the urge to bounce up and down with joy that she had asked to be baptized this morning.

She cleared her throat. "Are you done with that pot?"

He felt stupid. He'd stopped washing, lost in his thoughts.

"Sorry." He scrubbed off the remaining spots and handed her the pot.

He sneaked a sidelong look at her while he scrubbed the last dish. A lock of hair by her face stuck out sideways, curled up from the steam. He was tempted to straighten it for her, but forced his attention back on the dirty dish. He thought of something that would be safe enough to ask, that did have to be addressed.

Peter handed her the casserole dish and drained the dishwater. It sucked down with a loud slurp. "Who did you want to baptize you?" he got out, amazed the words were so hard so say.

She shrugged. "Who's available?"

"There's me," he said. He rinsed out the sink bottom and cleaned the trap. "Or Andrew."

It wasn't jealousy that didn't feel right about suggesting his brother. He wondered where Andy stood with Sienna; still, personal worthiness was Andrew's business, not his.

"Any Priesthood holder over age sixteen can perform a baptism. There's Bishop Greene, or . . . well, a whole lot of people who *could* do it."

He hungered for that honor; why couldn't he just say so?

Alyssa said, "I'm most comfortable with you doing it, if you don't mind."

Mind doing something I've dreamed of ever since I was sixteen? Peter thought. "Not at all," he said lightly. "I'd be happy to." His insides felt like they were playing ring-around-the-rosy. He kept talking to stop himself from picking her up and twirling her around the kitchen. "How set are you on doing this quickly?" he asked.

"Very. Once I'm ready for something, I'm ready."

"There are chapels with baptismal fonts in Liahona. The twins will be baptized there in the spring, but Mom just got back from the last trip. We won't be going again until Christmas."

"Too long to wait," she said.

Peter said, "I'll call Brother King and let him know we'll need the reservoir, then. He hates it when people show up without telling him. It's the only body of water close by that's deep enough for enough for immersion, but Alyssa—it'll be quite cold. It's never warm, even in the middle of summer. A font has warm water, like a bathtub. Are you sure?"

"Is it effective whether it's warm or cold?"

"Sure."

"Then I can manage it."

"All right."

Peter imagined Alyssa shivering, soaking wet and turning to him for warmth, and stifled the image before his imagination ran away with him. He needed a distraction, fast. He grinned and said, "Well, if it freezes this weekend, we'll just chip a hole through the ice."

That raised her eyebrow and made her think for a minute.

He patted her shoulder like he would his brother, and said, "I'll go talk to Mom and see about the other arrangements. Let me know if you change your mind." He left the kitchen quickly.

That night, Peter couldn't sleep. Never, since he joined the Church at sixteen, did he believe his wish that Alyssa would come into the Church would come true.

She had been studying intently, but he didn't expect her to accept it. Their way of life was hard, especially with the sanctions Article 28 placed on the expression of religion. Knowing her cynical nature, he expected her to say a polite "No, thanks," and that would be it.

Peter knew miracles alone didn't convert anyone. She'd had a marvelous experience; one that at first strained his own willingness to believe. He remembered how Laman and Lemuel saw angels, and afterwards they still beat up their younger brother, Nephi, and *he* was a prophet. Peter himself experienced a small miracle or two during his mission in China, but the people involved were not converted. A miracle alone didn't change a life. The Holy Ghost did. He knew that.

Alyssa had always been skeptical of anything and everything that didn't have concrete proof. She got that from her mother—although she wouldn't like hearing it put that way.

He had fully expected her to refuse the gospel. It sunk in how much that would have cost him. His heart would be crushed. Forever. For if she loved him, and not his religion, which would he choose? He ached at the thought. He couldn't imagine living without her, and intended to win her love or die trying.

Yet he couldn't face having to decide against his God and the doctrine that a man must take on eternal covenants of marriage, blessings available only inside the temple to worthy members, and without which he could never enter the highest degree of heaven. He was so torn that he had pushed it aside rather than choose in advance.

And without her acceptance of his faith—her pure testimony of its truth—their love would be confined to this life, ending with the finality of death. The temple promised eternity. He had seen marriages fall apart all around him after Article 28 passed, due to partners unequal in faith, divided. It was rare for such a marriage to last. He faced losing her, whether by death or divorce, unless he could be sealed to her forever.

It would be unfair to her if he could not promise his love for eternity.

As he lay in bed, his eyes refusing to shut, it became clear that this was why he held back.

He didn't want romantic advances on his part to influence her decision. If she thought once that baptism was a prerequisite to being with him—supposing that she wanted to be—it would not be a true conversion from her heart, a commitment first to the Lord, and not to him. The decision had to be her own internal choice, without his outside interference.

And now, it was.

Peter had kept his love wrapped in a sealed container in his heart, hidden away from anyone in his family. He didn't want his secret exposed. Andrew would tease and chide, especially if Alyssa did not return his feelings, and he refused to give his little brother the childish pleasure of getting a rise out of him.

Early on, he had a huge fight with his mother that Alyssa did not know about. His mother never told him Alyssa had called while he was on his mission. He was furious when he found out.

Then she brought up his failure to see through Jackie, and the torment that relationship had put him through.

As if he needed reminding.

He didn't throw it back in his mother's face that there would not have *been* a Jackie, if she'd just told him about that phone call.

Still, she had serious concerns that Alyssa's values and lifestyle would prove deficient, and did not want to see her son repeat a similar heartbreak. At the end of the argument, he was left with telling her he had no intentions in that direction, to put her mind at ease. It wasn't fully untrue. It wasn't until after that argument that the Spirit had opened his eyes and helped him realize the truth of his emotions.

He opened that sealed package now and allowed that love to wash over his soul, basking in the beauty and potential bliss that life with her might hold.

At length he slipped into a peaceful sleep.

* * * * *

The next morning, Kellie and Jordan came running into the house. "Lucy Mack's still in the barn!" Kellie said.

Jordan looked frustrated. "Andrew didn't saddle Thistle. Two days in a row!"

Beverly slammed her fist on the table and looked off in the distance. After a terrible silence, she said, "Just get to school, sweethearts." There was a catch in her voice.

"Who's going to saddle Thistle?" Kellie asked.

Beverly gave a deep maternal sigh of complete emotional exhaustion. "Peter?"

"I'm on it, Mom," he said, halfway out the door.

* * * * *

Andrew arrived home at dusk, walking, his head down, kicking up dust.

Beverly had watched out the front window all day. She met him at the door and kept her tone bright. "I'm so glad to see you home safe. Did you go to work today?"

He didn't look up. "I had the day off," he muttered. His clothes were wrinkled and dusty, and there was a hole in the knee of his pants that wasn't there when he left.

It was a lie. Dr. Hilbert had called the house to see if Andrew was sick.

He brushed past, refusing the hug she tried to give him.

He went to his room and did not come out.

Beverly leaned against the doorframe and wept silently.

CHAPTER 11

REFUGEES

The media is cooperating with our efforts to sterilize Central City. We have yet to achieve a high level of control, but public acceptance is steadily improving in the polls.

—President-General Leo Horne,
private log

Margret and her children hid in the underbrush and watched as a group of three or four hundred people neared their campsite, talking loudly, mostly ragged women and children. Not more than an hour ago, she heard prolonged gunfire from the direction of town.

They must be Central City refugees.

She knew of ATF now and knew terror. These people must have escaped the quarantine patrol.

"Stay quiet, Natty," she ordered. For once, the girl was still. They held their breath, watching. She'd had time to hide their gear and mess up their footprints and campfire, so their presence might not be noticed.

Near evening, men arrived in camp, hauling two cattle carcasses they had stolen and slaughtered from a nearby farm. They started fires and got it cooking.

The scent of sizzling beef wafted through the air.

Margret's mouth watered. She made a decision. David's money was as good as gone, and they had a long way to go yet. "They're like us, running away. They're not sick. We'll blend right in, and they have lots of food." Her kids agreed. It smelled too good to pass up.

They wound through the strangers, pretending they were coming back from the designated latrine.

Margret was right. They blended in. No one noticed they were new.

In camp, a blonde woman was complaining to the air. "We just want a fair chance. Everyone gets so hysterical! They won't even take our money!"

"Your money ain't worth squat," an old man said. "You just be grateful Doc saved the lot of us from that checkpoint."

"Checkpoint, my foot. Concentration camp is more like it."

Margret only had snips and bits of news from town. General Horne set up checkpoints every five hundred kilometers around the perimeter of Central City. You were supposed to check in to let people know you were alive.

Apparently, that would be your last mistake. She hoped Ralph got ATF. She took a perverse delight in imagining his eyeballs detaching from their sockets, him throwing up his own stomach, writhing in pain. Escaping that . . . the next thing she hoped, on hearing this, was that he'd sign in at a checkpoint.

She felt a nervous twitch thinking that he could be among any refugee group. Or that he'd left Central City before Outbreak, and was not at risk at all.

On the flip side, *he* might have to assume *they* were dead. An unusual form of safety.

That was good.

* * * * *

The weather turned chill. Their tattered jackets didn't keep the wind out, and blankets weren't passed around evenly. Those who thought of themselves as having wealth or prestige still demanded privilege.

Marcus and Nat trudged alongside Margret as they marched north. Marcus carried Natty when she stumbled. It pulled at her heart in a way that ached more than she could bear.

Their group was larger than most, she discovered. They had physicians, naturalists, and hunters in the group who taught survival skills as they could. Mostly, the men and a few of the women stole what they needed from townspeople, at gunpoint.

Marcus hated that.

"You have to eat," Margret urged.

"They stole it," he argued.

She could have slapped him. She held back. She had never struck her children in anger. This was no time to start. Fiercely, she said, "This is no time for a hunger strike, eh? I need you alive. *You eat!*"

He looked shocked, and pulled away from her.

Softer, she added, "Look. We didn't do the stealing, okay?"

After that he didn't argue.

Doc was their self-appointed leader, a retired doctor most of them respected—at first, anyway. He used an increasingly violent approach, causing more casualties in each town they passed through to get the ammunition and supplies he wanted.

In a town halfway between Shelby and Holstein, the firefight lasted much longer than usual. Margret, Marcus, and Natty crouched in a small stand of trees and underbrush apart from the others. Somehow during their time with this group, Natty had learned to hold still, to be silent. She no longer cried at every inconvenience.

"I'm scared, Mama," Marcus whispered.

"These people won't hurt *us*," she said.

Marcus said, "I don't like guns."

"Mama's always had a gun, *niño*." She was out of bullets, but that was beside the point.

"That doesn't mean I like it."

"We need food, and they feed us."

"We were doing okay," Marcus added. He pouted.

Not the hunger strike thing again, she worried. "Look. David's money is gone. If we didn't join them, they might have killed us. That, or we'd be eating leaves and roots and bugs by now."

Natty whispered, "I don't want to eat bugs!"

"I didn't need the comic book." Marcus' voice was small.

"My sweet baby." Margret hugged him. "That money wouldn't buy much else. No more guilt from you. Okay?"

"Okay," he mumbled into her shirt.

He read and re-read that thing, carefully stowing it in his tattered backpack. It was the best thing she'd done in a long time of mothering.

Natty perked up suddenly, losing her silence. "I want more bubble gum, Mama!"

"No."

She drew out a plaintive, whining, "Why?"

Margret buried her face in her hands.

* * * * *

Margret heard a woman weep over an antique Versace gown, bawling like she'd lost a child. She didn't know what "antique Versace" meant, until the woman carried on about its being worn to the Oscars in the original Hollywood by some old dead actress, pre-Blankenship. The dress was worth millions and burned in the Central City fires. Another woman consoled her, crying nearly as hard as the other.

Others complained about the food. Vegetarians. Or, "Are you sure that's organic beef?" Every night brought complaints about the lack of pasteurization or cleanliness. A couple of the naturalists looked ready to throttle the pickiest ones.

People reminisced about fancy restaurants they loved, as if talking about it would summon the food by magic.

Some hope died every day, especially for those born to luxury. Suicide won its casualties evenly with exposure.

* * * * *

Margret and her children accepted their rations with gratitude. It would take longer than a week for them to tire of fresh steak, normally a rare, rationed treat.

"You won't hear us complain, will you?" she said as they ate.

"I like eating with my fingers!" Natty giggled, meat juice dribbling down her chin. "You never let us eat with our fingers!"

"Don't get used to it. When we get to Alyssa's friends, the rules are back on. You behave like little angels."

"We will, Mama," Marcus grinned, and wiped his mouth with the back of his hand.

CHAPTER 12

O CANADA

I'm quitting soon. This place is just too depressing to work in anymore.

—Dinah Milton, R.N.
letter to a friend

Ockwen Oakley dreamed the seagulls flew north, to Canada, to freedom, out of this hospital-asylum-prison place in North Central City. Enemies of all seagulls brought him here. They shocked him with electrodes, fed him little white pills. Then the demons came to taunt him. Purple fear-monsters with rotten black teeth chased him at every turn, nibbling his extremities.

In Canada the demons would no longer find him.

"Vampiristic pain-sucking monsters!" he shouted, brandishing his fist. "Loathsome leech creatures of the dark! I will vanquish thee in the end!"

Somehow he knew this to be true: there would be an end, and he would conquer.

The seagulls flew north, fleeing the United States in droves.

This time, Ockwen flew with them.

* * * * *

The next morning he sat in the common area and willed his skin to grow feathers. Soon, it did! He flapped his new wings, squawking like a gull.

Nurse Dinah said, "Time for your medication, Mr. Oakley." She was a pretty thing, but standoffish. Oh well. Far too young for him anyway.

"I grew wings," Ockwen boasted.

"Sure you did." She handed him the little cup of water and the white pill.

He swallowed it and went back to flapping. He jumped on the table with a rattling thump and preened his fluffy white feathers. Nurse Dinah ignored his less-than-impressive landing, the rocking of the table on unsteady legs.

"Mites! Itchy things," he complained. "Nurse Dinah? How far away is Canada? As the gull flies, that is."

"Too far for you, Mr. Oakley." She turned away.

"My old bones won't make it, is that what you think?"

"No, I think you won't be leaving anytime soon," she answered, administering another patient's medication.

"But all seagulls migrate to Canada."

"Mr. Oakley. There are no seagulls in Central City, *or* Canada."

"Of course there aren't any here. The purple demons made them flee!" he exclaimed. The great flock of gulls in his mind's eye faded in the distance, leaving him behind. "There *are* seagulls in Canada, dear Nurse Dinah. And in Utah, eating up crickets. Are crickets on the menu this morning? I'm a mite hungry."

Nurse Dinah warned, "Don't make me get Dr. Gary. Stop that nonsense at once."

Ockwen gave a dramatic sigh and preened as he perched on the tabletop. Dr. Gary was horrid. *Fetid. Foul. Squalid. Putrid. Rancid. Rank.* He worked his way through his favorite synonyms for Dr. Gary.

The medicine worked its way through his bloodstream. His pretty feathers molted in an instant and dropped in a heap on the floor. Uncharacteristic for feathers. They should have floated down softly. They vanished and hysteria took their place. "The demons return!" he shrieked. "Did you check my room for demons?" He felt them circling the edges of his peripheral vision. He spun wildly. "Show yourselves!" he screamed.

Nurse Dinah tucked a bib under a drooling patient's chin. "Do I need to call Dr. Gary?" she asked, nonchalant.

Ockwen struggled to check his outward show of terror. He crawled under the table and sucked his thumb. No Dr. Gary. No straitjacket, no strapping to tables, no pain, no needles, please, not this morning. A moment ago it was such a fine morning.

He'd never succeeded growing a full coat of feathers before. Nurse Dinah utterly ignored this accomplishment as nothing.

"Please, please go check my bottom drawer. They hide in there. Please, dear Nurse Dinah?"

"I checked. It's empty," she said with a tired voice.

"Oh, thank you so much. It's safe to go to my room?"

"Sure thing, Mr. Oakley."

"Nurse Dinah?"

"Yeah, Mr. Oakley?"

"Would you please call me Ockwen?"

"I'm sorry, that violates protocol."

"Brother Oakley, then?"

"No, Mr. Oakley."

That name had such a wonderful ring. *Brother Oakley.* It was much friendlier than Mister, so right. He sighed. Nurse Dinah never budged.

He bolted to his room.

*   *   *   *   *

Later, Ockwen was absorbed in a topographic map of Canada when Dirk Mason appeared in his doorway. Map study kept the demons at bay. Concentration was vital. *Imperative. Essential. Fundamental.* His mind ticked through the synonyms. If his will broke but a moment, the waiting demons would bite.

"Ock. Ock. Hello, Ock!" Dirk pounded on the wall.

"Don't interrupt me!" he cried in anguish, then blinked dumbly at the figure in the door. "Brother Mason! How nice to see you." Ockwen stood up and shook Dirk's hand. But Brother Dirk Mason did not room in this wing. "Who let you over here to see me?"

Dirk said, "Can't you hear the riot! It's terrible. Just terrible."

The sounds outside finally registered.

"What is that awful noise?"

"People are sick everywhere, Ock. The patients and the nurses and the janitors and the doctors. And one of those *real* crazies in Ward B broke loose and unlocked the kitchen knives."

"Oh, dear." Ward B was for serial killers.

He went with Dirk. The killer had made rather a bloody mess of carnage. Lunatic. *Madman. Crazy. Psychopath. A few beans short of a full pot. A few bricks shy of a full—*

Dirk interrupted Ockwen's thoughts. "It was this guy, here. He's dead. Looks like he killed himself after doing all these in."

"That *is* how it appears, Dirk, I must agree." He gingerly stepped over the corpse blocking the hallway, and they picked their way to the common area.

The front door of the asylum was open wide. They looked at each other in disbelief. "I'll see if the electric fence is off." Dirk left him.

As Dirk said, everyone the psycho-killer didn't get was sick. People barely moved, puking on their own shoes. Vomit was splattered everywhere.

Nurse Dinah lay collapsed in a puddle of blood.

"Oh, no," he said, going to her. "My pretty Dinah." He stood over her mutilated body and cried.

"The fence is off!" Dirk yelled from the door, a silhouette. "I'm free! I'm gone, baby, gone!" Dirk vanished into the block of sunlight. Ockwen squinted after him.

Freedom. Canada.

Canada!

"Land of elk, moose, Mounties, and seagulls, my first-and-ever love, I am free! I come to you!" Ockwen raised his fist.

He had to pack. Blue Stuffed Bunny went first, of course. Next went the topographical map of Canada and his dog-eared, half-memorized thesaurus. He needed food: applesauce, salted peanuts, honey graham crackers. Au gratin potato chips. And *no* little white pills.

Water went on a trip. He filled a couple of liter-size bottles from the tap.

It would be too hard to fly with a heavy pack, but he needed the supplies. (Besides, his feathers refused to grow back.) He would walk it.

He passed Nurse Dinah on his way out and was sad all over again. He put down his pack and bent over her blessedly unmarred face. He kissed her cooling gray lips, and squeezed her bluish hands in an earnest goodbye.

"I do hate to leave you like this," Ockwen told her, a vague fuzzy feeling telling him there was nothing to be done for it. "But Canada awaits!"

* * * * *

He ran north, purple demons nipping at his heels.

Four days later he was in Iowa, southeast of Sioux City, vomiting blood, but no less determined to reach Canada. He was still unable to fly; no feathers grew. Flying would be ever so much faster. And he wished mightily the demons would stop making him throw up. It slowed him down.

The following morning he could no longer see. Demons had pecked out his eyes in his sleep, confound the beasts. And it was cold. Then hot as a desert. And cold again.

"Strange weather we are having," he said to no one, shivering.

Nothing so trivial as pain or cold or blindness could bar him from Canada now. Morning sun on his face told him north from east. He forged ahead. Shortly he fell into a rocky stream and got soaking wet.

Fresh water! The stuff in the bottle had gone a bit foul. Blind, he fumbled in his pack and poured the old stale water into the coursing stream. When it was empty, he squeezed the bottle and held it underwater. He brought it eagerly to his lips.

It held mud. He gagged and threw up again, dropping the bottle. He would have to cross; the stream lay between himself and mighty Canada. He felt his way out. Knee-deep in water, he drank his fill, and his ears told him he might be midway through. He waded through to the other side, glad he hadn't needed to swim, or been caught in a current. He crawled out to dry in the sun, exhausted. He must rest. He took Blue Stuffed Bunny out of his pack, who was soaking wet, and wrung out Bunny's ears and feet the best he could. He curled up in a ball and dreamed of seagulls and Canada.

Ockwen Oakley never woke up again.

CHAPTER 13

WORMWOOD

> *. . . And there fell a great star from heaven, burning*
> *as it were a lamp, and it fell upon the third part of the*
> *rivers, and upon the fountains of waters;*
> *And the name of the star is called Wormwood: and*
> *the third part of the waters became wormwood; and*
> *many men died of the waters, because they were made*
> *bitter . . .*
>
> —Revelation 8:10-11
> *Holy Bible*, KJV

"What do you mean the PR is all bad?" General Horne yelled at the screen. "I save all their sorry tails from dying, and this is the thanks I get?"

"We just need to be careful, sir," the major said. "We're working as fast as we can to buy out the media, but they're very resistant to go back to Jag's ways. They've tasted journalistic freedom. And we need more funding for it. A *lot* more."

"Irradiating the water was the only way!" Horne yelled. He needed a drink. He needed another cigar. He needed about fifteen women. None of which were present. "Don't they understand? There is *no more* ATF in anybody's water, except inside Central! It's contained! Play that up! Invent the money if you have to!"

"I understand, sir, and the troops are behind you one hundred percent. But the fact remains that the fish are dead, the rivers stink, and the water is still ruined, due to all the fish decomposing in it. What do you propose as a solution?"

"How fast can the recycling stations operate?"

"Probably fast enough to support the remaining population along the riverbanks, sir," the major replied. "But—"

"Get on it," Horne barked. "And get me some better press!"

"Yes, sir! . . . One more thing, sir?"

"Go ahead." He rubbed his face.

"An animal activist group is lobbying against you, sir. It seems they're upset about the fish anyway, but there's a certain species that may now be extinct . . ."

"Arrest the lot of them."

"Beg your pardon, sir, the press—"

"Screw the press! *Don't let anyone find out*, Major. That's an order."

"Yes, sir. Understood."

"Dismissed."

Horne groaned.

More troops would have to be reassigned to cleanup duty. They were spread out enough patrolling the whole perimeter of the City. Those dratted imbeciles inside kept trying to escape quarantine, spreading disease potentially anywhere.

Where to get more soldiers? Voluntary enlistment was at an all-time low. ATF had taken out his secret drafting pool, from those hidden slums deep inside Central. That option was lost. Well—few of those recruits were making good soldiers, no matter what incentives he offered. And he couldn't institute a nationwide draft with the media on his back. There would be a coup—and the world could ill afford his stepping down from power. Not until ATF was eradicated.

CHAPTER 14

INCOMMUNICADO

hey andy dandy how come your not answering my
emails? like it wasn't that bad, get over it all right? :-)
sorry for that thing i said you know i was just kidding
right. You are still steamin hot i still want to see you
again i had such an amazing time
luv
sienna xxoxo :-)

—email in Andrew's inbox

Something clicked in Alyssa's brain while she was feeding the chickens. It was a frosty morning, and the sharp frozen air hurt her lungs. She stood up straight, her mind spinning with realization.

Debra belongs to the same church as Peter!

She was late putting that together, for sure.

It was all she could do to finish her job, scattering the feed badly, before she ran to the stable to find Peter.

There might be a way to find her!

Peter was in the corral, walking Teancum. "What's wrong?" he said.

"Nothing!" Her words tumbled out fast. "I just figured something out. My best friend—Debra Gray—she's Mormon. It didn't connect until now. I ignored her whenever she talked about it—and lately, I've had so much else on my mind . . ."

With chagrin, she realized she'd forgotten her friend from so long ago. She shut so much out of her memory from those college days: her drug overdose, gettting involved with Rob, Caldwell's looming threats . . . it was better to forget.

Her worries lately focused so much on Margret, hoping she'd gotten out of Central City before ATF, whether she survived, how the two children might be doing. They hardly left her mind. She mourned for the ones that were most likely dead—Bert,

Crazy Mary, so many others she had loved . . . there had been no room, no time, for reminiscing beyond her years in the Gardens.

She felt terrible—Debra had carried her through the darkest hours of her life, and she'd hardly thought about her in over two years.

Peter halted the stallion. The great horse shook its head and snorted, but obeyed, regarding Alyssa with a watchful eye.

"And that means?" Peter asked.

"I have to find her. I have to see if she can come to my baptism!"

He wrinkled his brow. "That could be hard. Where was she when Article 28 passed?" he asked.

"With me. We were roommates still. She went off north with her family and her fiancé to go into hiding."

"Canada?"

"No. She was part of some trial group or something in northwest Iowa, closer to Sioux Falls. They called it New Hope. I'll have to look at a map."

"Oh! I know about New Hope," Peter said, brightening. He started the anxious stallion walking again. "That's just like Liahona, near us. We'll look her up when I get done with Teancum, all right? It should be easy. We'll find her." He smiled wide, and his eyes sparkled.

She could have hugged him—she was glad the horse blocked the way.

No sense making an idiot out of herself.

Liahona was the town Beverly visited every other month for supplies, hitching up the two mares to a large trailer. They sent a good portion of their crops, excess garden produce, and home canning to Liahona's storehouse in trade. Alyssa hadn't been there yet. Beverly usually took the all-day trip by herself, taking time off from her usual duties.

She knew Liahona had regular church buildings, shops, their own hospital, and other needed services—even a temple. The town's population was around five thousand people.

As her thoughts circled and settle in, she hungered to talk to her old friend, imagining their dialogue, picturing the look on

Deb's face when she answered the phone. Debra had no way to know she was no longer in Central City. She probably thought the worst—that was terrible. She had to tell her—not only was she alive, but about to join the same church! She fairly bounced on her heels with excitement. Debra would be thrilled.

* * * * *

"She was getting married," Alyssa told Peter. "Jon Pike was his name. Gosh, they've probably had time to have a couple of kids." That was a strange thought, picturing Debra as a mother.

Peter found several listings for Gray and Pike families in the Church's online members-only directory of New Hope, including one for a Jon and Debra Pike.

Eager, she made the call.

It didn't go through.

"Peter, what does this error message mean?"

He looked at the screen. "That can't be right. It means the servers don't exist."

After several tries, Peter concluded that either the directory was in error, or something had happened. He tried a few other New Hope numbers, with the same result.

Her disappointment was palpable. "I wanted to talk to her so bad. I know it's far, but I hoped she might be able to come."

Peter said, "I'll ring up Liahona and see what they know."

The same error message came up.

"Weird," he said. "Mom, when was the last time you called Liahona? Did you get an error message?"

Beverly came in from the kitchen. "That's not good," she said, wiping her hands on a kitchen towel. "I called Merrills a week ago about some feed, and the connection was fine. Bishop Greene didn't mention it when I made the baptism arrangements, either."

"Is he in Liahona?" Alyssa asked. Her local geography was iffy.

"No, he's only a few miles down the road." Beverly tsked. "You'd think if they were working on the lines, they would have told us."

"Maybe we'll find out at your baptism," Peter said. "I'll keep trying today, and see what I can find out. I'm sorry about your friend, though. Which is more important, finding her first, or going through with it?"

"The baptism," Alyssa said, firm. There was no question.

"I'm sorry," Beverly said with sincerity, resting her hand on Alyssa's shoulder a moment. "Listen . . . while you're making calls, have you thought about talking to your family?"

Alyssa looked up from her chair. She had to think a while about that before answering. Finally she looked down at her hands. "No. I can't bring myself to do it. Not yet."

"They should know you're safe."

She raised her eyebrow and flashed a wry look back to Beverly. "Mother won't think *here* is safe."

Beverly had to agree. She chuckled. "Well . . . think about it." She went back to tidying the kitchen.

"Think about it." Alyssa shook her head. It was liberating to think her mother and sister would assume she was dead. Why ruin that feeling? She brushed it out of her mind. "Peter, how far away is New Hope?"

"All the way across the state, and north." He punched some buttons on the computer and pulled up a map. "That's a long ride on a horse. And you're not experienced enough to make that kind of trip alone."

"The buggy?" she asked. They used all types of antique-seeming equipment to work around the gasoline deficit.

"No!" Beverly called from the kitchen.

Peter laughed. "You can't drive that, either." Then he sighed. "Either way you're looking at an eight-day trip, minimum. We can't be without our stuff that long . . . or without you, with all the work you're getting done. We need your hands. And with communication down, there's no way of knowing if you'd get there and back safely in the first place."

"There's no way to get fuel?" There were automobiles dissolving to rust in the Richardsons' garage. Even with gas, they may not run.

"I can't mortgage the farm just for a little trip." Peter smiled.

"Right," she said. A sigh escaped her lips. "Solar tractor?"

He laughed at the thought. "Do you know how ridiculous you'd look?"

"I'm just thinking out loud," she said.

He smiled at her. "Our tractors run off the solar panels built in to the garage roof, remember? Isaac didn't build them to be self-contained. They have to plug in at night. You'd only get so far before you stopped, with no way to recharge."

"This really stinks."

"You got that right." He paused. "Besides . . . Alyssa, we don't know what the error message means. I'm not sure why, but something about this feels wrong."

Alyssa knew it, too. She nodded.

He touched her hand with his fingertips. She looked at him, startled.

"Alyssa, if it means something has gone terribly wrong— because of Article 28 enforcement, or something else—will it change your decision? About baptism?" He took his hand away, then seemed not to know what to do with it.

Her heart fluttered. But he was emphasizing his question, nothing more.

"Peter," she answered, "I gave up on a normal life years ago. I can't deny what I know is true. Nothing can take that away from me."

He smiled. "I'm glad to know it."

She didn't know what to say next.

He turned to the computer screen and started a program. "This will test more of the connections," he said. "It'll take a while to run. Um, so . . ." He cleared his throat. "Tell me about Debra. You haven't talked about her much."

"Oh, wow," she said. Emotions and memories came flooding back. "She was the first true friend I found, after . . . after my mom split up your family and mine."

"She must be great, if you're willing to walk across the state of Iowa to find her," Peter said.

Alyssa nodded. "She sure is."

She reminisced with him, memories overflowing and spilling out—about Debra's house and family, the fun times spent there in high school, their two big dogs always knocking her over, watching Deb braid her baby sister's hair for hours and how Alyssa could never get the hang of it. Peter reminisced about his high school days, too—his friends, silly social mistakes, and playing soccer on the Varsity team. He laughed at her funny stories, and she got more animated in the telling of them. Soon they were both mimicking voices of friends, siblings, schoolteachers. Just like when they were kids.

Alyssa had forgotten just how many good things Debra had given her, how greatly she had balanced out the void left in her life by Peter's absence.

But she left out all the hard times Debra had pulled her through. It would complicate the moment. Right now, talking was easy. She felt unrestrained, happy. Comfortable. It felt like old times, before life twisted and turned and got complicated.

They laughed and talked together for hours.

CHAPTER 15

IMMERSION

> *. . . I am so lonely I wish I could die, to be with Phil. If he's even dead. The Lord has still not told me, and I don't know why I can't receive that revelation.*
>
> *I'm happy for Alyssa, true. It's just so hard to pretend all the time. To be strong. I feel like such an empty shell.*
>
> *I'm sensing a deep chemistry between those two. I'm not sure if they're aware of it yet. But it makes my loneliness even more profound, selfish though that is.*
>
> —Beverly Richardson,
> personal journal entry

The baptism day arrived, sunny but cold, late in October.

The reservoir water would be warmest in the afternoon. They set out after lunch.

Beverly knocked on the first door down the hall and asked, "Andrew? Aren't you coming?"

Andrew spent most of his time in his room lately, giving up even the TV news. He stuck his head out, barely. "Nah," he said. "I have things to do." He shut the door.

Beverly whispered to Alyssa. "I can't force him."

"I wouldn't want you to," she said. They went out to the stable together.

"Has he talked to you?" Beverly asked.

Alyssa made a noise. "Hardly. Why would he talk to me?"

"I know. I know. I just hoped . . ."

"I don't think he's talking to anybody," Alyssa said.

Beverly said, "I don't know what to do with him."

"I don't either."

Beverly's questions disquieted her. It wasn't like Beverly to be needy. Whatever it was, Andrew's problems weren't something she could fix. She knew that much.

Since the night Andrew failed to come home, he'd been sullen and different. But he went to work on time, came home on time, did his chores. He took care of Thistle before the twins went to school without forgetting. He didn't complain—or talk much at all.

Beverly took a deep breath and seemed herself again. "Well. That changes the riding plan a bit."

"Should I ride Lucy instead?" Alyssa asked.

Beverly said, "No, you're not as used to her. She likes to bolt. You'd better take Abish, I'll take Lucy, and put the twins on Thistle, instead of the twins riding with me and Peter. I guess you could take Thistle—"

Alyssa saw she was getting flustered. "Abish is fine. Don't stress about it."

They met Peter in the stable. "Is Andrew coming?" he asked.

Beverly shook her head.

He said, "I figured as much." His mouth formed a taut line as he cinched a saddle.

Beverly described to him the change in horses.

He nodded Alyssa's direction and smiled. "You want to ride with me, on Teancum?"

It put her on the spot. "Oh—I—" What *did* she want?

Beverly put in, "If she hasn't ridden him much—"

"I haven't at all," Alyssa confirmed.

"Then it's a bad idea. She's not used to his girth. If it was a short ride, fine, but she'll be much too sore before we get home."

"You're right, Mom," Peter said, and Alyssa didn't have to choose.

She put Beverly's worry and Andrew out of her mind as they readied the horses. She slipped on the straw as she slid the bit into Abish's mouth. Nerves. The horse neighed and tossed her head away from the bit and bridle. She worked the bit into the horse's reluctant mouth, then buckled the bridle properly. She normally had an easier time with the tack, even with the more difficult Thistle.

Alyssa had developed a habit of spending extra time in the stable. By now the work was routine and soothing.

Maybe it was the once-forbidden aspect of horses; maybe it was horse sweat inhaled deep into her lungs, maybe it was the simple rhythm of the muscle and bone moving in harmony. She couldn't explain how it satisfied a deep need inside her.

This would be her longest ride to date.

Bishop Greene met them on the way, riding up on a chestnut horse. Alyssa had met him two days ago, when he came to the house to interview her.

"Beautiful day for it, isn't it?" he called to everyone.

Beverly called, "Are the Wrights coming?"

"They're meeting us at the reservoir," was his answer. They needed at least two other witnesses to observe that the ordinance was performed correctly.

He soon answered the question on all their minds. "I found out today why the servers aren't working. The communications building in Liahona was destroyed by a laser missile at the same time Horne boiled the rivers."

Everyone exclaimed in surprise.

"It has to be Horne's work. And you know it wasn't reported on the news—that's worse," the bishop said. "It's a warning, obviously. But we don't know how to take it." He went on to say that Liahona had suffered three casualties, and gave their names; no one the Richardsons recognized.

Beverly was horrified. "How awful!"

"It would have been worse, except it was an office temple day," the Bishop said. "They were out."

Alyssa was suddenly anxious. *Casualties?* "What do you know about New Hope?"

He rode up next to her for a minute. "It's taking a long time to get the whole picture. I'm sorry, Alyssa. We don't have word from the other communities yet, but it's safe to assume they were hit. I'll let you know as soon as I hear. I promise."

Alyssa fell back to the end of the line.

Peter joined her shortly.

"Was Debra in communications?" Peter asked.

"It's not likely. She studied English, and Jon was in medical school. But it doesn't make this any easier." Pain showed in her eyes.

Peter offered, "Bishop says only the one building was targeted in Liahona. She might be okay."

It was small comfort.

* * * * *

When they arrived, Alyssa was a little sore on the dismount, but not bad. The leaves were crisp on the ground and crunched under her feet with a pungent autumn scent. She stretched her legs out for a minute while Jordan and Kellie called out with excitement.

The Wrights were there ahead of them. They had several young children, and Jordan and Kellie were thrilled to see their friends. Their joy was contagious. Alyssa's mood improved just watching them play.

The water before her was a vivid reminder of why she was here, and a thrill went through her that she could barely contain. This day would change her forever.

"Too bad we couldn't do this in Liahona," Sister Wright said, dipping her fingers in the lake. "Whew! That water's cold."

Beverly said, "She didn't want to wait for the next trip in. Don't worry, we brought plenty of towels and blankets. James—" she called.

The oldest Wright boy answered. "Yeah?"

"Can you get us a big fire started, for getting her warm afterward?" She handed him a box of matches.

His face lit up. "Thanks, Sister Richardson!"

There was a small lavatory, large enough for changing clothes. A few rough-hewn log benches were arranged along the shore.

Beverly handed Alyssa a duffel bag, and she went to change into white clothes.

She put on a long white dress that belonged to Beverly, and pulled the belt tight around her narrow waist. It hung very loose and was several inches too short. It was made of heavy polyester fabric; Beverly said it should stay decent, even wet.

Alyssa waited on a log bench in front, next to Beverly, while Peter went in and changed into white pants, shirt, and tie.

When everyone was ready, Kellie led the group in her favorite baptism song, something about rainbows and the earth washing clean, and wanting to feel that clean always. Alyssa liked it. Jordan said an opening prayer, after which Beverly stood and gave a few words about the meaning of baptism. Alyssa tried to listen, but she was anxious, tapping her feet out of jitters. The boy had gotten a nice fire going; it crackled and popped in the background, distracting her further.

"You're sure you're ready for this?" Beverly asked in the middle of her little talk, interrupting Alyssa's random thoughts.

"Nothing could stop me now," she said. A driving sense of urgency told her that this event was more crucial than anything else she had ever done.

Then it was time.

Peter walked to the shore and held his hand out. She took his hand, acutely aware of the electric touch of his skin on hers, taken back once again to the distant past.

She forced the memories away, focusing on the covenants she was about to make.

Her heart raced. *Remission of sins. Purity.* She craved them desperately.

The water felt like ice. They took about twenty sandy steps to where the water was waist deep. Merciless cold bit into her skin, and she held her breath and shivered.

Heaven itself seemed to hold its breath with her.

Icy water licked up against her belly. Peter explained that he would tuck her under the water and lift her back out. His right hand felt comfortable against the small of her back. He said, "Remember to hold your nose and bend your knees."

She smiled up at him.

Peter raised his right arm to the square and called her by name. "Having been commissioned of Jesus Christ," he said, "I baptize you in the name of the Father, and of the Son, and of the Holy Ghost. Amen."

Then she was under the water.

It was a shocking blast of sheer cold. Peter raised her up, and she drew a deep breath, shivering uncontrollably.

"I'm sorry about the cold," Peter said through chattering teeth.

"I'm okay," she stuttered. "Are you?"

"Better than ever," he stammered back. He couldn't stop his teeth chattering. It was a little silly. She had to laugh as they stepped back out of the water. Her teeth wouldn't stop either.

She had expected the bitter chill, and was anxious for the fire and the blankets.

What she didn't expect was the sudden surge of complete joy unlike anything she knew was possible. She felt buoyant, weightless, and as bright inside as the warm sun in the summertime. Her smile was as uncontrollable as her shivering body or her chattering teeth.

Peter kept his arm around her, steadying her, though she felt him shivering too. Beverly stood at the water's edge, holding up two quilts. She wrapped them each in one. "Thanks, Mom," Peter said. He sat down on a bench, motioning to Alyssa to hurry and change.

Her thoughts focused on immediate needs: getting warm and dry before the long ride home.

And if she felt Peter's arm rest around her waist longer than it had to, before Beverly wrapped her in a quilt and she went to change, surely it was her imagination.

CHAPTER 16

SABOTEUR

> *The operation is taking much more work than expected. We have barely covered half the City with our stealth flyers to spread the gas thoroughly without outside detection. Ground maneuvers to open and treat sealed buildings for thorough decontamination is to begin this week.*
>
> *Decontamination will take four to six more weeks, minimum. Your cooperation is appreciated.*
>
> —Pres.-General Leo F. Horne,
> Top-Secret Memo to the U.N.

Over the past weeks, Debra and Jon both got tired of attending funerals. Eight others died from their injuries; one died from a severe secondary infection. Yet two others with broken bones healed remarkably fast. One sister with a broken back was already walking with crutches, when by all medical knowledge, she should never have walked again. Brother Teasdale, a frail elderly man, recovered his full health. Small comforts like these came, piece by piece, as the intense initial shock gave way to the onset of healing.

New Hope gradually established a new routine, minus modern technology. President Weber made plans to run old-fashioned audio phone lines to connect themselves to one another, at least.

In the meantime, Jon and Debra had no phone and no TV, and Jon was gone longer hours at the hospital. She knew when she first met Jon, back in high school, that he was born to the field of medicine. She loved that about him. His passion for life, his career, and his work made him shine. His passionate side was something people often missed on a first impression. He was cool and soft-spoken. But she knew it well, and was glad. She knew the schedule went with the man, and she loved the man. Deeply.

* * * * *

Debra struggled through morning sickness and taking care of Zach, coping with a world flung upside-down. She hated asking for help. But ever since that night at scripture study, she didn't have to. Dinners came in, sisters came over and scrubbed the bathroom and kitchen, vacuumed, ran laundry, or just played with the baby and kept her company, talking.

Still, she felt like a burden.

She came up with a compromise, at least with her mother. She could do her little sister's hair while she sat on the couch, and it would take her concentration off her stomach and take a big chore off her mom's hands. Her mom agreed.

Jon's seventeen-year-old sister LaDell and her friend Tanya came over with her mom. LaDell worked on a Nubian twist in Tanya's hair. Tanya brought her three-year-old brother Dante along, but coloring books and paper kept him entertained.

She was twelve weeks along, too soon for morning sickness to be over, but the worst of it was easing off.

Debra took a comb and sectioned off a part in her little sister's hair to form the next cornrow. Rochelle didn't want straight ones this time, or plain braids. She wanted a swirl all the way around her head, which was trickier to get right. But it would be pretty.

"You're growing up," she teased, "if Mom's letting you have a style this fancy."

"It's not that fancy," Rochelle said.

She was nine, and not too squirmy anymore. She hadn't done Rochelle's head in a long while . . . not since high school.

Taletha Gray laughed as she folded Deb's laundry. "It's fancier than I'm willing to do on her, that's all."

LaDell and Tanya chattered about the available boys in New Hope. While it seemed a trite, silly subject, it kept them from discussing who had died in the explosion, who they missed most, arguing about why and how it happened and what was going to happen next. Thankfully, none of this group had lost family members or close friends, but grief still flavored every waking hour with its bitterness.

Deb sighed to herself and made a part for the next swirl. At their age she was already dating Jon, with an intense hope he would be the right one. Was that only four years ago? Life changed so fast. These girls knew nothing of pregnancy or childbirth or organizing an entire home or other things that were important to her current life. It was hard for Deb to fit into their conversation, but she laughed when the jokes came.

Zach bounced in his baby seat, cooing. He was growing fast, too. Nearly four months old. She couldn't believe it was already November; the year had flown. Thanksgiving was three weeks away.

"—And Bobby can't even call me if he wants to!" Tanya laughed.

"I guess he'll have to serenade you," LaDell said.

Debra added, "Or throw pebbles at your window!"

"Taletha, do you know when the phones are coming back on line?" LaDell asked.

Taletha answered, "They have to lay old-fashioned cable by hand. It's going to take a while, girls."

"Does anyone still know how to do that?" Debra asked.

"Some of the old folks remember. They used land lines when I was a girl, sisters—I'm not that ancient!"

Everyone laughed.

"Are those the two-piece kind connected with those funny twisty cords, like you see in old movies?" Rochelle asked.

Tanya said, "Yeah, those."

"It's going to take forever," Debra said, with dismay. She had more mature reasons for wanting a phone. Like calling Jon if anything went wrong at home.

LaDell said, "And you only hear the person's voice at your ear. Taletha, is it weird not to see people's faces when you call them up?"

Taletha laughed. "How old do you think I am, LaDell? Mercy. By the time I started using the phone it was all video."

"But not when you were born, right?" Debra teased.

"If you weren't so sick, I'd smack you, girl," her mother laughed. "Whatever you babies think, forty-two is not that old."

They all laughed. Taletha had never smacked anyone in her life.

"Dante, stay on the couch with those," Tanya warned.

The little boy climbed back up with his crayons. "Why?"

"I don't want you going anywhere," she answered.

"He's being good, Tanya," Deb said.

Taletha said, "I'm surprised he's been sitting there this whole time without complaining."

"I'm sorry my toys aren't more interesting," Deb told him. Zach's baby rattles weren't fun for a three-year old.

"I coloring. See?" Dante asked, holding up a scribbled page.

He was too little to make real pictures. It was a blob of blue, red, and green lines. "Oh, that's very nice," Debra gushed.

Dante grinned. "It's a horsie."

Deb looked back at Rochelle's head. Her work was shaping up nicely, which was a relief. She was out of practice. Her own hair grew loose and natural on her head, a lot longer than when she was first married, but she liked it this way. "Rochelle, did you want beads in this?"

"Beads are for babies. Debra, don't pull so hard. Ow."

"Sorry." Debra adjusted her tautness.

LaDell said, "Be glad you've got a big *sister* to do your hair, Rochelle."

"How come?"

LaDell laughed. "Jon braided my hair when I was your age. He pulled so hard, soon half my hair was on the floor."

"I didn't know that," Debra said, grinning.

"Mama had that job what took her away on Saturdays and she didn't have time. She wanted me to cut it off, but I wouldn't. So she stuck Jon with doing it."

"Girlfriend, you're crazier than I thought," Tanya said. "I'd have cut my hair."

"No way!" LaDell's hair was still long, in dreadlocks to the middle of her back. "Hey, did you know, when Jon was ten, he kept his head shaved close, so he didn't have to comb it? One day Mama saw he got all this dandruff going on. Turns out he hadn't washed his hair in a month! He thought if he didn't have no hair, he didn't have to wash his head, neither."

"Gross!" Tanya shuddered. "And you married him, Debra!"

Debra held up one hand in defense, laughing. "I never heard that story. I guarantee he's got meticulous hygiene now."

LaDell asked, "When I'm done with Tanya, you want me to do your hair, Deb?"

"No thanks."

"It's long enough."

"No." Deb shook her head for emphasis. Sometimes she put a knit headband around it, or pulled it back, but that was it. She liked the feel of it loose.

"Jon's making her grow it out, I bet you," LaDell said.

"He is *not*," Deb retorted.

"When Zach starts pulling it you'll do something," her mother laughed.

"Where's Dante?" LaDell asked.

"Dante! Cut it out!" Tanya got up, forcing LaDell to drop her hair. He was over by the kitchen. Tanya picked him up and hauled him over to a corner. "You stay there until I say you can get out."

"No!" Dante said. He stomped his feet.

"Yes you will!"

Debra couldn't drop her hands as easily, but she could see the wall from where she sat. He had scribbled himself a large "drawing" in several bright colors. "Oh, no!"

Taletha said, "Shoot. I'm sorry, Debra, I should have seen him."

Tanya said, "*I* should've noticed. Dante, that was naughty!"

From the corner, Dante gave his big sister a raspberry.

Debra didn't want to elaborate and make Tanya feel any worse.

"I'm so sorry. I'll clean it, I promise," Tanya said.

"Oh—don't worry about it, please. It's okay."

Crayon wouldn't come off anyway, even with good cleaners. She remembered well the many coats of paint they had used at home to cover Rochelle's wall drawings, at that age. She forced a smile. "It's all right. We needed some fancy artwork in here."

CHAPTER 17

THIRST

> *Peter confirmed me a member of the Church. He laid his hands on my head and blessed me, and in the blessing he said a weird thing. He talked about how my children would not all come in the usual way, and to let my heart be still concerning the matter.*
>
> *He has no idea how hard that hit me.*
>
> —Alyssa Stark,
> personal journal entry

Water was scarce.

Margret's company approached a small stream. Everyone scrambled down the short ravine to drink.

Brownish water gurgled and bubbled over the rocks. The mud was treacherous, and the kids could be trampled in the crowd. She asked them to wait a few paces away, and slid down the slippery bank.

Her thirst burned like fire. She splashed icy water on her face and ran wet fingers through her dusty, matted hair. The chill woke her to life, like escaping a dreary dream.

She dipped her hands to scoop up a drink.

A clear voice behind her said, "Don't drink that water!" She turned. Her children waited like they were told, a few paces back.

"Did you say something, Marcus?"

"No, Mama. Hurry and finish so it's our turn."

Her dry throat ached. The water smelled of mud and algae.

Again the voice spoke: "Don't drink it!"

She shuddered with abrupt terror, and the water spilled from her hands. Repelled, she backed away.

The other refugees drank heartily, laughing and bathing.

"We can't drink here, kids," she said.

"But you got a drink, Mama!" Natty complained, getting off Marcus' lap and stomping. "I'm thirsty!"

"No she didn't," Marcus chided. "She spilled it."

Margret reached them. "Did you hear a strange voice?"

"No," Marcus said.

"I heard a voice tell me not to drink that water. Do you believe me?" He had to believe. He *had* to.

"I believe you." His eyes showed it.

"Do you remember Bert, *niño?*"

"Yeah."

"Bert said he heard voices in his head, guiding him."

"Before they took him away, or after he came back all funny?" Marcus asked.

"Before," she said urgently. "It was before."

His liquid amber eyes held unasked questions. Natty kicked at the dirt, whining something unintelligible.

"Marcus—Natty—I heard one of those voices. I think God has spoken to me." The thought amazed her. She was far from believing in God; why, if there was a God, would he speak to her, and why now?

His amber eyes widened. "Bert was right all along?"

She whispered, "Maybe he was, *niño.*"

A smile burst across his face. "I know he was. I believe too!"

"You do?"

His whole being seemed to light up. "Mama, I did something, but I was afraid to tell you."

"What?" He looked happy about it—not guilty.

"Remember in the store when you said we had to steal? I prayed for us. I asked God, I said, if stealing was wrong, and He was really God, could He send us a way so we wouldn't have to break His laws," Marcus said quietly. "He sent David to us."

Margret couldn't have been more dumbfounded if the boy said he was abducted by aliens. Her mouth hung gaping open.

Natty broke for the water. Margret and Marcus each caught one of her arms and held her. Natty wailed.

"Quiet, Natty!" Margret ordered, scooping the girl into her arms. "You can't drink it!"

She was instantly silent, and sniffled. Fear loomed behind her eyes.

"I'll wait for a drink, Mama," Marcus said. "Natty will too. Won't you, Nat?"

"I'm thirsty!" Natty whispered.

"Sweetie, it could kill you! I promise we'll find water somewhere." It was a promise she doubted she could keep, but she had to offer some hope. The burning in her own throat was unrelieved. Marcus had to feel it too.

The stream bubbled over the rocks, mocking their thirst. She hugged Natty close, kissing her wavy brown hair. "I love you so much, *angelita mía* . . . try to understand. We have to wait for a drink."

Natty cried, burying her head in her mother's shoulder.

CHAPTER 18

YVETTE

My latest blessing said to be comforted, all is in God's hands, and that I will not experience these physical discomforts much longer.

—Debra Pike,
personal journal entry

A sonogram at twelve weeks showed Debra's pregnancy was proceeding normally; the baby had a strong heartbeat and was active. It was too early to tell the gender, and they didn't want invasive testing to find that out.

That was two weeks ago. Debra was gradually more at ease, looking forward to feeling its movement for the first time, a moment at least a month away.

After praying one night, Debra heard a faint female voice in her mind: *Thank you, Mama, for giving me my body.*

Debra's heart swelled with love, for the first time without fear and worry. The Spirit was strong within her heart, and she felt a communion with this child she had not felt before. She knelt several minutes, basking in the warmth of that peaceful glow.

She snuggled in next to her husband and whispered what had just happened. "Jon—the baby spoke to me. She told me thank you." Nothing like this had happened during Zachary's pregnancy. It happened to other mothers she knew; some even dreamed their children's faces before birth, and recognized them once they were born. She had never experienced such a thing.

Now, she had heard a daughter's voice.

Jon came awake. "That's awesome, Deb." He kissed her then, and the touch of their lips came so tender and delightful, they decided not to stop.

* * * * *

Jon left for work before dawn.

Later that morning, Debra sat on the bed, staring at two gallons of pale peach paint stowed in a corner. Tanya's baby brother Dante had left behind that nasty crayon scribble. Tanya fell all over herself apologizing, but that didn't erase it. Deb decided Zach could wait till he was twelve for crayons.

The afterglow from the night before hadn't worn off, either. She'd experienced pure heaven.

She felt wonderful. She took a deep, happy breath. Her stomach felt right this morning. And there was that little-girl voice she'd heard last night as she prayed . . .

Finally, the blessings were starting to come.

She felt a pinch in her abdomen as she stood up, and stretched out slowly. Zach was sleeping in their bed. She was vaguely aware of nursing him at some point in the dark, before Jon left.

She fixed herself breakfast, then got out the paint rollers, brushes, masking tape, pans, and drop cloths they had stowed in the closet. Jon wasn't getting to it. Work kept him busy and tired, and he hated painting anyway. Deb liked painting. And she'd been so sluggish and useless that she was itching to do something productive again.

She took only a minute to pull on grubby clothes and wrap her hair to keep the paint off. She had all the windows taped before Zach woke up.

She sang as she worked: mostly hymns, or old tunes her father taught her from the days of New York and Broadway. The roller swung up and down, making a cozy warm color change from boring white.

Zach did great. He played on the floor, rolling front to back and over again, grabbing at his toys. He couldn't do more than coo and smile yet, but he did more of both when she sang.

Her abdomen ached every so often, a stitch in her side. It didn't bother her much. It was wonderful just to feel active again.

She had two walls done by lunch. She made Zach his baby cereal and thought about how he'd been with them both forever and no time at all.

As she sat down by the baby seat, she suddenly realized she felt *awful*. It felt like she had menstrual cramps coming on. Shoot. She'd overdone it, and the job was only half-finished.

"Your daddy's gonna kill me for trying," she told Zach, spooning cereal in his eager mouth. If she left it half done, Jon would do it before bed, no matter how tired he was and how much he hated it. He would want to be chivalrous and save her from finishing it herself tomorrow.

Well—a quick nap might refresh her. After the cereal, she took Zach to bed to nurse him.

Before dozing off, she felt a mild worry that the cramping didn't seem to be letting up.

* * * * *

Debra woke up in severe pain. Something was very wrong.

Two seconds later, she ran to the bathroom before having an accident.

She panicked when she saw the volume of blood. She had no phone, and there was no one home next door. She couldn't just pound on the wall for help. The bleeding was too heavy for her to even leave the bathroom.

She was alone.

Bleeding happened sometimes. Octavia had a placenta previa with her third child. She bled the entire time and had to stay on bed rest for five months, but the baby turned out fine.

Her thoughts circled madly.

Was Zach okay. Would he wake up and cry. Would he roll out of the bed. She couldn't move to get him, even if he woke up. She hurt too much to move. *Why was I painting, anyway? Jon's going to freak out.*

The one thought she did not allow herself to have was, *What's happening to my baby?*

Belatedly she recognized the throes in her abdomen for miniature labor pains. The pain built to a peak, then ebbed away like ocean waves on the sand. She breathed and tried to bear it, willing it to stop.

She felt a large clot move through her, and she caught it on impulse before it fell in the water. Not until she looked at what her palm held did she understand. *It's the baby.* A tiny placenta dangled below her palm, about the size of a pancake, held there by a miniature umbilical cord—a bare millimeter wide. She gasped, staring, for several seconds, refusing to believe. The baby didn't move.

Her first, completely irrational thought was that she'd better try to get it back in there because it was much too small to . . .

No. No modern medical miracle had figured out how to reattach *that.*

She drew a long, ragged breath. Her heart clenched up inside. Tears didn't come right away.

Her next thought was, *It was fine two weeks ago. It was kicking, healthy, nothing wrong.*

She stared at the tiny body, its precious life gone. Broken membranes clung to the pinkish-brown skin of her palm. The smell of amniotic fluid surprised her. She studied its face, all its features placed properly. With care, she counted ten impossibly tiny fingers and ten tiny toes, small as the eye of a needle. She touched the limbs, and the joints moved with ease.

She can't be gone.

She lifted the placenta and inspected that too. Jon said miscarriage was nature's way of weeding out defects, but she saw no deformities anywhere that would indicate the cause.

She stood gingerly, supporting herself at the sink with her elbows. Gently she rinsed the tiny body, washing away the blood and amniotic fluid, careful not to damage the translucent skin.

She caught her reflection in the bathroom mirror. Splashes of paint flecked her face, her clothes, her head wrap, tiny light dots against the rich brown of her arms. She never wanted to see that perfect shade of pale peach again.

In a daze, she wrapped the whole thing in a soft washcloth. *It must be a bad dream. I took a nap, and I'm still dreaming.*

She heard Zach crying. It was not a dream. She was in the bathroom, she was wide awake, she had just delivered a miniature baby at fourteen weeks pregnant. Her baby was in a washcloth, lying on the counter. Her baby was dead. No. It was too horrible to accept.

She opened the door and put her head around the corner so Zach could hear her voice. "Hang on, babykins, Mommy will be right there!" She tried singing to comfort him, but her voice was plumb gone.

Rushing, she showered off, wrapped herself in a thick towel, and ran to Zach.

He was rolling at the edge of the bed. Debra ran, but not fast enough. He landed on his back with a thud. It took a single-second pause to get his wind before he shrieked in fear, surprise, and pain.

She sat on the floor by the bed and held him. She rocked back and forth, back and forth, crying. "I'm so sorry! Baby, babykins, hush . . . hush . . . you'll be fine . . . oh—I'm *so* sorry . . ." He was so angry that he refused to nurse. He just screamed.

She'd heard about babies falling off beds and figured their mothers were careless—that would never happen to *her* baby. But it did.

This was hands-down the worst day of her life. Worse than the comm building explosion by light-years.

When Zach was finally calm and she was clean and dressed, Debra wrapped the tiny body in the center of Zach's softest baby blanket. As she pulled over the last fold of fabric, a voice came to her mind, delicate as a spring breeze, whispering a name to her soul:

Yvette.

CHAPTER 19

FEVER

This organism is like nothing I have ever seen. It took the mind of a superior genius to design this. We find it in deceased victims in clusters of sixteen or thirty-two differentiated cells. This should be impossible. After 72 hours these cells are no longer viable. It is a great relief they can not survive long without a living host.

—Dr. Joel Kensington,
lab notes

Supplies grew more scarce for Margret's refugee camp. Cattle might be slow and stupid, but their owners weren't. The ranchers couldn't withstand heavy artillery, so they banded together, driving the herds far away from the cow-killing marauders.

The land was soon left to strays and wild deer.

Hunters reported a strange find. They discovered the decomposing body of a man by a stream, clutching a blue stuffed bunny in his arms. His ID tags pegged him as an escapee from the North Central Asylum for the Criminally Insane.

Margret sensed something odd about the story. Camp was unusually quiet. It didn't sit well with anyone that they had recently drunk from the same stream where the body was found.

She lay down with the tattered blanket she'd managed to snitch. She'd told Marcus a nice man gave it to them—he was so trusting. Pulling her children close, she tucked them in. November wind bit into her skin.

She coughed all that night.

When dawn came, Margret was shocked to see she had coughed blood. Red spots dotted the blanket. Another coughing fit took her, and she covered her mouth. When she drew her hand away it was spotted with fresh blood. She wiped it off on her jeans and swallowed, recognizing a familiar strange warmth that only comes from high fever.

Her stomach churned and she dry heaved. More blood spattered up with the bile.

Coughing blood was the first sign. Then severe vomiting.

ATF.

Few laws were enforced in the group, but the UN's policy on euthanasia was among them.

She groaned within herself.

Even if she refused lethal injection, the horror ahead would be a living nightmare. Her eyes and vital organs would fall out before she finally died in excruciating pain. Euthanasia was merciful. She had to be tested.

Bleak with grief, she shook Marcus awake. "Mama has to go to the doctors' tent, *niño*. I'll be right back."

He was groggy. "Are you sick?"

"I have a fever. I just need some medicine," she said. "Listen, if I'm not back—"

"You don't have ATF, do you?"

She cursed under her breath. His mind was too quick. "No." Maybe it wasn't a lie. Time would tell. "It's just a cold. But you hang on to this paper just in case they want me to stay there to get better." She handed him the tattered paper on which Alyssa had written her friends' names. Marcus tried reading it in the early light.

"Memorize that. And *don't* follow me, because there are sicker people than me at the doctors' tent. I don't want you catching anything. You take care of Natty until I'm better. Okay?"

"Okay," he said.

"If the camp moves on, and I'm not back, you know your north and south, don't you?"

He nodded, bleary-eyed.

"Stay with the group until they come to Holstein. Remember that. New Hope is west. Leave at night and don't tell anybody, or they'll follow you and hurt Alyssa's friends like they do in the other towns." She coughed, glad the predawn light was too dim for him to see blood. "I'll catch up later, if I need to."

"When you're all better?" He tucked the paper in his pocket.

She swallowed. "Yeah. When I'm all better. This is just *if* they make me stay in the doctors' tent. They might not. Alyssa's friends will take good care of you if you get there first."

"But you're just getting fever medicine?"

"That's right." She forced a smile. "This is all just in case. Do you understand?"

"I'm trying, Mama, but . . ."

She knew she was acting strange. Did he know about the UN policy? She'd tried to prevent him from overhearing the worst, keeping them at the outskirts of the camp.

"Repeat back to me everything I just told you."

He did, perfectly.

She mussed his hair. "You are so smart. Go back to sleep. Natty can sleep as long as she wants. They're hunting today, not walking. There should be food by dinnertime."

"Maybe we'll have venison again," he said, hopeful. He'd liked his first taste of it.

"Maybe so," Margret replied.

She hugged him until he fidgeted. Then she picked up her sleeping daughter and held her frail body in her arms. Natty stayed asleep. Carefully she laid her back down.

She wanted to kiss them, but didn't dare risk infecting them.

She ran her fingers through Marcus' hair for several minutes, humming "Amazing Grace." When she was sure Marcus drowsed again, she stood up.

"I love you with everything in my soul," she whispered. Her ribs ached when she stood. She blinked away tears and turned toward the makeshift hospital tent. She spotted a grove of trees near the camp, and without knowing why, headed there first.

She collapsed on her knees when she reached it, exhausted. Without planning to, she prayed with all her faith, which wasn't much, as she rode on the crest of her fever.

But Marcus prayed, and God sent David.

Can You hear me, too?

She whispered, with the little strength she had, "Dear God, if you're out there, bring my kids to safety. I haven't lived my life so good, but please bless my kids. Send someone good to care for them and let them live and grow up and be better than me. Please. I love them so much. Marcus believes in You . . . please don't let him down. Please be out there. Make my blood test be negative. Show us your great mercy. God, help us. Help me. Please." It was hardly the recited prayers of her youth. She hadn't touched a rosary or gone to confession in years. She prayed on, until she slipped in and out of sleep.

Maybe she would die here. But if she had ATF, it was better if she got to the tent for injection.

A voice came to her as she slept. Was she dreaming? She shook herself awake. The voice came again. *Your life can be spared, Margret, but your children are in grave danger. You must bring them over here.* She must be delirious. She struggled to form words. "I'll make them sick."

Go get your children. Bring them here.

It was harder to get up than she expected. She puked twice, staggering and crawling back to the place she'd left her babies.

She found Marcus, terrified. He had been crying. Tear streaks left clean pathways down his filthy cheeks. Natty clung to her brother, sobbing.

"I told you she'd come back, Natty." It was clear he hadn't believed his own words.

"I'm sorry, *niños*, it took longer than I thought."

"Did you get your medicine?"

She explained as best she could.

"If the voice said go, Mama, we better go."

His simple faith amazed her.

He gathered their sparse belongings, and strained to support his mother upright as they walked. Halfway to the stand of trees, an uproar of shrieks and screams burst from the main camp. Shots rang out—semi-automatic rat-a-tats.

"Get down!" Margret yelled, and dropped to her belly. They lay as still as frightened field mice. The ground spun beneath her in careening circles, and everything went black.

CHAPTER 20

MAGIC STEW

> *I do not know what motivated me. I injected a viable ATF cell cluster into a living rat.*
>
> *The rat died in 24 hours. Upon examination, the organism's cell cluster had multiplied from 32 to 188,000 differentiated cells. I destroyed the organism over a Bunsen burner immediately after the cell count. I am aware this is not appropriate lab procedure, but I am of no mind to discover what that organism was growing into.*
>
> —Dr. Joel Kensington,
> confidential ATF report

When Margret came to, she was staring into a man's eyes. She screamed. It came out with less volume than she hoped for. "I have a gun!"

His eyes were gentle. "Fear not, Margret."

"How do you know my real name?" She'd been calling herself Margarita here, to Marcus' dismay.

"I'm Phil. It's nice to meet you."

"Hi." She struggled for the gun, too weak to move fast. *No bullets anyway . . . Too sick to fight this one . . . dang, he's a big fella.* She looked around in panic. "Where's my kids?"

Were they hurt? If he intended rape or worse—

Phil laughed easily, and the sound soothed her. "Margret, you're all quite safe. I won't harm you. Marcus and Natty are over there, sleeping."

Memory came back in patches. She recognized the grove of trees. She saw the two humps of her children's bodies covered with thick blankets, and watched until she saw them breathing.

Relief flooded through her soul. "Who are you, and how do you know our names?"

"I told you, I'm Phil."

"Not enough information." She finally got her gun drawn and took unsteady aim between his eyes.

He wasn't afraid. He just smiled. "Margret. We both know that gun's not loaded."

"You willing to bet your life on that?"

"Margret, please trust me. I mean no harm to you or your children."

It occurred to her that he could have checked the cartridge while she was passed out. She tossed it down. The kids had to be warm under those blankets. She smelled a campfire and food cooking. The scent made her stomach roll over.

"Oh, I gotta puke—" It came up before she could turn away. "Sorry about that, man."

"No problem." Phil handed her a warm, wet towel. "There's fresh water heating on the fire. You can wash up with this."

Warm, fresh water? "Where'd that come from?"

"It's safe to drink," he assured her.

She rubbed the towel on her face. Heaven. It was clean and fresh and . . . fresh out of the middle of nowhere. She buried her face in the cloth, breathing in the steam. This couldn't be a dream, but if not, then what?

Her stomach somersaulted, and she managed to turn aside this time. Her body shook from the effort. "Hey, you got anything to stop me puking my guts up here?" She winced. Bad choice of words—ATF could make that phrase painfully literal.

"I don't, but I can help until you reach a doctor. I'll have some broth ready in a bit."

"It won't stay down."

"You have to try. You need the fluids."

Her fear subsided. If he was going to hurt them, he would have done it already. She dry heaved. Phil went to the fire and brought a fresh towel, taking the soiled one away.

"Thanks. What happened back there? The gunshots?" she asked.

"The camp has contracted ATF. They're fighting over who gets euthanized first—they don't have enough injections to go around."

Margret shook her head. "They got enough bullets, don't they?" She paused, certain dread sinking in. "Then I've got it too. I'm going to die." She hoped there was no puking after death. That would reek.

"You won't die. New Hope is only thirty miles away."

"Hey, buddy! I didn't tell *nobody* where I was going! Who *are* you?"

"Excuse me?" he said, like he suddenly didn't understand English.

A thought clicked into place. A thought that made no sense. "You're the *voice*," she said.

"I'm what?"

"You told me not to drink the water." She got excited.

Phil smiled. "You caught me."

"But how did you know?" Her fevered mind struggled to form logical patterns.

"A sick man died upstream and contaminated the water before the group reached it."

"The guy with the stuffed animal. From the insane asylum."

"That's right."

"But where were you? And if I didn't drink it, why am I sick?"

"A drop or two must have gotten in your nose or mouth. Rest now, Margret. I'm here to make sure you reach New Hope safely. Questions later. Relax and get some sleep."

He wrapped her in a thick, warm blanket, and she collapsed into fevered sleep.

* * * *

Phil was gone when Margret awoke. The fire was low, but not out. It was dusk. A stack of firewood lay nearby, and a large pot hung from a cast-iron hook above the fire. Beneath it was a square grill with legs that stuck into the ground, over the flames. She stared at it, blinking.

Her fever was down, and the nausea was present, but less intense.

None of this could be real.

Marcus and Natty were staring at her.

"Did you see that man? Or did I dream him?" she asked.

"He carried you here," Marcus said.

She'd been carried while unconscious. Of course. She had no memory of getting there, only of passing out in the tall grass when the shooting started.

"I like him," Natty said.

"He didn't hurt you? Touch you? Anything bad?"

Marcus said, "No, Mama, he's just nice."

"Where is he?" she asked.

"We woke up and he was gone," Natty said.

She had the chills. Her teeth chattered.

Marcus said, "Phil said to make sure you drink the broth."

"We'll all have some." She inched her way to the fire. "Put a couple of sticks on that, would you, sweetie?"

Marcus built up the fire, beaming. "Phil showed me how to do it before I went to sleep. You leave air between the logs so they can breathe, or it goes out."

"That's right." She was impressed. She hadn't taught him that.

Three tin cups waited by the fire, with three tin plates. A ladle rested in the pot. Margret was too weak to serve it out.

"Let me do it, Mama," Marcus said.

"Thanks, *niño.*"

She watched, helpless, as he ladled it out, giving his mother a cup first, then Natty, then himself.

It was pleasantly seasoned chicken or turkey, and tasted good even to Margret's ill stomach.

"What time is it?" she asked.

Marcus and Natty both shrugged.

She said, "Feels like time to sleep, to me. It's getting dark. Stay by the fire and keep warm, *niños.*"

Margret slept fitfully. She got up several times during the night, either sick and coughing or putting wood on the fire, but Phil didn't return.

Yet in the morning, there was more broth bubbling in the pot. She was startled. "What, is this some magic pot?"

"Phil came. He told me it's rabbit stew," Marcus said.

"How did I sleep through that?" She felt like she barely dozed all night.

"He brought more wood," Natty said. Sure enough, the stack was refilled.

"Friendly guy," she grumbled. "Doesn't stay long enough to say hello."

Footsteps crunched through the leaves. It was Phil.

"There you are," Margret said.

"Hi. Listen. You need to get on your way. The camp's lighting a bonfire for the dead this morning. You'll want to be long gone before then."

Margret didn't like being ordered around, especially by a man. "Why?"

"You're queasy enough, aren't you?"

"Oh . . ." By bonfire, he didn't mean wood. Dead bodies. Her mind spun, picturing human corpses, charred dead flesh. She got in control before throwing up, and forced her thoughts to more pleasant things.

Phil added, "You'll have to move fast not to get wind of it."

Marcus ladled broth into his mother's tin cup. She sipped, cautious of the taste. *Rabbit?* If she'd known that last night, it would never have stayed down. But it tasted okay.

"Can we bring the blankets?" Marcus asked.

"That's what they're for," Phil said. "Same for this little stove. It's not heavy, and it folds up. Marcus, do you think you can carry it, when it's cooled off?" He pulled the grill out of the ground and demonstrated how to fold it.

Marcus answered, "I think so."

Margret tried to stand up, and failed. "I can't walk."

Phil encouraged her and got her on her feet. "Sure you can. Head due north. Break camp as soon as you finish eating."

Phil went off to the right, and Margret forgot to ask where he was going, forgot to say thanks, forgot to say anything, much less ask when he was coming back.

Thirty miles might as well be a thousand. "We'll never make it," she said, wobbling on her feet.

Marcus offered, "Maybe not all in one day, Mama."

"I want to stay here, with the magic pot!" Natty said.

"Hush!" Margret couldn't cope with a tantrum right now.

"It's not a magic pot." Marcus was irritated too. "Besides, Natty, it's coming with us."

Phil didn't return, and they left in less than an hour. It was slow going. They stopped every few minutes to rest. Carrying blankets and camping gear made the trek harder, but they needed the supplies.

They kept low to the ground at first, hiding behind bushes and trees. From the direction of camp they heard moans and screams, wailing, and occasional gunfire.

They hadn't gone far enough when the bonfire was lit.

All three would remember that miserable stench for the rest of their lives.

CHAPTER 21

VISITATION

> *I am so angry! Jon wanted to take the baby's body to the hospital to do biopsies, then just have her remains tossed in the incinerator. I put my foot down. No way are they going to cut her up. She's my baby!*

> —Debra Pike,
> personal journal entry

Joan stood before Alyssa's bed. She pointed a finger at her daughter, startling her out of deep drowsiness. "Did you think I wouldn't find out how you wasted your father's money? Didn't you know Elation causes permanent acid flashbacks, you stupid child? And what do you think you're doing? I *forbade* you to come here ever again!"

The words came as a mental shout more than audible hearing.

"What are *you* doing here?" Alyssa squeaked, terrified.

"Looking for you! And to find you *here!*" She made a sound of disgust and rage.

Alyssa reached out to grab the bony hand. Her fingers passed through. She drew back in fear. "What are you talking about, Mother?"

"Didn't I worry night and day? Where have you been all these years? You could have called! Did you think I wouldn't notice your birth records *vanished*? You can't erase yourself from my *memory*! I knew I had another daughter, child! I never heard of such ingratitude!"

"I didn't do that!" Alyssa shot back, fully disoriented.

"Then who erased all those records?"

"Rob did! To protect me from the government. It had nothing to do with you!"

"Who's Rob?"

This was insane. "Who are *you?*" she asked. Was she dreaming?

"Don't you recognize your own mother? Ungrateful wretch!"

"Then *what* are you?" She stuck her hand through Joan's abdomen and waved it around, feeling only a chill.

That motion stopped Joan short. "I . . . I don't know . . . I was sick . . ."

Alyssa felt queasy. A question formed in her mind. "Did you catch ATF, Mother?"

Joan looked around, bewildered. She sobbed, "I was looking for you. Lauren betrayed me . . . I can't even say it. It's not true. It's *your* fault she—no, it was *you*. It was you in those disgusting pictures. Not my innocent, sweet baby Lauren!"

Alyssa remembered the dream of Joan and Lauren fighting, the shredded portfolio. *Was it more than a dream?* She gathered her quilts in front of her body to manage her growing fear. "It was *not* me," she insisted.

"It was not you," Joan repeated, her face blank.

Joan never conceded a point so easily.

"Mother. Did you have ATF?"

"I was quite sick . . ."

"You're *dead*." The realization struck like a hammer.

Joan dismissed the idea. "Oh, that's impossible."

"No it isn't. You're dead! You died!"

"If I'm dead I couldn't be talking to you, child. Dead is dead. A great nothingness."

"If you're alive, then how did you get here? Did you drive, or walk?"

"I was there . . . and then I was here. This must be a dream," Joan said with wonder. "How odd."

"You are *not* dreaming!" Alyssa felt too alert, the room too solid, for this to be a dream. "Mother. You died of ATF, didn't you?"

"I recall nothing of the sort. I was just . . . here. I was looking for you."

"Then go look for Dad. He's dead. If you find him, then you'll know you are, too." The idea came out of nowhere, but seemed logical enough.

"Oh, Chuck doesn't want to talk to me." Joan's confusion increased. "How do I know that?"

"I don't want to talk to you either," Alyssa said.

"What have I done?" Joan whined, about to cry.

"*Go away*," Alyssa said through clenched teeth. "And don't ever come back!"

"Is Beverly here?" she asked. She sounded hopeful, whiny, like a child who wants candy.

"Don't bother her! You've hurt her enough!"

"What have I done?" Joan repeated. "I have nothing now."

"So? You expected nothing after death. Go on. Go enjoy your great nothingness." Alyssa felt mean and small saying that, yet somehow justified. "Go!"

"Oh, all right." The image vanished; it was unlike Joan not to argue.

Was it really her? If it was, how could Alyssa know whether she was truly gone?

Alyssa pinched herself. She *was* awake. Drat.

She knelt in bed and prayed, coming up with things to be grateful for, until she felt a little better. The twins' gray kitten jumped up on her bed. It purred as she stroked its soft fur. That helped.

Then something Joan said hit home: *Don't you know Elation causes permanent acid flashbacks, you stupid child?*

She prayed again, much harder.

She never had flashbacks in the Gardens. She had blocked out the memories of those drug trips completely. Why were the crazy things returning, weirder than before, and without any drug to induce them this time?

Please, Lord. Help me understand.

* * * * *

The next day she canned tomatoes with Beverly in the kitchen. Earlier in the week they had picked all the vines, both red and green, before the first frost came and ruined the crop. It was messy work, with the tiniest cut or hangnail stinging from the juice as she peeled and cut.

She had to ask Beverly a question. There was no sense in hedging around it, and she couldn't think of a way to soften the blow. "Did you see Joan last night?"

"Did I see *who?*"

"Joan, my mother. She came to me last night in spirit. I think she died of ATF."

"Are you sure it wasn't a dream?"

"I'm not sure of much, but that was no dream! I *have* had weird dreams ever since I got here, but I was wide awake."

"She could have caught ATF, I guess," Beverly mused, standing at the stove while the tomatoes blanched in boiling water. "Tell me exactly what happened."

Alyssa went over the whole scene, noting Joan's confusion, and leaving out the references to Elation, as she peeled the warm fruit, slippery in her fingers.

"Well, if she *was* dead . . . it could make sense. But even if she came to me, I might not have sensed her presence. I don't have your gift."

"Gift!" She harrumphed. "This doesn't feel like a gift! It feels like a curse! I can't even trust my own brain."

"Alyssa." Beverly took her by the shoulder. "I've been praying for two solid years to know what happened to my husband, with no answer. I haven't so much as *felt* his presence near me, not once! Jordan and Kellie are both sensitive to spiritual things, too, like you are. But aside from normal feelings of missing their father, they haven't noticed anything either. We're all desperate to know what happened. Then you show up, and right off you start dreaming dreams, seeing visions, and now to top it all off, your own mother appears to you." She chopped the pieces to fit in the jars, her knife working fast and angry.

Alyssa tried to interrupt. Beverly didn't allow it. "I know you don't exactly want to talk to her, and I don't blame you, but think! You conversed with her back and forth and saw her clear enough to read her facial expressions. Yes! It is too a gift to have the veil be that thin. I'm envious. If I had a tiny fraction of what you have . . ." She stopped, pointing with the tip of the knife, before going back to chopping.

Alyssa used a rubber spatula to squish the air out of the jar she was working on. "This junk never happened to me before I came here! Are you sure it's not something in the house? Or the water?"

"That's ridiculous. If that was true, wouldn't we all have the same problem?"

Alyssa had no answer for that.

Beverly poured the chopped pieces into a jar. "Peter mentioned your vision of Ether. You said it happened a long time ago."

"That was different." She stiffened.

"How so?"

"I don't want to talk about it."

"Well . . . maybe you should."

It was still a choice.

She was too confused not to tell someone, but not Peter first. Andrew often called him Peter Priesthood or Peter Perfect, which Peter didn't like and which made Alyssa laugh, because it usually fit. He did think of himself as a little more righteous than most. She wasn't ready to know what his reaction would be to her former drug use.

She took a deep breath and held it a second. "I talked to Bishop Greene about this in my baptism interview, so before I say this I want you to understand it's all in the past."

Alyssa couldn't look her in the eye. She went back to peeling, staring at her fingers as they worked. "Back when my dad died, I got so depressed that I developed an Elation habit. Debra helped me recover, once she found out about it. I almost died. I'm not proud of it. It was my worst mistake, and I've been clean ever since." Her body shook. It was horrible to confess her worst mistakes to someone she cared for so much.

She looked up, tears in her eyes.

Beverly's look was one of compassion, not anger or judgment, as she half expected.

"Beverly, I've been afraid of what you'd think of me, if you knew. I try to forget I was ever that stupid." She worked to gain control of her voice and stop her tears.

"Alyssa . . . as you said, it's in the past. Don't be so hard on yourself. You were very young, and you were hurting so much—"

"I know, but—"

"Yet even so, you were strong enough to stop and never go back to it. That says a lot for your character. It's never easy." Beverly breathed a deep sigh.

"Thanks." Alyssa rinsed her hands before wiping her eyes with a napkin. "But there's more to be concerned about. Are you familiar with what Elation does? One of its components is LSD. A hallucinogen."

A funny look crossed Beverly's face. "I am. When it first came on the market, a handful of members took small doses, claiming . . . that it gave them visions . . . an easy access point to the Spirit World. They were all excommunicated, but a splinter group is still out there using it, last I heard. So you're saying that you saw Ether and the Jaredites while—?"

Alyssa finished for her. "While I was using Elation."

"Did you mention that to Bishop Greene?"

"Not exactly."

"You could go see him if you want. His farm is over—"

"I don't want to talk to him. I'm talking to you."

Beverly blanched more tomatoes and carefully dumped them in the sink for Alyssa to peel.

"I never had flashbacks in the Gardens. Not one. I had them right at first, in college, but only for a few months. Debra told me Jon gave me a blessing when I overdosed . . . that may have helped." She'd forgotten that detail until now. "I was unconscious when he did it."

"Wait a minute, you *overdosed* on Elation?"

"Yeah."

"How are you still alive?"

She laughed, humorless. "I don't know. OD'd on Elation, shot in that draft riot, got out of Central City just before ATF broke out. You tell me how I'm still alive."

"That's a miracle." Beverly continued, "Alyssa, when that splinter group claimed Elation accessed the Spirit World, I thought it was bunk. I couldn't reconcile how the Lord would allow a drug to be invented that would pierce through the veil. Still . . . it would explain a lot of what happened to you."

Alyssa said, "Elation activates the same part of the brain in use during a near-death experience. That's why it's dangerous—you might go all the way. It's why I picked it. I didn't care if I died, then." She shuddered. Life was far too precious to waste like that.

"And a drug wouldn't be selective as to where it took you, would it? It wouldn't only be good things . . ."

"Correct." She flinched with remembered horror. There had been a terrible Caretaker in charge of all the ugly beasts and creatures in the places of terror. That horror was not part of the dreams she had now. She remembered a conversation with Rob: scientists had suspected the hallucinations were real beings, possibly alien life forms. Rob didn't believe it. Neither did she. It was unsettling to think they might have been. Remembering him twisted her insides with gratitude, rage, and fear.

Her rare moments of bliss during a high seemed so artificial compared to the secure joy she now felt resonate within her soul on occasion. Back then, if she ever reached part of what must have been Paradise, she felt only shame, unworthy—like an intruder.

"I've heard horror stories about Elation," Beverly said. "Did the hallucinations, the spirits you saw—did they ever become visible when you weren't on the drug?"

"You heard of that? Yes—that was the worst part. They'd pop up out of nowhere and talk to me. I'd be in class, or walking through a hall, and . . . here's this *thing* . . ." She stopped her mind from remembering what they looked like.

"I don't imagine they were good visitations."

"They were evil." She was sure of that now.

Beverly thought for a few minutes. "Alyssa, I don't believe that what you're experiencing now is a flashback."

"Because?"

"If Elation pierces the veil between life and death, you might find similarities. But I believe this is new—a gift from God."

That explanation felt right. As she analyzed past and present experiences in her mind, she sensed the vast difference between the two. Her current dreams gave her peace, filling her with a sense of belonging or hope, not terror.

Fear did not come from God.

Still she held a deep-rooted, irrational worry. "What if—" She shut her eyes and forced the words out. "What if the draft riot was all a hallucination, or my entire healing was just a flashback? What if my memories aren't real? Then I worry whether I'm really even here, with you guys, or if even this is an elaborate figment of my imagination."

Beverly chuckled. "You're here, all right. And you're good help, too. You can drive yourself to distraction thinking like that—soon you start worrying if you're only part of someone else's dream world or we're all just part of a gigantic hologram . . ." She smiled. "It's true you don't have a scar from that bullet wound—"

"I wish I did. It would prove it was real."

"—but the clothes you had on are good evidence. Something happened to you."

"Did Peter pull them off the burn pile?" she asked. "I forgot all about them."

"He did. He told me you still wanted them."

"I'd like to see them."

"I think they're still out there."

Once the canner was boiling on the stove, they washed their hands and went to see. Alyssa put her hand through the bloodstained bullet hole in the left leg. It gave her an odd sense of reassurance. Tangible, real evidence that she could trust her own memory.

"Do you think DNA testing would prove this is my blood?" she asked.

"I suppose, but we do believe your story."

She felt something hard in the back pocket. "There's something in here." Curious, she pulled it out.

A memory disk.

She stared at it a full minute before remembering. "I forgot I had this!"

"How did we miss that?" Beverly asked. "Sorry. What is it?"

She smiled. "Part of my past come back to haunt me."

Beverly waited.

"My Elation habit had worse consequences than addiction. This disk holds classified information on Victor Caldwell. He wanted to find me, to . . ." It was difficult to explain. The very thought filled her with dread and horror. "I could see all these beings . . . talk to them . . . while I was on the drug. Sometimes I could see them when I wasn't high. Scared me to death. He wanted to use me as an ambassador, sort of, stoked on Elation forever in his laboratory."

"That's just evil," Beverly said.

She sighed. "I escaped, didn't I? This disk probably isn't important now . . . His building exploded in the fires at Outbreak, so Caldwell should be dead. Still, I would feel a lot better if I knew for sure."

Beverly nodded, her expression far away.

Alyssa remembered Phil, Peter's father, and realized how her sentence came across. "I guess you understand that feeling . . . for different reasons."

"Yeah." Beverly wiped away a tear.

They walked back to the house.

"So you've had dreams, too?" Beverly asked. "Not just this vision of Ether you remembered?"

"Ever since I got here. But I don't know what purpose any of this serves! I don't know why I'm seeing what I see."

"I'll help you understand whatever I can," Beverly offered.

Alyssa felt instantly lighter, like a burden was lifted from her shoulders. "Thank you."

But she wasn't about to share her journal, or many of the actual dreams. They seemed too sacred and personal to share. Something whispered to her soul that it was not for another to interpret for her . . . the dreams were something she would have to understand on her own.

* * * * *

The one thought that didn't sink in all that day was this: *My mother must be dead.*

Even if it was true, Alyssa was not sure she felt anything at all.

CHAPTER 22

DISRESPECT

> *my baby slipped out*
> *from my body away from me*
> *when she died i held her lifeless form*
> *still and silent betrayed and denied*
> *next to mine*

> —Debra Pike
> from "Poem for Yvette," unfinished

Jon came home from work to find Debra piecing wood scraps together on their tiny dining table. Sawdust littered the floor. "What's all this?" Jon said.

"I'm building a coffin for Yvette." She drove the nails in with such force they went in on the first or second blow.

"Where's Zach?"

"He's with my mother."

Finally the first answer processed. "Yvette? Debra, we talked about this. Where did you put it, anyway?" That tissue would decompose quickly. He worried about a smell.

"*She* is in my mother's freezer. Mom's under strict orders not to let you near her body, Mr. Incinerator."

"Debra—"

"I'm building her a coffin to bury her properly. Mom agreed to keep her until I can do it right."

"But—"

"She's my baby, and she's going in the New Hope cemetery where she belongs!"

"Debra, get a hold of yourself." He went toward her, but she held up the hammer, a wild look in her eyes.

"Don't you dare stop me!"

"Okay!" He backed off. "Baby, I'm really trying to understand here. I'm sorry."

"The service is in three days, in case you're interested in attending," she said, terse.

"Of course I want to go! I loved her too, Debra."

"You wanted to throw her away!" She pounded more nails, tears bubbling up through her anger.

"I thought she was too small, that's all," Jon argued. "And what I don't get is, you were the one carrying on as if being pregnant was the worst thing that ever happened to you, and if you remember, I was excited. *I* was fine with it."

"Yeah. And you're just *fine* with this too." She hammered away at the little oak box, the noise punctuating her words. She finished the third side and laid the fourth in place. "What are you, a robot? You're just fine with everything, no matter what happens!"

"That is unfair. I'm *not* fine! It's horrible, and I don't have any answers. I blame myself. I blame that blasted General Horne. If only—the comm building explosion was so stressful, maybe that set things off—or if I'd just gotten to the painting, then—"

"Don't you *dare* throw that back in my face!" she yelled.

"I wasn't! I just told you, I blame myself!"

"How dare you say I caused it! She had to have been dead before I even started painting that day. She probably died the night before, when I heard her voice. I can't believe you! Jon, you are one pathetic, asinine *jerk*!"

Jon stood and fumed. She hammered away at the tiny coffin, and didn't look up to see his fuming. Finally he said, "Debra, you know I didn't mean it that way."

She ignored him.

He went out, slamming the door.

*　*　*　*　*

Jon walked through the hospital door.

Jerry Marden, his mentor, saw him come in. Jerry oversaw Jon's medical training and residency. Jon's degree wasn't recognized by the rest of the world, but thanks to Jerry's excellent teaching, New Hope called him Doctor already.

"Why are you back?" Jerry asked.

"I forgot some paperwork," Jon explained. He went to the file cabinet.

"Jon." It was half reprimand, half question.

"Yeah?"

"How's Debra doing?"

Jon's shoulders fell. "She's ticked off because I said the hospital should do tests and dispose of the miscarriage for us. I backed off right away, but she won't let it go. Fourteen weeks along, and she wants a burial—in the cemetery, with a headstone and everything. Fine. I'm trying to give her whatever she wants, and she doesn't see that. She just gets in my face."

"Jon, working overtime won't help. Go home."

"Honest, I forgot to do these reports."

"Reports can wait. She won't."

Jon hung his head. He sure wanted to make her wait. When did it get to be her turn to be sorry? "Jerry, I can't do anything right. I bring her flowers, I make dinner, I do laundry, I scrub the toilet, but it's not enough. And the kicker is, she didn't even want to be pregnant this time! She complained the entire time—and she *never* complains. Now she treats me like I don't even have feelings, all because I wanted to run a couple of tests. Is that so evil?"

Jerry brushed lint off his lab coat. He had thin white hair, watery blue eyes, and a mouthful of perfect dentures. "Jon, pregnancy is hugely emotional for a woman."

"Tell me something I don't know! But what about my feelings? I was excited about that baby! I wanted her! I loved her just as much as Debra did!"

Jerry said, "Jon. Slow down. My wife told me that women in their childbearing years worry about pregnancy about as often as men think about sex."

Jon considered that. It was frankly a little alarming.

Jerry said, "And that's whether or not she wants a baby. Half of every month, pregnancy is a possibility, whether it's a fear or a hope. Think about it. See if you get a better idea where she's coming from. In fact, if she wasn't thrilled about the baby coming, as you say, miscarriage will hit her even harder. She'll feel guilty. She'll be worrying that she caused it by not wanting it. My wife felt that way for a long time."

"You went through this?" *Debra thinks like that?* It might explain her reactions—slightly. He almost softened, then remembered their argument and how she disrespected him, calling him names.

"Jon." Jerry's voice was kind. "Go home and work on your marriage."

"Not until she's good and sorry for what she called me."

"What did she say?"

"I refuse to repeat it."

Jerry's eyes twinkled. "You remind me of when we were newlyweds."

"We're not newlyweds," Jon grumbled. They were nearing their third anniversary, after all.

Jerry smiled at Jon's response, then got serious. "Jon, we're all going through hard times. This won't be easy for her—or you— to get through this extra trial. Please. Turn to the Lord together for help."

"Thanks for the input," Jon said, sullen.

He did paperwork for an hour before returning home. He hoped Debra had calmed down by then. He was sure he'd have to apologize first.

Again.

CHAPTER 23

MOURNING

I feel Joan's apparent passing as a terrible loss. I kept hope alive that even if she never accepted the gospel, or our way of life, that we could one day recover our friendship. With my affinity for psychology, I helped her work through some of the major trauma of her childhood . . .

I wonder if I should have ever taken that path. She needed a professional. Evidently she never went to see one. I was likely the only person who knew her, heart and soul. She told Chuck little, and her children, nothing.

Alyssa says life at home was easier after they visited us. I'm not surprised. Joan and I made private time for me to counsel her—it was her sole release from the horrors which haunted her. Her childhood can't excuse her adult choices or the emotional damage she inflicted on her husband and children . . . yet I intend to preserve the confidences she entrusted me with to the day I die.

—Beverly Richardson,
personal journal entry

Morning dawned cold and windy at the New Hope Cemetery. The undertaker had dug a tiny grave and chiseled a simple stone marker for the Pikes.

Debra had invited a handful of people, but more attended than she expected would come, about twenty people. Some brought flowers for the grave; others brought baby toys or colorful pinwheels. Deb could hardly keep any composure as she looked at that.

She started by thanking everyone for coming. "I know we've all had too many funerals to attend lately," she said. "It means a lot to me that you all came out for this."

Then she read from a paper in her hand. "Yvette, you were with me only a brief time. I've tried writing about you, but I can't finish anything I start. I want to apologize . . ." Her voice broke. "For every moment that I feared. For every moment when I lost faith that I could care for you. For not being close enough to the Spirit to understand you weren't going to stay very long." She couldn't finish the eulogy after that.

Jon wrapped his arm around her waist, and she sunk into him. He took the paper from her and read from where she left off. "Yvette, I pray you will always know your parents love you, and want to be with you forever . . ." Debra couldn't focus enough to listen, bawling as Jon's wavering voice continued to the end.

He added a few of his own words, and her heart swelled. He did care. He felt as miserable about all this as she did. She cried all the more, thinking about the hard words she'd said to him, how unfair and insensitive she had been. It wasn't his fault. He'd been trying; pretty hard, too, she realized.

Jon dedicated the tiny grave. People gently tossed pink roses over the miniature coffin. Jennie Soong added a pink blanket and a soft stuffed bear.

Debra couldn't watch. It hurt so much.

As the dirt was thrown over, the sisters came up to hug her in turn.

Jennie held Debra tight. She whispered, "It doesn't matter if you weren't ready for a baby. Don't let anybody say that. It's terrible, no matter what."

"That's so true," Debra sniffed.

Another sister told her, "I wish I'd done this after I lost mine. This helps me, and it's been ten years. Thank you so much."

"Thank *you*, for coming," Debra said.

"God bless you."

"We're praying for you every night in family prayer."

"I can't stop thinking about you. Hold on tight, and the Lord will get you through this."

Too soon, she stood alone with Jon, staring at the tiny gravestone, November wind whipping through her dark blue wool skirt.

Yvette, why couldn't you stay? she thought.

She heard only the sound of the wind and her own sobbing.

Jon embraced her. Gently, he whispered, "It's time to go, baby, but you can visit her anytime you want." He paused, holding her tight. "Deb, I'm so glad we did this. I'm sorry for the way I've acted. I was foolish. I'm trying to be strong for you . . . it's hard when I hurt so much too."

She nodded. "I'm sorry, too, Jon. I love you so much. I do." She was unable to take her eyes off the grave.

It was a good thing. She was glad she'd done it. People thought miscarriage mattered less than a full-term baby, or a child.

Not to her heart, it didn't.

Jon held her close. "I love you too, baby."

Slowly she turned away and let him lead her. She leaned into his chest as they walked together in the wind.

CHAPTER 24

SAFE HAVEN

Require not miracles, except I shall command you, except casting out devils, healing the sick . . . and against deadly poisons . . .

—Doctrine and Covenants, 24:13

Margret spied New Hope's lowrising buildings on the horizon.

"Look!" Marcus pointed. "There they are!"

"I see, *niño*. Almost there."

After more vomiting, coughing, and plodding forward, they were close enough to spot someone within earshot.

"New Hope? Hospital?" Her voice was too weak.

Marcus shifted Natty's weight on his hip and called out, loud. "My mama needs a hospital! Can you help?"

The person called back, "Stay right there! I'll get somebody!"

Everything went gray around the edges, and Margret collapsed to the ground. She was barely aware of being put on a stretcher and loaded into the back of a horse-drawn trailer with the children.

Horses? She had to be hallucinating.

"I love you so much. You babies take care of each other."

She vaguely heard Marcus before losing consciousness. "We will, Mama, I promise. I love you!"

* * * * *

Jon was on duty in ER when a sick woman was brought in. She'd come from the south.

She was probably another Central City refugee. Most moved on once they realized where they were. If they wanted to stay, they were welcome, but New Hope had to impose its lifestyle on anyone wishing to dwell there. Religion was a free choice, not part of the constraints.

Many people of diverse faiths found their place with them, sharing Article 28 in common. But New Hope's economic system shared all material things equally, and would fail to function properly unless each person committed to that system of their own free will. Most stragglers preferred to face the elements than live with those terms.

This patient was unconscious, and from the stains on her clothing, had been coughing blood.

Jon was busy charting another patient. "ATF?" he asked, anxious. ATF carried attributes of both virus and bacterium, resisting antibiotics, mutating, defying classification, in constant flux. It fascinated him. He had pored through every report Kensington rolled out, until communications went down.

"Can't rule it out," Hugh said, rolling the patient in on a stretcher. "Stand clear."

Dr. Jerry Marden pulled on his gloves. He called out, "Don't panic, everyone—ATF spreads only through bodily fluids and water. Safety procedures—gloves and masks on, STAT! Including patients! Paul—run tell President Weber we may have an ATF case. Find out what he wants us to do."

Paul ran out.

President Weber was mayor of New Hope and doubled as the head of local church government. There were no successful phone lines installed—they were having trouble acquiring cable. A staff of teens volunteered around the clock for the dozens of gofer jobs that cropped up.

"We're supposed to euthanize if it's ATF," Jon said, putting on his mask.

"Forget the UN. This is a human life!" Jerry said.

Using extreme caution, nurses drew blood, started an IV, and announced the woman's vital signs.

"She had two kids with her," Hugh said.

"Where are they?" Jerry said.

"Getting their blood drawn," Hugh answered. "They don't appear to be sick, though."

"Jon." Jerry caught his eye. "This could be your chance to study it firsthand."

Jon's heart thumped. Debra would never agree. He had only seen computer-generated images, downloaded from Dr. Kensington's National ATF Research Lab, before their servers were destroyed. To study it under his own microscope . . . what an opportunity!

On the flip side, Jon felt very sorry for this woman, if it was the disease they feared. She would die. And if Jerry refused to euthanize, the process would be torture. Jon was generally against euthanasia, but he wondered if forcing someone to endure that bitter death was too much.

"She's ready for you, Dr. Marden," a nurse said.

Jerry and Jon administered a Priesthood blessing. It was part of the holistic healing approach taught in New Hope. They used blessings such as these, herbology, chiropractic care, reflexology, and the like, in conjunction with modern science and medicine. Prayers for the sick and blessings for healing were as standard medicine as drugs or high-tech diagnostic imaging.

As he laid his gloved hands on her head, Jon realized how different his medical training had turned out than he'd expected. He provided better care for his patients this way, using all his faculties instead of part.

Jerry sealed the anointing. Jon felt a surge of energy flow through his gloves and into the woman's scalp as Jerry promised her she would live.

CHAPTER 25

MIDNIGHT AWAKENING

The patient tested positive for American Toxic Flu. The blessing promised her life, but that was before we ran the blood test. I'm not making bets. Neither of her children are sure how long she's been sick. Even so, the connective tissue should be deteriorating by this point. Her organs show no signs of damage or loosening.

The patient has some unusual scars on her body. Some appear to be cigarette burns, others knife wounds. The largest, on her left calf, was definitely not repaired by a medical professional. It appears these scars originated during the same time period, between three and seven years ago. Safe exams on the children show that neither has similar scars, or signs of active physical abuse.

Jerry assigned me to study her case. He says I'm better cut out as a research physician than a surgeon, whatever that means. We've taken so many precautions that there's no danger I'll get sick. I haven't told Debra yet—I hope she takes it well. She's still healing from the miscarriage.

—Dr. Jon Pike
personal log, lab notes

"*A*lyssa."

Awakened in the night by a voice, Alyssa's first thought was, *here we go again.* "Go away, Mother," she mumbled. She buried her head in the pillow.

"Alyssa."

It was not Joan's voice, but a sickly-sweet sound. Goosebumps prickled the hair on her arms, and she looked up.

A dark figure hovered in the corner by the dresser.

Alyssa bolted upright and pulled the quilts to her chest. Suddenly her long flannel pajamas didn't cover her near well enough.

"Get out! Now!" Old habit made her reach for her switch-blade. But she was so safe here, she'd quit keeping it under the pillow. It was in the top dresser drawer.

An ethereal figure stepped out of the corner. An inky black cape flowed around his shoulders as if a gentle breeze stirred. Another moment and she understood the blade would have no use.

She was too terrified to scream.

"I see you remember me." He stepped closer.

"Who *are* you?"

"Curious that you never asked before." His inky-black robe shifted to a brilliant silver. A rainbow-like corona shone about him. Alyssa blinked against the glare. If not for an underlying falseness, he could have appeared beatific.

The figure stretched out his arms and smiled. "I am the god of this world."

"You are not." She mustered all her confidence to defy this creature. Here was yet another relic from her Elation habit. When would that one mistake cease to haunt her life? "What do you want with me?"

"I *am* a son of God!" Loose papers flew about the room. "I am not pleased to find you *here*. We have missed you. It distressed me so when you left us." The flow of silvery robes and the rainbow aura surrounding him was mesmerizing, but there was a hollowness to those eyes, fathomless pits of darkness.

She shook her head and pushed down her fear, snapping away the hypnotic effect.

Her mind raced for a means to end the apparition. "I never wanted to please you," she said.

"I am the Caretaker of this world. I dislike misrepresentation of my character by these . . . deceivers. You must leave this place at once and follow me. I can give you everything you desire. Come with me, and I will guide you, care for you, and love you, always. Alyssa, be mine."

His smile, tone, and expression were unsettling yet seductive, drawing her toward him with an invisible gossamer cord. Doubt thrust its way into her soul, a black cloud overshadowing her burgeoning faith.

"If you will be my child, I can help you . . . I know you want Peter."

An image drove itself into her brain—Peter kissing her passionately, their bodies joined in a lover's embrace. It stirred up a potent arousal which she was unused to and didn't appreciate. "I can give you this, and more."

"No!" She rejected the image and fought off the unwanted sensation.

The creature before her was the terrible taskmaster she once feared on her drug trips, and facing him again she feared him still. Everything she had seen him do in the nightmare Elation realm where he reigned inspired only terror, pain, and misery. Could anything he said be true?

By their fruits ye shall know them.

She had read this simple verse earlier in the week, and now it flooded her mind with light, breaking through uncertainty. Whoever this being was, if it was real at all, it did not inspire love, goodness, or anything like it. She said, "You are no god. Leave me alone!"

He seethed with fury and waved his arm. The clock and lamp whirled off her dresser and shattered on the floor. "*I am a son of God!* Leave these wretched people and worship *me!*"

"No!" An unnatural wind whipped through her hair. She clung to her blankets. "You are *not* Jesus Christ. I have seen Him! *He* is the Son of God. You are nothing like him!"

He stretched his hand toward her and hissed, "If you will not come freely, I swear I shall destroy you!"

She managed a short cry of, "Peter! Help!" before her voice froze and she fought for air, choking.

Light spilled in from the hall. Peter stood in the open doorway, a silhouette. He flipped the overhead light switch. The figure whirled around.

In the light, it was just a dim gray shadow.

Peter cried, "In the name of Jesus Christ, I command you to depart!" His words rang with an authority Alyssa felt to the marrow of her bones like a thunderclap.

"No!" the figure shrieked.

Peter stepped in and repeated the command. It shrieked again and flew through the window and out into the night. The whole house shook. Glass rattled downstairs.

Its final screech lingered in the air before it faded into nothingness.

Alyssa exhaled slowly. Her throat felt frostbitten.

"Are you all right?" Peter asked.

Alyssa said in a small voice, "Please tell me that was only a *very* bad dream."

They looked around. The lamp lay in fragments. The curtains were in a heap opposite the window, next to the dresser. The curtain rod was crumpled. Papers and clothing were strewn everywhere.

"I didn't do that," Alyssa said, embarrassed. She felt small and strained.

"I know." He ran his hand through his hair. "Can I sit down? I'm a little shaky."

"Sure."

He settled into the wicker chair in the corner. He had on a faded purple terrycloth robe and needed a shave; dark circles showed under his eyes, and his hair stuck out in all directions. If he was that bad off, she must look even worse. Not that it mattered.

"Peter, what *was* that thing?" she whispered.

He furrowed his brow. "Some kind of demon, I guess."

"A demon? You *guess*?"

Peter nodded, grim.

She smacked her hand against the bed. "What *are* you people?"

"Hey! I don't know how it got in here any more than you do!"

"Didn't you hear me call you?"

He shook his head no. "Something woke me up and said to get up here right away."

They looked at each other for a long moment.

Peter asked, "What did it want?"

"He said he was the god of this world, and that I should leave this place and follow him. He got really mad when I said no, and that's when you came in."

"The god of this world." All the blood drained out of his face. He put his head down and rubbed his forehead. "That's worse than I thought."

"I'm sorry, what's worse than demons being *real?*"

"Oh, they're real." He was almost nonchalant. "But how did *he* get in? This house is protected!"

"Peter, make sense. Please."

He caught her eyes with his. "Alyssa, I think I just cast out Satan himself." His mouth hung open. His eyes were wider than she'd ever seen them.

"Excuse me?" She felt cold all over. "Do you mean to tell me—that that thing was Satan?"

The implication ran deeper than Peter knew. Where exactly was she during all those drug trips? She felt sick to her stomach and fought off gagging.

"Alyssa, I am so sorry. Here you've had all these dreams and stuff, we should have told you what to do just in case . . ."

"Just in case what? You're not making sense again."

"Evil things must obey the authority of Jesus Christ, if you command in His name. It's not hard to do, and it always works. But what I mean is, there's always a pattern. Once the Lord speaks, Satan comes around to put in his two cents. With me, it works more like, say, I'll get a good feeling that builds my testimony, then a doubt creeps in to test it. There's all kinds of precedents in the scriptures. You have Moses and the burning bush, Jesus himself fasting for forty days and nights, Joseph Smith in the Sacred Grove . . . Satan shows up either before or after someone has a major spiritual experience. From my observation, it tends to be balanced, little or big. You've actually seen Jesus. It was dumb of me not to tell you what to do just in case. It never occurred to me."

"That would have been *helpful.*" She scowled. "I could have taken care of him myself?"

"Yeah. Just do what I did." Peter's brow furrowed. "I'm really sorry this happened. Still, he shouldn't have gotten in the house. It's been dedicated. By Dad."

"Peter, this is too weird."

"I never had to do anything like this before."

"That's so comforting," she said.

"Maybe it's you," he smiled. "Nothing this weird happened before you got here."

She threw her pillow at him. "Thanks, I feel so much better!"

He caught it with a laugh.

Peter set the pillow on his lap and leaned on it. "Alyssa, there's something you need to understand. Two real, powerful forces exist in this world, one good and one evil, and each wants to own you. I don't understand why the fight is more intense for you than most people. But it is."

"How can I ever know if I'm safe?" Adrenaline still pumped through her system.

"Tonight you are, I'm sure of it. He won't be back. He's not allowed."

On impulse, she asked, "Peter, will you pray with me?"

She climbed out from under the covers and knelt on the far side of the bed. She felt vulnerable and afraid, and if it was undignified, she didn't care. She needed his help or she wouldn't calm down.

"Of course." Peter knelt on the opposite side. An odd feeling overcame her; there was something *right* about this scenario, both of them kneeling across . . . across a bed? No, that couldn't be it. It was something else. She didn't have words to explain it even to herself. The moment sang with a profound resonance.

"Would you offer it?" she asked, bowing her head.

Peter prayed for safety, understanding, protection through the night, and the guidance of the Holy Spirit. It was simple, but Alyssa felt much better when he finished.

"Thank you so much," she said.

"Anytime." Peter looked at her, his expression puzzled.

"I hope this *won't* happen again, actually," she said.

"Right, me too! But—" He bit his lower lip.

"What?"

"Did you feel something just now, when we knelt together? Something deep? Powerful?"

"Yes," she said, slowly. Her left eyebrow went up.

He reached across the bed and took her hand in his. It felt so natural, so right. "Alyssa?"

Giddiness rushed to her head. Peter Richardson was holding her hand. Memory rushed in, and she thought of something. She asked a question from the past. "What do you think you're doing?"

"Holding your hand," he quipped. The same words, from the day he first kissed her, years ago. But he didn't drop her hand as he had that day.

She said, "Do you remember every puny detail or something?"

"Absolutely everything," he said, looking in her eyes.

Her eyes went soft. She was afraid she might cry, right here, right now. "So do I," she said.

He leaned forward, and the tender kiss he gave her felt so right, that while she couldn't believe he was here, kissing her, part of her soul felt so connected by the touch of his lips on hers that it seemed they had never been separated a single moment. She kissed him back in earnest.

"Whoa." Peter blinked and shook his head when it was over.

She felt bashful. Was it too much? "Sorry?"

"Don't be sorry, of all things!" He took her hands in both of his and stared into her eyes. "Alyssa, I can't bear to lose you again. I believe we're meant to be together. Forever." He squeezed her hands. "Marry me, Alyssa. I'm dying inside, watching you every day and not being *with* you. I love you so much. I love you with everything I am, every fiber, every cell, every breath I take. I can't stand not telling you, even if you reject me. Please give me a chance. Please."

Is this actually happening? she thought, shocked, thrilled, her mind spinning.

Peter continued, "I won't ever be happy with anyone else. I know that now. If you won't marry me, I'll—I'll pine away forever in eternal loneliness."

His eyes showed he meant every word, otherwise she'd have smacked him for being so melodramatic.

She didn't know what to say, so she kissed him again.

"Does that mean yes or no?" he asked.

It was utterly crazy, too sudden. But who else would she be happy with? He was the only man she ever truly wanted. "It means yes!"

"Oh, you've made me a happy man," he said, beaming.

She was confused. "But I don't understand. Peter, we fought when I first got here. You didn't like things about me, my history, living in the City. We've been getting along, sure, but I thought you forgot where we left off—or if you hadn't, that you'd rather not be reminded. I didn't want to bring it up. And I haven't been able to *stop* remembering since I've been here. That's kind of pathetic."

"I was wrong to fight. It was judgmental and stupid, but I was scared, Alyssa. It didn't take me long to realize I never stopped loving you—and it scared me to death. If I didn't get mad, I'd have kissed you."

She thought back to those first few days here. "That night on the porch, when you asked me to stay, don't tell me you wanted to kiss me *then*."

"Yeah. I thought about it." He bit his lip, smiling. "I didn't think you were ready, and I wasn't either. But I promised you when I was sixteen that when we were older, I would rescue you and carry you away with me. I intend to keep that promise. If I could have found you years ago, I'd have done it. I tried."

This whole conversation was leaving her thunderstruck. "Why didn't you say so?"

"I've been trying, kind of," he said. "You didn't respond. You seemed afraid to be near me."

"I was terrified that my feelings would show! And you'd go, 'Alyssa, please, let's just be friends,' and then everything would get awkward. I couldn't face that possibility. I love being here too much."

"I didn't push it, because you had so much else to process— losing your friends in Central City, studying the gospel, your conversion—I about busted with joy when you asked to be baptized. I didn't want to burden you with my feelings—just like you said, it would be awkward. But I couldn't wait much longer. Awkward or not, I had to know, because it's you for me or no one. I mean that."

"Talk about putting pressure on a girl," she grinned.

He kissed her again, tender and sweet. She closed her eyes and soaked in the feeling.

Then Peter said, "When we knelt to pray just now, I saw the two of us dressed in white, holding hands across the altar . . . being sealed. When you said you felt something too, I knew it was time. I know it's sudden. But just so you know, I imagined this moment much differently."

She had to laugh. "I seriously doubt you imagined barging in, casting out demons, then going, oh by the way, will you marry me?" She felt giddy and nervous.

He laughed too. "But you *will* marry me?"

"I can't imagine spending my life with anyone else, Peter."

"Alyssa . . . you're so beautiful." Tears rolled down his cheek. "I can't believe you'll have me."

"Oh, Peter—I'm not beautiful anymore, if I ever was." She tousled his hair, the way she did to bug him when they were kids.

"Don't say that. You will always be beautiful to me."

She couldn't form a response to that for a minute. "I promise to be the best wife I can, Peter." She ran a finger down his cheek, wiping away the tears.

"And I promise to be the best husband you could ever dream of."

They drew back from the intensity of the moment. Peter stood up. She scooted herself back under the covers.

Alyssa surveyed the room. The nightmare that brought him up here seemed eons ago, almost a different life. "Should we clean up this mess?"

"No. I want Mom to see this first thing in the morning. And I should go . . . I'll see you in the morning. In a couple hours, that is."

"Peter," she said.

"Yeah?"

Peter leaned against the doorframe. She admired his muscular figure, even wearing that ratty purple bathrobe and mussed-up hair, needing a shave. He radiated love for her. How had she not seen it before? She'd been so afraid to hope that it made her blind.

She almost forgot her question. "Could he have killed me? He threatened to destroy me."

"He's after your soul, not your physical self. Be on guard—it's unlikely he'll attack directly like that again. It'll be smaller, more subtle, next time."

"And Peter—should we keep this quiet?"

"About us? Or the, uh, this other thing?" he asked.

"About us."

"I'm so happy, I want to yell it to the whole world! . . . But waiting is probably smarter."

"I'd like a little time to get used to the idea, myself, before everyone knows."

"I understand." His mouth twisted into a wry smile. "It'll be our secret?"

"Oh! You!" She tossed her pillow at him.

He caught it and sent it flying back to her. "Our secret, then." He blew her a kiss and left.

* * * * *

Peter went down the stairs bouncing on a cloud of delight. It felt like flying, or riding Teancum at a full gallop downhill. He guessed it was somewhere between two and three a.m. He stopped in the kitchen for a drink of water, and his thoughts turned somber. He cast out *Satan?* The thought of it shook him to the core. He hadn't seen anything with his eyes. He felt it, though—a menace of pure evil. He reacted from his gut to protect her. And it left. He hadn't tested that power before.

What was he thinking, proposing to her after that? Was that even fair? But—she loved him! She said yes!

His emotions tumbled all over the place. Joy, fear, faith, love, amazement, shock . . .

He passed Andrew's door and noticed the light on. "Andy? You okay in there?"

"Get off my case, Peter Priesthood. I'm fine."

"It'll be hard to get up in the morning. Can't you sleep?"

"Leave me alone."

"Okay, okay."

Peter went down the hall to his room. He felt a deep need to pray. He knelt by the side of his bed, opening his thoughts to his Father in Heaven.

He was filled with light and warmth. Tears welled up, and he wept, emotions boiling within his soul; worry for his brother, his mother, and the twins, along with his intense love for Alyssa— deep gratitude mingled with heartache. *Teach me what I need to do, Lord.*

Gradually he sensed a bright light form in his mind's eye. He couldn't bring himself to mentally look up, but a pure love emanated from a Divine presence, surrounding him with a blanket of comfort and peace. *I am with you, Peter.*

All his family waited on his leadership. Even his mother did; he knew it, and didn't like facing it.

I don't know how to lead them, Lord.

Peter saw himself then as a shepherd watching over a small flock; he knew they were his brothers, sisters, mother, and Alyssa. He gripped a knotty staff in his hand, the wood worn smooth, but it didn't quite fit his fingers right. This staff was made for his father. He had not yet made it his own.

How do I do that? he wondered.

The vision and spiritual presence slowly faded, leaving Peter with an intense, uncontrollable longing. Left to himself, he wept unashamed, releasing emotions he'd reined in since his father's disappearance, pouring out his whole heart to the Lord. He was tired of being in charge. He wanted his daddy back. He knew he hadn't accepted that this family was his to lead. Was Dad never coming back, then? He couldn't face that. He just couldn't. As irrational or impossible as it might be, he clung to a tiny hope that his father would come home one day soon and make everything right.

He couldn't remember ever having so many tumbling up and down emotions all in one night.

I'm doing a miserable job—Andrew thinks I'm a self-righteous dog, and maybe I am. Mom barely holds together. She's so sad. It affects everything around here, Jordan and Kellie the most. I have to do everything, read all the bedtime stories, do their baths, comb Kellie's hair, do all their bandages . . .

It wasn't quite that bad. His mother still functioned. It just felt that way. There was no joy in it for her like there used to be. He missed being little, being held in her arms. He missed how she used to sing him to sleep and rub his head. He missed being carried on his daddy's shoulders. He wasn't ready to be flung into carrying all of them on his shoulders, not permanently. Not this way. It was too hard.

But—Alyssa loves me! She wants to marry me!

Her kisses tonight were a thrill far beyond the physical. It tapped a vein of intense love so deep he could never discover its full dimensions. He wished to drink from that well eternally.

Still kneeling in prayer, his legs tingled with pain. Lost circulation forced him to shift his position. When he looked up, pale dawn filtered through his window. He took a deep breath and faced the morning.

CHAPTER 26

PILLOW TALK

As per your urgent request, I have continued my previous experiment with the ATF injections.

The laboratory results we obtained are as follows: I injected three rats with one 32-cell organism each. Upon their demise at 21, 22, and 26 hours post-injection, respectively, we located the ATF organisms and injected three other rats. The second set died at 46, 47, and 52 hours post-injection. I again located and removed the organisms, which had multiplied as I theorized. Each organism had attained a worm-like shape, barely visible to the naked eye. However, none of these organisms remained viable.

Of significant interest is a key detail which I must acknowledge my lab assistant noticed. I missed it myself. One of the secondary test rats was missing a toe on its right front foot from a previous injury. Upon examination of this specimen, the rat had regenerated that toe.

—Dr. Joel Kensington,
confidential report to Pres.-Gen. Leo Horne

Jon nudged Debra as she slept. "I have to tell you something. It's important."

"It's two in the morning. Can't it wait?"

"It's about work, and I'm not sure if you'll be happy about it. Please hear me out?"

"I'm so tired, Jon."

"We had a refugee patient test positive for ATF this week."

Debra shifted in bed. Her voice was more alert. "Did they euthanize her?"

He paused. "No."

"We could all die!"

"It's not airborne. Besides, she seems to be recovering." He bolstered his courage. "Deb, Jerry says I'm the best research physician they have on staff. He wants me to run the lab to find a cure."

"You tell him no," she said, more angry than he had expected.

"Deb! Don't you understand? This is an opportunity to find the cure for the worst disease ever known to man!"

Her voice came soft and trembling then. "So . . . my feelings aren't important to you."

That was worse than her anger.

He said, "No! You're my whole life, Debra! You have to believe me when I say curing this disease feels like a calling. You know how obsessed I've been with ATF."

"Yes, I've noticed, and I don't like it." She sat up and turned on the lamp. "Listen to yourself. Jonathan Clive Pike, Superman. Dr. Kensington and his staff in Des Moines are already working on it—scientists with years of experience, Nobel Prize winners. You're in your residency, for pity's sake! Name one thing you have that they don't. One thing."

"A recovering patient," Jon said.

The words hung in the air.

Debra let out her breath in exasperation.

With the light on, Jon saw the rage written on her face. There was hurt there too, and futility. "Debra, if she develops antibodies in her blood, we have a cure. *A cure.* And beyond that, a *vaccine.*"

"Until it mutates again! You told me yourself how unstable this thing is."

"Millions of lives could still be saved. Even with mutations, once we have an antibody—"

She interrupted. "Jerry can do the research himself. He doesn't have a baby at home to think of! Don't you dare leave me at twenty-three with a fatherless child and make me spend the rest of my life alone. Jerry's old. His grandchildren are in their teens!"

"That shouldn't make a difference, Debra."

"It makes a huge difference to *me!*"

"My life is not at risk. If I thought it was, the tiniest bit, I wouldn't do it, baby. Believe me."

"How can you know it isn't?"

"I wish you could have been there when she came into the ER. Jerry gave her an incredible blessing that promised her she would live, Debra, and she *is*. We don't know how or why. My job is to find out why she's surviving when no one else has."

"Just because *she* might survive doesn't mean she won't be a Typhoid Mary!"

That set him back a step.

She continued, "Why hasn't New Hope voted on this? Don't we have the right to know there's an ATF patient here?"

"It's classified. And you can't tell anyone either. I'm barely authorized to tell *you*."

"This is not right, Jon."

"President Weber gave us the green light *and* classified the information. There is so much at stake, I'm positive it will be worth whatever risk it takes."

"Even risking our lives? What about Zach's life? Are you willing to put your baby at risk?"

They looked at each other for an intense, furious moment.

Jon had one more card to play. "Do you want to know who she is?"

"That is so irrelevant. Why?"

"The patient had a paper on her with our names on it. Does anything on this look familiar?" He took the scrap out of his nightstand drawer and handed it to her.

She stared at the crumpled paper. Her hand went to her mouth. "If I didn't know better, I'd say this was Alyssa's handwriting."

"It *is* Alyssa's handwriting," Jon said.

"How can that be?"

"According to the woman's son, Marcus, Alyssa made friends with them. They were neighbors for a long time. They must have met after we left for New Hope."

"Alyssa—is she alive?"

He heard hope dawn in her voice.

He hated to crush it, but he must. "The boy doesn't know. They left Central City a couple weeks before Outbreak, and Alyssa was living there when they left."

Debra's face fell. He felt it too. There was a near-zero chance that she had survived.

"How old is this boy?" she asked.

"Eight. There's a little sister, Natty, who's four."

"Why did she send them to us?"

"I believe they were running away from a former stepfather." No matter how Jon or anyone else put questions to him, Marcus was not more forthcoming. "Alyssa suggested we were a safe place, and gave them money for traveling. That's all we know."

"What about these two kids? Are they sick too?"

"No, they're fine, except for being a bit undernourished." He cleared his throat. "They're staying with my mother."

"*Roberta* took them?"

"Yeah. She did." He watched Debra's face as she held the worn paper in two hands. He added, "If it was Alyssa in that sickbed, you'd beg me to save her."

"But it's not." She waved the paper scrap. "Knowing Alyssa was alive, at least recently—that's amazing news, but it doesn't change how I feel about this project."

"If the patient recovers, you can talk to her. You could find out everything that happened to Alyssa since we came here and you lost touch. Don't you want that?"

Debra gave him a look, shaking her head slowly. "That is so underhanded."

"I didn't mean to be. I'm just talking. Debra. Would you at least pray about it first? Please?"

"You're determined to do this whether I like it or not, so why should I bother?"

"Debra, I need your blessing. Please support me in this, I beg you. If you pray, you'll know." He hoped they would get the same answer, anyway.

"Why is it that you're begging, but I'm the one who feels powerless? I have to take this lying down because *you* have the final say. Don't I?"

Jon was flustered. "Where did *that* come from?"

"Don't I?" she repeated, terse.

He was cut to the quick. He hadn't seen the issue like that. He honestly thought she would come around, especially with the connection to Alyssa.

But if she would not bend, he would. He would tell Jerry tomorrow, and kiss his dreams goodbye, even if it left him feeling like a popped balloon, wrinkled, broken, and lifeless. Why did compromise always feel so one-sided?

"No." All hope deflated with that one word. "I don't want that, Debra . . ."

As Jon's voice trailed off he saw that, in his stubbornness, he was trying to force her to agree. Force belonged to evil. God used gentle persuasion, love unfeigned . . . never coercion or indifference to a loved one's tender feelings. He sensed anger percolating somewhere deep inside. Once again her feelings mattered more than his, and she wouldn't even look at it from his side.

He shoved the thoughts away. His marriage and family were more important than his work. He knew that, with both his head and his heart. He would not take the risk of causing a rift in his family that might never heal, losing her love.

"Debra, I can't do this without you. Please believe me. I won't do it unless you agree. I promise."

"Liar," she said. "I bet you've been working on it already, haven't you?"

Something must have shown on his face, because her next words were, "I knew it!"

She handed him his pillow and a blanket and sent him shuffling out to the couch.

He had never slept on the couch. He was dumbfounded and afraid. Twice during the night he went in to calm Debra's angry, ragged tears, but she shooed him back out, accusing him of only wanting to sleep in a bed.

* * * * *

In the morning, Debra's pillow hit him in the stomach, waking him from fitful sleep.

"I prayed about it, all right? Go do your stupid research. Your alarm is going off."

"What—huh?" Jon sat up.

"Go on. But don't ask me to be happy about it. I can't give you that."

"You'll let me do this?" He dared to breathe. Dark dread had hung over him all night that he had already damaged her trust in him and spoiled the love he cherished.

A glimmering thread of hope pierced through his doubt and fear, but he felt horrible about their argument. Their marriage had been so smooth until the last few months. He didn't know what to do. He hated how it seemed like any way he turned, he made a mistake. "I didn't mean for this to hurt you, Debra," he said, tears welling up in his eyes. "I'm so sorry."

"I'll fight with you, Jon, but I won't fight with God." She wiped her eyes and sniffed.

He went to hug her. She barely let him.

"Baby, I love you so much. I won't let you down," he said.

"You already have." Her voice was a soft, painful sound.

Jon winced. "I'll make it up to you. Say the word and I'll do it. And I'll be safe, I promise."

"I'm not so sure." She sniffed. "The answer I got was that I need to support you, but 'the danger lies not in the direction you expect.'"

He said, "I don't know what that means. Jerry takes every conceivable precaution."

"I don't either." She paused. Then she said, "Jon, I'm going to need another blessing."

"Sure. Do you want one right now?"

She took a deep breath and held it. "I want my dad to do this one."

He pulled back to look at her face. His voice was plaintive. "Why?"

"I just need my daddy right now, okay?" She wiped a tear off her cheek.

The request stung like straight alcohol poured in a wound. He felt replaced, even mildly offended, but he couldn't exactly blame her. He ran his fingers through her soft, wooly hair and rubbed the back of her neck, discovering a knot there.

"You can be there, of course, if you want to," she said, her voice softening as he relaxed the knot.

"If you'll have me," he said.

She nodded and leaned into his shoulder. He kissed her hair and held her close.

* * * * *

Jon had trouble concentrating as he compared test results and prepared the cultures for the day. It grieved him that he had hurt Debra so much that she felt the need to turn to her father rather than himself. She had every right to her father's blessing, but worry buzzed through his mind like an aggravating housefly that he had gone about this terribly wrong, and he couldn't swat it away.

* * * * *

Marcus and Natty stayed in a house with a nice grandma and grandpa, Sister Roberta and Brother Clive Pike. They were the mom and dad of the doctor who was helping their mama get better.

Marcus never had a grandma. Mama said his grandparents were mean and never took him to visit. He imagined to himself that Sister Roberta and Brother Clive were his real grandparents.

The Pikes were black and had African things decorating their walls. Marcus liked them. They had a wooden giraffe with yellow spots, ornate tribal masks, and his favorite, a painting of an elephant family done in black, gray, blues, and rich greens.

"My grandpa was black, too," he told them. "He married a Mexican lady, that's why Mama speaks Spanish so much. That grandma died before I was born."

"I see," said Sister Roberta.

Marcus asked to visit his mama every day. They said she was in a special room where germs couldn't get in or out. They wouldn't answer when he asked if Mama had ATF. She must have caught it. What else would make her that sick? He worried she would die. He worried they wouldn't tell him, if she did. He worried he would never, ever see her again.

He was angry. Couldn't he look at her in the special room? Did it have a window?

The TV-telephone on the wall was broken too. He was disappointed. They could watch movies on it, but he wanted to know how the phone worked. They never had a videophone.

"We had the old-fashioned kind in the Gardens," Marcus told them. Brother Clive was interested in that. He liked antiques. He told Marcus they were getting that kind of phone soon.

Sister Roberta hugged them and told him he was adorable. She cooked great food, and there was always plenty. He ate and ate. She looked at him funny if he talked about going hungry.

He started telling them how he was in charge of Natty all day while Mama slept, because she worked at night sewing shirts in a factory. He was proud he could do that. But Sister Roberta and Brother Clive whispered in each other's ears. So Marcus stopped talking about that, too.

Sister Roberta did everything for Natty like she was a baby. All that fuss would make Natty start up whining real soon, Marcus explained, but Sister Roberta didn't listen.

He had his own bed here, but he was used to sleeping with Natty. Natty had her own bed too, and liked being big and grown-up. She wouldn't share. It was hard to sleep.

He sat up late and read his tattered comic book so many times he memorized every line and picture, but he was really thinking about Mama. They'd never been apart this long, not even in the bad Ralph days.

He turned out the light and cried quietly in his pillow so nobody could hear how lonesome he was.

* * * * *

Sister Roberta figured out Natty couldn't read.

Marcus said, "She's only four!"

"My kids could read their letters by that age. And what about you? What grade are you in school?"

Marcus made a face. "I can read fine."

"What about math?"

"I know math."

"What's eight times seven?"

He made a face and hid his fingers behind his back while he tried to count, touching his finger to his thumb. Two eights was sixteen. Sixteen and sixteen made . . . thirty-two. How many eights was he up to?

"Marcus, have you been to school at all?"

"Of course!" Mama hadn't made him go since they moved to the Gardens. He had to babysit Natty.

"What grade were you in last?"

There was something about Sister Roberta. She got away without answering you, but you had to answer when she asked questions. "I finished first grade," he said, chin in the air.

"First grade! Child, you got some catching up to do."

"I don't want to go to school here!" He couldn't leave both his mama *and* his sister and go away to some school all day where he didn't know any of the kids. His lip trembled.

Sister Roberta smiled. "Don't you worry none. I can teach you both a good deal, right here at home." She gave him a huge hug and thumped him on the back.

"All right," Marcus grumbled.

Marcus then had lessons and books to go with the interesting toys, good food, drinks, and a soft bed. Everything he could want or think to ask for.

Except his mama.

CHAPTER 27

FULL DISCLOSURE

Kensington:
Your experiment bears repeating, to discover whether
the toe regeneration was a freak biological accident, or a
side effect of the ATF organism itself. Necessary funding
is granted.

—Pres.-Gen. Leo F. Horne
confidential memo

The morning after his proposal, Alyssa stole a whisper in Peter's ear. "Meet me in the hayloft after breakfast?"

He gave a nod, but there was a question in his eyes. *What?*

She gave his hand a quick squeeze and smiled, to mean it wasn't bad. But she feared it was.

After the meal, she casually strolled out to the stable, curried Abish for a few minutes, then snuck up to the loft and waited. Soon she saw the top of Peter's head as he climbed the ladder. She smiled.

He asked, "You haven't changed your mind, have you?"

She shook her head. "No way!"

"I wasn't dreaming, then."

"Nope. I just wanted to talk."

Peter sat and took her hand in his. He held up their hands, and she watched their intertwined fingers. "You really remember that day in the cornfield, on the Fourth of July?"

Alyssa said, "Every detail, like it was yesterday."

"When I think about it, and think how long we've been apart, and that a miracle brought you back to me, it amazes me so much that you still love me. I didn't sleep last night after I left your room."

"I didn't sleep either," she said.

"You're tired, huh?"

She laughed. "You could say that again. Well. I don't want to beat around this."

"Sure." He squeezed her hand, too hard.

She didn't want to keep him on edge. She began, "When you confirmed me into the Church, you said this weird thing about my future children."

"Something about that was in there. I remember wondering if that meant me, or if you were going to marry somebody else." He let out a nervous chuckle.

She grinned, then got serious. "You said my children wouldn't all come the usual way, and to let my heart be still. I wrote it down in my journal. But what you don't know is that I may never have natural children, Peter. My ovaries are dead."

She paused to let it sink in. "In the Gardens, the government forced us to get birth-control shots. I didn't—" How to word that? "I didn't *need* any, but refusing them was not an option. We had to go every few months, so I figured they wore off. The last time I went, the nurse told me the truth—they added a toxin to the serum that systematically destroys your eggs."

"My gosh," Peter said. "That's so wrong."

"Three years ago, I wouldn't even have cared. Kids scared me, I didn't like being around them, never wanted any. Marcus and Natty—Margret's kids—they changed my mind. Now it's just this unexpected, horrible, hole in my life. I'll never experience that joy." She blinked back tears.

"Why did they do that?"

"They let us live there and be poor, but they didn't want us reproducing. If you didn't get your shot, they would find you, and you'd disappear. I could have picked sterilization—but I didn't want to make a permanent choice, not then. Shoot. Getting my tubes tied would have been smarter!" She fought for composure and lost. Her tears came pouring out. "At least that's kind of fixable, sometimes, right?"

Peter stroked her cheek, wiping off her tears. "Alyssa, if you'd chosen surgery, it sounds like they would have just removed your ovaries."

"I hadn't thought of that."

"Besides, you were healed, by Jesus himself. Anything is possible, isn't it?"

"I thought of that. But human eggs are unique. Did you take biology class? Girls are born with every egg we ever produce. If they're gone, they're *gone*."

"The doctors in Liahona are excellent. I'm sure they could run tests and find out. But no matter what the reason is, infertility is never anybody's fault. It just . . . happens." He shrugged. "All the time."

"But if you want a family—with me—I can't give that to you."

"Alyssa, I love *you*. So we're a family of two. So what?"

She blinked. "Do you really mean that?"

"*You* are what matters to me. If it turns out you can have a baby, wonderful. If not, we'll still be happy together. I love you so much."

"I love you, too." She hated being weepy. But he was so sweet, it made her tears worse. "Peter, please, I don't want anyone to know."

"Not even Mom?"

She shook her head. "She'll figure out eventually that I don't have a cycle, but I'd rather wait. I don't need everyone feeling sorry for me. Peter, I've been so worried—if you were looking forward to everything life has to offer—"

"I am looking forward to being married to you," Peter said, and kissed her.

It was a delicious, long kiss, exploring the ways their lips could fit together.

She wished it would never end. She could kiss him like that for hours . . . days . . . weeks.

"Ha! Caught you!" a voice said.

With a startled noise, they broke apart.

Andrew peeked his head over the top of the ladder. "I thought I heard voices," he sneered. "You two want to explain yourselves?"

"We were just . . ." Alyssa was at a loss. She forgot Andrew had the day off.

Andrew folded his arms and laid his upper body on the loft floor. "I know kissing when I see it."

Peter was defensive. "How long have you been listening?"

"Long enough to get an earful."

"Andrew, don't say anything—" Alyssa started.

"And why shouldn't I?"

Peter stopped her with his hand on her arm. "What did you hear?"

Andrew gave a mean smile. "Enough. I got suspicious when neither of you were in the house or out in the yard. Thought I'd check to see if the horses were gone. And what do I find? Making out in the hayloft!" He headed down the ladder, saying, "And if you don't tell Mom, I will."

Alyssa asked, "Tell her we were kissing? So?"

"You know what," he said in a sing-songy tone.

Alyssa gave a terse whisper to Peter. "He *can't* tell her. That is so rude. It's my problem!"

Peter got up and helped Alyssa to stand, careful not to hit their heads on the rafters. "Andrew, before you do, make sure you get the story straight, why don't you? I'm not sure what you heard, but this was a private conversation! I proposed to Alyssa last night. We're engaged. Understand?"

"Married? So soon? Why the rush, I wonder?" Andrew's voice dripped with sarcasm.

"What's wrong with that?" Alyssa said, furious, climbing down after him.

Andrew snapped. "I heard what you said about having a baby! You're not having a cycle, and Mom's gonna figure it out, and you don't want everyone feeling all sorry for you! Peter, you are such a stinking, uptight hypocrite!"

Peter stopped in mid-climb. "*What* did you say?"

Alyssa felt violated. She yelled, "Next time you eavesdrop, why don't you listen to the entire conversation!"

She turned from the last rung, and it was all she could do not to push him. Andrew was shorter than Peter, but stronger than she was.

Andrew stood there, smug. "I heard all I needed to hear."

Peter jumped off the ladder and grabbed Andrew by the collar. "Get the cotton out of your ears! If you were listening, you'd know she can't get pregnant. The good old U.S. government killed her ovaries, all right? She wanted me to know before I marry her, and it happens to be a private matter between her and me, which is why we went up to the hayloft to talk about it. I've barely even kissed her four times. Do you feel stupid yet? If you don't, I'll keep going! You *jerk*!" He shook him forcefully.

"Back off, man!" Andrew pushed Peter away and stalked out of the barn.

Alyssa cleared her throat. She pulled his sleeve and whispered, "Five times."

"Huh?"

"You've kissed me five times. You forgot to count the first one."

He smiled and made it six.

* * * * *

By dinner everyone knew about the engagement, but Andrew didn't mention her infertility. Peter talked to him about it later in the day, once they both calmed down. Alyssa was quietly grateful.

At dinner, Jordan piped up and said, "Jackie was prettier."

"Jordan!" Beverly's tone was sharp.

Alyssa asked, "Wait a minute, who's Jackie?"

Peter looked away and swallowed.

"Well?"

Peter picked at his food. "Just an old girlfriend," he mumbled.

Kellie said, "They were gonna get married too. I remember. Mom had to take the flowers and clothes and stuff back and we waited forever while Mom argued with the store and we didn't even get our money back. Are you really really getting married this time, Peter? I hope so because I like Alyssa a lot."

Beverly said, "Kellie, you were only four. You don't remember."

Peter whispered, "Mom, you never told me—I would have paid you back."

"Peter, it's not like she says. She was too little to understand."

"I do remember!" Kellie said. "I was gonna wear a pretty green dress, and you took it back to the store!" She looked about to cry. Jordan held her hand and gave her a kiss.

"Why am I being ignored here?" Alyssa asked.

Peter said, "I'm sorry, Alyssa. Okay— I told you about the one engagement. I was engaged another time."

Jealous indignation rose up inside. "You were engaged *twice?*"

"Third time's a charm?" he offered, clearing his throat.

Something triggered in her memory. "She had dark red hair, didn't she?"

Alyssa got up, her appetite gone. She went out the kitchen door and headed for the stable. Tiny flakes of snow were falling.

Peter caught up with her halfway there. He stopped her. "How did you know that?"

"I just did." There was a clear image in her mind, but she couldn't place where it came from.

"How could you possibly know what she looked like? Tell me!"

Finally it clicked, with resignation. "It was a dream."

"Another dream? How long ago?"

"I was in college. I dreamed you were with a woman. She had this beautiful auburn hair—she was gorgeous, like a supermodel. She was stealing you from me, and I woke up wanting you back like I've never wanted anything in my life. It felt terrible. I didn't think it meant anything—I chalked it up to unrequited love or lack of closure or something."

"Wait, what year was that?"

"The year my dad died. Summer, 2045." She didn't add, *Right after my overdose.* She had only talked about that with Beverly . . . but with chagrin, she realized that was another issue she would have to bring up soon and take the consequences.

"Alyssa, that's the summer I was dating Jackie."

She felt a chill that did not come from the weather.

"I meant to tell you. She had a negative overall effect on me, you could say." He squirmed. "I don't want this to come between us. I'll tell you anything you want to know."

"I know you've had girlfriends, Peter. That's not it. I'm just going to the stable." She started walking again.

He walked alongside her. "The weather's no good for riding. This flurry's supposed to turn to rain."

"I'm not riding."

"You don't have your coat."

"I'm not cold."

"Alyssa—"

"Peter, the first thing you have to understand about me is that when I need my space, I *need* my space. Please. Let me go. I'll be right back."

He stopped following her. "You're not mad?"

She turned and walked backwards a few paces. "Why should I be mad?"

"I don't know." He shifted the weight on his feet.

She added, "Peter, I was almost engaged once, too. We'll talk about all this in a little while, I promise."

He registered mild surprise. "All right."

He stood in the cold, hugging his arms, and didn't follow.

* * * * *

In the stable, she brushed and curried Teancum until his mane and coat shone.

She absently rubbed the same spot over and over, lost in her thoughts. He stamped and snorted, looking at her with those gigantic brown eyes. "Sorry, boy. I'm not paying attention."

When she'd first arrived, she and Peter had talked about his first fiancée, the one with the stupid name. It was a "T" name . . . there it was. Topaz. But Peter shrugged that off as nothing, a childish crush, relieved the girl had married someone else before he came home from his mission.

This reaction was much stronger. Visceral.

And what was that last night, about *I never stopped loving you,* and *It's you for me or no one?* He was engaged before—not once, twice! This had to be at least his third proposal. Had there been girls who said no? Hmph!

Worse, there *had* been a woman in his life, at the same time, with the same color hair, as when she had that dream. That was the distressing thing. Couldn't she have any normal dreams? It was making her paranoid.

She leaned against Teancum's withers. He turned his head back and blew warm breath on her.

"I'm okay," she said.

He nickered a sound of disbelief. Stupid to try lying to a horse.

She was dating Rob when she had that dream. Afterward, memories of Peter consumed her, reminding her of the way love felt, and that she didn't feel the same way for Rob. It was after that dream that she broke up, refusing his offer to run away with him to Montana. Rob had risked his life to prevent Caldwell from discovering where she was. She was grateful beyond words; but the last thing she told him was that he was inextricably tied to a part of her life she desperately wanted to forget.

That still held true.

The horse whinnied and stamped, impatient. She reached up and stroked the jagged blaze that lent him the look of a warrior.

She resumed her currying. Her mind traced paths of unwritten futures, of *what if . . .*

Eventually she got Teancum a blanket and left the stable.

She laughed to herself. One reason she hadn't gone with Rob was that he planned to buy a ranch and raise sheep. She liked it here more than she expected; sheep ranching might not have been so bad.

* * * * *

Peter stood on the porch, shivering. She expected him to wait indoors—he must be frozen. He looked so forlorn.

The snowflakes turned to raindrops.

As she approached the porch, her mind locked onto something else. She stopped short and took a sharp breath.

"What is it?" Peter asked.

She looked in his starry blue eyes; they held worry and expectation.

"'Wait for me,' I said. I begged you to wait for me. In my dream. And you have."

Peter's face went white. "We need to talk, in private. Now."

"Peter, it's crowded in there, and you're freezing. We can't stay out in the rain."

"The garage. No one ever goes in there at night."

They ran for the large outbuilding as the rain came down in sudden sheets. Peter turned on the lights. Two rusty cars and three tractors were parked in a row. There was an electrical hum in the room. The tractors were plugged into giant outlets, absorbing the energy stored in solar panels on the roof.

Peter powered up the heater in one of the tractor cabs and motioned to her to get in.

Once they were settled, he began, "Alyssa, I never told anyone about the dreams I had when I was dating Jackie. Never. But I had a recurring nightmare of the day you broke your leg out at Camp Keomah. Remember that day? You were ten."

"How could I forget? It was terrible. Joan wouldn't bring us to see you for a whole year."

"In the dreams, you always said, '*wait for me.*' The day you broke your leg, that's what you said, when we raced. I didn't wait that day—I left you behind, and you were hurt. In the dreams, you said you were coming to me . . ."

Her heart pounded. She waited to see if he would finish.

"You said . . . I was the only one who could love you. Every dream ended the same way—I couldn't leave you hurt and afraid again. Jackie didn't want to wait, and she left me."

He squeezed her hand. "But I thought Jackie was so perfect then, that my dreams made no sense. You see—no one had ever measured up to you before. I had you on such a pedestal. I measured every girl I knew against what I remembered of you, what I fantasized being with you would have been like, had we never been torn apart. I figured those dreams were a subconscious extension of that fantasy, my unfulfilled wish that I could be with you instead. But it wasn't realistic. You were lost, and I had to accept that you weren't coming back . . . what choice did I have, but to go on?"

Alyssa didn't want to hear much about how perfect this woman was. "How did you break up?"

"Like the dream warned—she wasn't waiting for me."

"Meaning?"

Peter cleared his throat. "She wanted us to sleep together before the wedding, and I refused. You know that's not what the Church teaches—I was shocked. But I was so willing to forgive . . . so blind . . . I thought we worked through it, only to find out later that she was sleeping around behind my back. She said she had 'needs,' and if I wouldn't satisfy them, she had 'no choice' but to go elsewhere. We were getting married in the *temple*, Alyssa. She was supposed to—do you know what that means?"

Betrayal, hurt, and loss came through in his voice. She felt how deeply this had hurt him, but at the same time her heart did a little leap. It was so rotten that she was instantly relieved of worry that he might still have feelings for this Jackie person.

She answered his question. "I think I do." The temple was holy—a sacred place. More in-depth interviews were required than for baptism, interviews which established worthiness to enter the House of the Lord. Abstinence before marriage was one of the requirements. "What was she thinking?"

"She intended to lie through her interviews and never tell me what she'd done. But I found out." He sighed. "I haven't gone on a single date since. Some girls have asked . . . I couldn't bring myself to try. My dreams said, 'wait' . . . and I was so hurt, I figured I might as well wait, after that."

He forced out a humorless laugh. "I never expected you'd actually show up, though. Can you see why I was so shocked when you got here—why I fought it, at first?"

"Wow," was all she could say for some time.

They sat listening to the hum of the heater, the rain on the roof, the whistle of the wind.

"Can I ask how you found out about her?" Alyssa mused.

"Some guy left a mark on her, two weeks before the wedding date. We had a family barbecue, and we were all goofing off in the yard. Jackie was wrestling around with the twins, and her shirt kinda popped a button or something. It was great big, fresh, right over her heart—not something you'd normally have seen. I couldn't get that image out of my head for months. I felt like hitting something every time I thought about it."

"I can imagine." The story brought back an ugly memory from her own life. "I got a hickey once. It was horrible."

"Once?"

"Yes, once. You find that hard to believe?"

"No, I was just wondering if you want another one," he teased.

"Not if you don't want me to throw up," she said. "Joan beat me for it. It wasn't my fault—I was attacked. My sophomore year, this creep caught me in the hall and got his face all over my neck, and I couldn't get away fast enough." She took a deep breath. "I'm lucky he didn't do worse. I didn't know he left traces. Joan saw it when I got home. She went ballistic. I never saw her that furious, before or since."

"Oh, no," Peter said. He closed his eyes.

"Dad had to take me to the hospital. She broke my ribs."

He swallowed and stroked her hand. "I wish I could have saved you from that."

"Me too." She paused. "You remember, my first day or so here, that I wouldn't explain why Joan thought I had a bad reputation? That's why. I wasn't ready to tell you then. You weren't listening."

"I was kind of a jerk, huh."

She laughed. "I forgive you. I think we were both shocked to see each other."

There was another long pause. Rain drummed on the roof.

Peter spoke first. "Jackie hurt me so bad . . . it's not the same, I know, but I'm learning how hard it is to recover. The sense of betrayal runs so deep . . . and her betrayal can't be anything like how it must feel coming from your own parent, who's supposed to love you no matter what."

"I don't think Joan knew how to love anything. Not even herself."

"That's probably true of Jackie, too," Peter said.

She placed her hand on his arm. "I want you to know this. It is absolutely not in my nature to ever hurt you the way she did. I promise you that."

"Thank you," he said. It was heartfelt.

She brushed a tear off his cheek. "But while we're on hard topics . . ."

"Am I going to hate this?" He clenched his teeth.

"I'm not sure. I told Beverly already. Peter . . . after Dad died . . . I got into an Elation habit for a while . . ."

Once she got talking, she couldn't stop. Everything spilled out. She didn't glamorize the details, but Peter learned more than Beverly had. He took it better than she thought he would. She felt safe enough to talk about how Rob fit into the story, and how he had vanished into the vast unknown.

"I don't think I ever loved him," she finished. "I don't know what I was thinking. I was afraid you'd hate me for having drugs in my past."

"Alyssa, how do I know whether I could have survived that, myself? I doubt it. I'm just so relieved that you survived, so you can be here, holding my hand, totally in love with me and willing to be my wife. As I said last night—you've made me a happy man. All my dreams are coming true."

"That might be a bit too literal, Peter," she said.

He scrunched up his face. "Kiss me and let's not think about that too much."

She did. Then she said, "Let's go inside. This rain is making you get all mushy."

"I can't help it." He kissed her again, longer.

* * * * *

It was still pouring rain. They were soaked to the skin in the few seconds it took to run from the garage to the house.

"I'm so cold," Alyssa said. Peter's teeth chattered louder than hers. It reminded her of her baptism day, and she had to smile.

"I'm sure you two will find a way to warm up," Andrew said from the couch, flipping channels with the remote.

"What's that supposed to mean?" Alyssa said.

Beverly brought them towels. She chided, "Andy, apologize. That's uncalled for."

Peter flashed Andrew an angry look, but his brother wasn't looking. He worked the towel through his sopping wet hair. Alyssa tossed her hair upside-down to dry hers.

Andrew said, "I just can't say anything right lately."

Beverly softened her voice. "Try a little harder, that's all. You know we love you, Andy."

"Yeah. Love you too. My name is *Andrew*, Mom," he scoffed, and stood up. "Nothing's on TV. I'm going to bed."

Beverly asked, "Are you coming out for scriptures and prayer?"

He stepped around her into the hall. "Go on without me."

"Pajama time, Jordan and Kellie," Peter said, snapping his towel in their direction. "Let's go!"

The twins moaned disappointment. It was earlier than usual, but it offered a necessary diversion from Andrew's sulking attitude.

"When did he stop wanting to be called Andy?" Beverly asked.

No one had an answer for that.

CHAPTER 28

ALL IS WELL

Debra, you are the love of my life. I went about this all wrong, and I'm so sorry. Please forgive me. I need you so much.

—Jon Pike,
note card on bouquet of roses

Marcus sucked his thumb at Roberta's house in the dark in the middle of the night.

He was afraid in a new way. It wasn't the same fear he had of Ralph, but it made him want to hide in the back corner of his closet, like he did when Ralph lived with them. If Sister Roberta found him like that, she would ask questions. So he sucked his thumb, instead.

Sister Roberta told him, "You'll see your mama soon. She's getting better every day."

He didn't believe her.

Natty had made a friend.

Marcus didn't want to make friends.

He put his comic book away, except at night, and didn't let anyone touch his backpack.

* * * * *

Margret's mind swam through a haze of sickly green, wilted gardens of rotten vegetables, molding in frozen ground. Strange voices surrounded her, warped, slow, and distorted. Sometimes Bert cleared away the haze like wisps of smoke, and his face came into sharp focus. He sang gospel songs she had never heard before, with words like *come unto Jesus* and *all is well, all is well.* His large rectangular hands, with their long fingers and skin black as pure ebony, encircled her own with warmth, giving her strength, feeding her the will to live.

He talked in her dreams, real words instead of numbers, but the stories made no sense, and she could not remember them once he finished. They floated away like butterflies on the breeze. They were calm and peaceful and reminded her of Papa reading her bedtime stories, filling her mind with fairy tales and fantasies, castles in the sky, heavenly choirs . . .

Bert, Bert, te amo . . .

She had never told a soul. The love she had for him came on with power, different from anything she had ever felt for a man. It terrified her.

Then it was too late, and the government rendered Bert's Christian activist mind as useful as a potted plant on a windowsill.

He held her close until she believed it was real, that they had always been together and forever would be.

Faces of all the many men she ever loved flitted through her mind, laughing, taunting her as they took her, calling her names she well deserved . . .

. . . Her babies were crying, hungry, no food in the house . . .

Ralph appeared, with his unruly red hair and livid green eyes, chasing her with his cigarette butts, burning, burning . . . She screamed in pain.

She shouted at the Ralph-dream, calling him every filthy word she knew. She kicked him as hard as she could. Someone held down her thrashing arms, and she became vaguely aware of beeping hospital monitors, pale unfamiliar walls.

Bert came and cleared away the fear and haze and confusion. She wept in his strong black arms, her one anchor in this sick, green, fevered fog.

* * * * *

Alarms went off in Margret's hospital room. Jon rushed in to pin down her kicking legs, with little success. She bruised him badly in several places. He almost let go.

"What happened?" he yelled to the nurse.

Ginny struggled to free herself from her patient. "I was changing her IV bag, and she grabbed me. I can't get her off me!"

Her curly red hair had come loose from its barrette.

Margret's eyes rolled, the whites showing. She yelled in guttural, unpleasant-sounding Spanish, attacking Ginny with her nails.

"Get her off me!" Ginny shrieked.

Jon was trying to help. He got Ginny's uniform untwisted from Margret's hands, and the young nurse scooted out of reach, panting.

Dr. Marden ran in. "Her fever spiked, didn't either of you see that? It's right there on the monitor! How long has it been up that high?"

"I don't know!" Ginny burst into tears.

Jerry barked an order for a sedative. A nurse in the hall went running.

Jon held Margret down. It took all his strength. The nurse brought the sedative, and Jerry filled a syringe. He tucked it neatly into her IV, and within seconds the thrashing stilled and she fell into deep sleep.

Jon let go. His arms and ribs hurt. She had powerful legs.

Jerry ordered, "Get that fever down STAT. She doesn't need this in her condition!" He turned to leave.

"Jerry, you speak Spanish, what was she saying?" Jon asked, as he and Ginny brought out cooling, damp towels and prepared IV medication for lowering the fever.

"I refuse to translate that," Jerry said. "You don't want to know."

* * * * *

Toward evening, Jon was in the lab examining more endless samples. He put the next slide in the high-powered microscope for inspection.

Jerry snapped his briefcase shut and said, "See you in the morning, Jon."

Something on this slide looked different.

"Jerry, wait!" he called, excited. "I think we have an antibody, look!"

Jerry dropped the briefcase and hurried over to the scope. "I guess I'm not going home after all. And neither are you. Write a note explaining to Debra. I'll get a runner to deliver it."

The message runners were a primitive system, but it got the job done. Jon took out paper and pen. Debra might not appreciate his working late—they'd both gotten used to the regular daytime hours this project afforded. But this couldn't wait.

* * * * *

Margret came into a floating, fleeting state of consciousness. She was in a hospital bed. Why? A monitor beeped, indicating her heartbeat and vital signs, and her forearm looked like a pincushion of IVs and monitoring devices.

The room was dim. Night? She wasn't sure.

Her mind echoed the haunting tune Bert was last singing. *All is well, all is well . . .*

A black man sat in a chair by the window. Bert, here? She had something to say, now, if it was the last thing she ever did. Each word was difficult to form. Her voice came out raspy, hoarse, barely a whisper, but with feeling.

"*Te . . . amo . . . mi . . . amor.*"

"*Que - es - su - amor?*" the man asked, the broken Spanish of someone who never spoke it. Oh . . . she came late to the thought that Bert didn't speak Spanish, either . . . but this was not Bert's voice. Her disappointment was profound. It must be a doctor, or a male nurse.

Scant memories returned to her. The refugee camp. Puking. Lying on the ground, hearing gunshots. ATF. She had caught it. "When . . . am . . . I . . . die?" Margret struggled, choking on each slow word. She couldn't say everything she was thinking. It was miserable and frustrating.

"You're getting better."

"ATF. Whole . . . camp. No . . . cure."

"Rest, Margret. You're going to be fine."

"Where . . . kids? . . . Sick?"

"They're not sick. They're safe. They're being well taken care of, don't worry."

She faded into dreamless sleep.

* * * * *

Jon hurried out of the room as soon as the patient went back to sleep.

The patient is how he thought of her. But she had a name; it was Margret. And Margret had a voice.

That voice said *I love you* in Spanish.

She couldn't mean him. It was delirium, or a dream. But it was a husky, low, sexy voice, and it shot through him like a hot arrow.

Jon thought he was immune to such things. Once he made up his mind to marry Debra, he never entertained a single thought about another woman.

Now his thoughts went crazy all at once, the type of thoughts he normally experienced only for his wife. He was not given to wandering fantasies.

It occurred to him that this scarred, broken woman had likely never been loved tenderly in her life, and both wanted and deserved to be. With the thought came a vivid, if brief, image in his mind of giving her exactly that kind of loving.

It didn't help that Deb was physically recovering from the miscarriage, and he couldn't simply turn his energy toward her. Debra needed tenderness and closeness from him for the next while, not raw physical demands. Encouraging such thoughts, even for Debra, would do no good. They had no outlet. He'd managed to shut them off temporarily, and was doing well—until now.

He rushed to the hospital chapel and knelt down.

Heavenly Father, help me! he prayed, silently. He couldn't let anyone overhear. *I love my wife, I love my wife, I love my wife.*

He tried to call Debra's face to mind, but Margret's was stuck in his consciousness. He saw every line and detail of her face, how one eye tilted slightly more than the other, her full lips,

her oval fingernails, her delicate toes . . . He squeezed his eyes
shut, hoping to block out worse, but worse played out on the
stage of his mind regardless.

I'm a doctor! He was always professional. He never thought
about his patients that way—never.

Father! It was a mental shout. *Give me strength.*

Gradually the images faded as he fought them. He felt hollow
and stricken.

At length he could imagine Debra again; her sweet, passionate
kisses, their beautiful boy Zach, their good life together . . . except
for this contention in the last couple of months.

He would ask to be reassigned, if he had to. Jerry wouldn't like
that. He didn't want to have to explain.

It might only be a stray thought.

He took a deep breath and returned to duty—in the lab, not
Margret's room.

* * * * *

Margret slowly opened her eyes. The man she saw before was
there, going over her chart. Not a nurse, then. A doctor. It was
early afternoon, by the light.

"How . . . am I . . . doing?" Her words came much easier.

"Excellent. You're staying conscious today."

Deep in her body she felt something, a narrow glowing
thread spinning its way through her ravaged systems. It shone
like polished silver, winding through, cell by cell, restoring
health.

She took a good look at the doctor. He had a triangular
athletic torso, well-muscled arms, long legs. Small round glasses
framed his oval face. In the light, and fully awake, she'd never
have mistaken him for Bert. Bert was the color of ebony and a
good deal taller, and he was made of long rectangles—lanky
arms, bony elbows and knees. When they first met she told him
he looked like a walking lamppost with hinges. She loved Bert's
smile most, too broad for his face and filled with impossibly
huge teeth.

"Who are you?" she asked.

"I'm Dr. Jonathan Pike."

The name sounded familiar, but she couldn't place it. "Where are my kids? Are they okay?"

She felt guilty, daydreaming about Bert without giving them a second thought.

"They're healthy. They're staying with my parents, Roberta and Clive Pike. Your kids are terrific. My folks love 'em to pieces."

Relief washed over her.

"I'm going to live?"

"It's been touch and go, but you're going to make it." Dr. Pike smiled, showing a decent set of teeth. He looked maybe younger than she was.

She felt vaguely insulted. They put a green doctor on an ATF case? Why? No insurance? Or did they expect her to die anyway, so it didn't matter?

Her mind was fuzzy. She'd figure that all out later.

"You are one *muy* good-looking man," she said, as the thought came to her, delayed a stroke by comparing him to Bert. Tact wasn't her finest point, and illness only left her more . . . herself. "You married?"

"Yep. I have a baby boy too. He's adorable."

"Da-amn," she said, drawing the word out to two syllables. Rotten luck.

His eyebrows went up.

"Just kidding, eh?" she said, and coughed suddenly. A nurse appeared from nowhere and held a pan under her chin for the spit. When she finished, she said, "No offense."

"None taken," he said.

The nurse looked in the pan. "No blood."

"Good," Dr. Pike said. He wrote something on his chart.

The nurse was a young redhead with startling pale green eyes and freckled skin, not unlike Ralph's complexion, but with a kind smile.

"Who are you?" Margret asked.

"I'm Ginny Meier, your day nurse. I've been with you the whole time."

"Ginny takes care of all your detail work," Dr. Pike said. "IVs, catheter, bathing, all that stuff."

"Oh." She didn't know such things had been going on.

"That's my job," Ginny said, her voice bright.

Her mind worked out the forgotten puzzle. Finally it connected. *Jon and Debra Pike*—the names written on that tattered slip of paper she carried for so long. "I know who you are! Alyssa's friend, Jon Pike. The name on my paper. She didn't say you were a doctor. I'm sorry, eh. Your wife's name is . . . it's Debra."

"You got it. Good job, after being so sick." He laughed.

"I have ATF?"

"You did."

"You didn't euthanize me?" Margret wondered.

Ginny answered. "We didn't have to. You were in quarantine, and your organs never deteriorated—you're lucky your eyes are intact. Do you remember being in the bubble?"

"No. How long have I been here?"

"About two weeks," Ginny said.

It felt like two or three days.

Dr. Pike said, "We lifted the quarantine today. You can see your kids as soon as you're strong enough to manage a visit. They'll be so excited that it might be hard to contain them."

"My kids are okay . . ." Tears ran down her cheeks as it sunk in.

Ginny stroked Margret's hair, soothing her.

Dr. Pike moved to the door, as though remembering something forgotten and urgent. "Ginny, can you take it from here? I've got to run home."

"I've got it, Doc."

"It's good to see you up, Margret," he said, and left.

Ginny's touch on her head soon returned Margret to sleep, solemn peace filling her heart.

CHAPTER 29

TE AMO

Thanksgiving is next week, and we're having the usual discussions over whose parents we're having which meal with . . .

—Debra Pike,
personal journal entry

Outside Margret's door, Jon found Evie Jones, one of Dr. Wheat's nurses. "Can you find Dr. Wheat and see if he can finish my rounds? I don't feel well." His ribs felt sucked inward, like his heart was a black hole collapsing in on itself.

"I'll get him," Evie said. "Dr. Pike, are you okay?"

"I'll be fine. Could you tell Dr. Marden too, please? Thanks."

He climbed on his bicycle and rode. Guilt seeped into every thought, refusing to leave him be. Margret's words ran through his brain: *You are one muy good-looking man . . . You married? . . . Da-amn . . .*

He forced himself to concentrate on Debra and baby Zach. He could never betray them. They were his whole world. But conversing with Margret had brought back all his thoughts from before, and more, in a frenzy. The person behind that incredibly sexy voice thought he was attractive. A thought came . . . *what if it didn't matter . . .*

But it did matter; more than his own life it mattered. A mistake that serious would cost him his church membership, his eternal covenants, every blessing he ever held dear and sacred.

He pedaled through streets in a blur, not home, but to his dad's office. He went in and greeted the receptionist. "Hi, Sister Carmichael, is anyone with him now?"

"No, go on in, Jon."

He rapped the doorframe to get his dad's attention. Clive looked up.

"What is it, son? Shouldn't you be at the hospital?"

His words tumbled out. "Dad, I'm having a problem I never had before and never expected and I don't know how to make it go away." The black-hole sensation intensified, threatening to tear him apart. "I need a Priesthood blessing, please? If you would?"

Clive Pike furrowed his brow. His close-cropped hair was gray at the temples. He placed his huge brown hands palms-down on his desk and pushed himself up. He went to the office door and said, "Miriam, let us be for a while, would you?"

"Sure thing, Brother Pike," Sister Carmichael answered.

Clive shut the door and locked it. "What kind of problem might this be?"

Jon lowered his head and whispered, "Dad, it's too hard for me to say."

"Say."

"It's about a . . . a woman. I'm having all these thoughts about her, and I'm fighting them, I am. I've prayed so hard. I don't want a relationship with anyone but Debra—honest—but these awful thoughts keep popping up in my head. I need them to go away!"

There was an uncomfortable pause.

"Does this woman return your feelings?"

Jon shook his head no. Her words floated back into his mind . . . *You married?* . . . "It's not like I talked to her about it."

"That would be a mistake."

"I knew *that*."

"How long has this been going on?"

"Two days."

His father suppressed a smile. "I'm proud to know you keep your mind so pure, son. Tell me something. How are you and Debra doing? Really?"

It took him a minute to answer. "Ever since Debra lost the baby, she's gone crazy in the head, doing strange things I don't understand, and then we fight about it. I do all the work to make up afterwards, like it's never her fault."

The ATF research was still confidential. He had to talk around that part of their argument, but it was a sore spot.

"She says she's coping in her own way, and I need to deal with it, and I don't know how to deal with that. It feels like we don't even know each other anymore."

"And you don't think these thoughts could be a side effect of things not going smoothly at home?"

He hadn't considered that.

His father said, "You're most vulnerable when you're not close to your wife, Jon. Yes, I will give you a blessing. But I expect the real problem lies more in your marriage than in an inappropriate thought. Make good with Debra. The loss of a baby is terrible hard on a young mama."

Jon was aggrieved that his father took this confession so casually. Debra's answer to prayer about his research came to mind and haunted him: *The danger lies not in the direction you expect.* His heart raced in panic. "Dad, I know that's true, but I'm terrified this could get worse."

"I understand, son." Concern showed in Clive's eyes. He indicated an office chair, and Jon sat down.

His father stood behind him and placed those large, heavy hands on his head. The weight was comforting and familiar. Jon remembered many blessings from his youth, from being ordained to the different offices of the Priesthood, and further back in time, to his baptism. These same strong arms had immersed him in the warm water of the font, and he had felt clean and shining all that day. He wished he could feel that way again.

He felt tarnished, sullied, and unclean.

His father began the blessing, then took a long pause. Jon squirmed in the chair.

"The Lord God our Father loves you and knows your sorrows. In due time, you will receive further revelation concerning the child you have lost.

"However, in your time of grief, I remind you that Satan watches for weakness in his prey. Remember that he has no power to tempt you beyond your capacity, and as you continue in prayer, these unrighteous desires you are experiencing will fade.

"I warn you, Jonathan, that notwithstanding the great work you are called to do in the Lord's kingdom, if you do not heed every prompting of the Holy Spirit as you work on this project, that *you will fall*."

Jon felt a tear drip onto his hair, then another. It startled him. His father's hands trembled. Jon's own tears fell, sorry beyond words for telling that he had caused his father such pain.

Clive continued, "You must work harder to help your sweet wife cope with a loss she feels so intensely. Help her express the tender feelings of her heart, and rekindle the love you know you share."

He finished the blessing in the name of Christ and took his hands from Jon's head.

Jon wiped his eyes. His dad handed him a box of tissues and sat down behind his desk.

Jon waited, reminded of a time when he broke LaDell's doll on purpose and got told on by his little brother Danny. Jon shook off the image of himself as a little boy, facing his father with the broken doll on the desk, its head ripped off, cottony doll guts protruding out of the neck.

His father said, "Son, after my mama died from bad meth, my papa brought us out the 'hood of Detroit. He gave up drinking, drugs, cigarettes, every one of his vices. He raised us to be strong black men."

The tangent confused him. "You told me this before, Dad."

"What I seen as a kid in Detroit forty years ago was things you don't even imagine. Me and your mama sheltered you kids. But my papa worked hard to make his way and live right, to give us boys a fighting chance to make good in this world. By the time we found the Church, when I was sixteen, the Gospel fit us like a glove. Do you hear what I'm saying?"

Jon wrinkled his brow. "Sure, but . . ."

"Strong men keep their family together, no matter what it takes. I raised you to be a strong black man. I expect that of you. I'm saying, if your grandpa kept *us* together, you had better be a big enough man to keep *your* family together. You have it more good here than you'll ever know."

His father was so intense that Jon barely maintained eye contact.

"I seen the way people looked at my daddy. He was so poor, he got treated like a criminal everywhere he went. Didn't matter if he was polite, or how right he spoke. He was feared. Just for being poor and having dark skin. Feared in the bank line. Feared at the store. Feared just walking down the street. He hated it. *I* hated it. He was a good man. And you have *no* right to bring that burden back down on our people. It won't take much for even these righteous white people to revert to old ways. Those ways ain't been gone long, and they ain't full gone neither. They're just hidden, waiting for a reason to pop back out. If you don't believe me, just you watch and see what happens if you make a mistake."

His dad sat with his jaw clenched.

"Dad, I could never forget where I came from!"

Clive jabbed a finger into his desk to punctuate his words. "I'm saying, don't forget where we have trod as a people. What those much older than you have worked all our lives to correct and make better. Don't you dare mess that up for the rest of us."

Jon gave a humble, "Yes, Dad."

His father sat back in his chair, stretching his arms against his desk. He let out a puff of air.

"Now that I said my piece, Jon . . ." His father shut his eyes. "That's not the most important thing. You are. Son, I need you with us forever. I don't want to live to see you lost in the ways of sin."

"I won't be, Daddy, I won't."

"I'm proud of the choices you made in your life. You don't take your Priesthood for granted. You exercise it well. You married a fine woman, in the temple, for time and all eternity. Debra's solid. She's struggling now, but the bedrock of her faith is strong."

Jon nodded.

"I don't have to remind you that if you fall, Jesus stands ready to raise you up, or that *not* falling is forever better than having to work out a hard, miserable repentance. We taught you that your whole life." He paused. "But I want you to know your mama and I will always love you. We won't stand in the way of natural consequences, but however this turns out, we'll help you get by. But I'm begging you, son, *choose right.*"

"I told you this felt dangerous, Dad. You feel it too, don't you?"

His father nodded, somber. "You'll be strong enough to bear it, son. I have faith in you. When you look the tiger in the eye, as you have, it can't sneak up on you."

"Daddy, I'm so afraid!" Jon began to weep. Huge tears fell into his lap.

Clive came around the desk. He hugged him tight in his arms, until Jon had cried himself out.

Then Jon headed home to Debra.

* * * * *

Debra jumped when her husband walked in the door.

"Hi, baby," Jon said.

"I didn't expect you. Are you finished with the antibody work already?" Zach was crying, and she paced their small living room bouncing him in her arms. She had on the same gray sweatshirt that she'd worn to bed, and all the day before. Zach just spit up all down one sleeve. She hadn't combed her hair either, a mistake when it was so long.

The last thing she felt up to was her husband doing something unexpected and weird.

"No, I'm just taking a break." He kissed her cheek and took the baby from her arms. "I wanted to be with you. Mom's coming over to get Zach."

"You can't just leave work! Does Jerry know? I would have changed clothes—"

"Baby, it's just me. And it's not like I could call."

Zach kept crying.

"Hold him facing out," Debra said, irritated.

"I thought I'd try it this way."

"He doesn't like being held that way."

Jon turned the baby as she asked. "Does he need to eat?"

"I just fed him. He's fighting sleep, is all."

"How does holding him facing out help him sleep?"

"Did you come home special just to fight with me?"

Jon sighed. "Debra, I'm sorry, honest. I want to spend time with you. I miss you."

"You know Zach won't take formula, and I don't have a bottle pumped."

"He can eat cereal, then. He took formula for me once, when you were gone. Don't stress. She's coming for him, bottle or no bottle." He shifted Zach to face the other way, lying over his shoulder.

"I don't want *her* seeing me like this!"

"What's wrong with how you look?"

Debra recognized defeat. "Fine."

"Baby, we both need time alone, without him."

"My arms will feel too empty," she complained.

"I'll hold you," he offered.

"It's not the same." She saw the hurt look on his face and explained. "Jon, even Zachary doesn't fill up the empty hole Yvette left inside me."

"I just don't want us to fall apart. I love you so much."

Debra exhaled hard. "Fine."

She scratched her head. When did she last wash her hair? The days blurred together so bad that she wasn't sure. Not today, or yesterday.

Zach settled down to sleep on Jon's shoulder—facing in. Jon didn't show off the victory, either. He nuzzled the baby's head with his nose and lips.

The room was suddenly quiet.

"What did you want to do?" she asked. Jon always had a plan. No matter what his answer, she was determined not to like it.

Before Yvette made such a chasm in her life, she'd have pounced on this as prime time for intimacy. Fear now held her hostage. Fear of pregnancy, fear of another miscarriage, fear, even, of being too close to Jon. She had bricked up a solid wall between them, and wasn't ready to knock it back down.

Jon smiled that silly sheepish grin, the smile that intoxicated her when they were dating.

"I thought I could braid your hair, while we talk things out."

If he didn't look so cute, and if he wasn't holding a sleeping baby, she could have screamed. Out of the multitude of possible ideas, this one took her by surprise.

"N. O. *No!*"

"What's so wrong with that?"

"For one, you don't know how."

"I did LaDell's hair all the time."

"So I heard!"

"You talked to LaDell about my braiding her hair?"

Debra said, "You pulled half her hair out!"

Jon grinned. "She's my baby sister, not my wife. She wouldn't hold still, so I pulled. Come on, I won't do that to you."

"I happen to like it this way." Debra folded her arms. Her hair was strung out every which way, and only after she said it did she think about how bad it looked. "I'll look like a ten-year-old. I suppose you want to put beads in it too?"

Jon relented. "It was a stupid idea. I wasn't trying to upset you."

He looked so hopeless and forlorn that something inside Debra crumbled. She heard herself say, "It's okay, we'll spend the day braiding my hair." She rolled her eyes and went to gather Zach's things for Roberta.

"We can take it out, after," he offered.

"This is going to be a colossal waste of time," she muttered, out of earshot, stuffing diapers, toys, and a change of clothes into Zach's bag.

Man, she was gonna look scary. At least he'd let her take it back out without getting offended. He seemed more interested in the process than the result, like a three-year-old with finger paints.

That's exactly how her hair would look too—like a three-year-old's finger painting, braids in all different sizes on her head, sticking out any old way.

* * * * *

After Zach left with Roberta, the apartment was too quiet. "Are you sure she wants to keep him through dinner?" Debra asked. "He'll scream the whole time. He doesn't like those tribal masks on their wall, they scare him."

"He'll be fine. Does your hair need washing first?"

There was no getting out of this. "Yes." She headed for the bathroom.

He followed her. "Please—would you let me do it?"

"Now you want to wash my hair." She put a hand on her hip. "Why?"

"When I was a boy, I loved having mom scrub my head."

"Ha! LaDell said you wouldn't wash your hair for a month!"

He laughed. "You need to stop talking to that girl."

"Oh, no—I'm learning a lot." Her tongue went to her cheek.

"That's when I was ten! When I was five, I loved Mom scrubbing my head in the tub."

Debra's eyes narrowed. "Mm-hm. In the tub. Is this an elaborate plot to get my clothes off?"

"You didn't used to mind, baby," he said. "But no. That's not at all what this is about. I just want to take care of you. I won't peek. Not even if you beg."

"Oh, ho!" The challenge brought a smile to her face.

He placed his hand on her shoulder, serious. "Debra, I just want to do something for you that feels nice. That's all. How about one of those facials, instead?"

A facial now. Heaven forbid. At least Jon knew the basic *concept* of braiding.

Debra melted a little more from the warmth of his attention.

She felt as nervous as she had on their wedding night, when they had never been alone together before. For the first time in a month, she felt twinges of interest in that direction. But all she said was, "A bath is fine, if there's plenty of bubbles. You go on out until I'm in the water."

He smiled, and didn't make any of his silly teases about *I am a doctor, madam.* He just said, "Let me know when you're ready," and ran water, added lavender and chamomile, and started the bubbles before he went out.

* * * * *

The warm water made her drowsy. Jon lathered her hair and found all the tight places on her scalp that she didn't even know were there, relaxing her further.

He braided her hair as she soaked, and the gentle tugs as his hands moved the locks back and forth brought back memories of her mother's loving hands working on her head. They were good memories, happy carefree days, little-girl days filled with hopscotch, going to the swimming pool all summer, riding her pink-ribboned bike fast down the big hill, having none of these grown-up worries to weigh her spirit down.

Jon combed and parted each section with more care than she expected. He made single braids, and they came out about the length of her hand, half the thickness of her fingers.

"You do know how," she said. "I'm sorry."

"Apology accepted," he said, without gloating.

"The water's getting cold."

Jon turned on a trickle of hot water. She swished it with her toes.

Jon asked, "Do you want to talk about Yvette? I'd like to listen."

Debra took a deep breath, staring at her toes poking up through the bubbles.

"There's so many unanswered questions, Jon," she said. Their doctrine fell silent in a few places; miscarriage was one of them. "Do you think she's waiting for another chance to be born, or is she in the spirit world, passed on?"

Jon said, "I've wondered that too. She could have moved on."

That line of thought agreed with the voice she'd heard. "It's possible she was saying goodbye . . . I didn't think of it that way when she spoke to me. She said, 'Thank you, Mama, for giving me my body.'"

"It sounds like she moved on, but . . . I guess we'll know for sure someday," he sighed.

Deb said, "I don't want to wait. I want to know now. I miss her so much . . ."

Jon said, "Remember that dream I had when we were first married, where I saw a line of children and knew they were ours?"

Debra chuckled. "Yes. I got mad at you because you forgot to count them!"

"Yeah. I sure wasn't thinking. But there were at least four. Definitely more than one or two."

It was quiet a few moments while he worked, the trickle of hot water making an oddly cheerful splash into the bathwater.

She asked, "I wonder if she would've had your eyes, or mine?"

"She'd be so pretty if she had your smile."

"I wonder how she would have played with Zach. If they would have been friends."

Jon added, "If maybe they *were* friends, before they came here."

"I wonder if she would have wanted to be a ballerina, or play soccer, or if she'd ask us for a puppy when she got bigger. What kind of puppy would she want?" she asked.

"German Shepherd?"

Debra laughed. "No, she'd probably want a fuzzy lap dog she could brush and dress up and put pink bows on its ears." Suddenly she was crying. "My own baby girl . . ."

"She wouldn't want your dad's big old dogs," Jon said.

She had to laugh through her tears, agreeing.

"A baby girl would be so sweet," Jon said. "Pink ruffled dresses, pretty bows and lace . . ."

They daydreamed together about her possible features, likes and dislikes, wishes and aspirations, futures that could never be. Debra began to comprehend the depth of Jon's pain, and while he wasn't complaining, she realized she hadn't been good to him through any of this.

"I'm so sorry, Jon, I've been so involved with my own grief, I . . ."

"I understand, baby," he said, sympathetic and loving.

As she poured out her feelings, it felt like she was falling in love with him all over again. She found it didn't bother her that the bubbles were slowly popping.

At length she was able to whisper, "Jon, did I do something wrong?"

"Her death can't be a punishment. The Lord doesn't work that way."

"I know, but I was so scared. I wasn't ready for another baby. I didn't want her." Her voice broke. "Jon, how could I *not* have wanted her?"

"Baby . . ." Jon took her chin, caressing her cheek. She looked into his warm brown eyes an infinite moment, letting him see all the pain the past month had brought on. "It's not your fault we lost her."

"Are you sure?"

"I'm positive." He kissed away the tears rolling down her cheeks.

Debra reached her hands to his face and brought his lips to hers. He returned the kiss with exquisite tenderness.

With every braid he formed, Jon had been gently, quietly tapping away at each brick in that wall in her soul, until at last the wall was gone. Pure love washed through her in place of it, forgiving him, forgiving herself also, for everything.

Jon tried to break off the kiss before it went far, but she disallowed him, pulling him close, wetting his shirt in the bathwater.

"Your braids aren't done," he mumbled.

"Finish it later." She kissed him with increased passion. "Promise me. I want you to."

He murmured, "I promise."

"Oh, gosh, Jon, it's been way too long," she said.

He gave his tacit agreement.

* * * * *

Much later, Debra stretched out on her stomach, resting her head on folded arms. Jon leaned against his pillow and carried out his promise by candlelight, his fingers moving gently through her hair. Only a small section by the nape of her neck remained.

She had slept right through Jon's leaving and returning with the baby. "Are you sure Zach was okay today?" she asked.

"Mom said he played terrific all day. He fussed a little bit, but he stayed in a good mood." Zach was down for the night; Jon had taken care of him while she rested. Roberta had sent over a nice dinner, too.

She sighed contentment.

"Do you mean to leave these in?" Jon asked.

"As long as they last."

Jon leaned over so she could see him smile. "Really?"

She smiled back. "Really."

CHAPTER 30

HIS BROTHER'S KEEPER

The wormlike organism that results utterly fails to stay viable after the third insertion. I see great value in pursuing it, if it could possibly cause human tissue regeneration, but its DNA is too unstable to support life. I am perplexed.

—Dr. Joel Kensington,
private research notes

Peter woke in the night to use the restroom. Again he noticed light seeping under Andrew's bedroom door.

He knocked. "Andrew? Are you having trouble sleeping?"

"I'm fine," he answered.

Peter turned the knob and peeked in. "What are you doing?"

Andrew turned from his desk, surprised. "Hey!"

The picture on the screen registered with shock. "How did you get past Mom's web filters?"

"Relax, it's CGI, and it's not the internet. And as if you never saw a naked woman before. Cut the act."

"I wouldn't be proud of it, if I had! Turn that filth off."

"What are you going to do, tell on me?" Andrew said.

"That garbage isn't allowed in this house, and you know it." Peter averted his eyes.

"Come on, bro, don't tell me you never looked. Nobody's that pure."

"I had very good reasons not to." His eyes kept floating back to the screen; he squeezed them shut. Moral reasons were good enough; but Peter was once misinformed that Alyssa had taken on that career. He stayed completely away, unwilling to destroy his pure memories of her. He had since learned it was her sister, Lauren, who was involved with the filth, but his automatic avoidance was deeply ingrained.

Andrew laughed.

"Andy, turn that off. Now." He forced the words through clenched teeth and closed eyes.

"This is baby stuff! How dare you come down on me for this when you're upstairs doing *her!*"

"Doing *what?*" His eyes flew open and focused on Andrew.

"I heard you, sneaking up to Alyssa's room in the middle of the night. Tell me. If you're up there getting a real piece of action, what harm can my fake CGI girl do?"

Peter's jaw dropped. He clenched and unclenched his fist. "First, there is nothing like that between me and her: nothing."

"Sure there isn't."

"Second, I *did* go to Alyssa's room the other night. Mom knows all about it. Ask her! The Spirit woke me up and sent me running—not sneaking—to her room. I cast Satan out of her room! We didn't tell everybody, because there's no sense scaring the twins, and you don't care! You didn't even feel the earthquake. Mom did, and she's at the end of the hall, past your room." He pointed that direction.

Andrew looked puzzled.

Peter grabbed him by the collar of his pajamas, slammed him against the door, and hissed, "What harm does it do? *You let Satan into this house!*"

"I did not!" Andrew pushed him off. "Shut up!"

"You invited him in with this crap!"

Peter was livid. He pushed past Andrew to the computer. They hadn't wrestled each other down in years, but he'd do it. This was no childish quarrel.

Andrew said, "What are you doing?"

"I'm doing what Dad would do if he caught you." He yanked the screen off the wall and jerked the keyboard off the desk, ending the offensive program with a squawk from disconnected speakers.

"That's not what Dad would do! It's mine, I bought it!"

Peter said, "I knew I should check your hard drive. Did I do it? No. Why? I trusted you, Andrew. You blew it."

"You can't take that, it's mine." Andrew's voice was feeble.

"I can't make you quit, but I *can* keep you from bringing your filthy habits home. From now on it stays out of this house. Understand?"

"I don't believe this."

"You could at least act a tiny bit sorry or ashamed of yourself, couldn't you?" He shuffled the computer parts in his arms. "Couldn't you?"

They were silent, staring each other down.

"Fine," Peter said at length. He hauled the equipment out. Andrew offered no more resistance.

He felt dirty even touching the hardware. Peter couldn't blame him for normal hormones; this stuff wasn't easy to stay away from. But he seethed with rage. Andrew brought in this evil and broke the protective shield about the house. *Andrew* put Alyssa in grave danger. That was unconscionable.

He was too angry to see straight.

Without thinking, he flung open the front door and hurled out the equipment with all his might.

The pieces crashed to the ground and broke open. He stared at the destroyed, scattered pieces shining in the moonlight. Responsibility was a dead weight on his shoulders. How could he be both brother and parent?

Everything fell to him.

"Dad, where are you? What am I supposed to do?" Peter cried out, and his legs carried him out the door, around to the backyard, down to the stable. He climbed the ladder to the hayloft and collapsed in the straw, sniffling and crying like a little boy for a long time.

Memory returned the vision he had, the night he proposed, then had prayed until dawn.

Feed my sheep.

Again he felt the gnarled wooden staff in his hands, worn smooth to his father's grip, not his own. It didn't fit him any better yet. *How?*

It stopped his crying. He climbed down and thought about it all the way back to the house:

Feed my sheep.

* * * * *

A crash outside woke Alyssa from a sound, dreamless sleep. She heard Peter's voice under her window, loud and angry. Then footsteps.

She crept down the stairs, and flattened herself against the wall when she saw Andrew cross the living room. He looked furious. The front door was open. He went out, and she heard him cursing in the yard. She backed up a few stairs, so she wouldn't be seen, and waited to see what it was all about.

* * * * *

Andrew surprised Peter on the back porch, waiting in the shadows. "I am so sick of your hypocrisy, I could puke."

"Yeah? I'm tired of being called a hypocrite, especially by you!"

"At least I know what I am. I don't pretend to be something I'm not."

"Who says I'm pretending?"

"You are. You went back on your word."

"Excuse me?"

"You swore, after Jackie, you'd only marry a virgin. What do you call *her*?"

Peter reacted. He punched Andrew in the jaw and it knocked him backward. Andrew kicked Peter off balance as he went down, and they rolled together on the deck in their pajamas.

They kept their voices low and terse. Peter didn't want to wake anyone up. But Andrew had to be taken down for that. "You take that back!"

Andrew pushed him in the chest. "What is it with you? Why do you keep picking up trash?"

"Alyssa is not trash!"

"Yeah? Who died and made you the expert?"

They rolled. Peter tried to pin Andrew and missed. Through his red haze of anger, Peter heard Alyssa's voice: "Peter, stop it! Both of you!"

"Don't be stupid, man! She can't be a virgin, not where *she* came from!"

Peter caught his legs. "She was just baptized, you bonehead. If I say it doesn't matter, *it doesn't matter!*"

"So? Jackie lied! You can't know she isn't lying to get whatever she wants! You can't just trust her, you idiot!" Andrew rolled to the top. "Don't you dare make the same mistake—!" His breathing was ragged. He was tiring out.

Peter got out of the pin, grabbed Andrew's leg with his, and took the upper hand.

"Mistake?" Peter hissed. "She's not Jackie! It's not the same!"

"All Central City sluts are the same!" Andrew kicked and missed.

Peter swerved away and finally pinned him. "Take that back! Now!"

Andrew struggled as Peter got his knee on his brother's chest.

Andrew's right arm was stuck behind his back. "Get . . . off . . . me," he grunted, furious.

"You're jealous—is that it, creep? Watching that smut?" Peter raised his fist. "You'd better not be thinking like that about my future—"

"No!" Andrew tried to spit on him. He struggled to form words as Peter's weight compressed his lungs. "You . . . do better . . . than some . . . cheap piece of—"

Peter lunged so that Andrew groaned under him, then gasped for air.

"For what it's worth, you two morons, I *am* a virgin." Alyssa's angry voice barely registered.

Peter could sense her by the door, to his right, but his eyes were on Andrew. "The same mistake?" he spat out. Breathing hard, he forced Andrew's face toward his, one hand gripping his chin.

Andy refused to make eye contact.

"Peter, I'm talking to you," Alyssa said.

"I heard you," Peter said. "Not—me—the same mistake—twice." His breath came in panting gasps.

"Let him go, Peter!"

"You mean—the same mistake—as *you*," he finished, pointing a finger in Andrew's face.

Peter slid off his brother's chest. "This isn't about Alyssa at all, is it? Or your computer. This is about Sienna." Peter opened his clenched fist and stretched his fingers. Each word dropped into his heart like a lead weight. A dark feeling inside his chest swelled and broke open, releasing a torrent of shame and horror.

Alyssa was vehement. "Excuse me; do you have any idea how hard that was to say? I've kept that a guarded secret my entire life. Andrew's right. Virginity *is* unheard of, where I come from. If anyone finds out, they—" She stopped short, and swallowed.

Peter looked up at her at last, and they locked eyes. Anguish registered on her face.

"They try to take it from you," she whispered, more to herself than to him. "Oh, Andrew—I am so sorry."

Andrew scooted a few inches away. "I don't want your pity."

Peter said, "Andy, tell me you didn't. She *didn't*."

"I didn't say a darn thing."

Peter stared.

Finally, a trace of a nod. Then tears.

Peter gathered his brother up in his arms and rocked him. Where moments before were enmity and rage, Andrew now curled into Peter's chest like a baby and wept bitterly.

Alyssa sat down on the deck, next to them but apart, her arms wrapped about her knees, looking out across the shadows of fields and hills. The barest trace of dawn lit the countryside.

Peter watched the breeze blow through Alyssa's hair, his body keenly aware of the shaking of his brother's sobs as he lay in his arms, and knew he had never felt more lost.

CHAPTER 31

SOCIAL ADAPTATION

> *Peter overreacted with the computer. I don't know how I slept through all that. Andrew's face looks terrible—I guess Peter has a solid right hook. I was very upset. Those two haven't come to blows in years. They told me Peter apologized, and he's going to see if he can replace it on the next trip to Liahona. Still, I'm revoking Andy's wireless privileges, and I made it clear that that filth does not come in this house.*
>
> *They were all acting weird today. I have a nagging feeling this is only the tip of the iceberg.*
>
> *. . . Peter rededicated the house tonight.*

—Beverly,
personal journal entry

The silver thread Margret felt inside gained strength and dimension, working to restore her body to its proper state. She needed help getting up to void, but by noon the following day she could go by herself. Ginny promised Marcus and Natty would visit by nightfall.

By late afternoon, Margret felt up to eating. They brought her chicken broth and flavored gelatin.

Dr. Pike returned while she was eating. "How do you feel?"

"Lousy," she said, sipping the broth. "I feel like hell."

Dr. Pike choked.

"What?"

"Margret, I'm afraid you'll need to avoid that language as long as you're in New Hope. All right?"

"That's not even a bad word!" she said.

"Around here it is. You will not get on well with people if you talk like that. Try, okay?"

"Sorry, eh. I didn't know. What are you here for—didn't you do rounds already?"

"I just had a quick question for you before I go home."

"What is it?" She took another sip of broth.

The grin on his face couldn't get any bigger. "When you were a little girl . . . did you ever think you'd grow up and save the world?"

"That is one stupid-a . . . stupid question, Doc." It was hard not to throw in unacceptable words. "No half-breed poor runt like me ever saves the world. We're why it needs saving in the first place."

She was wrong. The grin got bigger. "But you may have done exactly that," he said.

"Say what?"

"You're producing an antibody to the ATF virus. And you are the only survivor we are aware of. The lab is busy manufacturing a vaccine. If it works, we'll inoculate New Hope . . . then the world."

He paused to let it sink in. "Congratulations!"

She put down her spoon. "You lie."

"Nope. We don't know why, but you fought this thing off rather than let it kill you. And that in turn could save everyone else. It's a good thing, too—we had two patients come down sick last night, hunters. They ate a sick deer without knowing it. Cooked it rare, too. They'll be first to receive the antibody. We have people working around the clock to produce it. Without you, New Hope would be in serious danger."

"What about the refugee camp I was with?"

"We found them—from a distance. We don't have high-tech environmental suits to get closer. But we pinpointed the contaminated river and sent a warning to Sioux City."

Dr. Pike was grim. "We have five thousand people here, and all modern communications are down. We printed flyers and announced warnings everywhere."

A vague memory surfaced. "What happened to that man? The one who helped us get here. He didn't get sick."

"You arrived with just your two children."

"No, no. There was a man. He gave us blankets and made rabbit stew. He knew we were going to New Hope . . . I don't know how he knew that. I hadn't told nobody, eh."

"What's his name? I can look him up, if he's one of us, by chance."

The name was on the edge of memory, but it floated away like evaporating mist. "I don't remember now." His features blurred in her mind; it was like her memory needed glasses. She frowned. "Maybe I only dreamed him. Could have been hallucinating, I suppose. Does Marcus remember?"

"You can ask him yourself in just a few hours."

That made her happy. "Doc, I'm tired." Margret suddenly pushed her tray away. "I'm so tired."

She fell asleep, still holding her spoon.

*　*　*　*　*

"Mama!" Two little voices chimed at once, waking her up.

"My babies!" Margret cried. Her tears of joy were instant. Her babies looked fed and happy and rested; well cared for, exactly as Dr. Pike said. Relief and exhilaration flowed through her.

"Be careful, Natalie, don't jump on her," Ginny warned.

"I'm *Natty*," the girl said.

Margret said, "If you jump, I might puke on you. Come here, *niños*!"

Ginny lifted Natty up on the bed, then quietly went out. Marcus climbed up with care on her other side, and she cuddled them close, one on each side.

Joy.

"You're not going to die, Mama?" Marcus whispered.

"No, sweetie. I'm gonna be here to love on you a long old time!" She rubbed his head. How bad she missed them! "Everything's gonna be fine now. Just fine."

"Why are you crying, Mama?" Natty asked.

"Because I just love you so much it has to leak out my eyes!"

The girl said, "I love you so much too, Mama! Look!" A tear ran down her cheek also.

"Me too, Mama. I missed you so much. I thought I'd never ever see you again," Marcus cried, his arms tight around her neck. She'd missed that feeling so much, those tiny fingers clinging to her skin.

"We'll never be apart again. I love you both so much." She kissed their tender cheeks and held onto them, one in each arm, with all the strength she had.

* * * * *

Marcus perked up as he saw his mother regularly. His acute fear subsided, replaced by joy and relief.

Mama had ATF, and lived.

He thought about the answer to his prayer in the grocery store. Now Mama's life was saved, too. Someone was listening. Someone knew he was there. He asked Sister Roberta questions about God, and she was happy to oblige.

He lapped up the gospel like a stray cat took to a saucer of milk. He added a *Book of Mormon* to the contents of his backpack, and it soon became as worn as his comic book.

* * * * *

Margret decided to leave her many pairs of earrings off. Nobody here wore that much jewelry. She left the belly ring out too, stashing the trinkets in a small tin Ginny gave her. Even lying around in hospital gowns, she was acutely aware how different she was. She made stupid social mistakes, cussing when she didn't know it, turning face after face bright red.

Her strength increased, and she saw her kids for longer time periods each day. After a while they set up a cot in her room, and the kids were allowed to sleep over.

Dr. Pike reported that the two hunters seemed to be getting better. They vaccinated her kids next on the list, once it showed signs of working.

They waited to release the news to the public until they had treated all of New Hope.

Dr. Pike was deeply disturbed by her scars, and got her working with a therapist, Dr. Vicky Lane. She wasn't sure about that, but Vicky was good people. They got along. Margret began to unburden her soul, and for the first time since her wedding night, her pervasive, overpowering terror of Ralph began to fade, if only in small degrees.

Their economic system here sounded a lot like the Gardens, where they had all taken care of Mary and Bert and the other crazies, sharing out work and the rooftop garden harvest. The main difference was that this community was super-organized about it.

Margret had been afraid of the huge bill she must be running up. In downtown Central, she'd be in danger of losing redundant organs or other body parts to pay. Now, if she understood right, there wasn't going to *be* a bill.

She was astounded.

The best part was, if she stuck by their economic rules and most of the moral ones, she could live here for free. The economic part was easy. Dumping everything you owned into a common kitty was only hard if you were rich.

The moral code was a tougher sell. All Ten Commandments, plus a few new ones.

A bunch of visitors came to see her one day. Some guy they called Bishop, Dr. Marden, Ginny, and a few others. It was some kind of interview, she guessed, to decide her future.

The Bishop guy asked her, "So, Ms. DeVray, what sort of skills do you have?"

She surveyed the room; some of the men present weren't half bad. She winked and said, "I'm darn good at sex, but I've never sold it."

Some faces went white, some went red, and the Bishop guy sunk his face into one hand. Dr. Pike let out a nervous laugh.

"Honest!" she added.

There was a nervous, group clearing of throats.

"Can't you guys take a joke?" she said.

"Oh, a joke!" somebody said. Relieved, forced laughter followed.

Margret rolled her eyes. "I'm a seamstress. Mainly women's clothes, but I had a couple jobs in upholstery. I'm just as good at that. I can clean or cook, any old drudge job you need done."

The Bishop guy smiled. "Great. I'll see what I can find. Meanwhile, we're getting a suitable apartment ready for you and your children." He and most of the others turned for the door.

"What's the rent?" Margret asked.

"Only trade for your work within the community."

Caramba! They were giving her an apartment. She'd bet her left eye it would be day work too, no crappy graveyard shifts.

Dr. Marden told the Bishop, "It'll be about four more weeks before she's well enough."

Four weeks! Life in the hospital was boredom incarnate. She let out a stream of expletives—in Spanish—expressing her disgust.

Dr. Marden turned and gave her a harsh look. "Not in my earshot, young lady!" In Spanish, he added, *"Have you no self-respect at all?"*

"Not much," she answered back, wishing she could spit—but that wouldn't help her get that new, free apartment. Dr. Pike was much more personable. She was glad he was her doctor, not that crusty old fart.

She complained to Dr. Pike after the old man left. "I can't even cuss in Spanish? I need an outlet, man, you people are gonna kill me."

Dr. Pike laughed. "Dr. Marden served as a missionary in downtown Bogotá. There's not much Spanish he hasn't heard."

"You ask for a lot, eh," she groused.

"We give a lot in return," he said. "Don't forget that."

CHAPTER 32

GIVING THANKS

> *I had another dream about my family. My sister was in it. She was so angry—more angry than I've ever seen her. She wound up spilling the urn with Joan's ashes in it by accident. She got out the vacuum and sucked her ashes up and ordered new carpet.*
>
> *Creepy. I seriously hope that one was only a bad dream.*
>
> —Alyssa Stark,
> personal journal entry

Julia and Derek came for Thanksgiving, which disrupted the sleeping arrangements a little bit. That made Beverly think about what would happen once Peter and Alyssa got married—and they hadn't set a date yet. They wanted to keep it small and quiet, and for the sake of propriety, Alyssa either needed to move out, or the wedding had to take place very soon.

Beverly fussed over how to rearrange all the bedrooms after the wedding, wanting to put them in her master bedroom.

Peter said, "Absolutely not. We'll be just fine in Julia's old room." Alyssa agreed.

"I could move the twins downstairs to your old room . . ."

Jordan squealed a complaint. "No, Mom!"

"What about the waiting period for new members, Mom?" Julia brought that up.

That was a glitch. There was a standard wait of about a year after baptism before new members could receive temple blessings, which included marriage and sealing together for eternity.

Beverly said, "We relayed the Liahona Temple to find out what the current flexibility is, but we haven't heard back yet." A Pony Express type relay had been set up for outlying members, such as the Richardsons and Bishop Greene's family, while

Liahona waited for communication lines to be rebuilt. It was old-fashioned, but they sent a letter as soon as they realized it had to be addressed. She added, "I heard the one-year rule isn't hard and fast since Article 28 passed. We lost a huge percentage of fence-sitters back then, and the few converts that do come in are coming to us one hundred percent dedicated."

Julia said, "Did you ever think we'd be the ones to see the parable of the ten virgins coming true?"

Her comment was all but lost in a hubbub of simultaneous comments.

"Wait—I have family in Salt Lake City," Derek said. "The farm satellite didn't get hit, right?"

Beverly said, "Right. We're fine."

Alyssa told Julia, "I'll move to Liahona, or New Hope, if it has to be a full year. I can't live here that long if we're not married. And I told Peter I don't want this at all unless it's forever." She smiled and squeezed his hand as they sat together, but neither was looking forward to an entire year apart. "Besides, he's looked forward to a temple wedding his entire life. I won't shortchange him on that."

Meanwhile Derek borrowed their phone and was ringing someone up.

Beverly added, "Alyssa is such a hard worker, too. I'm not sure how we'll get by without her. We were struggling a bit to fill your shoes, Julia."

Julia laughed. "I didn't mind handing them over." She was more of a city girl at heart.

"Hey, come here, Alyssa," Derek motioned.

"What is it?"

He grinned. "I have someone here for you to talk to. My oldest sister out in Utah is married to a Chavez. The grandson of President Chavez."

"President—!" she gasped. "Are you on the phone with—" *The leader of their worldwide church?*

"Calm down. It's not him, it's just my brother-in-law. Robbie, what's the latest word on Article 28 workarounds? I've got an almost-sister-in-law here with an amazing conversion story you have to hear. She and my wife's big brother have an unusual circumstance with their living situation, but they're both solid gold, just like Julia. Can you help us get the right paperwork, and help put in a good word?"

It was not as impossible as they thought, but there would be a few hoops to jump, and quickly. Alyssa would need to schedule several in-depth interviews via satellite with Church authorities in Utah, and they would both have to fill out a stack of paperwork. Alyssa was humbled to learn that for final approval, the highest councils of the Church would pray about her and Peter's situation during weekly meetings held by the First Presidency and Twelve Apostles. If everything was in order, their approval and paperwork for an early endowment and sealing could come through in less than a month.

"We could get married right after Christmas!" Peter said. "What do you think?"

Alyssa said, "Sounds like a plan. Derek—thank you so much!"

They looked on the calendar and set the date for two days after Christmas, when all the family would be together for the holiday anyway.

"Now, if it doesn't come through that fast—" Beverly started.

Alyssa was in high spirits. "We'll just keep setting it for the twenty-seventh of every month, until it comes through," she said.

* * * * *

Privately, Alyssa told Peter, "Let's be as safe as possible. I love kissing you . . . but let's wait, even on that, until we're married."

"Whew," Peter said. "That won't be easy."

"Okay, just short kisses then."

He laughed. "Alyssa, there is no way I'm going to come this far, to have the chance to be with you for all eternity, just to blow it by letting anything get out of hand."

"Andrew's problems scared me, Peter. We can't be too careful."

He swallowed hard. "I see your point."

* * * * *

Dinner was almost on. Alyssa whipped the potatoes for Thanksgiving dinner. The turkey rested on the carving board. Beverly stood at the stove, stirring the gravy.

The mixer hummed, gravy bubbled on the stove, and in the background the twins played hide-and-seek with Julia, Derek, and even Andrew, thundering through the house with squeals of delight. Earlier Julia and Alyssa had polished the silver and prepared a fancy centerpiece and table settings. Julia was very good at it. Alyssa just did what she said—she didn't have an eye for that sort of thing.

Peter came in the back door hefting a load of firewood. "This should about do it," he said, stacking the wood beside the fireplace. "Should keep us nice and cheery all evening."

As everyone sat to eat, chattering happily about the smells and sights of the Thanksgiving feast, Alyssa thought she saw Phil take his place at the head of the table and sit down. She shook her head, blinked, and looked again. He wasn't there.

Of course not.

When they were setting the table, a brief argument had come up between Julia, Peter, and Andrew over whether or not to set an empty seat for their father, like the Jewish tradition to set a place at Passover for Elijah. Lack of space settled the question, and Beverly sat at the head.

Still, it was so unsettling that she looked discreetly at each face several times, to be sure she had imagined it.

* * * * *

After the meal, Alyssa went to the stable, hoping to take a short ride alone to clear her head. After three days of company, the house felt crowded and claustrophobic, and she was starting to be on edge trying to be her best around Julia and Derek. They were terrific people. Just not quite like her. The endless questions about wedding plans and how they got together and all that romance-quiz business she was getting was driving her crazy.

Inside, she found Andrew currying Lucy Mack. The mare whinnied a greeting.

She said, "I'm sorry—I didn't know you were here." She turned to go.

Andrew said, "No, don't leave on my account."

"I thought I'd take Abish out for some exercise. Huge meal."

"Yeah, I'm stuffed too."

"What did you eat? Three plates?"

"Yeah," he said. "I'm slowing down."

They both loved horses, but each avoided this situation, being in the stable at the same time. She ran out of ideas, and brushed out Abish's mane in silence.

"Getting out of the limelight?" he asked.

"I guess so," Alyssa said.

"Me too," Andrew said.

"I guess you're as tired of their questions as I am." Andrew was polite through dinner, but Julia and Derek noted his sullen mood and quizzed him.

"Yours are easier to answer." Andrew worked on Lucy Mack's hooves with the hoof pick.

She finished with the mane and went to the currycomb. Somehow she didn't feel like rushing off on her ride. "Can I ask you something?"

"Your turn to interrogate the prisoner?" he asked, minus any emotion. His face was a blank slate.

"No . . . I'm just curious why you're so set against me, and if there's anything I can do to change that. I'm going to be your sister-in-law. I'd like to get along."

He set the horse's hoof down and straightened up. "Listen, I apologized for that stuff I said when I was mad at Peter. I didn't know any better. It was stupid, okay?"

"That's not it. There's something different that's always bugged you about me."

He paused.

She could sense him gearing up. But when he spoke, there was no emotion in his voice. Just flat words. "All right. You want to know? Why did Jesus come to you? Why not me? I wasn't always messed up, you know. I was a good kid. I followed all the rules, until . . . Listen, if the Lord can go fetch you from some pit of despair, why can't he bring Dad back? No offense, it's just—what makes you so special?"

"Do you think I *like* being 'so special,' Andrew? It's creepy."

He almost smiled. "Even if you are 'the one' Peter Perfect's been waiting for, I bet if you ask him, and if he had a choice, he'd pick getting Dad home over you."

She reminded herself that Andrew had never been known for tact. She held her tongue and thought about what he meant. "I'd like Phil back, too. I would. I can see how running all this drains Peter. He could use more support from you, you know."

Andrew's mouth hardened into a tight line.

She asked, "Andrew, I have to know. This . . . mistake . . . with Sienna—was it because of my being here, in any way? I feel like I should have known . . . or helped . . ."

"No. I was involved with her long before you got here."

She took a deep breath. She only observed the one "date" when he didn't come home all night.

"So—are you planning to fix it? You're driving this family apart with your crappy attitude. Can't you see that? Do you think any of us needs that right now? What about the twins?"

"Would you shut up?"

"No. Make it better, would you? Soon?"

"I *can't*," he said, finally with some passion.

"Andrew! You've been around the gospel most of your life, and you don't know what a priceless gift you have here? If Jesus himself dragged me out of Central City in time to save my life *and* my soul, why can't you believe He'll do the same for you now? I am *not* more important than you, in His eyes. I am positive of that."

She felt the Spirit burn within her as she testified.

Andrew's lower lip trembled, and he looked down at his boots. Alyssa stepped out of the horse's stall and latched it behind her.

"I can't make this better, okay? Leave me alone."

"No. Who are you to put limitations on the power of God? I swear to you, Jesus can heal this."

He wiped his eyes, regained some composure. "You can't just put virginity back once it's gone!"

He had a point. You either were, or you weren't. "He can make it seem like it never happened," she said. Ever since her baptism, her own former life tainted with drugs, addiction, and pain seemed like it belonged to another person, forgotten, fading away in the distance. "He stands waiting, offering you the power to be whole again, and you shove that incredible gift back in his face! I can't understand that," she finished.

He stood sniffling, eyes on the floor.

"Touch my hand, Andrew," she said.

He looked up, confused. He brought his hand up, and she placed his palm flat against hers.

"You feel that, don't you?"

"Sure."

"Can you believe that this hand once touched the hand of Jesus?"

He shook his head no.

"Okay," she said, a little shaken by his honesty. "Can you believe he wants to heal you?"

Again, a tiny shake of the head.

"Can you at least *want* to believe?"

"I do want to believe." He looked her in the eye, his brow wrinkled. His sorrow triggered a maternal response to hug him. To her surprise, he returned the hug and held tightly to her while he sobbed like a child. His tears made a soggy puddle on her shoulder.

"It's too big. I can't fix this," he cried.

"Not alone," Alyssa said.

* * * * *

The Saturday after Thanksgiving, Alyssa was flossing her teeth before bed at the bathroom sink when her reflection vanished, replaced by the Chinese boy she had seen in so many of her recent dreams.

Lately when she dreamed about him, he was not in the cage anymore; she dreamed of him living in a Central City library, not unlike the place she had last seen Rob in person.

The boy stared back at her in shock.

She screamed. The strand of dental floss fell to the floor.

He stood in a public bathroom, with stalls and a urinal behind him. He had on a normal pair of two-piece pajamas, not the strange gown he had worn in her first dream.

And she wasn't dreaming. She'd come up with rational explanations for these dreams—an odd manifestation of an inner child, perhaps. The explanations vanished.

The boy screamed too—she heard no sound.

She wiped the mirror on her side. He reached to touch her hand. Slowly she matched fingers with his and raised her other hand to the glass. He did the same.

She was afraid to blink as they looked at each other.

"Who are you?" she whispered.

He mouthed words she couldn't hear. She was no good at lip-reading. *I . . . am . . .* followed by what must be a name. His mouth shut, opened, and shut. It might have begun with P, B, or M.

"Why do you come to me?" was her next question, but the image vanished.

Staring back at her was her own startled reflection. She dropped her hands from the glass.

A knock came on the bathroom door.

"Are you okay in there?" Kellie asked.

"I'm fine, honey!" She forced her breath to slow down. She couldn't take her eyes off the mirror.

Jordan said, "We heard you scream."

"The floor's wet, I almost slipped," Alyssa said. It was not quite untrue. "I'll be all right."

"Okay," Kellie said. Their light footsteps moved off down the hall.

She stared into the mirror a long time that night, waiting for it to change back, but the boy did not return.

CHAPTER 33

SPECIAL REQUEST

Dearest Ethan:
  What a wild Holiday bash that was! The cleaning crew can't get here until Monday; can I stay with you for a few days?
  I hope to get the Braithewaite house on the market as soon as I can get it out of probate. I've always hated it.
  Much obliged, Lauren

  —Lauren Stark,
  e-mail to Ethan Fangren

Debra didn't look forward to Thanksgiving at all. They spent the morning with her family, and the big meal of the day with Jon's. She wished it were reversed, longing to spend more time with her own mother.

Roberta was also still watching Marcus and Natty, Margret's two children. Debra hadn't met them yet and was nervous. They were friends of Alyssa's, but that didn't mean she would like them.

All too soon it was time to leave Mom. Clive brought his horse and buggy around to pick them up. Jon and Debra used bicycles most of the year, with Zach strapped securely into a baby seat behind one of them, but it had snowed, and the roads were too slushy.

Her grumpy, out-of-sorts mood didn't help meeting Margret's children go any easier.

Roberta brought a young boy forward. He had curly dark brown hair and good color to his skin. "This is Marcus."

"Nice to meet you." Debra held out her hand, balancing Zach on her hip. The boy didn't take it. He shifted a tattered backpack on his shoulder and stared at her, sizing her up. "You have such pretty eyes," she said. They were a striking brown, almost gold color.

He responded by looking down at his feet.

"This is Dr. Jon's wife," Roberta told him. "Baby Zach's mama."

"Oh. Hi."

Debra asked, "Got some good stuff in your backpack there?"

Marcus squirmed away from Roberta and went down the hall.

"He's got a death grip on that thing. Won't even let go in his sleep. That's strange—he didn't talk much at all while his mama was sick, but he's been improving lately," Roberta said. "He might be upset his mama couldn't leave the hospital for Thanksgiving."

"She's doing well, isn't she?"

"Yes, but she still needs to be on the monitors," Jon said.

The girl, Natty, was a pretty little girl and talkative, but Debra was startled by her appearance. She looked almost white. Her brown hair was wavy, with a reddish cast, and she had light eyes and skin.

After Natty bounced away, Debra asked, "Not be rude, but what race is Margret, exactly?"

Roberta laughed easily. "We are all God's children, Deb."

"How do her kids look so different?" Their facial features contrasted nearly as much as their hair color.

Jon said, "Margret said her father is mostly black, and her mother mostly Hispanic. But she recited off a whole list of peoples in her ancestry, including Korean. I thought I told you that?"

"I guess so," Debra said, still puzzled.

Roberta said mildly, "The children have different fathers, Deb."

"Oh." Then she felt stupid.

Jon added, "She says her ex, Natty's father, was so white he glowed in the dark, and had red hair and green eyes."

"And the other father?"

"Mexican, I think," Roberta said.

"I see," was all she said. She wondered what kind of woman Margret was for Jon to be working with her so closely, and wondered again about the strange answer she got when she prayed about whether he should do this: *the danger lies not in the direction you expect.* But the thought left as quickly as it came.

* * * * *

Three weeks went by. A scattering of people in New Hope contracted ATF, were given the antibody, and recovered; only one elderly woman failed to respond to treatment and died, her body too old and feeble, giving out before the disease progressed far.

The vaccine inoculation was produced in small batches. Margret had to keep donating blood, in small quantities, for the task.

There was one week left till Christmas. The kids were so excited. Sister Roberta had a real tree in her house with lights and everything. Natty was talking about presents. Margret had no idea where *those* were coming from.

It wouldn't be the first holiday they'd gotten by with nothing. But this year, Margret found herself wishing for something to give, afraid to beg off anyone. She'd been mooching long enough, and honestly didn't dare ask what could be provided.

Ginny brought in a crochet hook, yarn, thread, and a book.

"Oh, no," Margret resisted. "That's not my style."

"I'll show you how," she said. "You're bored stiff. This at least gives you something to do."

It was bizarre how they didn't even try to disguise Christmas in this place. It hadn't been called *Christmas* since before she was born, by believers or not. It was strange to hear the word said openly, rather than the generic, politically correct *Winter Holiday.* Ginny brought in a tiny nativity set and holiday lights to decorate her room. She didn't mind the lights, or even the nativity. It almost made her miss her old rosary beads. But not quite.

Margret pushed her lunch tray back as Dr. Pike ushered Marcus into her room. Odd. Her kids visited as they wished, and the doctor had been in on rounds before lunch.

"What is it?" She wiped her mouth with a napkin.

"Marcus has something he wants to ask you." Dr. Pike smiled, nervous. Marcus looked at him, then her.

"You can tell me anything, *niño*. Come here."

Marcus climbed up on the bed and mumbled something.

"Louder, I can't hear you, and you're right next to me."

The boy focused on her eyes. He was dead nervous.

"What is it? Is somebody mad at you? You get in a fight, eh?"

He shook his head no. "It's something I want for Christmas, Mama, really bad."

She cast a frightened look at the doctor. Where was this going to come from?

He just motioned her to pay attention to Marcus.

"I can't promise you anything this year, but let's hear what it is."

His voice was soft and quivering. "I want to be baptized."

She was shocked. "You *what?*"

Louder, he said, "I want to be baptized. Please?"

Margret glared at Dr. Pike, an unspoken question in her eyes. *Who did this?*

"This is all his idea, Margret."

"I doubt that."

Roberta had visited the hospital. *There* was a suffocating woman, if she ever met one. She wondered how Dr. Pike stood being raised under her thumb. And her boy was living in that woman's house. Good thing they'd be together under one roof soon. She could undo whatever fantasies Roberta must be cramming into his head.

She wouldn't disrespect the man's mama in front of his face, but surely the doctor knew what sort of woman she was. Exactly the type to feed her little boy all kinds of nonsense.

Except Dr. Pike didn't believe it was nonsense.

Dr. Pike answered, "Hear him out. Tell her the story, Marcus."

"I've been thinking about God ever since we got here. Remember how he answered my prayer in the store and sent us David?"

"Yes," she said.

"And he sent the man with the rabbit stew, and the blankets, and the camp grill that folds up?" Marcus asked.

She vaguely remembered a fuzzy dream. "Who?"

"Don't you remember?" Marcus pleaded.

Margret frowned and shook her head.

"You talked about it when you first woke up," Dr. Pike offered. "You couldn't remember his name. Neither can Marcus or Nat."

The boy said, "The blankets and grill and the pot and dishes came with us, and they're at Sister Roberta's, but I don't remember his face anymore."

She said, "It's hard to remember anything from then."

Marcus unzipped his tattered backpack. He pulled out a book. "I've been reading this. I did what it says to at the end. I prayed about it to know if it's true, Mama, and God spoke to me that it is."

"He did that."

He nodded.

"How do you know it was God and not just in your head?"

"I *know*. Please, Mama?"

"You're too young."

"Eight is old enough. All the other kids here get baptized at age eight." His eyes glittered with hope.

"You can't make a wise decision at your age, *niño*. There's a lot about the world you don't understand yet."

His lip trembled.

Margret hated seeing that look; hated having to say no. But it was asking for too much.

"You're too little to understand what you're giving up. Don't you remember what happened to Bert?" She placed a hand on his shoulder.

"Yes. I remember. I want to do it *because* of Bert."

"Because of Bert?" She pulled her hand away.

"You heard a voice yourself!" He was trembling and close to tears. "The voice said don't drink the water, you told us! Then you didn't drink it and you said maybe Bert was right!" He broke into sobs. "You said Bert was right!"

"Yeah—and look at me! I got sick anyway!"

She felt disoriented, as if there was more to that event than she remembered.

"You didn't die! God saved your life!"

"He let me get ATF, didn't he?"

"And now a lot of people are getting better because of what you did. Doctor Jon told me so!"

That stopped her short. She rubbed at her temples, exhausted.

"Bert taught me right from wrong. He taught you, too. You listened to him even after he got funny and couldn't talk anything but numbers. Mama, Bert would want us to do this!"

"Whoa, back up. Us?"

"We can all get baptized, Mama. Natty's too little still, but—"

"Get that idea out of your head this minute, young man."

"Why not?" he pleaded.

Margret appealed to Dr. Pike.

"I didn't put him up to this, I swear." He held up both hands.

"We're going to live here anyway! Why can't I?" Marcus begged.

"I want to live here, but I don't want to *join* them. I have to say no. Maybe when you're old enough to make an informed decision."

Tears rolled down his cheeks. "But Mama!"

"That's not no never, that's no for right now. *Comprende?*"

He nodded, but the tears kept coming.

"I know it seems like forever, but it's not. You can't possibly understand what it means yet. When you do, we'll talk again."

"Will you read the book and find out for yourself, Mama? Will you ask God if it's true?"

She looked at the book he held out, worn and dog-eared. "Not now." She wasn't the least bit curious.

"You won't even try!" he cried.

Her refusal shattered his angel-image of her far more than asking him to steal to fill his belly had. She was dimly aware of that.

But no eight-year-old boy would hold her over a barrel on this point.

From this day on, her son might no longer worship her—but he would know the truth: his mama could not believe. His mama could not afford to believe.

"I'm sorry, Marcus. I can't."

Dr. Pike offered, "We have books on tape if—"

"I can *read!*" She flashed him an angry look and called him an equally angry name in English. He was properly taken aback. Something inside her relished his potent reaction.

"I'm sorry," Dr. Pike said.

"Why?" the boy wailed.

"Marcus, I said not now."

"So it's not no never?"

No doubt it was. Her heels dug in at the very thought. But at this point, a white lie to preserve the peace wouldn't hurt much more. "Maybe someday."

Marcus wiped his eyes. "How old do I have to be before you let me be baptized?"

Dr. Pike said, "We won't infringe on your parental rights. Nothing will ever happen in secret without your consent. I swear it."

Eighteen would seem too long, too unyielding. She didn't want to lose all his trust at once.

"Thirteen is good enough."

"Mama!"

"Okay, twelve. And that's final."

Marcus left the room first.

Dr. Pike whispered, "He's going to be crushed, Margret."

"Why didn't you tell him I'd say no?"

"We tried." He let that sink in. "If you let him go to church with us, he might feel better."

She wilted. "Who am I to stop a kid going to church?"

CHAPTER 34

CHRISTMAS GUEST

> *Ethan:*
> *No, unfortunately most of her crap is getting donated*
> *to the museum. I can't do anything about it. Some of the*
> *other pieces could be valuable, and I don't have an eye*
> *for what's what. Can you get that friend of yours over to*
> *help us figure it out?*
>
> —Lauren Stark,
> email to Ethan Fangren

The special papers arrived from Salt Lake two days before Christmas. Peter whooped with joy and swung Alyssa around in his arms. "We're getting married!" he called out to everyone.

"I know I'm trying not to kiss you that much, but this calls for it!" He planted an exhilarating long kiss on her lips as they stood under the mistletoe.

She whooped with glee. "It's actually going to happen!" She felt like she'd won a billion-dollar lottery.

The house was crowded. Isaac, Anna, and their two children came down for the holiday, and Julia and Derek returned as well. Besides the Christmas bustle and preparations, they also had last-minute wedding plans to marshal. As the days ticked through, no one thought the needed approval would come in time. Again the rooms were rearranged. Andrew slept in Peter's room, and the twins moved in with Alyssa, on the floor, to make enough space.

Alyssa barely remembered the oldest son, Isaac. He was outdoors checking his solar handiwork and helping Peter with multitudes of farm repairs most of the time. She liked his wife Anna and their two-year old daughter Kira right away. The baby, Isaac Jr., was a doll, with big blue eyes like Peter's.

* * * * *

At Christmas Eve dinner, Peter passed a note to Alyssa under the table at dinner. She tucked it in the back pocket of her jeans, curious.

Julia announced that she was pregnant, causing even more excitement. She was only a few weeks along, and they hadn't known at Thanksgiving. Alyssa felt a twinge of envy, but let it pass. She had hope—maybe, someday.

Peter only smiled and said, "What note?" when she asked what it meant.

It read:

> *Alyssa—*
> *Meet me at the Christmas tree at midnight.*
> *Love, Peter*

Everyone gathered in the living room after the holiday dinner for *family traditions*, Beverly called it. Alyssa felt a thrill of excitement. Never in her life had she spent a real Christmas Eve celebrating the birth of the Christ child. In her home there had been Santa Claus and Rudolph, cheery jingle bells, stories of selfless giving and peace, but no mention of how the much-commercialized Winter Holiday came to be.

The twins and young Kira were keyed up, anticipating presents and filled stockings in the morning, bouncing about the living room, checking the presents already placed under the tree.

They read the Bible story of the nativity, and sang many songs celebrating the birth of Jesus.

She couldn't remember ever being so happy and excited for this holiday.

* * * * *

Jordan and Kellie were sent up to bed early, and everyone else turned in by eleven.

Alyssa had spent hours in the past month making simple crafts to give for presents. Beverly helped. She felt her offerings were painfully inadequate, but she managed to wrap a small present for each person.

The joy of the season even seemed to catch up with Beverly. Her mood lightened, and it seemed some of the burden she carried no longer weighed her down as fully.

Peter had spent a full day away from the farm in the past week doing Christmas shopping in Liahona. He rode out long before dawn and didn't get back until well past bedtime, arriving with full saddlebags. He double-checked with the officials at the Liahona Temple personally to ensure that all was prepared, should their papers arrive in time.

Alyssa went to her room last, gazing at the lights on the tree, anxious and excited to learn the meaning of Peter's cryptic note. One more hour. And in about sixty-four hours, she would be a married woman.

She stopped with her hand on the doorknob. She heard the twins inside, whispering. Beverly checked on them over an hour ago—they should be asleep. She stood outside the door a moment, listening.

"I *saw* him, Jordan, I swear it!" Kellie said, sounding irritated.

Alyssa worried that something about the evening's grown-up activities had gone awry. She knocked lightly.

The twins made hushing sounds before Jordan whispered, "Who is it?"

Alyssa nudged the door open. It was dark inside, and she could barely make out their huddled shapes. "It's just me. Did I hear you guys talking about Santa?" she asked.

"No," Kellie said, defensive.

"I couldn't help overhearing something, I'm sorry," she explained.

"She's talking about Dad. She says she saw him standing over in the corner when we were reading the Christmas story."

"I did," Kellie insisted.

"You can't have," Jordan said.

"I did."

Alyssa remembered the funny sensation at Thanksgiving when they sat at the table. She whispered, "I thought I saw him once too, but not tonight."

"When?" Kellie asked. Alyssa could hear the girl's rapid breath.

"It was Thanksgiving. I thought I saw him sit at the head of the table, but then he wasn't there."

She heard Kellie smack her brother lightly. "See? I'm not crazy, Jordan. I told you."

"That doesn't prove anything," the boy said, sullen.

"Yes it does. I saw him at Thanksgiving too, Alyssa. Just like you said. See, Jordan? He sat at the head of the table. Then he was gone."

A chill ran through Alyssa's spine.

"There was another time I never told anybody about," Kellie said. "I was just getting tape from the drawer. It was like remembering, only not remembering. It was like I *saw* Dad get a piece of tape, just like I did. I was making paper dolls, and they ripped. I dropped the dispenser on my toe and my toenail turned black, do you remember that, Jordan?"

"No," he said. "Why don't I ever get to see Dad?"

"You get your funny feeling, Jordan," Kellie said.

Jordan said, "Don't tell her about that!"

"Alyssa, I don't like remembering Daddy," Kellie said.

"Why not?"

"I miss him too much, and it makes me cry. And then I just remember dumb things like that, like Daddy pulling tape off the dispenser. I wish I could remember how his voice sounds when he reads me bedtime stories. He did it better than Peter."

"You can talk to your mommy," Alyssa suggested.

Kellie said, "If I talk about Dad she always cries, and I never know what to do when she cries."

"Maybe just let her cry, sweetie." She knew it was crummy, but didn't have much else to offer.

"Please, Alyssa, don't tell anybody I saw Dad in the corner? I don't want everyone teasing me. Jordan's bad enough."

"Okay, Kellie, I promise."

Jordan added, "And don't tell anybody we were awake, either! Please?"

"Have I told anybody about your little gray kitten that's not supposed to be up here?" she countered.

Jordan whispered, "She knows about the kitten?"

Alyssa had to smile. "It sleeps with me a lot. Purrs real loud right in my ear."

"So that's where he goes!" Jordan said.

"You can trust me, sweeties."

"Alyssa?"

"Yes, Kellie?"

"If you see him again will you tell me?"

"You bet I will," she replied. "Goodnight."

"Goodnight," they echoed, in whispers.

* * * * *

At the stroke of midnight, Alyssa crept downstairs to find Peter sitting on the floor in front of the tree.

"What's all this about?" she whispered.

He put a finger to his lips. She sat down cross-legged, facing him.

"Merry Christmas," he whispered, and handed her a small velvet box.

"Oh, my gosh—Peter!"

She opened it to find a half-carat diamond engagement ring inside.

She gasped, unable to take her eyes off the glittering facets. It flickered with rainbows, reflecting off the colorful lights on the tree. "It's fabulous!"

He cleared his throat. When she looked up she noticed he'd gotten on one knee. "I felt a bit stupid the first time . . . so I'd like to get this right. Alyssa Stark, will you marry me?"

"Peter, don't be silly."

He was very serious, waiting for an answer.

"Yes! Of course. In fact, let's get married in two days! Does Friday work for you?"

"Perfect! Oh—I was so afraid you'd say no," he joked. He sat down again, leaned over and kissed her. "Let me put it on," he said.

It fit perfectly. "It's so beautiful! When did you get it?"

"In Liahona last week. I had Jordan measure your finger with a string, that day you were taking a nap. I hope you like it. We can exchange it when we're there, if . . ."

"No, it's perfect. I didn't even think . . . I just—I've been too busy, so worried whether the papers would come in or not . . ."

"I'm surprised you never asked about a ring," Peter laughed. "I'm sorry I couldn't get it sooner. Anyway, Dad taught us boys, you're not formally engaged until you have a ring and a date. So . . . we are now officially—*engaged!*" His voice got louder on the last word, and the lights came on.

"Congratulations!" said a quiet chorus of voices.

Alyssa had to laugh, looking around. Everyone silently herded in from the kitchen, except for the twins and two grandchildren.

"You set this up!" she exclaimed.

"I sure did," Peter admitted, grinning.

"We're so happy to have you as part of our family," Julia said. "And I have a present for you. Mom and I were talking . . ." She went to the kitchen table and brought out a large, flat box. "This is for you. Open it."

Alyssa couldn't think what Julia would have to give her. She lifted the lid and went speechless when she saw billowing folds of white fabric. She looked up with surprise.

Julia bubbled with excitement. "It's not mine, either," she said. "I've been sewing ever since Thanksgiving. I hope it suits you—while I'm here we can make alterations, fix anything on it that you don't like. I brought extra fabric in case you don't like the sleeve or something, I can use Mom's machine, and . . . well, there it is!"

"Julia . . ." was all she could say. She lifted the satin wedding dress out of the box, and the fabric rustled, smooth under her fingertips. "I never imagined wearing anything this beautiful." She had never been to a formal or had occasion to dress up, and had talked herself into the thought that it wasn't that important what she wore, not compared to the blessing of being with Peter for eternity.

As she looked at the dress before her, tears of gratitude welled up, and she didn't bother holding them back.

"I didn't want you to have to borrow everything of mine," Julia said, wiping her own eyes. "Besides, Mom told me you like things simple. We both thought my dress would be too lacy and ruffled for you."

She was right—Alyssa had seen pictures of Julia's dress. She hadn't wanted to bring up the subject after Thanksgiving, when Beverly had assured her that the temple had dresses she could choose from. The pattern Julia used was perfect—simple yet elegant.

Alyssa shook her head. "You had me fooled," she said to Beverly, who was grinning.

"We wanted it to be a surprise present," Beverly said. "Merry Christmas!"

Alyssa hugged Julia, and hugs of congratulations to her and Peter went all around.

"Congratulations," Andrew said, offering her a brief hug as well.

"Are you feeling all right?" she teased. They'd gotten along better ever since their talk at Thanksgiving.

"You're almost my sister, so I better be nice, right?" He smiled.

Beverly hugged her last and longest.

* * * * *

Phil watched his family's activities all evening, including Peter's whimsical second proposal.

Beverly wasn't alone until well past midnight. She sniffled through tears while she put on pajamas. She climbed on the bed, reached for Phil's pillow, buried her face and wept soundlessly.

Does she end every night this way? It wasn't the bedtime routine he remembered. His heart ached to capacity. Her emotions could be keen due to the holiday stress, and the wedding.

He couldn't normally watch them so closely, lest they sense his presence. Kellie especially had remarkable perception and had to be accounted for.

Phil wanted to swing his wife around in circles with joy, but it might give her a heart attack.

Then she pulled a piece of paper out from under her pillow, unfolded it and read it. It was worn and tattered . . .

Phil recognized it—the same note he had left her, so long ago.

Beverly looked up at the ceiling, the letter in her hand, tears falling. She spoke quietly. "Why can't you tell me what happened, Lord? I've given everything I can, and I still have no answers. I know Thou knowest where he is. Even if it's terrible, I can handle knowing now. Just tell me where my husband is, please . . . ?" Her voice trailed off.

The pain on her face was more than Phil could bear.

"Beverly, I'm right here," he said softly.

"What?" she whispered, startled.

"Beverly . . . Sweetheart . . . I'm here." Phil caused himself to become visible, not too bright for her mortal eyes to handle.

She blinked. "Phil?"

"Don't be afraid."

"Is this a dream or a vision?" She rubbed her eyes, and the letter floated to the floor.

"Neither." Phil slowly crossed the room.

"But I locked the door—Oh, it's true—it's true." She started to cry. "You're dead. I hoped somehow maybe . . ."

"Beverly, I've missed you so much." He sat beside her, pulled her precious body into his arms, and kissed her tenderly, as he had longed to for what seemed like eons.

She kissed back—then let out a scream and shoved him away. "I thought you were a spirit! Who are you? *What* are you?" One hand scrambled for the rifle under the bed.

"It's me. Phil. Your husband!"

"If you're a ghost, how come I felt that kiss? Otherwise why are you glowing, and how on earth did you get in here?"

"Bev—Bev—don't shoot that thing, it'll wake everyone up, and I'll have to go. Beverly, I've been resurrected."

He'd meant to soften that information, but if she made a commotion, he'd have to vanish. Literally.

She dropped the rifle barrel. "It can't be."

"I've been allowed to show you I'm all right. I'll be at the wedding Friday. You most likely won't see me in the sealing room, but if you keep the seat open to your right, I'll sit by you. Further, you must keep this knowledge sacred, even from the rest of the family, along with everything else I tell you tonight, until the appointed time. Do you promise to do that?"

She was dazed. "Yes . . . I promise."

Briefly he related the story of his kidnapping and the events afterward. The specifics of his angel-work remained private; she did not press for more information than he could give. He admired that strength in her.

They held hands as they spoke, the touch on his skin delightful.

"When we go to build the temple in Zion, I will be with you to lead the family there," he finished.

Her eyes sparkled. "It's not far off, then? And we're to be included?"

Phil smiled. "You can't mention *that* to anyone, either."

"I won't."

Phil was in awe.

The beauty of her spirit, her loveliness, and his tender love for her, overflowed his heart. It was incredible to be *together*, speaking, touching. At last.

"Phil, why did I have to wait so long?" Her voice held only sorrow. "I can keep secrets, I'm able to—"

"You weren't as ready as you thought you were, darling . . . It took you so long to turn your suffering over to the Savior so He could heal you. We've been waiting for that to happen."

"I was just so angry . . . Phil, I didn't understand . . . I'm sorry . . . I never thought it was me . . ."

"Beverly, I knew it would take time. I've ached every hour to be with you."

"I imagined you missing me, in some prison, or tortured, or getting therapy treatments and living without your mind and unable to remember us, but it never occurred to me that I could keep you away . . . Phil, please forgive me."

"Beverly, there is nothing to forgive. I love you so much."

She kissed him then.

She looked him up and down. "Even if you *are* my legal and lawful husband, it's bizarre thinking I've just kissed an angel."

"I am both. I'm still the same Phil Richardson you fell in love with thirty years ago."

"Only you're perfect now?" Beverly half-closed one eye.

"I'm trying my best to be." He didn't always feel like *a just man made perfect*. Yet it was true Satan had no power over him anymore; he couldn't commit sin with the light and knowledge he held.

She ran her hand over his right forearm, turning it over. "That scar is gone. Do you remember how you got it?"

He rubbed at the spot where the scar used to be. "Is this a test?"

"Humor me, Phil. Look at yourself."

"Do I look so different?"

"You look young and perfect." Her eyes were misty. "And I don't."

"Beverly—I literally see your spirit shining through. You're breathtakingly beautiful."

She sniffled and gave him a bashful smile.

"My scar . . . I slipped off the baling machine, ripped my arm open to the bone, and fainted in the car before you got me to the hospital. Isaac was little—still in a car seat. It took sixty-eight stitches."

Her hand stayed on his arm, her fingers running over his skin. Her touch was far more potent than he let on; sheer exhilaration and euphoria.

"That's right," she said softly. "Your belly is gone too. Do you get resurrected with all that fat still attached? Please tell me no. Please."

Phil laughed. "Mine happened immediately after death, which is sort of unusual. The fat was there at first, but it metabolized fast."

"I like this beard. It's so soft!" She reached out and touched it. Phil didn't say so, but resurrected hair follicles were live with sensitivity, not dead protein like mortal hair. Her touch on his beard sent him reeling.

"I can get used to it," she said.

"That's good. I know you never cared for beards, but shaving isn't exactly part of the picture."

"So I've wasted years of my life shaving my legs and underarms?" Beverly laughed.

He laughed at that. The things she thought about in five minutes were issues he hadn't given any attention during two full earth-years in his new state. "Probably, but don't worry about it."

There was a pause.

"Phil, how does it *feel?*"

He was at a loss. Experience was the only thing that could answer that, and as far as he knew, that was a long way off, for her. "It's hard to explain. I'm never tired or sick, I don't feel pain . . ." But those were surface answers. "I feel *whole*. I'm linked with every cell in my body, as though this is what our bodies were designed for, which is true . . . this is the state we were destined for."

He floundered, unable to put the rest into words. How could he describe a color invisible to mortal eyes? Or a sense of smell that identified every molecule? He drank in the familiar, sweet perfume of her body as a parched man who reaches an oasis in the desert.

"And from what I can see, you have a perfect body." Beverly sized him up with a look in her eyes, an unspoken question, her head cocked. "Which belongs to me, as your wife?"

"Beverly!" Phil felt nervous and bashful.

She gave him a familiar look. "Come on, let me look at you. Please? I'm just curious."

"I can't *do* that."

"I'm sorry—is it forbidden?" she asked.

He opened and closed his mouth. "Well, no." The Spirit wasn't warning him to leave; instead he felt its warm presence, encouraging him forward, not away.

"I just want to know what this perfect man of mine looks like." She tickled his ribs, apparently warming up to the concept of what he had become.

Phil rolled his eyes, smiling and helpless. "Do you have any idea what that's doing to me?"

Fifty years old, she giggled like a schoolgirl. "Do I?"

"Beverly—"

"Prove to me that I'm not dreaming, Phil," she said.

"You're not," he said, and pulled her close to kiss her.

* * * * *

Phil hated to leave her side in the morning. But he was strong enough to endure the parting, and now, so was she. Yet a while longer, and they would be together always.

He whispered one final thing into Beverly's ear before leaving, something she could not fully comprehend, not until her own resurrection:

Darling, my joy is full.

CHAPTER 35

TIDYING UP

> *Every passing day increases our risk of public discovery.*
> *The media is suspicious, but they are keeping their*
> *choppers out of shooting range. Ground troops must*
> *move with stealth. It is most frustrating to have to move*
> *this slowly. Kensington is on my back.*

—Pres-General Leo. F. Horne

private memo

No telephone meant that Jon couldn't figure out the mood Debra was in before he got home. He missed that the most. Debra's good days didn't outweigh the bad, not yet. But Christmas had been good the day before, and the natural holiday cheer lingered.

Zach was too small to open presents or understand what was going on, but he'd been adorable chewing on the wrapping paper and batting the bows with his fists.

Jon parked his bike in front of the house and steeled himself as he held the front doorknob. A strange noise met his ears. Old-style gospel music, blaring and irreverent, screeching about Jesus. Where on earth did she dig that up? And why?

Inside, Debra walked the floor with a crying Zach, swaying to the music. She looked strung out, dark circles of fatigue under her eyes, but not unhappy.

"Let me take him," he offered.

"No, he's almost out. He'll be asleep in a minute." She held him facing out, at waist-level. True enough, the baby's eyes were starting to roll up, precursor to sleep.

With that crazy music blaring? Jon wondered.

"Let me make dinner," he said. "Did you have a menu plan?"

"I sure don't. Thanks, baby." Zach's fussing wound down— music and all.

Jon peered in the fridge and moved things around. "There's some leftovers from Relief Society," he offered. They hadn't brought anything home from Christmas dinner at her folks'.

"Oh! That stuff was nasty!"

"I thought it was okay," Jon said.

"Then you eat it," Debra laughed.

"There's not much here. I can make you an omelet."

"Sounds great."

Jon fixed it the way Debra liked, with green peppers, mushrooms, ham, and shredded cheese.

The music blared on. Jon tried to ignore it, but as the omelet set, he couldn't help it any longer. He went over to the player to see what on earth he was being constrained to listen to.

"Dottie Peoples?" Jon said, looking at the case. "Debra, this stuff is fifty years old. Where'd you dig this up?"

"Mom lent it to me yesterday. She cut her teeth on this, and so did I." She laughed. "I'm surprised it took you this long to say something."

Zach had indeed collapsed into sleep. Debra went to put the baby down in his bed. Jon held his breath.

"Whew," she said. "He didn't wake up."

He exhaled. "He's getting better at that, isn't he?"

"Thank goodness. Come on, out with it—what's your problem?"

"It's just not . . . appropriate," he said.

Debra said, "I don't care about 'appropriate.'" She picked up Zach's toys and put them in the red plastic toy bucket, then folded a baby blanket.

"Her doctrine's kind of mixed up, that's all," he said.

"It won't damage my testimony, Jon. This music comforts me." She was smiling.

The omelet! He rushed over and pulled off the lid. It was puffed and perfect.

"Trust me, Jon, I need my roots right now. Some syrupy Mo-Tab version of 'O May My Soul Commune With Thee' is just not going to cut it."

"Okay, I can see that," he laughed.

He set her omelet on a plate and decided to make one for himself, tossing the idea of reheated casserole.

Debra said, "I borrowed CeCe Winans, Shirley Caesar, and the Dixie Hummingbirds, too."

"So I'd better get used to it?" he asked. "What's wrong with Christmas music?"

"I'm tired of Christmas music. You're cute when you're worried," she teased him.

He whipped the eggs for his dinner. A plain cheese omelet.

Debra came up behind him as he worked at the stove and wrapped her arms around his waist, leaning her head against his back. She sang along, "*When God is silent, he's listening . . . giving you more time to pray . . .*"

Jon said, "When you put it that way . . . it's kind of pretty."

"It'll sink into your bones. Give her a chance." She patted his shoulder and went to put away a few Christmas decorations. She took down a string of lights and wound them around a piece of cardboard.

"Taking things down already?" he asked.

"I feel up to it," she said. "I might as well."

Even with that wild background music, Jon felt peaceful.

Over dinner they talked about how the vaccine production was going, and somehow they got on the topic of Margret and Alyssa's friendship.

Debra had liked Margret the instant they met. Jon was inwardly surprised they got along, but the meeting went well.

"Back when I went to meet Margret, and we talked about Alyssa, it hardly seemed like we were talking about the same person," Debra told him. "Except for Alyssa's appearance and family details. She changed a lot over the last two years. For the better, it sounds like. That girl was so used to having money— I didn't think she'd make it if she had to be poor."

Jon said, "Me, neither."

"Margret said they called her the spoiled little rich kid until Alyssa realized it was true and got over it. She would never let me get away with that!" She laughed. "But there's just something about Margret. Don't you think?"

"I hadn't noticed." Jon shrugged. His thoughts were staying in check, and now that things were smoother with Debra, he felt haunted that he'd ever had impure thoughts about Margret. Like the blessing promised, it was fading away. But he wished it had never happened.

"I can't believe I didn't feel like meeting her. She's so interesting to talk to. I'm ashamed to admit this, Jon, but I was jealous of her for a while. Especially at Thanksgiving, when I met her kids, and they have different dads, and that answer to prayer I had, saying the danger in the project wasn't what I might expect? And we'd been fighting so much, right after the miscarriage—I got a little worried."

Jon worked to remain calm. He just let her talk.

"I'm sorry I thought that about you, Jon. I feel bad. I do trust you." She squeezed his hand.

"Baby, I love you so much. I would never hurt you like that," he said. And in that moment, he knew it to be absolutely true. It was just—gone. Like a bad dream. Even the guilt he'd clung to floated away.

"I know." She paused. "Then she recovered, and none of us got sick, which leaves me thinking either the danger is past, or there's still some other unexpected direction I haven't figured out yet."

Jon said, "I prefer to think it's past, and that we avoided it."

"Me too," she said. "I guess we might never know, huh."

She got up to put their empty dishes in the sink.

"Did she tell you Alyssa babysat her kids? I'm still getting over that. Alyssa taking care of kids. That's just not like her. For free, too." She told Jon a few related stories, then stopped. "When Margret left Central City, Alyssa had no job, no money, businesses were closing, people in that place were rioting . . . then ATF broke out everywhere . . ."

Jon said, "I know it doesn't sound good for her survival."

Debra sighed deeply. "But you were right, Jon. I know I was mad when you first told me they knew each other. I didn't appreciate it then. But it's so good to have someone else around that knew Alyssa. It makes her memory more real, somehow."

CHAPTER 36

LIAHONA TEMPLE

Jerry gave me the honor of recording the press release. President Weber approved a car to deliver the disc to a news station in Sioux City.

Margret has requested that neither her name or photo be used in the press release, due to the off-chance that Ralph might be alive and looking for her. I have to agree it's a wise choice, though I'd like to give her the public credit.

Margret should get to come to Mom's house for Christmas Eve. She is well enough for an overnight visit, but Mom will have to monitor her vital signs. Her apartment won't be ready until after the New Year.

—Dr. Jon Pike,
research notes

Friday morning, everyone was up before dawn. They loaded a trailer full of farm produce and hitched the two mares to it. Jordan and Kellie huddled in the back with their mother. Liahona would give Alyssa a glimpse of the life Debra lived, across the state in New Hope.

Andrew drove the trailer. He cracked the whip and it lurched forward. Isaac and Anna drove a two-horse carriage with their children, and squeezed Julia and Derek in with them.

Alyssa rode behind Peter on the stallion.

"Nervous?" Peter asked.

"Not about marrying you, just about its actually happening."

He laughed. "Amen to that."

The sun rose on a cloudless, bright day.

Beverly was markedly more cheerful since Christmas, and seemed to be daydreaming often, sometimes talking to herself out loud.

"Is your mom okay?" she asked.

"She seems terrific. I was worried that today would be hard on her."

"She seems as happy about our getting married as we are."

"I thought it would remind her of when we were sealed as a family, and that she would miss Dad today even more than usual. He's . . . he's the only one not here, see."

She thought of Kellie's secret, and hers: maybe Phil *was* here—somehow. She left that thought to herself. "Doesn't she seem a little *too* terrific, though?"

Peter shrugged. "I'm not going to complain."

* * * * *

They stopped the trailer at the outskirts of Liahona behind a large, plain brick building. Peter helped Alyssa out of the saddle. "The Bishop's Storehouse," he told her.

"Brother Richardson!" a man called. "Good to see you."

Peter shook hands. "How are you, Brother Grant?"

"Fine, fine. Any word on your dad yet?"

"No." Peter shook his head.

"We still miss him here."

Peter nodded.

"Well—let's get these supplies unloaded, shall we?"

They unhitched the trailer and left it there. The Richardsons would pick it up, filled with supplies, on their way home. Alyssa and Peter were to return on Teancum in a few days after a brief honeymoon.

* * * * *

Alyssa's nerves mounted as they approached the temple.

It was a modest granite building with a steeple and pillars, and while of a simple design, Alyssa felt immediately that the structure was much more than a place of worship.

On the front were carved the words, "*Holiness to the Lord - The House of the Lord.*" It possessed a quiet elegance, and while less elaborate, *castle* was the descriptive word her mind clung to: *Behold, the Castle of the Most High God.*

And she was allowed inside, to make further covenants with God and become sealed for all eternity to the man she loved.

Kellie said, "We got to go inside before it was dedicated, but I don't remember much except that it was pretty and sparkly."

Jordan added, "Mom says the sparkle was all the crystal in the chandeliers."

Andrew was lucky in one respect: since he hadn't been through for himself, he was not expected to be inside. His job was to watch the twins and Isaac's kids and wait for everyone to come out. It saved him from any need to explain to Isaac or Julia that he couldn't go in, and would not be worthy to enter for some time.

At Thanksgiving, Julia had brought up once how neat it would be if Andrew received his endowment the same day. Beverly nipped that thought in the bud by changing the subject.

* * * * *

The sacred words of the ceremony poured over Alyssa like a calming, beautiful wave of living water. She felt a deep strength grow at the core of her being that she did not realize she possessed.

A magnitude of peace seeped through her entire being. By the time everything was completed, all the words were said in more beautiful language than she could have imagined, and she kissed Peter across the altar, she could not restrain tears of joy flowing down her cheeks.

* * * * *

The reception in Liahona was simple, possessing a handmade charm. Many people came, bringing gifts, and Alyssa was amazed to see how included and accepted she was.

As they received guests in the line, one little girl nearly picked Kellie up in her excitement, twirling her around.

"Lily!" Kellie said. "I missed you!"

Jordan greeted his buddies with hand slaps and signals. "Alyssa, you remember the Wrights, from your baptism?" he said, finding his manners.

"All of you?" The group coming through included several children of nearly the same age—many more than she remembered. Sets of triplets? Had they left some at home, before? It was a few too many even for a Mormon family.

"We're all Wrights," Lily Wright said.

Another child joked, "Yep, we're *fine!*"

"Our dads are three brothers," Lily explained. "We're sisters, brothers, or cousins, all of us."

"Yeah, the Wright brothers," another said, spreading his arms like the wings of a plane. He swooped after Jordan, who ran off laughing. "No relation to the airplane guys, though," the boy finished, breathing hard.

"How long are you staying? Can you sleep over?" one of the boys asked Jordan.

Jordan asked, "Alyssa, can we?"

"Yeah, can we?" Kellie echoed.

"I'm not in charge. Ask Mom!" The children ran, escaping the dreaded line; Beverly was off working at the refreshment table.

Peter whispered, "They have a model of the *Flyer 1* at Kitty Hawk on their front lawn made of rusted scrap metal."

"Please tell me their names aren't Orville and Wilbur."

Peter gave a hearty laugh. "No. They're Joe, Brett, and Aaron. Brett's family came to your baptism."

She smiled to greet Brett and his wife Jane.

The reception was a daze, as Alyssa processed the day's events, meaning and import, and tried not to stress over the evening ahead, afraid Peter would find her a terrible disappointment.

Alyssa caught half a minute to whisper to Beverly over the punch bowl: "Beverly—I'm extremely nervous about tonight. I don't know if I'll be . . ."

Beverly giggled. Her odd mood held all day, and she seemed giddy as a little girl. But compassion lit up her eyes. She squeezed her new daughter-in-law's hand and smiled.

"No need to worry," she whispered back. "It's like riding a bike; once you learn, you never forget. Only it's much easier to figure out and a whole lot more fun." Then she turned to filling punch cups for more guests, and that was all the information Alyssa got on the subject.

* * * * *

Soon she was riding off alone with Peter and the evening was still young, not quite eight o'clock.

"Where to first?" he smiled.

"Dinner? I didn't eat anything but that piece of wedding cake you shoved in my mouth." They laughed, in part from knowing it was a fond memory, past, done, theirs to share forever.

They went to a delicatessen. Prices were listed above the counter, but Peter pulled out his temple recommend, and that was all they needed.

"That seems too easy," Alyssa said.

"There might be a fuss if an able-bodied person came here three meals a day out of sheer laziness. We give as much as we take, by ability. Brother Johannsen has run a corner deli his whole life. But here, he serves the community without ulcers over profits and losses, and his shop brings income from non-member visitors."

That explained the prices listed above. The economic puzzle began to take shape in her mind. It was like an elaborate co-op.

Brother Johannsen came to their table. He was red-faced and smiling, with a mouthful of yellow teeth. "Are the sandwiches to your liking?"

"Delicious, yes," Alyssa said.

"Great food, as always," Peter said through a mouthful.

"Can I bring you anything else?"

"We're fine," Peter said.

"Good, good." Brother Johannsen patted Peter on the back as he left.

"I didn't want to say we just got married. He might sing."

Alyssa said, "Good thinking."

"But he likes his customers happy," Peter whispered. "Look really happy, or he'll come over again. He'll think you don't like the food. Aren't you happy?" he asked.

"Yes, very!"

"What's wrong?"

She shook her head and took another bite. She felt so shy. Peter put his sandwich down. "You're *nervous*."

"Is it that obvious?"

He took her hand across the table. "I'm nervous, too."

"What if I freeze up and it goes terrible and you hate me?"

"Honey." When did he start calling her that? Today. Odd how a ceremony changed everything. He said, "First, I would never, ever hate you. Second, we'll go slow. I've never done this either, remember?"

"Deep down, Peter, I'm afraid." She got her worst thoughts into words: "And if Joan *is* dead, what if she shows up in the middle of everything and yells—I mean, she never liked you—"

"You have a horrible imagination!" Peter laughed.

She laughed at herself. "I know."

"We'll just cast her out if that happens."

That seemed rational enough.

"For all I know, that's against spirit world rules. Alyssa, I haven't waited this long not to be sure we're both perfectly comfortable. I never want to do anything that hurts or frightens you."

She felt worlds better.

He looked in her eyes, and she melted into their starry blue. "Alyssa, I need to know how you're feeling and what's important to you. And nothing says we can't take our time."

They stayed at a bed and breakfast in Liahona. It was a beautiful room with a canopy bed that was like stepping back two centuries. Both felt silly and nervous and unsure what to do or say. It was weird to share a sink to brush their teeth— weirder still to be so very much alone and undisturbed.

Finally Peter took her in his arms and began kissing her, long and slow, without stopping.

CHAPTER 37

PRESS RELEASE

This "Doctor" Pike sent us DNA and antibody samples free of charge. We are working to replicate the antibody ASAP. However, as I suspected, this man has no real credentials and his research contains glaring errors. This causes a premature hope which may prove false. He should have consulted with our lab before making his wild claims public.

Obviously we must perform the omitted procedures at once to ascertain its safety and effectiveness, along with doing independent studies. As Operation Cleanup is yet incomplete, I beg you to please allow my staff inside the Central City quarantine to search for potential test subjects. If we find other survivors with antibodies, or (better) living victims of ATF, it may reduce the need to infect healthy human hosts.

—Dr. Joel Kensington,
email to Pres.-Gen. Leo Horne

Jon didn't go with the car headed for Sioux City, though he wanted to. It had a great send-off, with people lining the streets, cheering, throwing confetti. A band played. He was needed in the lab, manufacturing ATF antibody and overseeing immunizations.

President Weber himself called Jon and Debra into his office shortly after the send-off. They left Zach with Deb's mother for the interview.

"Thanks for coming," he said as they sat down.

"President, what's this about?" Debra asked first.

"First I wanted to say I'm proud of you. You've done great work, Jon, in the actual research, and you, Debra, for supporting him. I'm sure this hasn't been easy on either of you."

Debra looked in her lap.

"We sent copies of the press release and antibody samples to labs in Salt Lake, Quebec, and Mexico City. They left yesterday. A hired courier is en route to Dr. Kensington in Des Moines with samples, to verify your results."

"All those places?" Jon asked.

He looked serious. "The vaccine is working, Jon, and we need to share your find with the world. But I'm concerned something could go wrong. While your appearance on the press release is well-earned, I don't want any backlash on you personally. We must use caution."

"How?" Deb asked.

"We've tapped into one comm line that keeps us in touch with local news—when it works. If General Horne doesn't like this, we mean to protect you and your family against anything he might do, if he gets personal."

"And he wouldn't like it because he doesn't like us," Jon said.

"The comm building was just a sample of his hatred, I'm sure. Now, there's a secure bunker in the basement here," President Weber said. "It should keep you safe if we need it to. The entrance is well hidden."

Debra was hesitant.

President Weber smiled. "Don't worry, I don't think it will be necessary. But you should be prepared."

"What about our families?" Debra asked.

"There's room for them too. But I wouldn't worry them just yet. Let's wait and see how it works out."

* * * * *

Horne was livid.

For the umpteenth time he wished he had even half Jag's control of the press. If ATF could be cured, wonderful. But *not* by those treasonous, psycho, religious wing-nuts.

He watched the newscast as Kensington tried to refute it. The man was an excellent scientist, but Horne made a mental note to get him a double for reporting to the media. He was either boring, with that droning voice, or too arrogant and unlikable.

However the man had a point.

Those zealot outposts . . . the plan was afoot. They were waiting, all this time, waiting, for Horne to clean up their dirty work, then take over the country and proclaim it the Kingdom of God on earth and announce the Second Coming.

They must have engineered ATF.

Even if the upstart doctor's story was true, if the Mormons showed up with a working cure, the world would herald them as miracle workers, giving "God" the glory, making believers out of the masses.

And the masses were too great to cure the resulting wanton psychosis all at once. Their opinion would rule, sane or not. They would want Article 28 repealed. They would make demands. They would want to punish those who enacted Article 28 in the first place, which included himself. He'd be out of a job. Perhaps worse.

He wasn't about to allow it. Mass conversion was likely part of the insidious master plan.

He called a conference with his favorite commanders to determine his next course of action.

CHAPTER 38

RICOCHET

Kensington:
  *Be patient. I am formulating a better plan. Do not
violate quarantine.*
  *However, in the meantime you may select from
subjects remaining at the checkpoints.*
  Contact Major Griffin at HQ.

—P-Gen. Leo Horne,

memo

The Richardsons went straight home after the wedding,
leaving Peter and Alyssa on their honeymoon in Liahona.
"I wouldn't want to camp for my honeymoon." Julia made a
face. "Gross. And in the middle of winter!"

"There's no other choice," Beverly laughed. "They have all the
equipment they need, and they'll have three nights in Liahona
first. I told Peter to take their time getting home. I'm glad you
and Derek stayed to help us clean up for a few days." Isaac and
his family needed to get back. He didn't have as much vacation
time with his job.

* * * * *

Tires rolled down the Richardsons' gravel driveway.
Beverly hadn't heard that sound in ages. She peered out the
front window, worried. It was a black luxury sedan.

She didn't know what to think. "Andrew—lock all the doors.
Where are the twins?"

He followed directions and located the young ones playing in
their room.

"Keep them there," she said. "Go upstairs until I figure out
what this means."

"A car, visiting?" he looked out, too.

The driver got out, and Beverly's jaw dropped. "I can't believe it," she said. "That's Lauren."

"No, her name is—" Andrew stopped mid-thought, turned beet red, and said, "I'm going upstairs now, Mom. Fill me in later." He went up.

"Andrew? Are you all right?" Beverly processed what her eyes were seeing. Alyssa's sister? Here?

The woman went to the trunk, lifted out a cardboard box, and came to the door.

Beverly opened it before she could ring.

"Hi. Glad you still live here, man. I'd hate to waste all that gas. I couldn't find your number or remember the dumb address, but for some ungodly reason I remembered the driving directions. Crazy how things work out, isn't it?"

"Lauren . . . This is such a surprise . . . I'm sorry, Alyssa's not here right now." Then she remembered Alyssa hadn't ever called her family.

"I came to see you—wait a minute, you've seen her? Recently?"

"Yes, actually . . ."

"Wow, I thought she was dead." It was mild curiosity. "Well, that's news to top ATF, isn't it? But I came out to give you something. Stuff of Mother's." She indicated the box on her hip.

Beverly's mouth hung open.

"Crud, sorry—I forgot to start off right. You don't know, do you? Joan passed away in October. She caught ATF when it first broke out—she was off in Central hobnobbing with her archaeology cronies."

"It's true," Beverly gasped. "Please—won't you come in and sit down? I think . . . I think I need to sit down."

Lauren chucked the box on the coffee table and perched carefully on the edge of the sofa. Beverly took the brown armchair, reaching for tissues before she sat.

"I've been going through her effects. I'm executor of her will, and she stipulated I had to go through her personal effects myself. If I'd known before the old bat went off and died, I'd have changed it—I'd rather hire it out. I lose the inheritance if I don't comply, so there you are. I found all these notebooks way back in a corner, and I . . ." Finally some emotion showed through. "I don't want to keep them around, but it seemed wrong to throw them away. With the holidays and all, I got to thinking that she'd want you to have them . . . they're a bit revealing."

It clicked; Beverly thought she knew what the notebooks contained. She said, "So you know."

Lauren nodded. "It helped me understand her life. I still can't forgive her, but no wonder she suppressed me so bad and I turned out the way I did. If I'd known my own grandmother was such a . . . Interesting as my career has been, I don't touch kids. That's just too wrong. Dad told us Joan's mom was a tramp, but letting all those men . . ." She shook her head.

Beverly was grim, at a loss.

"She mentioned in these that it was you who told her to write it down. You did help her. A lot. I see that now. I sort of wanted to say . . . thank you."

"I couldn't do enough, though. You and Alyssa ended up with so much to recover from."

"Yeah, my therapist has been digging too deep lately." She gave an empty laugh. "I thought about getting a new one, but that defeats the purpose, doesn't it?"

Beverly flipped through the top notebook. "I kept telling her to write it out, but she never told me she actually did . . ."

"You never saw these? I assumed—" Lauren reached for the book.

"Lauren, I've heard most of it," she replied. "You know by now she was never quite . . . right, mentally. Given the nightmares she survived, it's understandable, but it does *not* excuse her adult behavior, or her refusal to get professional help."

Lauren scoffed. "You got that right."

Beverly sighed. "It was probably a mistake for her to ever marry, much less have children. I'm sorry, I shouldn't say that out loud—"

"I've thought the same thing myself," Lauren said dryly. "So—Alyssa? You've seen her?"

Beverly took a deep breath. "She's been living with us since September—just before Outbreak. She and Peter are . . . they're on their honeymoon." She got up, returning with a wedding photo to show her.

Lauren laughed out loud. "Mother will roll over in her grave. That's just great." She paused. "September, huh? I guess she didn't want to tell us, then . . . yeah. I can see why. Well—tell her congratulations for me. We never talked, but . . . I always wondered if she had something more going on with him, when we were kids."

"I'll tell her," Beverly offered. It was awkward.

"Mrs. Richardson—don't stress. If I could have disappeared from Joan like that, I'd have done it. I always envied her for that. I never gave Alyssa anything but misery, myself. If she's happy, then I'm happy for her, but I'll never hold it against her for not trying to get in touch. Serious. I understand."

"I did try to get her to call. She couldn't face your mother, especially about living here."

"It's all right, she might not have gotten through anyway. I sold the old Braithwaite house, and my number's unlisted, of course. I'm living with Ethan Fangren these days. You may have heard of him . . . movie director?"

Beverly shook her head.

"I doubt you'd see his work, come to think of it," Lauren said. "I'm thinking about changing careers, actually. Ethan's more jealous than you'd think. I'll be too old soon—might as well take the money and run." She gave another empty laugh. "Twenty-six, and too old to work. Well—I have a call time at six, I have to go."

Beverly went to the shelf and handed her a book. "Lauren, would you take this, as a holiday gift? I think Alyssa would like you to have it. And I'm positive Joan wouldn't like it at all." She smiled.

Lauren took it. "Sure, thanks. But you don't owe me anything. I'm not sure myself why I came here. Closure, maybe. Like I said—that therapist is getting under my skin. I didn't . . . I never understood what your friendship meant to Joan."

Lauren swallowed hard. "She was much too rough on you. You didn't deserve to be cut off like that."

Tears welled up in Beverly's eyes. "It means a lot to me to hear you say that."

Lauren said, "See you around, maybe. Say hi to Alyssa. Congratulations and all that."

They said goodbye. Beverly watched her drive away.

* * * * *

Lauren didn't mean to make the woman cry. She wasn't about to do it herself, and she hadn't expected she'd feel like it. She tossed the book on the front seat next to her.

The Book of Mormon. Another Testament of Jesus Christ. Hmph. Well, Alyssa could have whatever life she wanted.

Halfway to Des Moines, moving at top speed, she pitched it out the window.

* * * * *

"Mom, you have to see this!" Andrew called from the living room.

It was a live special report. The anchorwoman said, "This prerecorded press release just in from our sister station in Sioux City. Dr. Jon Pike, of the Mormon community of New Hope, announces their community has developed a working immunization for ATF."

The doctor's face came on the screen, reporting details of an unidentified ATF victim and her amazing recovery, and the development of an antibody in her bloodstream.

"Jon Pike . . ." Beverly muttered. "Why is that name so familiar?"

The station played the tape three times in a row.

"Oh! New Hope!" Beverly exclaimed. "I wonder if that's Alyssa's friend from college."

"No way to find out till they're back," Andrew said.

"Andrew, record this for Peter and Alyssa," Beverly said.

Andrew pushed some buttons. "Got it."

Dr. Joel Kensington came on, live, shortly after. He refuted Jon's claim and said it was physically impossible for any human being to survive infection.

"I prefer to believe we have found our culprit!" Kensington said. "I and my staff have been working around the clock, using proven scientific methods, without this measure of success. It is simply unreasonable to expect their claims to be accurate."

The anchorwoman said, "They claim to have found a survivor."

"Listen, Ms. Tyler. First, *no one* survives this disease. Second, this location is much too far north. *There is no ATF* that far from Central City. President Horne's laser irradiation worked perfectly, and the quarantine is strictly enforced. You saw the tape yourself—that man doesn't look past twenty years old! He's very likely not even a real doctor. They are doing this to call attention to themselves. That is all. It is either a cruel hoax or an attempt to absolve themselves of guilt. Do not forget, Ms. Tyler, this press release comes directly from a group of known lunatics who refuse psychiatric treatment. Who among us knows their true intentions? You must take that into account before you believe anything on that tape."

Andrew said, "He's blaming us for ATF! Did you hear that?"

Mandy Tyler shot back, "After working with you for the past few months, Dr. Kensington, I'm more inclined to believe you wanted the glory of discovery for yourself! Isn't it possible you're jealous someone beat you to it, Doctor?"

Kensington blustered a bit, then she cut him off and replayed the press release. This time, she included a disclaimer explaining the mental instability of the source.

"He can't blame us without proof!" Julia said.

"It's just that one community," said Derek. "New Hope."

Andrew said, "Yeah, but that 'one community' is connected to the rest of us."

* * * * *

Julia and Derek left for their own home in the morning, cutting their stay short a few days. Derek was anxious to get back and check on his family in light of the news. A few of his many siblings lived near Sioux City, close to the place the news said ATF had been located.

That evening, a special broadcast again interrupted regular programming.

The twins complained together, "Not *again!*"

Beverly hushed them.

Anchorwoman Mandy Tyler said, "We have live, breaking news. When the ATF survivor story broke, one brave cameraman and pilot chose to violate President Horne's strictly enforced no-fly zone. We wanted to investigate what General Horne *is* actually doing inside Central City and see for ourselves whether it is true. Are there, or are there not, survivors of ATF?

"We are distressed to report the pilot and cameraman both sacrificed their lives to obtain the video you are about to see. The plane was shot down by U.S. military aircraft moments ago."

Tyler was unprofessionally distressed.

The video was alarming. Two-thirds of Central City lay in blackened ruin. At the northern edge of the line of destruction, fighter jets were releasing a green gas cloud. Wherever it descended, any remaining trees, grass, or bodies melted into black ash. The plane turned 180 degrees to show the untouched northeast quarter and zoomed in. There was movement on the ground.

People.

Not many, but human life was clearly visible.

"As you can see, our previous report that there were no survivors in Central City was a grave error." There was an explosion and the video feed went to static. Mandy Tyler's face returned to the screen. "We are attempting to locate President-General Horne for an immediate press conference. We strongly suspect he was aware of this situation before beginning this maneuver. In light of these new photographs, we must ask ourselves: what have we done, allowing this ruthless man to lead our nation? We can only hope that the loss of innocent life is not as terrible as this video would have us believe."

There was silence among the family members. They stared at the replay of the video feed.

"'Not a yellow dog left to wag its tail . . .'" Beverly whispered, in shock.

Andrew said, "Horne knew exactly what he was doing. That's why he ordered the no-fly zone. People are gonna be pissed."

"Watch your language," Beverly said, on automatic.

"Mom, Andrew said *piss*," Jordan tattled, in the same instant. She snapped to attention. "That doesn't mean copy him, Jordan! *Try* to be a good example, Andrew."

Andrew muttered an apology.

Softer, Beverly said, "You're right, though. This can't be good."

Kellie said, "I hope Peter and Alyssa are okay."

"They should be," Beverly said, "But I'll feel better when everyone is here."

* * * * *

Alyssa sat up from a sound sleep, disoriented and afraid. A moment more, and she remembered where she was. They were camping now, heading back home, their fifth day married. She listened to the quiet winter silence of the forest surrounding the tent. Outside, Teancum stamped a hoof in his sleep and snuffled.

Peter slid his arm about her waist and she jumped.

He mumbled, "Is everything okay?" He sat up.

"It should be—I don't know. I feel something. I'm scared."

"We're safe here."

"Are you sure?"

"We prayed, remember?"

Yes, she remembered. They dedicated the campsite before pitching the tent.

Peter kissed her, his lips eager, hungry. She felt tingling energy rush through her spine, and leaned into him, banishing her fear to a small place inside her mind.

Minutes later, they heard galloping hooves pounding along the road. Teancum whinnied wildly, pulling at his tether.

"What's that?" Alyssa's fear returned in force.

"It's too far and too dark to see, even if I go out there," Peter said.

"I don't want you going out there. But why are they riding so hard?" Two horses.

"I don't know," Peter said. The galloping passed by and began to fade. "But they're going toward the farm. It could be Pony Express from Liahona."

"Pony Express doesn't ride that fast. I think we should get back home and see if anything's wrong," she said.

"I agree, but not now. Let's wait for first light."

The sense of urgency fell on both. They packed the camp site and were away before dawn.

* * * * *

Everyone was relieved to see them. By lunch Beverly had filled them in and showed them the recorded broadcast. News programs were still on—no station was broadcasting regular programming.

Alyssa was stunned just to see Jon's face plastered all over the news, but as it sunk in what General Horne had done, she was physically ill. She thought of Margret, Marcus and Natty . . . Bert . . . all the many friends she knew in the Gardens. From the map on the screen, the Gardens sector was fully destroyed.

All those people . . . gone forever.

Alyssa had pointed Margret to New Hope, but it didn't mean she ever went there. Had she settled down somewhere inside the City? Alyssa clung to slim hope that she'd made it out in time.

Yet—Jon was alive and well—she had proof. And he'd done something incredible.

"He shouldn't be out of med school yet," she commented. "He's my age."

Yet Dr. Jon Pike had discovered the cure for ATF. She was astonished.

She was consumed with wondering whether or not Debra was okay; if she and Jon had married, as they planned; whether they had children. Her guts hurt from missing her friend.

* * * * *

Alyssa unpacked from their trip in Julia's room—now to be hers and Peter's room, together. It felt so strange to take his clothes out of "their" bag and put them on hangers in the closet. Peter was downstairs talking with Andrew. World events swum through her mind, sadness and anxiety mingling with cherished thoughts of the last few magnificent, blissful days alone with Peter. She wished it hadn't had to end.

Beverly came up to the room as she finished. "Alyssa, while you were away, something else happened that I need to talk to you about. You'll want to sit down."

She did. Beverly sat next to her on the bed.

"Lauren came to see me."

"Did I hear you right?"

"She didn't know you lived here, of course. She came to give me a few things that belonged to your mother." Beverly's expression was hard to read.

"I don't understand. Why did she just up and do that?" A grave feeling swirled in her chest.

Beverly said, "Joan did pass away, just like you feared. She was in Central City at Outbreak, and died of ATF. Lauren brought me some of your mother's effects."

"Then it *was* her . . ." Alyssa was stunned. How many shocks could she take in one day?

She and Beverly were silent.

Alyssa craved maternal love and acceptance, which never came from Joan, but "love" was not an emotion she remembered ever feeling for her mother. Hearing the truth that Joan was dead upset her in a far different way than the news of her father's death once had. It was hard to sort out. She didn't miss her; she didn't feel sorry Joan was gone. But it hurt. Joan had carved so many wounds in her soul, so many invisible scars.

"Did I tell you Mother blamed Dad's death on me? As though my growing up was what made him drink himself to death? What's worse is, for a while I believed her. I believed that something I had absolutely no control over—something natural and normal and predictable—caused my father to give up and die." As she spoke, her worst memories surfaced. "And the day I left home, she told me she wished she'd had an abortion. What kind of person tells their daughter something like that? Is that a *mother*? You know what? I'm glad she's gone. Maybe I'm not. I can't figure this out."

Beverly wiped away tears of her own.

Alyssa forgot that Joan's death might register as more of a loss to Beverly than it did to herself. "I'm sorry. I never did understand how you two could be best friends, when you're so nice, and she . . . she . . . was so horrible. What did she ever do for you? It was so one-sided. She just took and took and never gave anything back to anybody."

Beverly took Alyssa into her arms.

Her body shuddered, weeping. "I never had a real mom . . . Chuck wasn't much of a dad, either . . . he didn't save me from her . . . he let her go on hurting me. I feel like I've been an orphan my entire life." The entire pain of her childhood deluged her with uncontainable anguish. In Beverly's arms, she felt tiny and helpless, as if she were seven years old all over again. Memories flashed through her mind's eye one after another. Oddly, she also felt the warmth of the Spirit surrounding her, easing the pain, whispering that it was time to let it go. A new thought came to her mind.

"I want you to be my mom," she said suddenly.

That set Beverly to crying more. "You could always call me Mom, sweetheart, even if you hadn't married Peter."

"I mean forever, as in temple sealings," Alyssa said. "I wish it so much. I don't want them. All I ever wanted was a real mom and dad that would love me forever and ever," she sobbed.

Beverly kissed her hair and held her close.

CHAPTER 39

FALSE WITNESS

Public outrage obliged President-General Horne to cease the gassing of Central City. We were grateful to learn that the destruction didn't reach our valued historical sites in Independence.

However, the quarantine is still enforced, and New Hope's claim to a cure is universally doubted.

I fear the rise of a new Hitler. Polls agree that the destruction was a necessary evil. They say Horne's precautions are working, since ATF has not been found except in that one tributary. According to the reports, that was a direct result of a failure in the quarantine patrol. Horne is blaming the error on insufficient ground troops, calling for a nationwide draft. He sent fighter jets over the small tributaries to purify them of disease, and they are repeating the missile irradiation of the two large rivers.

The ends do not always justify the means. There have to be other ways to combat this plague. How many innocent lives has Horne destroyed, that would not have been at risk otherwise? He terrifies me.

Mandy Tyler isn't on the news anymore.

No explanation—she was just gone. The new guy has to be Horne's puppet.

—Beverly Richardson
personal journal entry

Horne made a phone call. "Kensington!" he barked.

"Yes, sir?" The scientist blinked.

"Did they manufacture ATF, or not? I have to know now."

Kensington frowned. "I can't prove it either way. The antibody isn't an exact DNA match to the ATF samples in our lab. That doesn't mean they *didn't* manufacture it, but I can't establish concrete evidence from this particular sample, either."

"Get me something I can pin on those freaking rebels so I can shut them down. I want hard evidence in my office by the end of the day. Get to work!"

Kensington said, "Shut them down? If you hadn't hindered scientific progress, we would have had the antibody weeks ago. You wouldn't let my staff break quarantine. You informed us your surveillance found *no* survivors after day six. You refused to let us harvest the checkpoints for test subjects. We have *not* had all the tools we needed, as you promised. Speaking frankly, sir, I don't think you have the people's best interest in mind in this crisis. You're a power-hungry tyrant with the brilliance of an amoeba. Millions of lives have been lost on account of your rash decisions!"

Horne's mouth twisted down. "If you value your life, you will not insult me again."

Kensington held his ground. "I'm the only man alive with the skill to do what you ask, and you know it. You won't have me killed. But I'll have you know, I won't go down with this ship you're sinking."

"Joel." Using his first name got the doctor's attention. "You have to trust me. Everything in my gut tells me this group is the culprit. They *did* invent this plague. Therefore, I don't care if you make up the evidence today—because the real evidence will turn up soon enough, and it *will* be them behind it. Of this I have no doubt. They must be stopped before they can complete their master plan. That is why I'm asking you to expedite the establishment of proof. I will not have the media make either martyrs or Messiahs out of them!" He growled out the last sentence.

"Frankly, *Leo*, I'm not sure whom to trust at the moment," Kensington said. "I believe in science. I believe in proof. I *don't* believe in your 'gut.'"

"My gut has never been wrong. But I also have strong evidence that they have both opportunity and motive. This group was my primary suspect from the outset. Now they're showing their colors. Listen to me. There are numerous references in their literature to a mass takeover of Central City—they call it 'returning to Zion.' My intel sources have turned up all sorts of wild 'prophecies' they believe in, including clearing out their sacred land of everything within it, down to the last yellow dog, so they can return en masse and live there and wait for Jesus, while they rule the world!"

"I was unaware of this." Kensington pondered the new information.

"I assure you, President Garrison was not. One reason he pushed Article 28 so hard was to prevent a crisis like this one. Untreated psychopaths are dangerous. They're more dangerous in groups, and the most dangerous when every last one of them believes the same thing. There is a strong *scientific* probability that such groups often try to fulfill their own prophecies. Did you never study basic human anthropology, Doctor?"

"More people will suffer if you go through with this, Horne, and I don't want any part of it."

"I'll double your salary." He hesitated a beat. "Plus I'll lift your restrictions. You'll have the test subjects you need, full access to quarantined areas, and I'll cover you if your procedures are ever called into question. Once we get a vaccine on the market, I'll give you twelve percent of the net profit."

The key to leadership was knowing what motivated your people. Greed was Kensington's.

"I'll get right on it. I should be able to have something plausible by morning, at the latest."

* * * * *

Major Cougar Eye approached Horne's desk, saluting. "President-General Horne, sir?"

He returned the salute. "What is it, Major?"

"We have the bootlickers you asked us to find, sir. You were right to suspect that these zealots have more enemies than you do—they weren't hard to find."

"Who are they?"

"These are from some group that split off from the main religion a few years ago. They got kicked out and are still fighting mad about it. They're only too happy to talk to you, sir."

"Perfect. Bring them in."

Horne stood as two middle-aged men were brought in, under guard. They wore crumpled suits and hadn't shaved in a few days. He sniffed. They hadn't bathed, either. He made a mental note to order everyone cleaned up who came for personal interviews. He offered them seats, but did not shake hands.

"This interview is being recorded by the camera you see behind me," Horne told them. "Guards—at your posts."

Two armed guards stood at attention on either side of the entrance.

The yokels sat there looking awed and dumbfounded. "President-General Horne, sir," the first stammered. "It's an honor, sir."

Horne smiled; it was well-practiced, designed to bestow confidence on those unused to meeting with people of importance. "And you are?"

"Ned Smith," he said.

The second said, "General Horne, sir, my name is Ripley Panfrey."

Horne noted that. Some mothers should be shot before naming babies. "Nice to meet you both. I understand you have information that might be helpful to me."

"Yes, sir," Ripley said.

"Absolutely," Ned added. "We're on your side, sir. These Mormons are dangerous. We know all about their secret plans to infiltrate the U.S. government, the military—begging your pardon, sir—and the U.N. Their ultimate goal is to take over world government, proclaim the Kingdom of God on earth, and subject everyone to their rule, forcing everyone to convert to their faith."

"We used to subscribe to that doctrine, but we have repented. Absolutely," Ripley said.

"We saw the light," Ned said.

Ripley said, "We feel certain they created ATF. Central City was Babylon, Babylon is to be destroyed, and the abomination of desolation must be seen before the Second Coming, that's in all the prophecies and scriptures everywhere, absolutely. They got tired of waiting is all, decided to take it on themselves. They're losing membership because it's taking too long for Jesus to return. Absolutely."

Horne decided Ripley could shut up anytime. "Ned? What's your opinion?"

"Abomination of desolation. That's right, sir. I agree with Ripley, President-General, sir. We're grateful to be operating through the Greater Light. We were saved."

"I was told you were kicked out."

Both men grimaced. "That's a lousy way to put it, sir, beg your pardon," Ned said.

"Absolutely," Ripley chimed in.

Horne could slap the man if he said *absolutely* one more time; but he probably *would* say it, and Horne wouldn't strike, because he needed their testimony as evidence.

Plus there was the camera behind him.

He tapped his foot quietly on the floor.

"We were not allowed to stay because our practices differ," Ned added. "We were given more sure ways to receive revelation, which the Church leaders refused to accept as true."

"At that point we parted ways," Ripley said. "We didn't need them anymore. They were fallen. They didn't understand the Greater Light."

"Please just make your point. Where is your evidence they created ATF?"

Ned produced folded-up papers from his pants pocket. "We have the proof of our visions. That's all *we* need to believe. I got copies here of the words of our enlightened Prophet."

Horne took the papers. They were highlighted in parts. "Prophet?" he asked. The writing was religious drivel.

"Our Prophet is the *real* prophet. Theirs is fallen. You can't believe anything they say, it's all lies, absolutely." Ripley again. Horne wanted to shove his tongue down his throat.

"Boys, this isn't much to go on." He smiled again. "What I need are a few good men. Men willing to help out in a pinch. Especially if it will help take down these false, vile unbelievers. Are you that kind of men?"

They looked at him, then at each other. "We believe so," Ned said.

"Would you be willing to make a statement?"

"What kind of statement?" Ripley asked.

"I need witnesses to state, for the record, that New Hope did create the ATF virus. We have scientific data to back it up, but what we don't have are eyewitnesses. Can you do that for us?"

Ned asked, "You want us to lie?"

Lovely; honesty was a value. Horne thought fast. "If you testify you knew they were doing this and tried to stop them, then along with the scientific evidence, it's enough to take them down. They will be utterly stopped. In addition, you become heroes. You do believe they did this?"

"Absolutely!"

Horne could have shot him—but he'd asked for that one. He clenched his teeth. His foot kept tapping. The cigar craving returned with a vengeance. He had managed to fight off smoking for the most part.

The men hesitated. Ned said, "I'm not sure, Rip . . . we were long gone before they started building all those little United Order villages."

Suddenly both men jumped to attention, focused on a spot behind Horne.

Horne turned. There was nothing there. "What?" he barked.

They looked back at Horne. "We'll do it!" they said in chorus.

Ripley added, "The Greater Light guides! This is the path! We are chosen! Absolutely, absolutely, absolutely!" He stood and clapped his hands with glee, an enraptured smile on his face.

Ned stood also and bowed low—but not to Horne; to an empty space behind the General.

"Guards—restrain these men!" he ordered.

Immediately the men were handcuffed and held by the arms. "Explain this nonsense at once!"

Ned said, "President-General Horne, sir, you are the Chosen! You are the One! Why do you not believe?"

"He can't see," Ripley said to his friend. "He hasn't taken on the Gift."

Ned realized this and explained. "Sir, *you are not alone.* The Greater Light has sent One to guide you."

Not much fazed the General, but these two spooked him.

"Go on," he said, out of sheer morbid curiosity. Horne heard nothing, saw nothing, felt nothing—except the heebie-jeebies.

"Your Guide honors you," Ripley said. He stared at the air, pausing as he spoke, as if translating. "The honor had always belonged to you . . . the honor he once believed was meant for him . . . Now he knows. Now he understands. And you must both continue in the path to fulfill the plan."

Both men struggled against the guards, but it was only to kneel before Horne. "We are your humble servants, and shall do all your bidding," Ned offered, bowing his head.

That part wasn't so bad.

Ripley's eyes stayed fixed on a point in space. He said, "You don't believe . . . but I can show you." He focused back on Horne. Horne liked it better when he didn't. "The Guide gives me a sign. You have not smoked in years, but you have been craving cigars. In fact, you want one at this very moment. This is the sign your Guide is present and wishes to communicate with you.

"He is here now. He speaks to me. I see him! Ned! Ned! Do you hear him? *He says he is the Maker!* He is the Maker of the Gift, the Sacred Elation! We must bow before him!" He tried to prostrate himself flat on the floor, but the guard yanked the man upright.

"You're insane," Horne spat out. "Get them out of here and take their statements!"

"He has much to teach you, if you would only listen and believe!"

The guards ushered them out roughly.

He slammed the office door after them. He was furious and shaken by this interchange.

"Sometimes a cigar," he said through his teeth, "*Is just a cigar!*"

* * * * *

He oversaw the taping of their statements. What complete psychos!

As he observed at the one-way window, more reports came in. More willing witnesses already turning up. How many would crawl out of the woodwork before he was through? He decided he would not meet any more of them personally—just in case.

He wasn't *that* into being bowed down to.

When the taping was finished, Horne met the guards.

"Yes, sir?" one asked.

"Take these cuckoos over to Psychiatric and have them treated. Immediately!"

"Yes, sir!"

"No!" Ned and Ripley screamed at once.

Ripley begged, "You can't, sir! You are the Chosen One! We pledge thee our devoted service! We cannot serve that which we cannot remember to worship!"

Ned burst into wailing tears. "Please don't take away our Gift! Not the *Gift* . . ."

The men were hauled off, their raucous bawling causing a commotion the entire way.

* * * * *

By day's end, Horne surveyed a well-produced press release and was pleased. "I'll have to promote you for this work, Major. This should do quite well."

The major beamed.

Earlier, Horne made an executive, necessary decision to yank the media back into his control, like it or not. The first thing he did was pull that stupid broad Mandy Tyler off the job. Her words grated on his nerves. *"What have we done?"* she said. Live, on the national news broadcast. *"What have we done, allowing this ruthless man to lead our nation . . . ?"*

Hardly professional journalism. How could he solve this crisis if she turned public sentiment against him? If he was not in charge, chaos would reign. That, he knew. The public never understood when death and sacrifice were necessary evils. Some healthy people may have died in the gassing. But it was impossible to know who would turn out to be a carrier, or where else it might spread if he let them go. Containment was necessary at whatever cost. The square kilometers comprising Central City seemed massive, yes, until one considered its ratio to the rest of the globe. Even accounting for population.

It was a major accomplishment that ATF was not cropping up in Europe, Asia, Africa . . . it was found nowhere else but within those limits. And the world was not even grateful.

Fools.

He could not entice the public to understand his methods and reasoning unless he was the only one doing the explaining.

The story broke on the evening news. From here the tide would turn.

People would forget their anger with Horne's drastic but necessary measures in light of the new information. Their outrage would shift to the Mormons, and the public would demand retribution.

He meant to punish Tyler for her crimes personally.

CHAPTER 40

PROTECTIVE ACTION

General Horne:
We are alarmed by your evil and groundless accusation. You have placed blame on the innocent for the sole purpose of increasing your power and material gain in a time of crisis.

DNA samples were sent to us in Salt Lake City, Mexico, and Canada, and we have reproduced and forwarded these reports to labs around the world. We are aware you have control of national news broadcasts and that United States citizens may not discover the truth of your deceit, but you have worldwide reactions to consider. We will not be silent in proclaiming our innocence.

We are a peaceful people. We have no design for world power. We allow all men to worship how, whom, or what they may, or not at all.

We beg you to please have mercy on our innocent people. Please allow our members in outlying areas to leave the country if they wish. You have shed much innocent blood. Do not add more to your hands. We fear your fate at the last day shall be terrible and eternal. We admonish you to repent.

—Ricardo C. Chavez, President
The Church of Jesus Christ of Latter-day Saints
Salt Lake City, Utah Nation

New Hope was on edge.

President Weber had a crew working nonstop to connect cables to large screens in New Hope's community center. They managed to hack in to one local station. Equipment to restore the Church's satellite connection had been sent from Utah by horseback.

It was the only way to get news, so people were constantly packed into the building to listen.

Jon, Debra, and their families crowded into the gymnasium, standing room only. Jon leaned against the wall, holding a sleeping Zach, with Debra comfortably squished next to him.

The story came on that New Hope had invented ATF at the direction of Church leaders. Witnesses came on saying the Church destroyed Central on purpose to bring about the abomination of desolation—exactly as Blankenship had destroyed L.A. to "prevent" the Tribulation. "Now *they* look crazy," Jon pointed out. "Nobody knows what 'abomination of desolation' means, anyway."

Debra agreed. "How many times can that guy say 'absolutely' in one sentence? And his eyes—he looks like he's on drugs."

The story progressed to show matching DNA strands in the antibody and the ATF organism, "proving" the disease and the cure came from the same place.

Jon was shocked. "That's not what I sent! They made that up!"

Debra groaned inside.

They put a spotlight on President Weber, who was standing at the front of the gymnasium. He knelt with a microphone and began a prayer. That alone kept the crowd from rioting, and allowed for a strange calm.

A few members ran off as soon as the news broke and were never seen again.

During the prayer, someone tapped Jon on the shoulder. "Brother and Sister Pike? Could you come with me, please?" he whispered.

"What is it?" Debra whispered back. The President was still praying; they should have their eyes shut, no talking.

"President Weber wants me to take you to the bunker. We'll let your families know where you are."

"Our families are right here," Jon whispered. His mother was peeking out the corner of her eye.

"My wife will explain it to them," the man offered. "I'm sorry—we haven't met, but I know your face. I'm Brother Jameson. Please—come."

"Now?" Debra asked, but they were already moving out of the gymnasium. Debra mouthed the words, *it's okay*, catching her mother's anxious stare.

Once in the hallway, Brother Jameson picked up the pace. It was crowded everywhere, and they hurried through with bumps and jostling.

Outside, he said, "President Weber asked me to get you out during the prayer when nobody was looking. He's not just worried about Horne—he's afraid some people might want your head on a platter."

Debra asked, "Without Jon, we'd all be dying right now! Don't they remember about the asylum guy that fell in the stream? Or the two hunters?"

She felt rightfully proud. Indignant. In that moment, she forgot she ever hadn't wanted him to work on ATF research.

Her husband was a hero.

"People tend to forget things when they're angry. If they want to blame someone right now, that's you."

Jon said, "We all voted on the press release. It's too important to keep it from the world!"

"President Weber understands. I understand, too. We just want you to be safe."

They reached the administration building. Zach was awake. They took an elevator into a basement level and went through a hallway with many unmarked doors. Brother Jameson opened one with a key, a supply closet.

"If you could help me move this?" he asked.

Jon gave the baby to Debra and helped push a metal shelf away from the concrete wall.

A steel door lay behind it.

"Jon, I don't like this," Debra said. She was amazed Zach stayed so calm. He looked at his mother, blinking.

"I don't either, but what else can we do?"

"Not to worry," Brother Jameson smiled. He unbolted the door and swung it wide. "You'll lock it from the inside, and this door is so heavy you should be able to push the shelf out of the way."

"Oh!" Debra exclaimed. She assumed "bunker" meant dismal and gray. Inside, it was decorated like a living room with comfortable chairs and paintings on the walls. Several doors and passages led away, giving the feeling it was very large.

He explained, "It's fully stocked. The lights are full-spectrum, since there's no windows. There's water, hot and cold, a kitchen, tons of food, bathrooms, bedrooms, laundry room, everything you'll need. Even diapers."

Jameson went to a screen on one wall. "This is the only sort of phone we have connected. It's more an intercom, really, that goes direct to the President's office."

He pushed a button, and they saw the empty office on the screen. He changed a channel. "This is that local channel, if you want to watch." He muted the volume and left the news on.

Debra's lip trembled. Although nice inside, it still felt like prison. "But it can be locked from outside."

"Trust me, we have no desire to."

She sighed.

"We only want to protect you. When any danger is past, we'll let you know. We'll bring your families down too, if it seems they're at risk, but we wanted to secure you first."

Debra didn't relish the thought of sharing quarters with *both* sets of parents at once, plus siblings, plus nieces and nephews.

"It's way better than Liberty Jail, Deb," Jon offered.

His chuckle fell flat.

"I feel like I got sent to my room," Deb said. "Only Mama sent the wrong child. I didn't do anything wrong."

Brother Jameson was sympathetic. "I understand. I wish it was different myself. I almost forgot—if there's anything you want from home, make a list, and your family can bring it. All right?"

They nodded.

"All right. Good luck. Consider it . . . a vacation."

He explained the lock, which was controlled by an electronic keypad by the door, shook their hands and left.

They stood dumbfounded for a few minutes, then investigated their new surroundings.

* * * * *

Debra and Jon sat powerless while the world fell down around them.

General Horne gave a speech the following day to a large crowd. He said, "For public safety, Article 28 shall be strictly enforced. Those who refuse psychiatric treatment are ordered to enter the quarantined area of Central City. Utah shall retain its sovereignty for the time being, but the former leniency President Garrison allowed will not be tolerated. The former President failed to disable a known threat. Central City's millions of lost lives could have been prevented, had the law been enforced!

"Since these terrorists say they have a vaccine, we shall use the quarantined area to hold them. We shall see whether their 'cure' is effective against ATF."

Cheers rang out on the screen.

Horne then gave an ultimatum that all illegal communities, including New Hope, were to be dissolved within two weeks and remove the inhabitants to Central City, or face military action.

"He can't do that," Deb said in shock.

"Yes he can," Jon said. "We're under martial law. Article 28 was already the law. We only hoped this would last . . . It's gone so well here, I took it for granted."

"What are we going to do? Jon, this isn't how we're supposed to be called back to Independence to build Zion!"

"I never expected the call to come like this, either," Jon answered. "But Horne didn't ruin Independence. So I expect that whatever happens, we can build Zion in the appointed place. The Prophet Joseph built Nauvoo out of a mosquito-infested swamp."

"Yes, but this sounds like a roach motel, not Zion. He'll wait to get us all in one place, then—" She closed her eyes in fear.

"Debra, baby. We've made it this far. We'll make it through this." Tenderly he kissed her, pulling her close.

* * * * *

A few days after Horne's ultimatum, Margret strolled near the southern outskirts of New Hope, finally well enough to walk. It was a warm spring morning, and she held hands with Marcus and Natty as they went. She hadn't decided yet what to do.

She saw tanks approach on the horizon.

"Marcus! Pick up Natty and run!" she yelled. She moved as fast as she could to the administration building. She was weak. Marcus was much faster.

He called out, "Help! Horne has tanks coming!"

The offices became a blur of commotion as the warning spread. New Hope was defenseless against heavy artillery.

President Weber rode his horse out to meet them, and Margret went outside to watch. The long line of tanks moved slowly into formation, surrounding the town. The President spoke to the commanding officer of the unit for some time. Many gathered near Margret to watch and wait.

When he rode back in, he spoke to those gathered. "They're here to deliver the commands and make sure we comply," he said. "They won't fire unless we try to stay. We have ten days left."

* * * * *

The intercom rang in the bunker. President Weber told Jon and Debra about the tanks. "They're not looking for you after all," he said. "But I have a story ready, in case they change their minds. In that case, a small lie to save an innocent life would be justified."

"Can we come out then?"

"I'll come down and get you myself. I imagine you're as safe as the rest of us. You do need to pack your things, but Jon, try to stay indoors. You're a celebrity of sorts—any of those soldiers could recognize you. Work on a disguise, okay? "

* * * * *

New Hope took the most caution with closing down their beloved temple. Everyone planning a wedding, or even thinking about getting engaged, got married within the next three days.

Then the temple was permanently closed, and sacred items were carefully packed away under lock and key.

Debra hated thinking it would soon be overrun and probably destroyed. She had been married there; it was *her* temple. It seemed during the remaining week, packing boxes, helping her mother, brothers, and sisters, that she never stopped crying.

CHAPTER 41

PERSONAL EFFECTS

> *. . . I haven't dreamed about the Chinese boy ever since I saw him in the mirror. He's just . . . gone from me. I worry about him though. I wonder even more if he's real, or if my mind is playing serious tricks.*
>
> —Alyssa Richardson,
> personal journal entry

Local police dropped by the Richardson farm to make sure they were leaving. Beverly assured them they were, and sent them away. The farm was closer to Central City than Liahona, so they would first join Bishop Greene's family, and the King's, and wait for the Liahona crowd to catch up.

"I can't stand to leave this place," Beverly said, over and over. "Phil's grandfather built this house over seventy-five years ago."

The Richardsons left the Church satellite on day and night. The Prophet sent words of encouragement over the satellite. He sent three of the Twelve Apostles and several other authorities from Utah by car, to assist relocation efforts and go with the Saints into Central. There were five villages total to disassemble, all north or east of Central City.

"We can't survive in there," Peter said. "Horne killed off everything organic with that gas. Nothing's going to grow. Any ground there will be poisoned for years."

"He didn't finish," Alyssa said.

"It sounds like Salt Lake is working on it," Andrew said, glued to the screen. "Listen."

A report came on that the Prophet was negotiating with General Horne on terms. He had arranged a location for the Saints to gather, outside the perimeter, for all to receive vaccinations first. To refuse them that small courtesy would be sending them to certain death, and even the U.N. wouldn't agree with that.

"I *had* wondered about that detail," Alyssa said dryly.

The report continued to say that several thousand head of vaccinated cattle, sheep, and other livestock had been sent from Utah. There was no risk of ATF out west. The antibody samples New Hope sent were used, initially, on the needed animals. Other food would be shipped if wholesome food was not found inside City borders.

"Where are we going to put those?" Peter mused, holding Alyssa's hand on the couch. "Didn't you say it's all paved, with enormous skyscrapers? Cattle need fodder and pasture."

She shrugged. "It was that way in the parts I've seen. I've never been to the northeast quarter."

"We'll need the animals, though," Peter relented. "We'll have twenty-five thousand people to feed, and with all the power grids blown, nothing's going to be fresh. Not for a long time."

"It's a big cage," Alyssa said. "I wish we could go to Canada or Mexico instead."

"The border's closed," Andrew piped up. "Nobody gets in or out. Horne doesn't want us escaping without 'justice.'"

Beverly came in from outside, listening a moment to the conversation. "I never thought this would happen in America, either. But get up everybody, we have to get the gear together."

They all stood, with a collective, "Sorry, Mom."

"I can't find our old camp stove," she said. "Have any of you seen it?"

"The little fold-up one?" Peter asked. "I thought it was buried in the garage somewhere."

"I've torn it apart. It's nowhere."

"How about the regular grill?"

"It's too big, remember? Directions from Salt Lake are to take only personal effects, items of sentimental value, journals, genealogy and stuff. And any livestock. There's a city full of goods we can use once we get there."

Andrew said, "Who knows how long it'll take to immunize everybody?"

"More camping," Peter whispered in Alyssa's ear.

She giggled, blushed, and squeezed his hand. "Sh!"

"The grill will pack fine, Mom," Peter said. "We're not taking much, when you think about it."

"A bunch of the tin pots and plates are missing too. I'm positive they were all together with the little stove."

"Are there other things we can use?" Alyssa asked.

Beverly grumbled and went off to the kitchen. Ten minutes later, she was back. "Andrew, I asked you three hours ago to work on the chicken cages."

"I did," he said.

"I wanted them loaded on the trailer."

"I fixed the broken ones, made sure they fit, and took them down. We can't put the chickens inside yet. I thought that's what you wanted."

Beverly made a frustrated puff of air, blowing her bangs upward. "Isaac and Anna are getting here tomorrow. Where's their stuff going?"

"In the garage," Peter said. "There's plenty of room, Mom."

Beverly said, "I don't want the same room arrangements as Christmas. I want Isaac and Anna in my room with the babies, and I'll take Peter's old room. But where do I put Julia and Derek? We can't put the twins in with you two."

"Mom, we don't mind," Peter said. Beverly rolled her eyes.

"Relax, Mom," Andrew said. "They can stay in my room,"

They spent the day packing boxes with journals, photo albums, trinkets from each of their childhoods that Beverly couldn't bear to part with, including their old baby blankets and clothes.

"Will we ever see this place again?" Alyssa whispered to Peter.

"I don't know, honey . . . I don't know."

* * * * *

Ruby said to Jon, "Would you hold still, boy?"

Rudy was sixty-eight, Octavia's mother, and the best hairdresser in New Hope for gluing on hair extensions. They fell out of fashion eons ago. Ruby carefully attached a twisted lock permanently to his head.

Octavia had donated her long, dreadlocked hair for Operation-Get-Jon-a-Disguise. LaDell had offered her hair, but Jon knew too well how hard it would be for her to cut it. Octavia's hair was much longer. She still had eight inches of hair left, but Debra couldn't get used to seeing her with the short style.

The hair was half on, half not. Jon pointed to LaDell and said, "What are *you* laughing at?"

Debra couldn't hold back her laughter either. She never imagined her husband with long locks.

"I'm gonna stick out *worse* this way," Jon complained. "And I can't go to work, right when the vaccine cultures are taking off. Jerry says they're multiplying like crazy."

"They'd better," Octavia said. "We got twenty-five thousand people to inoculate."

Debra said, "Jon, you can't be seen. We don't know if Horne's men will suddenly change their minds and think they need you. Everybody—call him *Nathan* outside now. That's the end part of Jonathan, with my maiden name, Gray. *Nathan Gray.* Got that?"

The other sisters laughed heartily.

Jon was utterly miserable. "Are we *sure* this is necessary?"

"It better be, boy, at this stage," Octavia said, giving him a friendly smack. "You were committed the minute Mama got out those scissors."

Ruby said, "It wasn't easy for me to cut off my baby's hair. You take good care of it."

LaDell said, "Sistahs—shall we do his nails next?"

"That boy looks like he could use a pedicure. Bring that foot over here," Ocatvia said.

Jon wriggled his feet away from her teasing. "No, no, no!"

"Hold still!" Ruby smacked the top of his head.

He fingered the two-week growth on his chin. "But the beard stays, so nobody goes around thinking I'm one of you-all women."

* * * * *

Margret struggled with her choice. She wasn't a believer; she could go free. But Marcus nudged her over the edge. He had his daddy's mellow eyes and a tender heart that she couldn't crush any further. He had already pulled away since she refused his baptism request, and he wanted to go build Zion with the Saints.

They offered good work, and good friendship, once she restrained herself a little.

Once they got there, it could be like the Gardens again . . . only not so poor. She'd have a day job, and maybe even a house with a yard. She never lived in a house in her life.

It sounded good.

They wanted to put her on an animal for the trip. She said no right away. Let Marcus and Natty ride some, stinky, sweaty old pony if they liked it. She was too weak to walk, though. She found a carriage with room for one more person, and the kids' pony plodded alongside.

The Salt Lake people sent up two semi-trailers per town for everybody's personal stuff. Not for furniture—only for sentimental stuff they couldn't part with. Margret didn't have anything to put in. Everything she and her children owned fit in their packs.

Margret was amazed to learn four other towns just like New Hope existed. Gasoline costs would be astronomical to move twenty-five thousand people.

Horne wouldn't cough up military transport, either. Soldiers and tanks were visible along the road, a hundred yards off the pavement, silent shepherds, making sure no one ran off.

President Weber made a little speech about how his ancestors traveled months across the prairie in wagons with no roads, and encouraged everyone that walking a hundred miles or so in honor of that pioneer heritage would do them no harm.

It shut up a lot of the grumblers.

At night, she dreamed she lay in Bert's arms.

* * * * *

Beverly finished unhitching the mares to camp for the night.

She felt a kiss on her earlobe. "Hello, Sunshine," Phil's voice said in her ear. She jumped and spun around. There was no one there.

"I'm here, but you can't see me right now." He squeezed her hand. She squeezed back. That was a strange thing, to hold air and feel Phil's warm hand.

"These soldiers make me nervous," she whispered. They were everywhere, watching, with rifles and tanks. She'd never seen a tank up close. What if they opened fire?

Phil said, "Trust me. This is the way."

"When will I see you?"

"Tonight. After everyone's asleep."

Peter came up. "Who are you talking to, Mom?"

"Oh—just talking to myself, that's all. I don't like the looks of these soldiers."

Peter said, "None of us do."

* * * * *

That evening, Andrew took a long walk with Bishop Greene. They were gone for two hours.

When they came back, Andrew's eyes shone with hope.

* * * * *

Liahona was first to arrive at the designated meeting place, a campground near Mt. Pisgah. They spread out in evenly-spaced rows of tents, organized by ward and stake.

Ten semi-trailers carrying everyone's personal effects were there, parked in a large lot.

The Richardsons arranged their four tents together in a cluster. Each married family had their own, with the largest, a three-room tent, going to Beverly, Andrew, Kellie, and Jordan.

Alyssa was relieved to see public bathrooms on the grounds.

"Are all twenty-five thousand people going to be here at once?" she wondered.

The enormity of it sunk in. She knew that many people fit in an average sports arena, but spreading out to live took much more space.

Peter said, "I hope not, but until New Hope gets here with enough vaccine, we're stuck."

* * * * *

The town of Moroni, which lay north of Liahona, arrived second. The Nauvoo settlement along the Mississippi, and one from Kirtland, Ohio, had farther to travel and would be last.

After a week, scouts reported New Hope parties should begin arriving by noon.

Alyssa said, "I'm riding out to meet them, Peter—don't try to stop me."

"Stop you? I'm going with you," he said.

They saddled Teancum, and Peter spurred him into a gallop.

* * * * *

"We're looking for Jon and Debra Pike," Peter said to those in front, breathing hard from the fast ride. "Can you tell us where they are?"

"Why do you ask?"

Alyssa said, "They're old friends of mine."

They were met with suspicion.

Allysa added, "Her maiden name is Debra Gray? Jon has to be here somewhere—we saw him all over the news."

"Who's asking?"

"We're the Richardsons, from Liahona," Peter said.

"Oh! Why didn't you say so? Because of the soldiers, we're trying to keep him undercover."

A woman pointed out a caravan. Peter spurred the horse.

When they got close, she dismounted and called at the top of her voice, "Debra! Debra Gray? Debra Pike?" A female figure held a hand to her forehead, squinting.

"Debra, it's Alyssa! I'm over here!" she called.

Debra ran faster. When she recognized Alyssa, her hands flew to her mouth. Alyssa wrapped her in a huge hug and almost picked her up in her excitement. "I'm so excited to see you!"

Debra wept for joy. "Alyssa, is it really you?"

"It's really me!" They drew back and looked at each other. "I tried to call but by then your servers were blown—I have so much to tell you! I got to Peter's house right before Outbreak, then I got baptized, and we got married in the Liahona Temple three weeks ago! I wished you could have been there! I've missed you so much—all I can think about is how I wanted to let you know I'm alive."

Debra couldn't speak beyond, "Alyssa . . . Alyssa!"

Peter dismounted, and Alyssa made introductions.

Jon came up with Zachary, and Alyssa reached out to hold him. "He's beautiful! He looks just like both of you." She brushed off a thought that she might never have children that looked like her or Peter—no need to dampen the joy of this moment. "Jon, what happened to your hair? It was short a month ago when we saw you on the news!"

He grinned. "They're hoping it will disguise me. It's not working, huh?"

"I wouldn't have recognized you." He looked good, just very different. Debra's always-short hair had grown too, and she wore it in braids all over her head. It was pretty.

Debra exclaimed, "I can't believe I'm looking at you! And what you said—it's all true?"

Peter beamed. "It's all true. When there's time, she has quite a story to tell you."

A clear, young boy's voice called out. "It *is* Alyssa! Mama, come quick!"

Two children burst through the crowd of people. They tackled Alyssa to the ground in their exuberance. She laughed and laughed, tears streaming down her cheeks, recognizing the children she loved so much. She sat in the shallow snow and held their little bodies tight and close. It felt so good, so perfect. "Marcus! Little Natty! You made it! I can't believe it, you're okay!" But where was their mother?

She recognized Debra's mother Taletha, holding Margret up, coming slowly.

"Let me up, babies, I want to see your mama." They let go.

Jon said, "And coming toward you is our miracle worker, our recovering ATF patient."

"It was Margret?" She was dumbfounded.

"She didn't want her picture to be on the news, in case her ex-husband might see," Jon explained.

"Oh—of course." She could think about that later. Alyssa hurried over to wrap Margret in a hug. "You're alive! Oh I'm so glad I found you! I've been so worried—"

"I'm alive! You mean *you're* alive!" Margret shook in her arms from the tears. "I thought you were dead, I thought you were dead," she repeated, over and over again. Finally she pulled back to look in her face. "I missed you every day, man!"

"You're the one that survived ATF?" Alyssa asked.

"That's me," she said. Marcus and Natty clung to their legs. "I'm still mending. But look at us! Both of us, survivors. How incredible is that?"

Natty said, "Mama, Debra said Alyssa has a *husband!*"

"You lie!"

Alyssa showed Margret her ring, smiling so wide that her face hurt.

"Where'd you find a man so quick, girlfriend?"

"Remember the man I could never forget? Peter? It's him!"

"*Caramba*, you mean it?"

"Come meet him, he's right here!"

Introductions went around again, and the little group talked and talked as they went along, with years of catching up to do.

Alyssa's jaw hurt from all the talking and smiling by the time they got back to camp.

* * * * *

The DeVray's set up a tent next to Alyssa's. Soon it was dinnertime. Marcus scurried around gathering firewood, and set up his little stove.

Peter did a double take, seeing it. "Marcus . . . I'm just curious, where did you get that?"

Natty set out three tin plates and cups on a blanket, and Peter's jaw dropped.

He whispered in Alyssa's ear, "If I didn't know better, I'd say those were ours."

"That's impossible. Those things look alike, you know that."

Marcus answered, "A nice man brought them to us when Mama first got sick. He helped us get to New Hope and showed me how to build a good fire."

Peter watched the child stacking the wood with a sense of déjà vu. *That looks exactly like the way Dad taught me to make a fire when I was in Scouts . . .* Peter asked, slowly, "What was this man's name?"

"I don't remember." Marcus shrugged. "Natty and Mama don't remember his name either. Mama doesn't even remember the nice man now, but we know he was real because we still have this stuff."

Peter felt a strange chill.

Beverly came up. "Peter, do you have the—?" She stopped short and stared at the stove. "So that's where the stove went. Peter, you should have told me you found it—it would have saved me a lot of trouble."

Peter said, "I didn't find it."

Alyssa said, "Marcus just said a nice man gave it to them, when Margret first got sick."

Beverly intoned, "Phil . . ." She drew it out funny—as if she were scolding her non-present husband. "You took it, didn't you!"

Alyssa whispered to Peter, "She's cracked!"

He shared his wife's concern. "Mom?"

Beverly paused like she was listening to the wind, but there was no breeze blowing. Then she smiled.

"Kids, I have something to tell you. Come with me. Now."

She gathered the family inside their large tent, all six children, three spouses, and two grandchildren.

"I know where your father is," she announced.

There was instant commotion. Beverly silenced it with a whistle, two fingers in her mouth, the way she called them from play as children.

When it was quiet, she spoke again. "He's right here."

Alyssa whispered, "She's lost her mind, Peter, now what do we do?"

But a faint light appeared in the tent and grew brighter until it materialized into a person. Peter recognized the shape and form and carriage . . .

"Dad!" Peter couldn't believe his own eyes. His father stood before them, smiling with joy.

Everyone gasped.

Kellie and Jordan called *"Daddy!"* and threw themselves into his arms first. He picked them up and kissed them, squeezing tight.

Peter stood open-mouthed. "Mom? Dad? What's going on here?"

"It's a long story, but today, there's time to tell it all," Phil said. "Hugs first!"

On Peter's turn to be hugged, he melted into the comfort of his father's arms. "Dad, I miss you so much." It was hard to let go and allow Julia to go next. Phil reassured him, "I'll be here for a while."

Phil embraced each of his children in turn. Andrew hung back, last.

"Andy . . . come here." Phil held him the tightest, and Andrew wept like a baby in his father's arms.

CHAPTER 42

GATHERING

Find out who invented the hallucinogenic drug known as Elation. Find out if he ever smoked cigars. STAT.
If he's alive, bring him to me.

—Pres.-General Leo F. Horne,
memo to Major Cougar Eye

The camp held an atmosphere of tedious waiting.

Horne's armies kept their distance, but the camp was surrounded. More groups arrived in Mt. Pisgah daily. Dr. Jerry Marden headed up a well-organized immunization project, setting up temporary labs in tents to manufacture more vaccine. It would take time.

New Hope was already immunized; that helped. Two Apostles from Salt Lake went with President Weber and took most of New Hope's citizens down into Central City, not long after their arrival. A third Apostle stayed to preside over the growing, waiting company.

Phil wasn't visible often, and felt like more of a guest than a resident to the Richardson children. His presence was not known to the general camp.

But a great burden lifted off the family's shoulders. They were all comforted and more at ease, grateful when they could see him.

Peter hoped his father's return meant the mantle of patriarchy would be removed, but Phil smiled and told him no. "That's your job now, Peter. I am part of this, yes. But no longer a mortal part."

"Why can't it fall to Isaac? He's the oldest and he's right here."

"You know their present needs better than he does. He hasn't been around home as much."

Peter was grieved. "But . . ."

Phil embraced his son in a warm hug. "You must learn to lead, Peter. But I'm here to help."

* * * * *

Debra and Jon stayed behind when New Hope and their families left, basking in Alyssa's long-lost company. They built new friendships with Peter and his family and got along well together.

Margret stayed also. She didn't want to leave Alyssa either, and neither would Marcus or Natty.

* * * * *

The livestock arrived with some fanfare, coming from Church land in Idaho, Utah, Montana, and Wyoming. The dust cloud the hooves kicked up was visible miles away.

Alyssa had never seen so many animals gathered in one place.

Late the same afternoon, Alyssa checked on their chickens. Andrew had set up a temporary wire coop, so the ckickens didn't have to stay in the cages, but the wires needed frequent repair to keep the chickens from escaping.

She didn't notice the dusty, unshaven man in a cowboy hat, threading his way through crowded tents and supplies, one of the ranchers just arriving.

He spotted Alyssa, stopped, and watched her work for a few minutes. Alyssa was focused on twisting the wire into place with long-nosed pliers.

He cleared his throat and tapped her shoulder. "Excuse me . . . you look like someone . . ." he said.

She turned and looked up into his face.

"Alyssa, it is you! I thought I'd lost you forever!"

She dropped the pliers. "Rob! Is that you?"

He caught both her hands and held them. "It is so good to see you—you're every bit as beautiful as I remembered." He made a move as if to kiss her, and she gently pushed him back.

"Rob, what are you doing here?"

"I could say the same for you. I'd never have looked here to find you . . . I thought you might be dead, but I never gave up hope."

Delight shone in his eyes. His fingers noticed her wedding ring and his expression shifted; he let go of her hands.

Peter pushed his way through the milling crowd. "What's going on here?"

Her gut twisted. "Rob, this is Peter Richardson . . . my husband. Peter . . . this is Robert Giles." She watched his face—yes, Peter recognized the name.

They shook hands. Peter wasn't overly pleased, and didn't hide it. "I've heard of you."

"You haven't said why you're here," Alyssa said.

"I came with the cattle drive, but how is it *you're* here? You escaped Caldwell. That's such a relief. But you with the Saints? You never cared for organized religion."

Peter stood with his arm protectively about her waist.

"Rob, I think you should know right away that Peter is the man—the one I could never forget, my first love. We found each other again." She took Peter's hand in hers and gave it a squeeze. She felt no inner conflict whatsoever. It was a relief to know that about herself. Rob's whiskers looked prickly, too—*Peter won't be growing a beard anytime soon. Ick!*

She added, "It turns out that Peter never forgot me, either. He never married. So . . . we got together, and we were married in the Liahona Temple." She didn't tack on how recent that event was.

She wished Peter would say something. The way they stood side by side, she couldn't see his face well to read into what she should say or not.

"She does get a hold on you, doesn't she?" Rob got a bit misty. Then he straightened up, swallowed. "I'm glad to know she found you."

It was just plain awkward.

"I'm not doing a good job here," Rob apologized. "Peter, I'm a man of covenant, as you are. I would never come between a man and his wife. What's more, if you are that first love . . . I knew even then that her torch for you would never go out, even if she came with me instead. I would have lived forever in your shadow, because you alone possessed the power to make her truly happy. I honor you."

He was so sincere that Peter was touched. "I appreciate that," he said, finding his voice.

Rob said, "When I got to Montana, I felt so terrible about my whole life, especially the mess I got Alyssa into, that I searched every religion, seeking out truth, something I could cling to. I craved redemption. I found it here, in this church, and I have not strayed from its teachings ever since.

"Also . . . Alyssa—I could never think of you without wishing I could apologize for everything terrible that I put you through. I can't delay an opportunity that I've prayed for every day for years. I know now that what I did was wrong and caused you so much pain, that I can't begin to express how sorry I am. Please accept my deepest apologies. I hope you can someday forgive me."

Alyssa stared at her feet. She'd rather it wasn't brought up, frankly. She leaned slightly deeper into Peter.

Forgive him? Have I done that?

She looked up and took in the sincere intensity of Rob's brown eyes. "I will try." She meant it. "Apparently, I haven't spent as much time in deep thought about it as you have. But I would not want to deny forgiveness to anyone."

Rob exhaled, a look of peace coming over his countenance.

Debra came up carrying Zach on her hip, and Margret came with her. "Who's this, Alyssa?" Debra held her free hand out to shake Rob's. "Hi. I'm Debra Pike, and this is Zachary."

Rob said, "You look so familiar. Have we met?"

"It's Rob Giles, Deb," Alyssa muttered. "Remember?"

"I've got it!" he exclaimed. "You're Alyssa's roommate. You never liked me. What a day this is!"

Debra made the connection and got as defensive as Peter. "What are you doing here?"

"I came in with the cattle drive. You—you're a Latter-day Saint too?" Rob was befuddled.

"Dyed-in-the-wool, back to the pioneers," Debra said. "Alyssa didn't know that when we roomed together, not until the end. After you left."

"And who's your friend?"

Alyssa said, "She's an old friend of mine. Margret DeVray, Rob Giles. Rob is . . . well, he's an old boyfriend."

Margret shook hands. "Girl, you never let on you had such fine taste in men!"

Alyssa laughed with her.

Rob *was* rather attractive; he didn't strike her that way now, but she knew that it once made her choice to leave him harder than it should have been.

Peter didn't care for Margret's comment, either. He wrapped his arms around Alyssa from behind and held her even tighter.

"Peter, I can't breathe," she whispered, to get him to loosen up.

It was almost funny.

Rob smiled at Margret. "I take it you're single."

"Very," she answered.

"She's got two kids, Marcus and Natty, ages eight and four. They're around someplace," Alyssa said.

Margret popped her on the arm. "Gee, thanks, what are friends for?"

"Margret isn't a member," Debra offered.

"You guys are so good to me," Margret teased. To Rob she said, "I'm just along for the ride. Got mixed up with these guys along the way. Debra's husband saved my life."

Debra beamed. "Jon just discovered the antibody, Margret. You're the woman responsible for creating it."

Rob asked, "You're the ATF patient who lived?"

Margret said, "You're looking at her. That's me."

Rob took Margret's hand in his and kissed it. "Bless you. You worked a miracle for the entire world. I'm honored to make your acquaintance."

Margret looked at Alyssa. "Whoa, girlfriend, was he always like this?"

Alyssa laughed. "No. That's new."

She sensed that Peter's nerves were still on edge, the way he clung to her. She would reassure him later that Rob was indeed correct—Peter was the only man who would ever possess the power to bring her happiness.

As the circle of old and new friends talked together, the conversation becoming smoother and more relaxed as it went along, something about it struck Alyssa to the center.

The dear friends she had once lost to unknown fates were all found.

Before her in one place stood those she held dear, whose associations she cherished. Most important was Peter, best friend and husband, clinging to her side with an attractive, sweet sort of jealousy. Her other two closest friends, Debra and Margret, stood side by side, laughing together, different as two women could be, but sharing a type of camaraderie. They had all survived, including herself—beating incredible odds. To be together like this, in one place, in one piece, was a true miracle. Peter's father was also found, another mystery solved with joy, relieving much of the burden Peter felt.

Now, last of all, even the mystery of what happened to Rob had been unraveled. Her heart felt like it could finally rest, after spending a long sleepless night wandering in disquiet and worry.

Although the immediate future seemed bleak—no heart untouched by grief—in that moment Alyssa felt more happiness, joy, and peace than her heart could contain.

❧◆☙

Acknowledgements

First, I need to thank my dear husband Steve, as always, for providing the nurturing support I need to keep going and never give up on my dreams. I am also very grateful to my children for their continued encouragement and support, and for the wonderful spirit each one of them possesses. I have truly been blessed. I'm also grateful for rare, true friends in my life. It's good to know you're out there to pick me up if I should fall. (Danielle, you can start waving your hand now.)

BJ Rowley and the authors with LDStorymakers, Inc. (including my editors: BJ, Josi, Julie, and Tristi) have more than earned my profound thanks for their hard work and dedication in producing this book. I am pleased, honored, and mostly humbled to be counted among them—these are some amazing and wonderful people to know and work with.

I would like to thank my manuscript readers, Arlen, Ashley, Danielle, Emily, Jeanette, Katie, Michele, and Steve, with thanks to Arlen for hunting down that elusive chapter heading scripture during the final read-through.

In case anyone is wondering, Liisa is my sister, and spells her name with two 'i's—it's not a misprint, but a nod to Finland.

Sincere thanks are also due to Janice Kapp Perry for giving me permission to reprint the lines from her beautiful song, "A Child's Prayer."

ABOUT THE AUTHOR

Linda Paulson Adams was born in Baltimore, Maryland, moved to Hollister, California in 1978, and attended Brigham Young University in Provo, Utah for four years.

Linda married her husband, Steve, in 1988 in the Manti Temple. They are both lifetime active members of the Church. They reside in Jackson County, Missouri, with their six children ages fourteen and under (three girls and three boys) and several pets.

Prodigal Journey, her first novel, was released in 2000 by Cornerstone Publishing. Cornerstone ceased operations before *Refining Fire* could be printed, and she is now pleased to be aligned with LDStorymakers, Inc. She has published poetry and short fiction in a variety of literary magazines, including *Irreantum, Meridian Magazine,* and *Lynx Eye.*

Linda became fascinated with the history and future of Jackson County shortly after moving to Missouri around twelve years ago. Soon this story grew and flourished, bits and pieces of chapters written between changing diapers and sorting mismatched socks. She has made the content of her two novels a matter of prayer, research, and study. However, in no way are the fictional events portrayed intended to be anything more than a fanciful exploration of possible ways that latter-day events could play out.

Her hobbies include yoga, knitting, thread crochet, drawing, singing, writing music, and of course reading (especially science fiction). But with all this she is quick to add that she can't do crafts, scrapbook, tole paint, or decorate.

Visit her website at: www.alyssastory.com
Sign on to her email fan list.